D0259197

FOR BETTER FOR WORSE

As Britain recovers from WWII, Annie Royal is looking to the future. Recently married to Henry, and with a baby on the way, she and her husband are happily settled in the seaside town of Worthing. But a knock at the door brings Annie's world crashing down. On her doorstep stands Sarah and her two young children. Sarah reveals that she is Henry's wife and has been searching for him for over a year. Annie is forced to accept the truth when Henry is arrested for bigamy. In her darkest hour, with the baby imminent, Annie finds support in the most unlikely places.

FOR BETTER FOR WORSE

FOR BETTER FOR WORSE

by

Pam Weaver

Magna Large Print Books
Long Preston, North Yorkshire,
BD23 4ND, England.

British Library Cataloguing in Publication Data.

Weaver, Pam
For better for worse.

A catalogue record of this book is available from the British Library

ISBN 978-0-7505-4056-8

First published in Great Britain by HarperCollins*Publishers* 2014

Cover illustration by arrangement with mirrorpix

Published in Large Print 2015 by arrangement with HarperCollins Publishers

Magna Large Print is an imprint of Library Magna Books Ltd.

Printed and bound in Great Britain by T.J. (International) Ltd., Cornwall, PL28 8RW

This novel is entirely a work of fiction.
The names, characters and incidents portrayed
in it are the work of the author's imagination.
Any resemblance to actual persons,
living or dead, events or localities
is entirely coincidental.

Acknowledgements

I am grateful to my agent, Juliet Burton. You are always there to encourage me and spur me on to greater things. You're the tops!

My thanks also to my editor Helen Bolton and the wonderful team at Avon. I am forever in your debt.

This book is dedicated to Tony and Audrey Hindley and Polly McLelland. Thank you for all the times you've encouraged me. If they gave out medals for encouragers, you three would share the winner's podium.

One

July 1948

It was gone. Really gone. She'd spent the past hour hunting high and low for it, but it was no use. She couldn't find it anywhere. She'd tried all the usual places first: the drawer, the kitchen dresser, her coat pocket, but she quickly drew a blank. She'd even been outside and looked down the street in the hope that it hadn't fallen from her pocket, but she couldn't see it. Her stomach was in knots. After everything else, this couldn't be happening. Having tried the obvious places, for the past ten minutes she'd been looking in the pram, the toy box and the outside lav, places where she knew it couldn't possibly be, and yet she hoped against hope that she'd find it.

'Have you seen Mummy's purse?'

Jenny pushed her silky brown hair out of her eyes and looked up at her mother with a blank expression. She was a pretty child with long eyelashes. Born in the middle of the war, she was Sarah's first child.

'My purse,' Sarah said impatiently. 'Have you taken it to play shops?'

'Oh, Mummy,' her daughter tutted, one hand on her hip and her mother's scolding expression on her face, 'I'm not playing shops. This is dolly's tea party.'

Sarah frowned crossly. 'Don't get lippy with me, young lady. I asked you a question. Have you seen my purse?'

Her daughter looked suitably chastised. 'No, Mummy.'

Sarah's heart melted. She shouldn't have spoken to her like that. She wasn't having a good day either. Just an hour ago, Jenny had come into the shared kitchen with a worried frown. 'Mummy, Goldie isn't very well.'

Sarah had followed her back up to the bedroom and sure enough, her pet goldfish was floating on the top of the water. Slipping her arm around her daughter's shoulder, Sarah had to explain that Goldie wasn't ill; she had died and gone to heaven.

Jenny had stared at her mother, her wide eyes brimming with tears. 'But why?'

Why indeed, thought Sarah. 'It just happens, darling. Fish get old and die. It was Goldie's time to go.'

'Is that what happened to Daddy?' Jenny's words hung in the air like icicles and Sarah had swallowed hard. Her heartbeat quickened and she felt very uncomfortable. It was at that moment she realised she should have talked to her daughter before. She had no idea the poor little mite had been thinking that Henry was dead. 'No, darling,' she'd said, drawing her closer. 'Daddy isn't dead. Daddy went to live somewhere else.'

'Why Mummy? Didn't he like living with us?'

Sarah had taken in a silent breath, wondering how on earth she could answer that. She didn't really understand herself, so how was she going to explain to a six-year-old why her father had simply packed his bags and walked out? Up until that moment she had thought Jenny was coping well. She'd seemed to accept that Henry had gone away, but as they'd talked Sarah could see that that Jenny hadn't really understood after all.

'I'm sure Daddy loved living with us,' she'd said, kneeling down to look into Jenny's face, 'but he had to go away.'

Suddenly, Sarah's youngest daughter Lu-Lu crashed into them and tried to kiss her big sister. Jenny laid her head on her mother's shoulder. 'Did it hurt?'

Sarah frowned. It was hard to follow the child's reasoning. 'Did what hurt?'

'Did it hurt Goldie when she died?'

By now Sarah had drawn her arms around both her children. 'No. I don't think it did and I'm sure Goldie had a very happy life.'

Jenny had put her hands on the goldfish bowl. 'Can we bury her?'

'Of course,' smiled Sarah. 'I think I've got a little box we can put her in and we'll bury her in the garden.'

They laid the fish on a bed of cotton wool inside a box which once held three man-sized handkerchiefs and Sarah put the lid on. Goldie was all ready for burial, but they couldn't do it there and then. It was raining hard and Sarah didn't have anything suitable for digging in their tiny courtyard garden so she promised Jenny they would bury the goldfish after school the next day.

'Can I ask Carole to come to Goldie's frunrel?'

Sarah hesitated. Her sister Vera made her feel that Henry's disappearance was somehow her fault, and although Jenny and her cousin Carole got on well, she wasn't too keen to have her sister around.

'Please, Mummy. Please,' Jenny pleaded.

Sarah nodded reluctantly. 'I'll talk to Auntie Vera,' she promised.

It had brought a lump to her throat as she watched her daughter drawing a picture for Goldie, so she decided to give the girls a little treat. It was almost lunchtime, and the corner shop closed from 1 p.m. until 2 p.m. Sarah still had some coupons and if Mrs Rivers next door would take them in, she just had time to run and get some sweets.

Mrs Rivers was only too glad to have the girls. She was fond of Jenny and she loved spoiling Lu-Lu. Sarah had promised to be as quick as she could. She'd used her sweet ration for the first time in months to buy them a small bar of Cadbury's each. Given their normal circumstances, it would have seemed extravagant, but with the guinea Mr Lovett had pushed into her hand, she told herself it was only 3d a bar and she knew the girls loved chocolate. The purse had been in her basket when she came out of the shop because she remembered stuffing it down the side. After that, she couldn't remember seeing it again. She'd collected the girls and come home, so somewhere between the sweet shop, Mrs Rivers' place and home, the purse had been lifted or dropped out of the basket. She shifted the pile of papers on the kitchen table. She'd already searched through them once but she was irresistibly drawn back to look yet again. The purse wasn't there.

Lu-Lu toddled across the floor and sat down to eat a crumb which had fallen from the table. At fifteen months, everything went straight into her mouth. Sarah bent to take it from her hand before she put it in her mouth, and as she lowered herself back onto the chair, the terrible realisation dawned. Her purse with all her money in it was well and truly lost. What was she going to do? That purse contained the coal money and everything they had to live on for the next week. There was no nest egg to fall back on, no Post Office book with a secret stash, no money in the jar on the top of the dresser. She couldn't ask her sister to help either. Since her brother-in-law had landed a job with Lancing Carriage Works, Vera had become rather sniffy. She'd been friendly enough when Sarah lived in the house in Littlehampton, but since she'd come to Worthing, Vera's attitude had changed. If she didn't know better, Sarah might have thought she was ashamed of her.

Lu-Lu asked to be picked up and Sarah pulled her onto her lap, kissing the top of her golden hair as she did so. Jenny had inherited her mother's light brown hair and hazel eyes but Lu-Lu had blue eyes and fairer hair. Cuddling her daughter, Sarah shook all thoughts of Henry away. She felt the tears prick the backs of her eyes, but what was the use of crying? That never solved anything. She hadn't cried when he'd buggered off and she wasn't going to start now. Besides, it was no good going back over what might have been. That was all in the past and right now her most pressing problem was what to do about her missing purse. She didn't have a lot before it went and now she had absolutely nothing. How was she going to manage? As a woman deserted, she had no widow's allowance. Henry contributed nothing towards the care of his children. Every penny they had was what she earned. Thank God she'd already got the rent money together. That was tucked into the rent book on the dresser, but she still had the children to feed.

Their home was two rooms on the first floor of a run-down fisherman's cottage in Worthing where they shared the downstairs kitchen and toilet with another tenant. They were just across the road from the sea, but being at the back of some larger buildings meant that there was little incentive for the landlord to improve the property. The old woman who lived below them had been taken to hospital a few weeks ago and it was Sarah's greatest fear that she wouldn't come back. If that happened, there would be new tenants. The landlord had intimated several times that once the other tenant, an old family retainer, passed away, he planned to sell the property. Even though the place was damp and badly in need of decoration, Sarah had done her best to make it a nice home.

'A bit of soap and water works wonders,' she told her sister Vera when she'd first moved in, but she couldn't help noticing her sister's look of disdain. It was a far cry from the lovely house Sarah had shared with Henry, but without his wage, and because of a steep rise in the rent, it was impossible to carry on living there. Sarah and her girls had moved here three months after he'd gone, and up until today, everything had been going fairly well. To save money, Sarah had always made the children's clothes and it had been her lucky day when she went to Mrs Angel's haberdashery shop to get some buttons and bumped into Mr Lovett.

The shop was a jumble of just about everything. There were the usual buttons and embroidery silks, but Mrs Angel also stocked ladies' underwear in the glass-topped chest of drawers under the counter and a few bolts of material. She would also allow her customers to buy their wool weekly and would put the balls away in a 'lay-by' until they were needed.

'Madam, I have a proposition to make to you,' Mr Lovett had said as he spotted Jenny's little pink dress.

'Mr Lovett has been admiring your handiwork,' Mrs Angel explained. 'I told him how popular your little kiddies' clothes are.'

'If you could make another little girl's dress like that and a boy's romper suit,' Mr Lovett went on, 'I think I could find a London buyer.'

'It takes me a week to make one of those,' Sarah had laughed. 'The smocking takes ages.'

'I can tell,' he smiled. 'And before you say anything, there will be no monetary risk to your good self. I shall supply all the materials.'

Sarah hesitated. Could she trust this man?

'I'm sure Mrs Angel will vouch for me?' he added as if he'd read her mind.

'Mr Lovett is a travelling salesman,' Mrs Angel explained. She was a matronly woman with a shock of white hair. Rumour had it that it had turned that colour overnight after her beloved husband was killed by lightning on Cissbury Ring.

Sarah had been slightly sceptical, but with Mrs

Angel only too keen to provide the cottons and any other material she needed, the deal was struck. When she'd finished making the dress and romper suit, Mr Lovett was as good as his word. He'd been right. He'd had no trouble selling her handiwork to a shop in London where rich women were willing to pay the earth for things of such good quality. She knew he'd kept back some money for himself, and yet each time he'd taken an order he'd given her a whole guinea, more money than Sarah had had in a long time. He'd extracted a promise that if the customer liked her work, she'd be willing to do some more. Sarah didn't need much persuading, even though, without a sewing machine, she'd had to sit up all hours to get them finished on time. She'd been so pleased with the money she'd saved, she'd decided to buy half a hundredweight of coal.

Outside, a lorry drew up and the driver switched off the engine. Lu-Lu wriggled to get down. Sarah let her go and looked out of the window. Oh no, Mr Millward was here already. She couldn't take the coal without paying for it. How frustrating. Wood never gave out the heat that coal did, and after the horrors of the winter of 1947, she had thought that this coming winter was going to be one when they didn't have to worry about keeping warm. Think, she told herself crossly. Where did you last have that purse?

There was a knock on the kitchen window and Peter Millward, his wet cap dripping onto his face streaked with coal dust, smiled in. 'Shall I put it in the coal shed then, luv?' He was a kind man with smiley eyes, skinny as a beanpole, and at about thirty-four, was five years older than her. He had been married but his wife had died in an air raid, which was ironic because Peter, who had seen action in some of the worst places, had come through the war unscathed.

Sarah shook her head and rose to her feet. 'I'm sorry,' she said, throwing wide the front door which opened onto the street. 'I'm afraid you've had a wasted journey. I've changed my mind. I shan't need any coal today.'

'Shan't need...' he began with a puzzled expression. 'But you only came to the yard and ordered this stuff an hour ago.' He waited for an explanation and when one wasn't forthcoming he said crossly, 'I can't be doing with being mucked about.'

'I know,' she said, 'and I'm sorry.'

He stood for a second staring at her. Lu-Lu headed for the open door and Sarah bent to pick her up. The child was wet.

'Was it Haskins?' he blurted out. 'Has he given you a better deal? Normal price is five bob a bag but I can knock another tanner off for the summer price.'

'No, no,' Sarah cried. 'It's not that. I won't be needing it, that's all.'

'If you leave it until winter I may not be able to help you out,' Mr Millward persisted. 'And you won't get it at the summer prices either.'

'I know,' said Sarah.

As she began to close the door, he said, 'If it's about the money, I can't give you the whole five bags but I could let you have one if you and I could come to some sort of arrangement.' He raised an eyebrow.

Sarah felt her face flush and taking a deep breath, she said haughtily, 'I shall not be requiring your coal and I'd thank you to keep your special arrangements to yourself, thank you very much Mr Millward,' before slamming the door in his face.

He was raising his hand as the door banged and he called out something through the wood, but Sarah turned the key in the lock and took Lu-Lu upstairs to her bedroom to change her nappy. As she washed her daughter's bottom with a flannel, Sarah smiled at her child but inside she was raging. How dare he? What was it with men? Ever since Henry had gone, half the male population of Worthing seemed to think that she was either 'up for a bit of fun' or 'gagging for it' or available for 'an arrangement'. Little did they know that after the way Henry had treated her, she didn't care if she never saw another man again.

Putting the baby down, Sarah had another thought. Maybe Lu-Lu had taken her purse out of the basket while she and Mrs Rivers were having a cup of tea. She hadn't stayed long because Mrs Rivers' son, Nathan, had come home a bit earlier than usual, but there had been plenty of time for Lu-Lu to carry it off somewhere. As soon as Mr Millward's lorry had gone, Sarah popped Lu-Lu into her playpen at the bottom of the stairs and knocked next door again.

'Please don't take this the wrong way,' she began as she stood in Mrs Rivers' doorway, 'but did you find a purse after I'd gone?'

'No, dear,' said her neighbour. 'Why, have you

lost one?'

'Yes,' said Sarah. 'I had it in the shops ... obviously, but when I got back home and looked in my basket, it wasn't there.'

The door was suddenly yanked open and Nat Rivers pushed past his mother. Sarah jumped. She didn't like him. He was a big man with a generous beer belly, a mouth full of brown teeth and greying stubble on his chin. She'd never once seen him looking smart. Today he was wearing his usual grubby vest, no shirt and his trousers were held up with a large buckled belt. Nat Rivers had been in and out of prison all his life.

Mrs Rivers looked up at him anxiously and slunk back indoors.

'Are you accusing my mother of pinching something?' he snapped.

'No, no of course not,' said Sarah. 'It's just that…'

'Then bugger off,' he said as he slammed the door.

Sarah turned away despondently. She'd never be able to prove a thing of course, but she couldn't help noticing that Mrs Rivers was looking rather flushed as she spoke – and her son's attitude wasn't exactly neighbourly. Almost as soon as the door closed, she could hear the sound of raised voices and what sounded like a slap. She hovered for a second, wondering if she should knock on the door again, but then she thought of the children. What good would it do if Nat came out into the street and hit her in front of them? It was a relief when everything went quiet.

Back home once more, Sarah had a heavy heart.

It was so hard not to become bitter. She had thought that she and Henry were doing all right. He'd been looking forward to the birth of their second child. In fact, the whole time she'd been pregnant, he'd been like a big kid himself.' He'd fussed over her and bought her flowers. He'd helped with looking after Jenny when her ankles swelled. Towards the end of the pregnancy, he'd taken Jenny out every Saturday so that Sarah could have a rest. When she and Henry were alone, he'd spent hours with his hand on her belly talking to his unborn child. He was so sure it would be a boy and she knew he was more than a little disappointed when Lu-Lu came, but she was such a beautiful baby right from the start.

'You're as good-looking as your daddy,' she'd told Lu-Lu, knowing that Henry took pride in himself.' He fancied that he looked like Ronald Colman with his light-coloured hair slicked down and his pencil-thin moustache. Sarah couldn't see it herself but didn't contradict him. Henry wouldn't like that.

As Sarah told him time and again, it didn't matter that they hadn't got a son yet. The baby was healthy, that was the main thing, and eventually he seemed to accept that she was right. But then one day she came home from picking Jenny up from school to find that he wasn't there. She'd reported him missing but the police seemed to think that because he'd taken a suitcase, there was nothing amiss, so she was left to soldier on by herself. She had hoped he would return, but it had been almost ten months now and she had to accept the fact that he wasn't coming back.

Sarah was terrified that the welfare people would come and take the kids away, which was why it was imperative that she ask no one for money. She didn't want anyone thinking she was an inadequate mother. She was determined to provide for them whatever happened. Over the months since he'd been gone, Sarah had pawned everything of value and only kept body and soul together by earning the odd shilling or two by cleaning the local pub in the morning and a couple of big houses during the day. It wasn't easy because she had to take the baby with her and sometimes Lu-Lu was fractious because she had to sit in the pram all the time. Her sister had slipped her the odd five bob in the beginning, but she hadn't offered anything lately and Sarah hadn't asked. Mrs Angel had seen her skill with the needle and given her the occasional job mending a petticoat or making a baby dress, so when the children were in bed, she'd carried on working. In short, Sarah was willing to do anything which would raise a few extra funds provided it was honest, which was why meeting Mr Lovett had seemed like a godsend. All she could do now was hope and pray that he came back quickly with another order.

Despite how she felt about Henry, Sarah had kept the few personal things he had left behind. There was a brown suit, a little old-fashioned with turn-ups, a couple of jumpers she'd knitted him and a silver cigarette case. It was hallmarked and she'd often wondered why he hadn't taken it with him. There was an inscription inside, *Kaye from Henry*. She had no idea who Kaye was and Henry had certainly never mentioned her. Sarah turned the case over in her hands. It was time to let it go. She could get good money for it and it would do far more good helping to feed her children than gathering dust at the back of the wardrobe. If he came back she would explain and hope that he would understand. She searched through the pockets of the suit and found a pair of baby's booties. They looked brand new but she didn't recognise them. The girls had never worn them and she could only surmise that Henry had bought them intending to give them to her but forgot. They would do for Jenny's dolly. With determination in her heart, Sarah bagged everything else up ready to take it to the second-hand shop. She'd take the cigarette case to Warner's antique shop by Worthing central crossing in the morning.

'Vera,' Sarah called out to her sister as they dropped their children off at school in the morning. 'Could I have a quick word?'

Vera glanced around as if to see who was looking. Sarah quickly explained about the goldfish and the funeral Jenny had planned for it and Vera agreed to bring Carole along. 'Only for a minute, mind,' she cautioned. 'Bill will be expecting his tea.'

Back home, Sarah used a tablespoon to dig a hole in the postage stamp garden. When she'd finished, she'd stared down at it hoping it was deep enough. It definitely wasn't the regulation six feet, but that would be ridiculous, wouldn't it? How deep do you need to go for a fish? When she'd got up that morning, Jenny was already up and decorating Goldie's coffin. She'd drawn flowers all over the sides and she'd even stuck some bits of ribbon on the lid. There was a note as well. Sarah's eyes pricked as she read, 'Gudbi Golldy.'

The rest of Sarah's day was full. She took Lu-Lu to the pub where she cleaned the bar and toilets. Lu-Lu sat in her pram playing happily with some old beer mats and eventually fell asleep. After work, she took Henry's suit and other things to the second-hand shop on North Street, where Lil Relland gave her five bob for the lot. The man in Warner's valued the cigarette case at twelve shilling and offered her ten. Sarah was in no mood to argue. She took the money.

After school, Vera and Carole came around and Jenny organised everybody for the fish's funeral. As they stood in the small yard, Lu-Lu in Sarah's arms, Carole read a poem something along the lines of:

No more Goldie swimming round and round the water,
swimmin' like a little goldfish aughta...

while the two sisters, in a rare moment of shared pleasure, struggled to keep a straight face. Then with a clear voice, Jenny put her hands together, grace style, to say thank you to God for Goldie.

'Dear God, please look after Goldie in heaven. I know it's a big place and she might get lost if the angels don't look after her. And ... please remember she gets scared if she's left on her own. Amen.'

Sarah dared not look at Vera as she put Lu-Lu down and began to fill in the hole.

'Wait a minute, Mummy!' Jenny turned to run indoors. Sarah looked at Vera and gave her an exaggerated shrug. They waited, each avoiding the other's eye, until Jenny came back out with the metal bridge from Goldie's goldfish bowl. Everybody watched as Jenny knelt reverently beside the hole and placed it on top of the box. 'She likes to swim around that,' said Jenny.

As she stood up, Sarah pushed some earth over the edge with her foot and eventually the hole was filled.

When it was all done, Carole wanted to sing a hymn, so they plumped for *All Things Bright and Beautiful*. As they sang, Sarah's heart was heavy. Not so much for the little fish lying there but for her little girl, having her first encounter with death and loss. What with Henry going, Sarah wondered how this might affect Jenny. Would she become terrified that she was going to lose everyone she loved? Vera sniffed (or was it giggled?) into her handkerchief. They marked the grave with the only piece of wood Sarah could find. Made out of two broken pieces of fence panelling and held together with a six-inch nail, the cross was ten times the size of the little body in the ground.

After the service was over, Sarah gave Jenny the baby booties for her dolly, hoping it would soften the blow. Apparently it did, because before long, the two older girls were playing out on the street, while their mothers sat at Sarah's table with a cup of tea. Sarah held Lu-Lu on her lap. Vera seemed very quiet, so Sarah took the initiative. 'How's life treating you?'

'Very well,' Vera beamed. 'Bill has just got a promotion. He's foreman in the coach works now and since they nationalised the railways, the firm thinks they'll get a lot more work.'

'That's good,' said Sarah.

'Well, you can't have a railway without carriages, can you?' Vera joked. She frowned. 'I hardly like to ask, but any news of Henry?'

Sarah shook her head. 'Not a dickie bird.'

Vera tutted. 'I still can't believe it. The swine. He took us all in, didn't he? I mean, fancy leaving you in the lurch like that. He always seemed such a nice man. You didn't say anything funny to him did you?'

'No!' Sarah frowned crossly. Vera only knew the half of it. She'd never told her sister how demanding Henry had become and how difficult to live with. When he'd left, he'd taken all the money in the house, including the rent money and the emergency money in the jar.

'Bill is still convinced something's happened to him,' said Vera. 'They were such good mates.'

Sarah shrugged and stared into the depths of her cup. 'The police said he'd gone of his own volition.' What else could she say? As far as she knew, Henry had never contacted any of their friends or relations, and yet before the war, the four of them had had some good times together before the kids came along. As soon as Jenny and Carole were born, the men became occasional drinking companions, sometimes in Littlehampton and other times at the Half Brick. She smiled as she remembered one occasion when they lived in Pier Road, Henry came home on his bicycle, telling her that on the way to the pub he'd nearly fallen off when a lone Home Guard stepped out into the road and put his hand up.

'Whatever for?' she'd gasped.

'He wanted to know what I was doing out at this time of night,' Henry had chuckled. 'I looks at my watch. "It's only 9.30," I says and then he wants to know where I'd been. "To the pub," I told him. "Aren't there any public houses nearer home?" he asks me.' By now, they were both laughing.

'But why on earth would he do that?' Sarah had wanted to know.

'He was a just a rookie having a bit of a practice,' Henry had chuckled.

'If you were a ruddy German,' she had laughed, 'you'd hardly invade the country on your own ... and on a pushbike.'

Vera interrupted her thoughts. 'You seem to be managing all right then?'

'Oh yes,' Sarah smiled. Pride prevented her from telling her sister just how hard things really were. She couldn't bear to hear her sister say, 'I told you so…'

'If you need a few bob,' said Vera, reaching for her bag, 'I suppose I might be able to spare...'

'Don't worry,' Sarah interrupted as she felt her face heat up. Perhaps she could have done with a few bob, but Vera's grudging and condescending manner meant that her pride got in the way. If the boot was on the other foot, she thought darkly, would I embarrass you the way you embarrass me? I think not. They drank their tea in silence. Sarah had little to say and the atmosphere between them had become rather awkward.

'Did I tell you we're moving?' Vera asked.
'No?'
'We're buying a house in Lancing,' Vera beamed. 'Annweir Avenue. The railway is helping us with getting a mortgage and Bill wanted to be closer to the carriage works anyway. I can't wait.'
Sarah swirled the tea in her cup. 'Sounds good.'
'Bill is going to do it up and we may take a lodger. You know ... someone respectable.'
Vera's husband had done well for himself in the Lancing Carriage Works and the workforce was a close-knit community. During the war years, they had been kept busy repairing bombed-out carriages because the shortage of petrol meant that the railways had to be kept going whatever the cost. Henry had worked in a jeweller's shop in Littlehampton until he was called up. It was through his friendship with Bill and the local cricket club matches that he and Sarah had met in the first place. Life was strange. It may have dealt her a bad hand but she was happy for her sister. They seemed to be doing really well.
'The new British Railways have some brilliant new ideas,' said Vera. She was on a roll now. 'There's talk about having an open day next year and inviting families and friends to come and have a look around. If they do it, you must come too.'
'Sounds fun,' said Sarah.
'It's free but they're raising funds for the Southern Railway Servants' Orphanage and Homes for the Elderly. You will come, won't you?'
'Try and keep me away,' said Sarah, stifling a yawn. It was becoming more and more difficult to talk to Vera. As they'd got older, they had less

and less in common. She felt uncomfortable and the conversation was always very one-sided. 'How long before you leave Worthing?'

Vera shrugged. 'Two weeks, a month? There's still a bit of paperwork to do but the house is already empty.' She stood to leave, calling her daughter to her and explaining that she had to get back for Bill's tea.

'It was lovely seeing you again,' said Sarah, planting a kiss on Vera's proffered cheek

'By the way,' Vera said in a rather loud voice as she stepped out onto the street, 'I've got a few bits and bobs you can have that belonged to Carole when she was a baby. They're a bit worn but they might come in useful for Lu-Lu.'

A couple of her neighbours were walking by. Sarah averted her eyes. 'Thank you,' she said quietly as she felt her face colour. 'That's very kind of you.' She couldn't say no. The children needed clothes and she knew she shouldn't feel this way, but did she have to tell the whole street? She closed the door, grateful that Vera and Carole had gone.

Later, when the children were in bed and asleep, there was a knock on the door. Sarah was surprised to see Mrs Angel and Peter Millward, the coalman, on her doorstep. Mrs Angel looked much the same as she always did, with her snow-white hair falling from her loose bun, but Peter was all spruced up. He was wearing his demob suit, a white shirt and a black tie. His thinning hair was slicked down and he was holding a bunch of lily of the valley.

'May we come in Sarah, dear?' said Mrs Angel.

Tight-lipped and angry, Sarah kept her back to them as she made a pot of tea. If Mr Millward had been there on his own she would have slammed the door in his face, but having Mrs Angel by his side meant that she felt the need to be polite. She'd carelessly cast his bunch of flowers onto the draining board without a word of thanks. In fact, she hadn't said a word since the pair of them walked in the door. How dare he come back! And how dare he get someone as nice as Mrs Angel involved as well. She put a cup of tea in front of them, making sure she slopped some of Peter's drink in the saucer, and sat at the table, her eyes fixed on Mrs Angel.

'Peter wants to ask you something,' said Mrs Angel.

'Does he now,' said Sarah coldly. 'Well, I'm sure I have nothing to say to him.'

Mrs Angel put up her hand. 'It seems there's been a terrible mistake, dear.'

Sarah opened her mouth but then Peter said, 'I'm a man of few words, missus, and sometimes they come out all wrong.' Sarah turned to give him a cold hard stare.

'I need a bookkeeper,' he blurted out.

Sarah blinked in surprise. 'A bookkeeper?'

He nodded.

'I don't know why we didn't think of it before, dear,' said Mrs Angel. 'It's something you could do from home. What I mean is, you wouldn't have to get someone to look after the children.'

'A bookkeeper,' Sarah repeated. 'I used to be good at sums at school, but I've never done anything like bookkeeping.'

'Perhaps not, dear,' said Mrs Angel, 'But I can help you get started and there's nothing to it. You just have to be methodical.'

Sarah's gaze went to Mr Millward. 'I can't pay you,' he began. 'I've only just started out myself, but I could pay you in kind.'

Sarah felt herself relaxing. 'With a bag of coal?' He nodded furiously and she began to laugh. 'You know what?' she said. 'You've got yourself a bookkeeper.'

Mr Millward beamed.

'I owe you an apology,' said Sarah, but he waved a hand and shook his head. 'Yes, I do,' Sarah insisted. 'It's just that since my husband disappeared, a few people have made some rather improper suggestions.'

Mrs Angel looked away but Mr Millward continued to stare. 'Henry has disappeared?'

'Yes,' said Sarah. 'Didn't you know? He walked out on me and the children some time ago.' She picked up her cup and tried to appear nonchalant. 'I haven't seen hide nor hair of him since.'

'A terrible thing to do,' said Mrs Angel, shaking her head. 'Those poor little girls need a daddy.'

'But your Henry hasn't disappeared,' Mr Millward exclaimed. 'I've seen him.'

Sarah was aware that her mouth had dropped open, but the news had rendered her speechless.

Mrs Angel clutched at her throat. 'You saw him?'

'My old Mum lives in Horsham,' said Mr Millward, addressing Mrs Angel. 'I go to see her every week. I was there last Sunday and I saw him just down the road from Mum's place. He didn't see me, but I saw him.'

Sarah took in a breath. 'Did he look all right? I mean, was he well?'

'Yeah, he looked fine.' But as he looked at Sarah, the colour in his face rose and he shifted uncomfortably in his chair. 'I don't know how to tell you this, missus, but he wasn't alone. He was arm in arm with some young woman.'

Two

Annie Royal crept downstairs and into the kitchen. It was 6.30 a.m. and Henry would be up soon. She had laid the table the night before, so there wasn't a lot to do. Today was his birthday and she was planning a little surprise. Tying her ash-blonde hair up with a scarf, she put an apron on over her nightdress.

She loved her little house. It was the sort of home every girl dreamed of. Fairly near the centre of town, it had its own backyard and even a tiny front garden. She had a dining room and an upstairs bathroom with hot and cold running water. When they'd moved in, they had spent several happy weeks redecorating. All the dark greens and browns of yesterday were gone so that the house was light and airy. The country was still suffering hard times after the war so their furniture was utility, but it was clean and sturdy, and Henry promised that as soon as he got a raise, they would look for some more modern stuff like the furniture she'd shown him in her magazines.

Their wedding had been a quiet affair. It wasn't what she'd dreamed of but she tried not to mind too much. She had always wanted a big do with all of the family there, but when Henry had worked in her father's jewellery shop they had fallen out over something. She'd tried to find out what had happened, but both men were too stubborn to say. Henry had tried to make it up to her as they'd planned their wedding almost a year ago. The registry office was full of flowers and the woman who cleaned the brasses on the front door and a passer-by had been their witnesses. All through the ceremony, which was breathtakingly short, Annie kept looking around, hoping that Mum and Father would come dashing in muttering apologies that their car had broken down or the bus was late or they'd missed the train, but it never happened.

Of course, Henry could see how upset she was and he was kindness itself.

'It'll be all right, darling,' he'd nuzzled in her ear. 'Don't let it spoil our special day,' and his tender kisses helped to take some of the disappointment away. So long as she did what he told her, Henry was her hero, her knight in shining armour.

Instead of a reception, they'd had a meal in a pretty restaurant. Somehow the people found out that they'd just got married (probably Henry's doing again) and they'd made a huge fuss of them, giving them a free glass of wine each and handshakes all round. Annie blushed modestly and thought herself lucky or blessed or a mixture of both. Henry was light-haired, suave and sophisticated and, in her eyes, even better looking than

Ronald Colman, the star he so much admired. He was so loving and caring as well. Her honeymoon nights spent right here in their own home were full of his lovemaking and her days packed with his kisses. He paid her compliments all the time and she was convinced that she would be the envy of all her friends if ever she got to tell them. Henry wasn't one for visiting. He said he preferred them to spend their weekends by themselves, so she hadn't seen anybody for ages. Still, it didn't matter. Not really. She smiled to herself. Henry was so romantic, just like the film stars at the pictures. Whenever she and Henry went out, he was even mildly jealous when other men looked at her. She'd laugh gaily and tell him it was his own fault because he would keep buying her pretty dresses and scarves as well as things that were for his eyes only in the bedroom. Henry was exciting, passionate and all hers...

When she'd written to tell her parents they were married, Mum wrote back protesting that they'd never received the invitation.

'Of course they did,' Henry had said crossly. 'I posted it myself.'

'I'll pop over and see them,' she'd said, but Henry didn't feel it was wise.

'Why ever not?' she'd protested.

'Leave it for a while,' he'd counselled. 'Let things settle down.'

Annie was reluctant, but then her new husband had given her a wounded look and complained that everyone was ganging up on him, so she'd let it go.

Annie had settled down to domesticity and

looking after Henry. He wouldn't hear of her getting a job. 'No wife of mine will ever have to go out to work,' he'd declared stoutly. It was fun at first, but she soon got bored.

She had only been married for five months when she discovered she was pregnant. Henry was over the moon and did his best to treat her like a piece of delicate china.

'I'm only pregnant,' she'd laughed, 'not ill.'

Henry had screwed up his nose. 'Don't use that word, darling,' he said. 'It sounds so vulgar.'

She was taken aback. 'Then what…'

'Say you're in the family way,' he said, kissing her ear. He was funny like that. Prudish over some things and yet such an accomplished lover in the bedroom. She supposed it might be because of his Rhodesian upbringing. Henry had come to this country as a boy to get an English education and for some reason far beyond Annie's understanding, had never gone back.

As soon as she heard Henry moving about upstairs, Annie put a pan of water on the gas stove and lit the flame underneath. She took the loaf out of the breadbin and unwrapped it. She always kept it covered with a damp tea towel to keep it fresh. Her neighbour, Mrs Holborn, had given her that useful tip. All she had to do now was make the tea.

Annie had met Henry just over a year ago. He didn't talk much about his past or his wartime experiences because he had been captured in the early days and spent almost all of the war years as a POW. He was a lot older than her. She was eighteen and he was thirty-six today. She'd adored him from the start, but her father, who had taken Henry on in the jewellers' shop, had been more cautious.

'He's deep that one,' Father had said. 'He may be a good worker, but we don't really know much about him.'

Of course, her parents were concerned because their courtship had been so short. 'All I know is that I love him and he loves me,' Annie had said stoutly, and now that Henry was her husband and she was expecting his baby, she had high hopes that Henry and her father would make friends again.

'I know Father can be difficult,' she'd pleaded with Henry, 'but please try and like him just a little bit.'

'I do, darling,' Henry protested. 'Really I do, but the man is impossible.'

She sighed. Perhaps he was right. She'd written to her parents several times, but they'd never replied.

She could hear Henry coming out of the bathroom, so she put the eggs into the boiling water and two slices of bread under the grill.

'What are you doing up so early?' he asked as he walked into the kitchen.

She indicated his chair and he sat down. Putting her arms around his shoulders, she kissed the top of his head. 'Two boiled eggs, three minutes, just as you like them, coming up,' she said, putting the toast and butter in front of him.

Henry smiled. 'Thank you, darling.' He patted her arm. 'When I've gone to work, I want you to go back to bed.'

'Henry, I'm fine,' she said, reaching for the teapot.

'A woman in your condition…' Henry began again.

'Please don't worry about me,' she protested as she put one egg in the egg cup and the other on the plate. 'I'm fine.'

'Please don't argue with me,' he said, his pale eyes narrowing slightly. 'I think that as your husband, I'll be the judge of what's best.'

'Yes,' she faltered. She mustn't make him angry. It was a bit scary when he shouted. 'You're right. I'll go back and lie down once you've gone to work.'

'I only have your best interests at heart,' he said, slicing off the top of the egg smartly with the knife. The yolk, a thick, rich orange, spilled over the side of the egg cup and onto the plate. 'Yours and the baby's.'

'I know,' she sighed. She sat opposite him and drank her tea, but she was in no mood to eat.

As her pregnancy advanced, Henry was most insistent that she lead a quiet life. 'First babies can be difficult to carry,' he told her. 'I want you to rest as much as possible.'

As he constantly reminded her, Annie had promised to love, honour and *obey* him, but at times it was very boring. She cleaned the house and did the shopping, always remembering to buy his favourite coffee crunch sweets and settling into a weekly routine. On Mondays it was washing, Tuesday cleaning upstairs, Wednesday she did the ironing and Thursday she tackled the downstairs. On Friday it was a little light gardening until she got too big and then it was time to get the sewing machine out and make a layette for the baby. On Saturdays and Sundays Henry was home so she read books and knitted and sometimes they went for a walk. She loved the little market town. It seemed so bright and cheerful after the war. She loved the striking façade of the Black Horse Hotel with its pretty window boxes, and the Carfax, a sort of market square with its own bandstand. Even the posh new toilets in the Bishopric were a talking point, but with so little else to stimulate her mind, Annie could hardly wait for the baby to come.

A man came to decorate the nursery. He was good-looking, funny and friendly, but Henry said he didn't like the standard of his work, so they had to find another. The new man turned out to be rather dour, but despite his advancing years, he got the job done eventually.

She set her teacup down on the table. 'I thought I might write to my mother and ask her over,' she said as he tucked into his second egg.

'I don't think so,' said Henry tartly. 'You know how awkward your father can be and I won't have you upset.'

Disappointed, she showed no emotion as she handed him a present. 'Happy birthday, darling.'

'Birthday? Oh! So it is.'

She was slightly surprised that he hadn't bothered to remember his own birthday, but his enthusiastic praise for the box of handkerchiefs she'd given him put her in a better mood. She went with him to the front door but he kissed her in the hallway.

'Don't let anyone see you looking like that,' he said, pushing her behind the door. 'Back to bed now.'

Using the door as a shield, she lingered in the hallway and blew a kiss as he closed it. After that, she went into the sitting room to watch him go towards the station. Across the street, she saw a woman walking in the opposite direction suddenly dart into the gateway of a house. Lifting the net curtain, Annie watched her husband's back until he reached the end of the road and walked out of sight. When she turned her head again, the woman was still there. She seemed to be watching Henry as well, but who was she? Annie had never seen her before. She was elegantly dressed in a lilac two-piece. The jacket had a nipped-in waist and the flowing skirt was a perfect imitation of the New Look. She wore a small, brimmed hat with a circle of netting on the side. She seemed rather nervous as she watched Henry go to the end of the road, moving her clutch bag from one hand to the other. She waited until he'd turned the corner before she came out onto the pavement again and, opening her bag, she took out a cigarette case. Annie watched her take one out and put it between her lips and, as the woman fired her lighter, she turned towards the house to shield the flame. Her cigarette lit, the woman looked up and their eyes met. They stared at each other for a split second then, as the woman took a long drag on her cigarette, Annie let the curtain drop. A moment later, the woman turned and walked on.

'That's funny,' Annie murmured to herself as she turned for the stairs.

She found herself trembling from head to foot and her heart was racing like the clappers when she saw him. She hadn't expected to bump into him in the street. If she'd been on the same side of the road, she would have walked right into him. Luckily, when he'd come out of the gate, he'd had his head down and was brushing something from his trouser leg. That had given her just enough time to dart into the nearest garden, but she had watched him walking briskly down the street with his head held high until he'd turned the corner. Arrogant sod. Now that he'd gone and she was back on the pavement, she didn't know why she hadn't confronted him there and then. It would have been the perfect opportunity and they were quite alone in the street.

She hadn't expected to see the girl either. So young ... she only looked about sixteen. She threw the half-smoked cigarette into the gutter and hurried on. Tears were biting the backs of her eyes, but she wasn't going to give way. She knew exactly what to do.

Her car was at the end of the street. She opened the door and threw in her handbag. Once in the driver's seat, she fumbled for another cigarette. Drawing deeply, she felt the rage inside her subsiding slightly but not the anger. That was cold and calculating. Nobody wanted their dirty linen washed in public, but enough was enough. She was rational enough to want it all done properly and that would take time. He was not going to get away with it, not this time. It might be unpleasant, but he had to be stopped. Putting the key in the ignition, she revved the engine a couple of times and set off.

Sarah could hear raised voices next door. She tried to block out the sound because she was concentrating on Mr Millward's books, but then she heard the sound of a loud thump, someone falling and Mrs Rivers crying out. Sarah took off her shoe and banged on the wall. She wasn't brave enough to confront Nat Rivers face to face, but she wanted him to know that someone was listening. She heard him curse and a few moments later, the door slammed and he walked by the kitchen window. Sarah dashed to the front door and slid the large bolt at the top seconds before Nat tried the doorknob. Her heart was pounding as she turned the key in the lock and shot the bolt at the bottom of the door. On the other side, Nat kicked the wood. 'You stay away from my mother,' he shouted through the letter box. 'Keep your interfering nose out of my business.'

Sarah pressed herself against the wall and said nothing, but as soon as he'd gone down the road, she went to the wooden partition between the kitchen and the scullery. 'Are you all right, Mrs Rivers? Mrs Rivers? Shall I come round?'

'I'm fine,' her neighbour called shakily. 'I dropped the coal bucket, that's all.'

Sarah respected her wish not to be disturbed, but she wished she could have gone in to check.

'Sarah dear?' Mrs Rivers called a few minutes later.

'Yes?'

'I think it better if you don't come round for a

while. Is that all right?'

Sarah swallowed the lump in her throat. 'Are you sure? I'm not scared of him.' It was a lie of course, but there was nothing to stop the two of them getting together when Nat wasn't around.

'I think it's best, dear.'

Reluctantly, Sarah went back to her paperwork, but her mind was all over the place. She hadn't wanted to believe Mr Millward when he'd told her about Henry. She'd tried to tell herself he was wrong, or that it was a case of mistaken identity, but the man was adamant. He had definitely seen her husband in Horsham. All the same, Sarah had to see for herself. Her greatest problem was getting over there. She had no spare money for the bus fare and besides, who would look after the girls? She could try Vera, but she was finding it increasingly difficult to ask her for help.

It took quite a while to plough through the mountain of paperwork Mr Millward had given her, but gradually she made sense of the books. Over the past few weeks, he'd been delighted with her work and they'd become friends. He was no oil painting but he was a good man, she could see that now. He was ambitious too. He'd lost everything in the war, his wife and his home, so he had to start all over again. The coal yard, he'd told her, was only the beginning and now that his books were straight and he could see that he was doing quite well, it was time to expand.

Then this morning he'd turned up at her house unannounced. 'I'm planning to go into the haulage business,' he told her. 'I'm not getting any younger and humping coal is a young man's job.'

She'd smiled encouragingly as she'd passed him a cup of tea. What was he trying to tell her? That he wouldn't be needing a part-time bookkeeper anymore? That she'd lost the position?

'I need a couple of lorries,' he went on.

Sarah stirred her tea, trying not to notice his protruding nasal hairs.

'So I'm going to Horsham next Thursday,' he said. 'This chap I know can get hold of ex-army surplus stuff at a knock-down price.'

Sarah nodded. 'I hope it's all legit.'

'It is,' he said. 'I've checked. The thing is, if you want to see that husband of yours, you and the kids can come with me in the lorry if you like.'

Sarah hesitated. Confront Henry outright? It was a tempting thought.

'I have to pick Jenny up from school at three,' she said cautiously.

'I'm not seeing the bloke until six-ish,' said Mr Millward. 'I can pick you up after you've got the kiddie, if you like.'

Sarah's hand went to her mouth. The timing couldn't have been better. It was an opportunity too good to miss.

Annie Royal lifted the net curtain to dust the already dustless window ledge then glanced back at the clock. Ten thirty. Mrs Holborn from next door would be here at any minute. Annie returned to the kitchen to boil the milk in readiness for their morning cup of Camp coffee. She had only just put the pan of milk on the stove when there was a sharp rap on the back door. 'Come on in, Mrs Holborn.'

Her neighbour took off her coat and hung it over the back of her chair and after swapping comments about the weather, the two women sat down. They were as different as chalk and cheese but their shared loneliness had drawn them together for their twice a week coffee times. On Thursdays, Annie would go next door to Mrs Holborn's place and today, Tuesday, Mrs Holborn came to her. They were both housewives. Mrs Holborn, a woman of fairly mature years, spent her time looking after her sick husband. She also had the responsibility of caring for her aged mother-in-law who lived a couple of streets away and, on top of that, she had three strapping but lazy sons living at home. Annie was easily twenty-five years her junior, but the two of them enjoyed their little chats together.

'How's your Oswald?'

'Much the same. He's coughing up blood now.'

Annie frowned with concern. 'Have you seen the doctor?' Since the advent of the new National Health Service, it was so much easier to get medical help. Annie knew that if this had happened only a year ago and Mrs Holborn had to pay for the doctor to come, Oswald would have waited in vain.

Mrs Holborn nodded. 'He's sleeping now so I can't stay for more than a minute or two today. They're taking him up to the sanatorium in a couple of days, so I won't be able to have you over for coffee on Thursday.'

Annie squeezed her hand. 'Oh, Mrs Holborn, I'm so sorry ... for your husband, I mean.'

'It's for the best, dear,' said her neighbour. 'I

know it was Oswald's wish to die at home but it can't be helped. The TB has got a terrible hold on him now.'

Annie knew Henry wouldn't like it if he knew Mrs Holborn was here. Because her husband was so sick, Henry was afraid she might 'pass something on' to the baby and had forbidden Annie to be with her, but how could she turn away a friend in need? Mrs Holborn had been so kind when they'd moved in and had given her such a lot of friendly advice. There was so much more to being married than she'd realised, and Henry liked everything just so. Annie had been at a bit of a loss to begin with, and when Henry got annoyed, she'd cried bitterly. Mrs Holborn had helped her master the New World cooker and had given her tips on how to make the rations go further. It wasn't easy managing on an ounce of bacon, two ounces of butter and a shilling's worth of meat a week, and Annie welcomed Mrs Holborn's inventiveness when it came to making interesting meals. Her own mother hadn't been near the place, but Mrs Holborn had not only been on hand to give her motherly advice, but she'd also been a pal to laugh with and sometimes a shoulder to cry on. Now the tables had turned and it was her turn to be there for her friend.

As they sat in Annie's immaculate kitchen, Mrs Holborn took a small package out of her apron pocket and pushed it across the table. 'A little something for the baby,' she smiled.

It was wrapped in blue tissue paper, and when she opened it, it was a tiny matinee jacket with matching booties knitted in snow-white wool.

'It's beautiful!' cried Annie. 'Whenever did you find the time to do it?'

Mrs Holborn blushed. 'Actually I didn't. My mother-in-law can't get around like she used to but she's still a good knitter. I bought the wool and the pattern and she did it for me.'

Annie fingered the lacy pattern. It was so soft, so snowy white, just perfect for her baby.

'How long have you got now?' asked Mrs Holborn.

Annie put her hand over her bump. 'Two and a bit months. It's due in the middle of November.'

'About the same time as the royal baby then,' Mrs Holborn grinned. 'I wonder which one of you is going to be the first to tie the good news on Buckingham Palace gates?'

Annie chuckled. The whole country was already excited about the forthcoming birth of the Princess Elizabeth's first child, and King George VI's first grandchild. The papers had gone quiet since the announcement and the princess hadn't been filmed or photographed since the summer, but everyone knew the baby was due in November.

'Did you notice that woman was back?' said Mrs Holborn suddenly. 'She was waiting across the road again this morning.'

A feeling of unease wrapped itself around Annie's stomach. 'What woman?'

'Attractive, well dressed. She looked as if she was worth a bob or two,' Mrs Holborn went on. 'I saw her hanging around a couple of weeks ago.'

Annie frowned. 'Is she still there then?'

The two women, their eyes locked, stood up together. They walked quietly to the sitting room and, standing well back from the window, scanned the street, but there was no sign of her. Annie was secretly relieved. She had no idea who the woman was, but it was a bit disconcerting having her outside the house.

'The car's gone too,' said Mrs Holborn, sounding surprised.

'What car?'

'I saw her heading towards a car at the other end of the road,' said Mrs Holborn.

'She must have been waiting for someone,' Annie remarked.

'Maybe,' said Mrs Holborn. 'I get the feeling that she'll be trouble.'

'Ah well, thank goodness she's not there now,' said Annie, steering her back to the kitchen.

Three

On Thursday afternoon, Annie washed up her cup and saucer and wiped the draining board. Her jobs were all done, the house was spotless and the ironing basket was empty. What on earth was she going to do for the rest of the day? Once the baby came there would be plenty to think about, but right now, with no friends living nearby, she was bored, bored, bored. If only one of her friends from Worthing would answer her letters. She wrote nearly every Sunday and Henry posted them on his way to work, but it was as if she faced a wall of silence. A glance through the window told her that the rain was holding off, so she decided to go for a walk. Maybe she'd take a sandwich, buy herself a magazine and sit in the park for a while.

Annie put on her swagger coat and sensible shoes. She decided against an umbrella, but she took a ten bob note from the emergency jar. She wouldn't spend it all of course, but she might buy something from the shops ... some chocolate or maybe an ice cream. Surely Henry wouldn't object if she treated herself now and then? Feeling suddenly daring, she kicked off the sensible shoes and reached for her high heels. She hadn't worn them for ages but they did make her feel more feminine. Just because she was pregnant, she didn't have to be a complete frump, did she?

Annie had no problem finding a seat in the sunshine. Earlier in the month when they'd held the Horsham Festival and the fairground rides were there, you could hardly put a pinhead between the people on the grass, but there were few in the park today.

It was a lovely place. If she had been with Henry and she wasn't pregnant, they might have gone to the outside swimming pool or played a game of miniature golf followed by cucumber sandwiches and a pot of tea at the park café. Today, she'd bought a quarter of coffee crunch for Henry and had been daring enough to buy a naughty cake. She settled down to eat it. Henry would have been annoyed if he'd seen her. 'Eating in the street?' he would've said. 'How slovenly,' but for the moment, she didn't care. She bit into the sponge and the imitation cream tickled her nose. Delicious. Her magazine was enjoyable too and she was soon engrossed in a story about an actress who felt miscast as a housewife (oh, how she sympathised), when a shadow fell across the page. When Annie looked up, the elegant woman she'd seen in the street the day of Henry's birthday was standing right in front of her. Immediately her pulse rate shot up and the baby kicked inside of her.

'Excuse me. Is your husband Henry Royal?'

The woman's voice was soft and well educated and yet she didn't appear to be at all toffee-nosed. All the same, Annie didn't want to talk to her. Snatching up her magazine, Annie stuffed it into her bag. She didn't know why but this woman was unnerving her.

'I'm sorry,' said the woman. 'No, no, don't get up. I didn't mean to startle you.'

'Who are you?' Annie challenged. 'And what do you want with my husband?'

The woman made as if to speak and then seemed to change her mind. As she moved her arm, a waft of expensive perfume filled the air. 'Is there somewhere we could talk?' she said softly. 'Somewhere a little more quiet. A café or some tea rooms?'

Annie's heart was bumping as she looked the woman up and down. She was older than she was; mid-thirties or perhaps more. She was dressed in orange and brown. Her hair under her lopsided burnt orange hat was curled, but it looked natural rather than a permanent wave. Her complexion and make-up were flawless. She wore an orange and white spotted blouse underneath the jacket of her brown suit, which had a long line pencil skirt ending way beyond the knee. Her dark brown suede court shoes sported a neat bow on the front. She wore elbow-length gloves which matched her hat and she carried a lizard-skin clutch bag. The woman was polite enough and her voice was gentle but somehow Annie didn't want to hear what she had to say. 'I can't stop now,' she blurted out. 'I have to get home and get my husband's tea.'

'You're pregnant,' the woman said as Annie pulled her coat around herself. She sounded a little surprised.

'Yes I am, but I don't see what business that is of yours,' Annie said haughtily.

'It makes things a little more difficult,' the woman conceded, 'but I still need to talk to you.'

'Not now. Not today.'

In the distance, the town hall clock struck the half hour. 'It won't take long and it is rather important.'

'I have to go,' said Annie, wishing she'd worn the sensible shoes now. Hurrying in high heels which she hadn't worn in ages was not a good idea, but she couldn't bear to be near the woman a second longer. Annie didn't look back as she hurried away. She was shaking inside and she'd gone most of the way home before she'd managed to calm down. Thankfully the woman hadn't followed her.

As she turned the corner of the street, there was an ambulance outside Mrs Holborn's and when a stretcher came out of the house, she saw Oswald, pale-faced and with sunken cheeks, under the blanket, blinking up at the sky. He looked terrible and Mrs Holborn was crying. Annie didn't have time to say anything to them but she did stop to give her neighbour an encouraging smile before the ambulance doors were closed on them both. As it roared away, she somehow knew that was the last time she would ever see Oswald Holborn. The woman in the park had shaken her up, but her discomfort was nothing compared to what poor Mrs Holborn was going through.

When she got indoors, Annie hid her shoes at the back of the cupboard and put the radio on full blast. Henry didn't like a lot of noise, but Annie wanted to shut out the memories of Oswald's pain-filled face and every trace of that woman in the park. The one thing she couldn't stop were the questions reverberating around in her head. Who was that woman? Why did she keep coming back and what did she have to do with Henry?

Before long the potatoes were peeled and the cabbage ready in the pan. Tonight Annie was going to cook lamb chops as a special treat. She had just laid the table when there was a sharp rap at the back door. Her neighbour, Mrs Holborn, must be back from the hospital already. 'Come on in,' she called.

The door opened and a woman she'd never seen before stepped into the kitchen. Annie jumped and gasped in disbelief. Now what? Her first thought was that the woman was a gypsy, perhaps selling pegs or lucky heather, but a more considered look told her this woman was no gypsy. How strange, and what were the odds against two completely different women accosting her on the same day? She was just about to shout at her and threaten her with the police when she noticed she had two little girls with her – one was in her mother's arms while the other leaned against her body.

Annie felt her blood run cold. 'Who are you? What do you want? My husband will be here at any minute,' she said, hoping to frighten the woman away.

'Your husband?' Sarah sneered.

Her words seemed to hang in space. Annie put her hand protectively over the baby under her floral apron. The woman stared at her bump and Annie held her head high.

'You don't know, do you?' said the woman. 'You haven't a clue.'

'Don't know what?' said Annie, doing her best to sound in control of the situation.

'Henry Royal isn't your husband,' said the woman, the words tumbling out. 'My name is Sarah Royal. I've never been divorced, so you see Henry can't be your husband – because he's still mine.'

A deafening silence crept between them. Annie, still holding the salt and pepper pots ready to put on the table, was conscious that she was staring at this stranger with her mouth open. Clearly she must be quite mad. She'd got Henry mixed up with somebody else. In a couple of weeks it would be their wedding anniversary. A year ago, they had had a proper wedding with a registrar and witnesses. And wasn't her marriage certificate in the drawer? Her husband came home every night and was with her every weekend so how could he possibly have another wife and family? As the silence deepened, the smaller child wriggled in her mother's arms to get down. Her mother put her onto the floor and straightened up again.

'I'm afraid you've made a terrible mistake,' said Annie, taking a deep breath and willing herself to stay calm. She continued with putting the condiments on the table and tried to sound firm yet gentle. It was obvious that the poor woman must be deluded. Annie had heard of things like this before. The war had only finished three years ago and there were stories in the papers all the time about women who still believed their husbands were coming home even after they'd been officially informed to the contrary. Annie chewed her bottom lip. 'Please,' she began again. 'I know you are upset but I really must ask you to go. My husband...'

They all heard a key turn in the front door and a blast of cold air propelled the kitchen door open and tugged at the tea towel hanging over the back of a chair. Annie and the woman stood facing each other, their eyes locked. At the same moment Henry called, 'Darling, I'm home.'

The older child beamed. 'Daddy!' she cried and as she darted towards the hallway, her mother grabbed her arm. 'No Jenny, wait.'

'But that's Daddy,' she cried. 'I can hear him.'

Annie's stomach went over. She looked down at the girl. She was about six years old with light brown hair done up in plaits. Her pinched face had an earnest expression. She was clean and tidy but thin and pale. Her coat was far too small for her. The sleeves ended above the wrists and the buttons strained across her middle. It barely reached her knees. The other little girl looked about eighteen months old.

Henry's heavy footsteps echoed along the passageway. 'Didn't you hear me call, darling? I'm home.'

Annie remained rooted to the spot. She didn't know what to do. He'd be furious that she'd let this stranger in and even more annoyed that the uninvited woman in his kitchen was unhinged enough to be making such ridiculous accusations. 'I think you'd better go,' she hissed, but it was already too late.

A bunch of chrysanthemums heralded his arrival and then Henry himself stood in the doorway. When he saw the woman, his face froze. 'What the hell are you doing here?' he thundered.

'Daddy,' said the child again, but he ignored her.

Her mother pulled Jenny back to her side. 'You know perfectly well why I'm here,' she said defiantly. 'How could you do this to us, Henry?'

'Get out,' he bellowed. 'Get out or I'll call the police and have you arrested.'

Annie gasped and put her hand over her mouth.

With a defiant look, Sarah squared up to him. 'Why don't you do just that,' she retorted, but he'd thrown the flowers onto the kitchen table and was already bundling her roughly through the kitchen door. 'Call the police,' she shrieked as she was being manhandled outside, 'and it's you they'll lock up, Henry.'

'Get out, you witch, and don't come back!'

'You owe me, Henry!'

'I owe you nothing.'

'But we've got nothing. You've got to help us.'

By now both children were crying, but Henry

didn't seem to care. 'Get out, get out, the lot of you...' he shouted as he slammed the door after them. There was the sound of a fall and Annie listened in horror as the little girl tried to comfort her mother and sister.

'Oh Henry, I forgot to bring the washing in,' Annie cried. 'She's fallen over the tin bath.'

She ran towards the door but Henry grabbed her wrist and rounded on her. 'Why did you let them in? Haven't I told you time and time again not to have people in the house when I'm not here?'

'I didn't realise she was there,' Annie protested. The wails outside began to fade and they both knew that the woman and her children were leaving. 'I thought she was Mrs Holborn.'

'And why would you think that?' he bellowed.

Annie gulped. Why had she blurted that out? She dared not tell him that she and Mrs Holborn met on a regular basis.

'You've had her in here, haven't you?' he cried, swinging his arm around and sending everything from the table onto the floor. The plates smashed and the knives and forks fell with a clatter as he yelled, 'Why can't you women do as you're bloody well told?'

'Henry...' she said in shocked surprise. He'd been cross with her in the past but she'd never seen him in such a rage before. She gasped at the broken plates and the bunch of flowers scattered everywhere, but he was totally unrepentant. His feet crunching on broken glass, he stalked angrily out of the room.

Annie's heart was thumping as she surveyed the mess. This wasn't how she'd wanted the evening to be. A smell of burning chop wafted towards her and she realised too late that the dinner was ruined as well. Miserably, she began to clear up. When she opened the back door to put the pieces of broken crockery into the dustbin, the woman and the two children had long gone. There was no sign of them. The washing was still in the clean bath, so she picked it up and brought it in. Putting it onto a chair, Annie fought her tears and began to fold it ready for the iron.

Could the woman's words be true? Annie had been ready to dismiss her fantastic accusation out of hand until the little girl recognised Henry's voice. The child was so young it seemed impossible that she would make it up, and if she really was his child, how could he have been so cruel? Annie caressed her bump. What if he was that horrible to her baby? She heard a footfall behind her and realised he was back.

'Sorry, darling,' he said in a contrite tone of voice. 'Bad day at the office.' He took her in his arms and held her tightly.

'She said you were her husband.'

'I've never seen her in my life before,' he said firmly. He leaned down and kissed her tenderly and she melted in his arms.

'But the little girl seemed to know you,' Annie said. 'She called you daddy.'

His expression darkened. 'What is this? Are you calling me a liar?' he challenged.

'No, no, of course not,' Annie said. 'It's just that…'

'They train them to do that,' he said.

Annie was aghast. 'Train them?'

'Don't you see, you silly goose?' he smiled, relaxing his expression. 'It was some sort of racket. She wanted money, that's all. They come round and make a scene, the kid pretends the husband is the father and we pay her to go away and say nothing.' He put his arms around her again.

'Poor little things. They did look rather thin,' Annie remarked.

'Let's not talk about them anymore,' said Henry curtly.

'The tea,' she said miserably.

'Don't worry about that,' he said. 'We're going away.'

'Going away?' she said faintly. 'But you never said. Where are we going?'

'It's a little surprise,' he said. 'I've got a few days off work. Now go upstairs and pack, there's a good girl. We'll eat on the train.'

'What train?' she asked.

'Stop asking bloody questions!' he snapped impatiently.

Annie fled. The suitcase was on the bed. He'd obviously been up into the loft to fetch it. She packed what she could but had no idea how long they were going for or even where they were going. Why couldn't he have mentioned the surprise this morning? It would have made the day so much better, having something to look forward to, and she could have done a little ironing ready to pack the suitcase. Still, it was a good time of the year to be going away. Most boarding houses would welcome late guests. The summer season was over and yet the warm autumn days were as good as, if not better than, August. She wondered where they were going. They certainly couldn't afford to stay in a hotel. Henry was always very careful with his money.

'Finished?' he said, coming through the bedroom door.

'I hope we're not going to be too long,' she said. 'I have to see the midwife next week.'

'For God's sake!' he snapped and, pushing her roughly aside, he slammed the lid of the case and locked it. 'Stop bleating on, will you? Go and get your coat on.'

'We're not going right away, are we?' she gasped.

'Yes we are, now get a move on.'

He was hurrying her down the stairs so quickly she almost stumbled. He helped her with her coat and then she remembered the rice pudding still in the oven. 'I have to turn the oven off.'

'Leave it,' he growled.

'Don't be silly, Henry,' she said, hurrying back. 'If I don't turn it off we'll burn the house down.'

She heard him opening the front door as she put on the oven gloves. A second later he came rushing through the kitchen, knocking her against the cooker as he went.

'Mind the pudding!' she cried as it slid from her gloved hands and onto the draining board. But Henry wasn't listening. He'd flung open the back door and was charging out into the garden. He didn't get far. Someone was standing in the shadows waiting for him. 'Going somewhere, sir,' said a man's voice.

Annie gasped as a policeman walked her husband back into the kitchen. Henry looked around helplessly as another policeman came into the kitchen from the hallway.

'What's happened?' Annie cried. 'Is it my mother?'

'Henry Arthur Royale,' the policeman was saying, 'I am arresting you on suspicion of bigamy. You do not have to say anything...'

'The bitch is lying,' cried Henry. 'I got a divorce.'

With a horrified sigh, Annie lowered herself onto a chair.

Four

As soon as Sarah stumbled out onto the street, she was filled with remorse. What on earth had she been thinking of? When Vera told her she was unable to have the girls, she should have let it go. She should never have brought them to Horsham. They could be traumatised for life by what their father had just done to them. She still had Lu-Lu in her arms and Jenny was clinging to her skirts. They were all crying now and when she knelt on the pavement to put her arm around Jenny, the little girl was trembling.

'I'm sorry,' she whispered as she choked back her own tears. 'Mummy is so sorry about what happened, but I want you to remember that Daddy is cross with Mummy, not with you. He didn't mean it.'

Jenny looked at her, her eyes brimming. 'But he called you a witch.'

'It was a silly grown-up's joke,' she said in a measured tone. It cost her dearly, but Sarah was determined that her gentle and loving daughter wouldn't be damaged any further. She had never once expected this sort of reaction from Henry, but she must have been mad to come, especially with the children.

To her surprise, a couple of minutes later, a police car drew up and several policemen got out. They went into Henry's gate. Sarah hoiked Lu-Lu back onto her hip and took Jenny's hand in hers. An expensive-looking car had also pulled up beside the pavement. The driver, a woman, seemed to be waiting for something but she didn't get out.

'Move along now if you please, madam,' said a policeman coming up to Sarah. 'This is no place for little ones.'

Sarah didn't need any more persuasion. Whatever Henry was mixed up in, she was well out of it. Her only thought now was to get her children away from here.

As they hurried back along the street, Sarah turned her head to see the same policeman who had told her to move on leaning into the expensive car's window. A few seconds later, the woman drove off.

Before long, as they waited on the corner for Mr Millward's lorry, Jenny was swinging around the bus stop and Lu-Lu was giggling as she watched her big sister play. Sarah was grateful that she'd thought of bringing the baby reins. They gave Lu-Lu a little freedom but also kept her safe. In the distance, Sarah saw what looked like Henry being bundled into a big black car.

That girl in Henry's kitchen had looked as fresh as a daisy and as innocent as a virgin, only she wasn't a virgin, was she? She was pregnant. Before Sarah realised the girl's condition, she had hated her without even knowing her. Now that Henry had been arrested, she was beginning to think there was something about the girl that reminded her of herself. It probably wasn't her fault. He'd most likely lied to that girl in just the same way he'd lied to her. For a moment back there she'd felt … oh, she couldn't put it into words ... protective or something like that. She'd wanted to prepare the girl for what was to come. It wasn't logical and her thinking was muddled. She certainly didn't feel like that now. Because of that girl, everyone had been let down. Her friends, his friends, even the people where he'd worked. Sarah was both frustrated and angry. The silly trollop had ruined all their lives.

Jenny sidled up to her and leaned into her body. 'Who was that lady in Daddy's house, Mummy?'

Sarah smiled down at her eldest daughter. 'Nobody important, darling.'

'You all right, dear?'

Annie was still in her kitchen with the back door wide open. Her eyes were puffy and her throat was sore from crying. Henry was gone. Bewildered, she had followed him to the front door and watched the police take him away in a big black Humber, spitting feathers and using ugly swear words she'd never heard before.

'Get me a solicitor,' he'd bellowed as they'd pushed him onto the back seat of the car.

Her mind was in a whirl. Should she follow him to the police station? How would she get there? More to the point, where was it? If it was too far to walk, she'd have to go on the bus and it was gone eight o'clock. If they kept her at the police station for a long time, how would she get back home? She didn't like the thought of being out at night on her own, especially in her present condition. He wouldn't want her getting a taxi. Henry had always insisted taxis were a terrible waste of money.

She had returned to the kitchen and sat at the table doing her best to gather her thoughts. There must be a terrible mistake. That woman at the back door – Sarah was it? – seemed normal enough, but she had to be deluded. Either that or it was a case of mistaken identity. Henry probably reminded her of her lost husband. He must have said something, or walked the same way her husband walked, and the poor woman had convinced herself that he was the same man. Annie cast her mind back to the late summer of 1947 when she and Henry had first met and were strolling along a country lane. She'd caught sight of a girl with long red hair just up in front of her. From the back, the girl had looked just like Ellen Slattery and her heart had missed a beat. Annie had grown up with Ellen and knew her very well, but Ellen had been killed in an air raid in 1940. At the time, Annie hadn't taken into account the fact that Ellen would have been five years older, and that when you lose someone, they stay in your memory exactly as when you last saw them. The woman who had knocked on her kitchen door must have done exactly the same thing. In the cold, hard light of day, surely she would realise her mistake?

'Annie dear...'Annie became aware that Mrs Holborn was standing over her. 'I've made you a cup of tea. You look as if you could do with one.'

'They took my Henry away,' she said dully.

'I know, dear,' said Mrs Holborn. 'I saw them taking him away as I got off the bus. I wasn't sure if I should come in…'

Annie stared at the cup and saucer being pushed in front of her. 'Where can I get a solicitor? He told me to get him a solicitor.'

'I shouldn't worry about that now, dear,' Mrs Holborn soothed. 'Plenty of time in the morning.'

'Yes, but where would I find one?' Annie persisted.

Mrs Holborn shrugged. 'I'd ask the police when you go to see him tomorrow.'

Annie nodded dully and shivered.

'Are you cold?' asked Mrs Holborn. 'I suppose you are. You had all the doors wide open. I'll put the oven on and leave it open to warm the place up a bit.' She glanced at the clock. 'It's a bit late to light the fire in the sitting room. You'll be going to bed soon I expect.'

Her neighbour left the room and Annie looked up. The clock was already ticking its way towards 9.30 p.m. She blew her nose and sipped her tea. A few minutes later, Mrs Holborn was back with a hot-water bottle. Annie watched as she emptied it out and refilled it with hot water.

'I'm sure everything will come right in the end,' said Mrs Holborn. 'Your Henry is a good man.'

'A woman came to the house,' Annie began.

'That woman we both saw in the street?'

'No, a different one,' said Annie. 'She said Henry was her husband.'

'Her husband?' cried Mrs Holborn. 'Well, that can't be right, can it? Didn't you tell me you were married in the registry office?'

Annie nodded.

'Well then,' said Mrs Holborn. 'She's made a mistake. I shouldn't worry, dear. The police will soon sort it out and he'll be back home before you know it. I'll just pop this hot-water bottle in your bed for you.'

Annie listened to Mrs Holborn climbing the stairs. The baby moved and she rubbed her stomach. What if Henry really was still married to someone else? Her baby would be illegitimate, wouldn't it? Her throat tightened. She was an honest woman. She'd been a virgin on her wedding night. Henry was experienced, but then you expected that; didn't you? Young men and their wild oats and all that... But he wouldn't have deceived her about something as important as having another wife, would he? Would he? Supposing he *was* still married? That would make her an adulteress, wouldn't it? If she'd broken the seventh commandment and she didn't know, would that still make her a sinner? He'd told the police he'd got a divorce. Annie never even knew he'd been married before. Why hadn't he told her? That wasn't the sort of thing a husband should keep from his wife.

Mrs Holborn was back. She looked tired and drawn.

'How is your husband?' Annie asked

'I'm going back first thing in the morning,' she said grimly. 'They tell me it's only a matter of days.'

'I'm so sorry,' said Annie, catching her neighbour's hand.

Mrs Holborn squeezed her hand back. 'Don't you go worrying about me. We've had a good innings, Oswald and me. All good things come to an end.' As she spoke, her face coloured and she looked embarrassed. 'Sorry, dear. Me and my big mouth. Now it's my turn to be sorry.'

'Do you think I should telephone the police station?'

'Leave it until the morning, dear. I'm sure they won't tell you anything you don't already know.'

As Peter Millward drove her and the girls home, Sarah couldn't stop thinking. In truth, she'd wished she was still in the kitchen when the police had knocked on Henry's door. How she would have loved to see his smug face change when they'd arrested him. What on earth had he done? If she could have had anything to do with it, she would have enjoyed pointing the finger and watching him squirm. How could he have left her and the kids like that? She was at her wit's end. Someone in the pub had told her that if a person was missing for seven years they could be declared dead. But he wasn't dead, was he? He'd walked out of all their lives, taking everything portable with him and, somehow, Sarah had struggled on. Seeing the lovely house where Henry lived made it even harder to keep a lid on her anger. She and the girls managed in one room and a bedroom upstairs and a poky little kitchen which she had to share with the tenant downstairs. They had an outside lavvy while the rat who'd put her in this position lived in a three-bedroomed house with its own little garden.

Henry had once accused her of being dippy and said that she wouldn't be able to cope without him. Well, she'd proved him wrong, hadn't she? She may not have such a grand house, but she'd kept a roof over their heads and the girls knew they were loved.

'I take it that it didn't go well,' said Peter cautiously.

'It didn't,' Sarah said. The only sound in the lorry was the hum of the engine.

'I won't pry,' he said, keeping his eyes firmly fixed on the road, 'but just to let you know, if ever you want to talk…'

'Thank you, Mr Millward,' she said stiffly. 'You're a kind man.'

'Peter, please.'

'Peter,' she said shyly.

And with that, he left her to her own thoughts for the rest of the journey. The minute Henry had pushed her and the girls out of the door, Sarah's hopes and dreams had been finally dashed. In her haste to get away, she had tripped over a metal bath full of washing and fallen onto the path. Poor little Jenny was distraught. Sarah had hauled herself to her feet and, ignoring the graze on her leg, limped away, her only thought to get her children as far away from Henry as possible. For the first time since it happened, she became aware of a throbbing in her leg. She glanced down and in the headlights of a passing car, she caught sight of a dark stain creeping down her leg. Her stocking was shredded.

'Do you need to stop and sort that leg out?' said Peter.

'No, I'll be all right,' said Sarah 'I'll wait until I get home.'

Jenny had already leaned into her mother's side and promptly fallen asleep. Lu-Lu was dead to the world in her arms and although Sarah was dog-tired, she couldn't sleep. Her brain was racing. Lu-Lu was far too young to understand, but how would her gentle Jenny survive knowing that the daddy she adored had no time for her now? How could he be so heartless and cruel? Sarah kissed the top of her daughter's neatly plaited head. 'I'm so sorry, darling,' she whispered to her sleeping child. 'From now on, I promise to protect you. He may not want you, but Mummy loves you to bits.' And, she thought to herself, Mummy will never let you down.

Mrs Holborn left soon after she'd put the hot-water bottle in the bed, making Annie promise to lock the door when she'd gone. The suitcase stood accusingly in the hallway as Annie wearily climbed the stairs. She would unpack it in the morning. As she undressed and crawled into bed, she wondered vaguely where Henry had been planning to take her. She turned out the lamp. It was lovely and warm between the sheets but already she missed Henry's bulk beside her. *Oh Henry ... where are you now? They must let you come home soon.* Her silent tears were making her pillow damp. She turned it over and closed her eyes, but sleep didn't come easily. Her mind wouldn't stop going over and over what had happened. When she finally drifted away, her last thought was of him. *I need you, Henry. I simply can't have this baby on my own.*

Five

Annie woke up with a thumping headache but there was no time to feel sorry for herself. Two aspirin with her cup of tea would have to suffice. By 9.15 a.m. she was already walking down New Street. She didn't have a plan but she knew she had to do two things: one, to make sure Henry was all right; and secondly, to find a solicitor. As she reached the bus stop, a Southdown bus pulled up to let someone off. Annie climbed aboard. There was no room on the lower deck so she went upstairs, and how providential that turned out to be. As the bus turned towards the Carfax, she spotted a sign engraved on a first floor window. D.C. West, Solicitor and Commissioner of Oaths. Annie got off at the next stop.

The entrance was in between a café and a greengrocer's shop and up a steep flight of stairs. A door at the top was open and Annie found herself in a small office. A woman behind the desk was typing but she stopped as soon as she saw Annie.

'Can I help you?'

Annie stated her business and the secretary asked her to wait. She knocked on the glass of another door and a rather squeaky voice called 'Enter.'

Mr West turned out to be an amiable man with a jolly face and a bald head. He was dressed in a pinstriped suit and when he offered her a handshake, she could see he had well-manicured fingernails. The first thing he did was to ask his secretary to bring some tea. As soon as she left the room, Annie started to explain what had happened when suddenly Mr West put up his hand.

'Before I begin my consultation,' he smiled, 'I'm afraid I must ask you for two guineas up front.'

Annie swallowed hard. Two guineas? There wasn't even a pound in the emergency jar and that was all she had. She had already eaten into the ten bob note when she'd seen the posh woman. Henry kept all their money in the bank.

'My husband handles all our affairs,' she faltered.

'The balance can wait until the case is cleared,' Mr West said, 'but I need something on account.'

Annie opened her purse and, keeping back a florin, tipped five shillings onto the desk. 'I'll bring the balance tomorrow,' she said firmly.

'Two guineas,' Mr West insisted. He leaned back in his chair and studied her face.

Annie stood up, moving slowly and exaggerating her bulk. 'Then I'll have to go home and fetch it,' she sighed.

'Perhaps…' he began as she headed for the door, 'er … um ... in view of your condition, I could, make an exception.'

'Thank you,' said Annie, lowering herself into

the chair again.

For the next few minutes, she told her story and Mr West took everything down.

'Do you have your wedding certificate with you?'

Annie shook her head. Ever since she got on the bus she'd had a feeling she should have brought it with her, but it was still in Henry's drawer.

'Bring it when you come back with the balance,' said Mr West, rising to his feet and offering her his hand. 'Like you say, I'm sure this is all a silly misunderstanding. Leave it to me, Mrs Royal.'

'Next.'

The receptionist at the Old Town Hall was a tight-lipped woman with a severe hairstyle and a lazy eye. A young woman with a small child on her hip walked to the desk and began speaking in hushed tones. Annie, who was next in the queue, had been directed there from the police station after the desk sergeant had explained that Henry had been sent to the magistrate's court which was held in the Old Town Hall. It was so annoying. If they had told her that straight away, she would have been here a lot sooner, but instead they had kept her waiting in a bare room for twenty minutes and then a detective had asked her a lot of questions. Had she seen the other Mrs Royal before that day? Did she know Mr Royal had been married before? Where did she meet Mr Royal? How long had she known him? The questions went on and on.

The young woman moved away from the desk and the receptionist called a second time, 'Next.'

Annie explained that she had come here to see Henry. She addressed one eye before realising that the woman was actually looking at her with the other. It was most disconcerting and even more so when the woman told her she was already too late to see Henry.

'Mr Royal has already appeared before the magistrate and is now in the cells,' she said, lifting her head. 'Next.'

Annie was aware of other people behind her in the queue but she hadn't finished yet. 'In the cells?'

'He's been sent for trial at the next Lewes Assizes,' the woman said curtly. 'And before you ask, no I'm afraid you can't see him. Not in here anyway. Next.'

'But how long will it be before the trial?' Annie asked. A man shuffled towards the desk.

'Three weeks,' said the woman.

Annie stayed rooted to the spot. Three weeks? Henry would be stuck in jail for three weeks when he hadn't done anything? 'So what do I do now?' said Annie, more to herself than to anyone else.

'You can visit him once he's been transferred,' said the woman. 'You don't have to apply for a permit for prisoners on remand. Next.'

'Thank you,' said Annie faintly. She moved out of the way and the man shuffled forward again.

'If you want my advice,' the receptionist muttered, 'you'll choose your friends more carefully next time.'

Annie felt her face flame and she turned on her heel. 'Well, nobody asked you for your advice so I'll thank you to keep your opinions to yourself,' she snapped.

The woman looked deeply offended, but with head held high, Annie walked back to the door, ignoring another person in the queue muttering a breathy, 'Well, really...'

In desperate need of refreshment, Annie wandered into the café next door. She felt a bit guilty being so rude to the woman in the town hall, but how dare she judge her. Henry was innocent, and even if he was caught up in something, she wasn't going to be a doormat, nor the brunt of other people's ill-informed opinions. Sitting in the window seat and watching people going about their normal business had a calming effect. She had resisted having a quiet cry all morning and when at times her hands had a visible tremor, she'd made a point of gripping her handbag on what was left of her lap so that no one would see how upset she was. She wasn't about to let that silly old cow in the town hall reduce her to tears now. The waitress put the teapot in front of her and the rattling teacup and saucer brought her back to the here and now.

'Nice day,' the waitress remarked.

Annie managed a thin smile and her mouth said, 'Yes, yes it is,' and at the same time thinking, *well, it may be for you but my world is falling apart...*

Left to her tea and her own thoughts, Annie wondered about little Jenny and her mother. Henry had insisted it was all trickery; but the child had seemed genuinely upset. What sort of a mother would expose her child to such an awful scene? If she had something against Henry, why didn't she confront him when they were on their own? What the woman said couldn't possibly be true, and yet the magistrates had believed her story. They must have done if Henry was to be sent for trial. Annie's eyes drifted towards the newsagent across the road and in particular the billboard outside. What if the newspapers got hold of the story? She shuddered at the thought of being the object of shame and gossip and gripped her cup with both hands to stop them shaking the tea onto the tablecloth as she pictured herself trying to dodge the reporters in the same way people did on the Pathé newsreels.

And what about Henry? This could ruin him. For the first time since it happened, Annie suddenly remembered his job. She would have to tell them where he was, but how could she? Once they knew he was in Lewes prison, he'd get the sack. He had already lost his freedom, and if she let him lose his job, he would be totally humiliated. It was grossly unfair. She couldn't let it happen. As soon as she'd finished her tea, she would go round to the jeweller's shop in the High Street where Henry worked now and make some excuse. But what on earth would she say? She could explain away a day or two with a bad cold or a hacking cough, but three weeks? Think, she told her jumbled brain, think carefully and logically. Rhodesia. He'd told her that he'd grown up in Rhodesia. She knew that much anyway. It was only as the detective asked her questions that she realised how little she knew about him. Did he have brothers and sisters? She didn't know. Where was he educated? She hadn't a clue. She'd told the policeman that Henry had been a POW during the war but when he'd pressed her on that one, she had no idea where he'd been. She'd never thought to ask and she'd never really realised before that even if she did mention something about his past, Henry always changed the subject. The policeman had exposed her lack of knowledge and she'd felt such a fool, but she'd made up her mind that as soon as Henry was back home, she'd make a point of finding out everything she could.

But for now what was she going to tell the people where Henry worked? If she couldn't tell the truth, she'd have to make something up. What if someone out there, his mother or his brother, had sent for him? His father was dying ... yes, that was it. She would tell them that his father was dying in far-off Rhodesia and that his mother had sent for him. He'd gone at once and he'd be back in three weeks. Of course he didn't have the plane fare and there was no question of waiting to save up, so they'd sent the plane ticket by wire from Rhodesia. What with all the changes, it took four or five days to fly out there which was why he needed to go at once and why it would take at least three weeks to sort everything out. She drained the last vestige of her tea and took a deep breath. She was no good at lying. Her parents always knew when she wasn't telling the truth. She thought back to 1940 and the last time she'd been with Ellen Slattery shortly before she was killed. They were both ten and supposed to be going to GFS after school. The Girls' Friendly Society was fun, but Ellen had persuaded her to play Kiss Chase with the boys instead. They'd had a great time and when it was time to go home, they'd synchronised their stories. Ellen got away with it, but somehow Father had known that Annie was lying. If she closed her eyes she could still feel the unbearable sting of his wide hand as it met the tops of her bare legs. She'd been sent to bed with no tea and spent the next few days pulling her dress down to hide the bruise marks from his fingers, which were still clearly visible. This time she had to get her story right if the people Henry worked for were to believe her.

Sarah was going through the motions. She'd got the children up and Jenny to school, but she kept away from her sister. She was still annoyed with Vera that she had refused to have Jenny and Lu-Lu for a bit and she certainly didn't want to have to talk about what had happened in Horsham. She did her shift in the pub, which was particularly unpleasant that day because someone had been sick in the gents, and then a little shopping. She avoided Mrs Angel's shop because she couldn't face putting what happened yesterday into words there either. She tried not to, but she couldn't help wondering what Henry was doing now. She hoped his cell was freezing cold and that they'd taken away all his clothes. She hoped his bed was made of rusty nails and that he had rats for company. Of course, in this day and age that was impossible, she told herself, but she wished for it all the same. The puzzling thing was, why had the police arrested him? If only she had stayed outside the back door a bit longer, then she might have heard.

Where did she go from here? She should jolly well make Henry pay for his children's upkeep, but how did she go about it? Besides, if she flagged herself up to the welfare people, they might decide to take the kids away from her and if that happened, she couldn't go on. Without Jenny and Lu-Lu, she might as well be dead. She had no money for solicitors and the like, so she was in a cleft stick.

Before picking Jenny up from school, Sarah went to the phone box to look in the dog-eared Directory Enquiries book for the number of the Horsham police station. Then she lifted the receiver and asked the operator to connect her. Once she had pushed the money in the slot and the operator told her she was connected, she pressed button B and heard a gruff voice saying, 'Horsham Police. Desk Sergeant.'

'I'm enquiring about Mr Henry Royal,' she said in her poshest voice.

'He's been sent for trial at Lewes Assizes.'

Sarah swallowed hard. 'On what charge?'

'Who are you?' said the sergeant.

'I'm his wife.'

'Then you already know,' said the sergeant. He sounded irritable. 'Seeing as how you made the complaint.'

Sarah hesitated. What was he talking about? 'But I've made no complaint,' she said.

There was a pause at the other end. 'Say your name again?'

'Mrs Sarah Royal,' she said deliberately.

The sergeant must have put his hand over the mouthpiece because although his response was muffled, Sarah heard him gasp, 'Bloody 'ell. Call the Inspector. There's another one on the phone.'

She hung up.

Back home and exhausted, Annie stood in her bathroom and put a cold flannel to her forehead. What a day. The meeting at the jeweller's where Henry worked in the office went quite well, although she'd hated having to lie to them. She'd used her pregnancy to good effect and even had them fussing around her with a chair and a glass of water before she'd left the shop.

'If there's anything we can do to help, Mrs Royal,' the manager had said as she left, 'please don't hesitate…'

Annie had kept her head down, not daring to look him in the eye, but she told him of her appreciation for his kind offer. It was so embarrassing and she went away full of shame, but for Henry's sake what else could she do?

The next pressing thing was to find some money and her wedding certificate for Mr West and that left her with another dilemma. Henry kept all their important papers in the dresser drawer, but she didn't have the key. Henry kept all the keys to himself, while she only had the front and back door keys.

After reviving her flagging energy levels with a sandwich, Annie tackled the drawer. She tried sliding a knife along the top, but as soon as it hit the lock, that was that. She found a bunch of keys in the outhouse but nothing fitted. She tried picking the lock with a piece of wire, but her attempt soon convinced her that she'd never make a good burglar. What looked easy on the Hollywood silver screen was far from simple in real life and it was also very frustrating. The emergency money was almost gone. If only she hadn't bought that cake and magazine. True, the cake had only cost 3d, as did the *Woman* magazine – hardly high-class living – but right now every penny counted. And then there was that pot of tea she'd had this morning. Mr West already had five bob and the rent was due in two weeks' time. Annie held her head in her hands. What on earth was she going to do? She wasn't even in a position to earn any money. Who would employ a woman about to give birth? She lowered herself into a chair as her thoughts grew even darker. How was she going to visit Henry with no money? She hardly had enough to feed herself for three weeks, let alone travel all the way to Lewes. Then she remembered the gold watch Granny had given her for her birthday. She could pawn it for the time being. Once Henry's trial was over and he was proven innocent, she could get it back. It was heavy, so it must be worth a bob or two. Annie searched the place high and low, but she couldn't find it. It was all very puzzling. She had it on the day of her wedding because she remembered that Henry had remarked how much he'd liked it. She was sure she'd put it back in the box but it wasn't there now. She racked her brains but she couldn't remember seeing it again. Where on earth could it have gone? Having drawn a complete blank, there was only one other way forward. She had to open that drawer.

Angry and frustrated, Henry Royale lay on his cot facing the wall. How could he have ended up in such a place? He didn't ask much out of life. A little money, a loving wife, a son ... and yet it had come to this. He drew his knees up as he thought of Annie. Why, oh why, had she let that witch in? If he'd told her once, he'd told her a thousand times, 'Don't let anybody in the house while I'm at work.' Of course, he'd never for a minute believed that Sarah would track him down, but if Annie had done as she was told, he could have bluffed his way out of it, same as he always did. And if she'd got a move on with the packing, they would have been long gone before the police arrived as well.

Lewes prison, No. 1 Brighton Road, turned out to be a castellated flint and brick building. Built in Victorian times for far fewer inmates, he and another 149 prisoners were incarcerated two together in a one-man cell, with the stinking toilet stuck in the middle of the room. Only a wooden lid kept the body odours in check and, from where he lay, it wasn't very effective. They'd told him that if he'd been a convicted man rather than a prisoner on remand, he would have been put in isolation straight away. Frankly, he would have preferred to be on his own. He hated having no privacy and, to add insult to injury, he only had a thin mattress, a stained and smelly pillow and a prison blanket on his bed, so no comfort either. He didn't even have any more of his favourite sweets. He'd eaten the last coffee crunch before he'd been remanded in custody.

A noxious smell filled the air as the other prisoner farted. 'Whoops, sorry mate.'

Henry pulled the blanket over his nose. His cell-mate, a skinny man with a broken tooth who had obviously been drinking heavily the night before, wasn't the only animal to share his room. Before he'd turned his back on his fellow prisoner, Henry had seen at least two cockroaches running around the perimeter of the room.

The fat solicitor Annie sent seemed to think that if he was convicted, he'd get three months. Three months wasn't too bad. There was a vague possibility he'd miss the birth of his son, but he'd be back with Annie before the child was more than a week or two old. He could have done with the man earlier but he'd arrived too late for the short hearing in the magistrate's court where Henry had elected to conduct his own defence rather than wait. He realised now that he shouldn't have been so hasty, but what was done, was done. Right now there were more pressing things to think about ... like getting his story straight and winning the sympathy of the jury.

Six

Annie stared at her reflection in the mirror and sighed. Her cheeks were pale and her lipstick reduced to a fading thin line. She took out her compact and began to repair the damage. This wasn't what she'd planned at all. Until two days ago, she'd never even been in a police station before and now here she was waiting to be 'interviewed' again.

They'd made her tip everything out of her handbag, and then she'd watched them picking through her lipstick, powder compact, her purse, the wedding certificate and the brooch. They took the brooch and they'd already taken her bank book earlier on. Having put on her lipstick, she rubbed her lips together and wondered how much she should tell them.

Having stared at it for several days, she had managed to get the drawer open earlier that morning, but the wood had split when she'd levered it away from the lock. She'd gasped in horror knowing that Henry would be very cross, but once she'd calmed down, she'd told herself it couldn't be helped. Her hand had trembled, and after all that effort, the results were disappointing. The contents of the drawer looked a bit dull. Would the police be interested to know about the papers and the photographs? As she'd sifted through everything, the milkman had clinked the milk bottles outside the back door and she'd almost jumped out of her skin. She'd felt like a thief, but then she remembered Henry saying, 'what's mine is yours,' and relaxed a little. Of course, he only said that when they were in bed together, and she knew he didn't mean she could take his personal things when they had married, but hadn't he promised 'all my worldly goods I thee endow'? When her heartbeat had returned to normal, she'd lowered herself onto a chair and spread everything over the table.

There was a pretty amethyst brooch in the shape of a flower. It was in a blue box, the kind her father used in the shop. Henry must have been saving it for her for when the baby came.

The papers were completely incomprehensible, a neatly folded pile which looked as if she'd need the services of someone like Mr West to decipher them. There was one marked Southern Rhodesia Tobacco Company, which looked like it had something to do with shares belonging to Grenville Hartley. She also found a life policy in her name with the SunRise assurance company, the house insurance and her wedding certificate. She had known about the SunRise assurance company because the man came once a month for the premium.

The photographs were of Henry with another woman. Should she tell the police about that? Henry was much younger and in swimming trunks. He stood next to the woman who was wearing a one-piece bathing suit. She had a long cigarette holder in her hand and her hair was tied up in a white turban. She seemed vaguely familiar although Annie knew she'd never met her. Perhaps she was a film star? She certainly could have passed for one with her slim figure and long legs. Annie didn't recognise the beach but it looked hot and sunny. They were both laughing and looked so happy that Annie couldn't help feeling a little jealous, but she would keep that to herself no matter what. The other photographs were of people unknown to her; a man in a deck-lounger in a field and another of Henry standing next to the same man with the woman, this time without her turban. There was something written in pencil on the back of one of the photographs. 'Priory Road, Chichester, August 1927.' Having looked at them for some time, Annie decided that the unknown man was probably the woman's husband and that they were friends of Henry's from before she knew him.

Annie remembered feeling uncomfortable and a little bit angry as well. This was a part of Henry's life that she knew absolutely nothing about. Who were these people? Had they died in the war? Were they relatives or just friends? Why hadn't he told her about them? Pushing the photographs back into a pile, she'd wiped a renegade tear away from her cheek and stood up. The bank book had been a pleasant surprise. It was in their joint names and there was a healthy £500/14/6 in the account. £500! She couldn't believe her luck. This, she had felt sure, would keep her very well until Henry was released. Of course, she would use it frugally, but it did mean she could travel to Lewes by train to see Henry as often as she wanted. A wave of relief had swept over her. Everything was going to be all right after all.

Considering that the lock on the drawer was already broken, she tucked the wedding certificate, the brooch and the bank book into her handbag for safekeeping and put everything else back into the drawer.

It didn't take her long to get ready to go back into town. She had planned to take the wedding certificate to Mr West as soon as she had drawn some money from the bank. She'd never actually written a cheque before but she had seen her father do it hundreds of times. She'd handed it to the cashier who'd studied it for a few seconds and then stood up. 'If you will excuse me Mrs Royal, I have to check something with the manager.'

Annie was puzzled. 'Is everything all right?'

'Yes, yes,' the cashier assured her, 'I won't be a minute.'

He'd left the counter for a few minutes and came back with the bank manager. The manager was very polite as he asked her to step into his office, Annie thought it a little odd, but as they were both being so pleasant, she didn't dream anything was amiss.

'Is this your bank book?' he'd asked. Annie sat opposite him at the desk.

'Mine and my husband's.' Annie smiled pleasantly. 'My husband has had to go away on business and I need a little cash.'

'I see,' said the manager. He was turning the book over and over in his hands. 'I was a little concerned because the signature in the book and your signature are different.'

Annie returned his gaze. 'My husband usually draws our money.'

'This book hasn't been used for ten years,' said the manager, 'and to be perfectly frank, I don't believe it's yours. You've stolen it.'

Annie leapt to her feet. 'That's not true!' And at the same time a policeman walked into the office. The two men conferred together while she protested her innocence, but it was no use. She had been asked to accompany the policeman to the station, which was a few doors away and where she now waited. She glanced up at the clock on the wall. How much longer were they going to keep her here?

She replaced her compact and closed her handbag just as two men in plain clothes came into the room. They put a file onto the table.

'My name is Detective Sergeant Hacker,' said the first one, 'and this is Detective Constable

Green. I'm sure that in your present condition you don't want to be here any longer than you have to, so I'll get straight to the point.'

'I appreciate that,' Annie nodded.

'Good,' said DS Hacker. 'So perhaps you would explain to me why you tried to access someone else's account at the bank and how you came to have that brooch in your handbag.'

So Annie told them. She told them that Henry was on remand, and that he was innocent. 'It's all a terrible mistake,' she said quickly as the policeman raised his eyebrow. She told them about his locked drawer and her desperate need of money. She told them about Mr West and that she had only gone to the bank to get two guineas for him and a few shillings for her own needs. She pointed out that the size of the cheque she had written was tantamount to proof of that. Wouldn't she, she asked them, have written a cheque for the whole of the five hundred pounds had she been a thief? They listened without interruption until she sat back in the chair.

'Umm,' said DS Hacker, looking sceptical. 'There's only a couple of small problems with all that, Mrs Royal. The names on the bank book are for a Mr and Mrs Royale, spelt with an "e" and the brooch has been reported stolen.'

Whenever Sarah saw Mrs Rivers now, the older woman hurried on her way without speaking to her. Sarah was deeply hurt. They had been such friends before. Nat seemed to enjoy creeping up behind her in the butchers or the pub and shouting 'Boo!' or something silly like that. If only she could do something about him. She was sure he was still knocking his mother about but she knew that until Mrs Rivers made a personal complaint, the police treated all such incidents as 'domestic'.

One ray of sunshine in a series of dark days was the fact that Mr Lovett had secured several orders. The number and the timescale was a bit daunting – six romper suits and five dresses in a little under three weeks – but if he paid her as well as he had done before, Sarah would give it a go. However, she was shrewd enough not to show her excitement just yet.

'I've no money for materials,' she said. They were in Mrs Angel's shop and there were no other customers because Mrs Angel had pulled down the blind for a few minutes so that they could speak in private.

'Just tell Mrs Angel what you require and I'll settle up with her later,' he said.

The relief Sarah felt was palpable. If she could carry on with this, life would be so much easier for herself and the girls. All she had to do was get through the next few weeks on what little money she did have, although after seeing Henry's lovely house, it galled her that she still had this perpetual struggle. It wasn't right that she and the girls should be scrimping and scraping, barely able to keep body and soul together, while Henry and that trollop lived so well.

'So,' Mr Lovett beamed. He was holding out his hand. 'Do we have a deal, Mrs Royal?' Sarah put her hand in his and shook it warmly as he added, 'Then I shall be back in the middle of the month.'

As soon as he'd gone, Sarah rushed around the counter to hug Mrs Angel.

'No need for that, dear,' said the old woman, stepping back, her cheeks pink with embarrassment. 'I only did what anyone else would do.'

'You did more than that,' Sarah insisted. 'You are the only person in the world who has offered me any practical help and I can never repay you for your kindness.'

'No need to,' said Mrs Angel, getting a couple of bolts of material down from the shelf. 'I hardly like to ask, but how did you get on when you saw your husband?'

Sarah told her briefly what had happened and explained that, given what she had seen, she wanted to claim maintenance for the children.

'You'll have to get a solicitor to deal with that,' said Mrs Angel.

'And that takes money,' said Sarah sourly.

'You can apply for a legal certificate,' said Mrs Angel. 'That means you don't have to pay. Would you like me to ask around? I shall be discreet.'

'You're very kind, Mrs Angel,' said Sarah, 'but I don't want everybody knowing my business.'

Mrs Angel nodded sagely. 'My dear, it's already in the paper. Didn't you know?'

Sarah's mouth went dry. Mrs Angel went into the back room beyond her shop and came back with the *Gazette*. The front page was dominated by a story about a woman's body being found near the pier, but Mrs Angel opened it to page five and pointed to a small paragraph headed 'Worthing man remanded in custody,' In the brief article, she read that Henry Arthur Royale had been remanded in custody to appear at Lewes Assizes on two charges, one of bigamy and another of theft. Sarah felt the colour drain from her face. She had blanked everything else out and had been so consumed by Henry's reaction and the way he'd treated Jenny; but now things looked really bad. Henry really had married that girl and, to top it all, he was being accused of theft as well.

'When he comes up before the judge,' she said, 'I need to be in court.'

'Haven't the police talked to you, dear?' Sarah shook her head. 'Then he must have been married to another woman,' said Mrs Angel. 'Don't you see?' she added as she saw Sarah's puzzled frown. 'Someone else has made a complaint.'

Sarah gasped. 'You mean it's not just me?' She remembered the comment the desk sergeant had made when she rang the police.

'If you make a complaint as well,' said Mrs Angel, 'they will get you to court.'

Armed with two yards of material and some embroidery silks, Sarah had plenty to think about as she walked back home. One thing was for sure. She would do as Mrs Angel suggested. She would report her marriage and go to court.

The detective who had interviewed Annie was terrifying. In his forties, and with a greasy, pock-marked face, he was very much a dominating force, aggressive and loud. Annie was respectful and did her best to field his questions, whilst at the same time, struggling not to cry.

'Where did you get this bank book?'

'I've already told you, from my husband's drawer.'

'You must have seen the name.'

'I didn't notice the "e" until you said.'

'But it was obvious.'

'I know. I can see that now, but I honestly didn't notice at the time.'

'Is your initial "K"?'

'No.'

'Then you must have known the book didn't belong to you.'

'No ... that is... Maybe I saw it but it didn't really register. I was upset…'

He banged the book onto the table, making her jump. 'I think you knew very well what you were doing, young lady,' he shouted. 'You saw a bank book with £500 pounds in it and you thought, Ah, I'll have some of that.'

Annie was alarmed. 'It wasn't like that!'

'So you passed yourself off as Mrs K Royale.'

'No,' Annie protested again. 'I only wanted enough money to pay Mr West and to go and see my husband.'

'But you haven't got a husband, have you?' he sneered. 'I can see you are having a baby, but you're not married. You're living in sin.'

'I am not!' Annie cried indignantly. 'How dare you say that! I *am* married and you've got my wedding certificate to prove it.'

The two men looked at each other, then DS Hacker closed his folder and stood up. 'All right, Mrs Royal,' he said. 'For the moment we're giving you the benefit of the doubt. We're keeping the bank book, and the jeweller concerned doesn't want to press charges, but remember that impersonation is a very serious offence. You are free to go.'

As they led her away from the poky little room and back to the entrance, Annie struggled not to give way to tears. She wasn't going to give that horrible man the pleasure of seeing her break down, but when she reached the front desk all her plans went out of the window. A man and a woman stood up as she came through and the woman called her name. With a loud sob, Annie threw herself in her parents' arms.

Seven

When she told the police why she had come, Sarah was shown into a small room near the reception area. As he opened the door, the desk sergeant shouted over his shoulder, 'Constable, get Bear and get this lady a cup of tea.'

'He's with the relatives of that woman found by the pier, Sarge,' said the constable.

'Tell him all the same,' said the Sergeant, nodding kindly at Sarah. 'I think he'll want to see Mrs Royal.'

The tea came first and Sarah struggled to control her hand. She was trembling. Perhaps she shouldn't have started this. Maybe it would have been best to leave things as they were. Twenty minutes later, she had finished the tea and was just thinking about making her escape when the door opened and a huge man entered the room. He leaned over the table to shake her hand, 'Detective Sergeant Truman,' he smiled. 'I am so sorry I kept you waiting. How can I be of help?'

Sarah immediately understood why they called him Bear. He wasn't fat and flabby, far from it. Broad-shouldered and powerfully built, he had a warm smile and kind eyes. He was surprisingly softly spoken and he listened attentively as she told him about Henry. He took everything down and when he'd finished, he said, 'We would want you to say all this in court. You will come, won't you?' Sarah hesitated. 'If it's transport that's the problem, I can arrange that for you,' he said kindly. 'And should you need to employ someone to care for your children, that can be arranged as well.'

He saw Sarah to the door and they shook hands once again. Bear watched her as she hurried down the street towards the school.

'Everything all right?' the desk sergeant asked.

Bear shook his head. 'Things will never be the same for her, poor girl, and there's something about that Henry Royale that sticks in my craw. Something's not quite right.'

'You can say that again,' chuckled the desk sergeant. 'Looks like he's already married half the bloody county.'

'It's more than that,' said Bear, turning to leave. There was a frown on his face. 'But don't you worry. I'll find out what it is and then I'll have him.'

The rest of the mothers were already waiting and

the teacher had sent the children to meet them as Sarah reached the school gates. Jenny came running towards her holding a piece of paper in the air and with her cardigan only on by one sleeve.

'I drew you a picture, Mummy,' she cried happily.

Sarah smiled at the drawing as she put her daughter's arm back into the sleeve and gave her a kiss. Her plaits were untidy and she was missing a ribbon. 'It's in my pocket,' Jenny said as Sarah waved the bare plait in front of her nose.

As she stood up, Sarah suddenly felt her elbow being held in a vice-like grip. 'I need to talk to you,' her sister Vera hissed in her ear.

'I have to get back...' Sarah began.

'It won't take a minute,' Vera insisted. She pulled Lu-Lu's pram into a corner of the playground and slapped a newspaper into Sarah's hand. 'What have you done?'

Sarah didn't need to look at the article to know what it was about. *Worthing man on theft and bigamy charges*.

'What have *I* done?' said Sarah, snatching her elbow away. 'I did nothing except marry someone who apparently wasn't free to marry.'

'Bill isn't happy about this being in the paper,' Vera went on crossly. 'You need to get it cleared up quickly.'

'Vera ... it's not my fault.'

'How could you?' Vera spat. 'Dragging the family name through the mud.'

'You haven't heard a word I've said,' said Sarah. Jenny and Carole were playing tag and thankfully out of earshot. Lu-Lu sat bolt upright in her pram sucking her thumb and twiddling her hair, obviously concerned by the tone of their conversation. Sarah caressed her daughter's cheek and smiled, while inwardly thanking God she didn't understand what was being said. 'This is none of my doing.'

'You must have told the police about him. Why didn't you tell Bill and let us deal with it in the family?'

'Actually,' Sarah said deliberately. 'I wasn't the one who reported him and I've only just been to the police station to tell them that I'm his wife as well.'

'What do you mean *as well?* Are you saying there's more than two of you?'

'Apparently,' said Sarah.

Vera took in her breath. 'Bloody hell, Sarah.'

'I have to go to court,' Sarah went on. 'I may not have to testify but I have to be there.'

'When?'

'Three weeks.'

Her sister looked thoughtful. 'Well, it's a good thing we don't share the same surname anymore, but I don't know what Bill is going to say about all this.'

Sarah felt her cheeks flame, but she resisted the temptation to hit her. Her sister had always been self-centred, but now she was being crass. Where was the sympathy; the concern? 'I need someone to look after Jenny and Lu-Lu while I go.'

'I don't think...' Vera began.

'The court will pay a small fee to whoever looks after them for me.'

Vera hesitated. 'All right, I'll talk to Bill about it,' she said, 'but for goodness' sake, keep away from any newspaper reporters.'

It was raining hard when Annie got home. She had been glad to be in her parent's car. She would have been soaked had she caught the bus and had to walk from the bus stop. What a terrible day. Her relief when she saw her parents in the foyer of the police station was enormous, but the explanations as to why they were there had to wait. Her father was anxious to get her back home to Worthing, but before setting out on the twenty mile journey, they took her back to the home she and Henry shared first. While they waited in the sitting room, Annie packed her suitcase.

It was then that the full import of her predicament slowly dawned. If what they said was true, then she wasn't married, and what was worse, through no fault of her own, she was an unmarried mother. She had been horribly deceived. In one fell swoop, she had lost her identity, her status in life and probably her lovely home as well. She had agreed to go back to her childhood home for a bit, but now she was wondering how could she possibly manage to come back to Horsham without the support of a husband? She would lose this house and all the furnishings she had made. Ever since that night when the police came, she had clung to a flimsy belief that maybe, just maybe, there had been a ghastly, mistake, but faced with the evidence they'd put before her, Annie had a sinking feeling that it was all true.

Her mother had appeared in the doorway and

offered her some help.

'Take as much as you can, dear,' she had said quietly. 'You won't be coming back here, will you.'

Their eyes met and Annie had felt her throat tighten as another thought drifted into her mind. She'd have to face everybody in Worthing. What was she going to say to her friends? Her hand rested on her bump. If only she wasn't pregnant, she could start over again quite easily. Now that she had a baby growing inside of her, everything was changed. She would have a miserable time for a while, but hopefully with a bit of help she could get her life back on track eventually. 'Oh Mum,' she'd mumbled sadly.

'I know, I know,' said her mother, holding out her arms to her.

'Hurry up, you two. We haven't got all day,' her father shouted up the stairs, startling Annie and her mother into action again. All her clothes were in the suitcases her mother carried and as Annie had left the bedroom she picked up the case containing the baby's layette.

'What's that?' said her father as he took the case from her at the bottom of the stairs.

'Baby clothes,' said Annie.

'Well, you can leave them behind,' he said gruffly. 'You won't be keeping it, will you.'

For a second, Annie was taken aback. She didn't want her baby dismissed so lightly. It made her feel uncomfortable. And she certainly wasn't going to give him up. She must have looked startled because her mother's expression softened.

'Even if she isn't keeping it, Malcolm,' she'd said, 'the clothes might come in useful for whoever has him.'

Her parents walked on ahead as Annie stood in the small hallway for the last time. She was exhausted and drained. More than anything, she wanted to get away because this home only held sad memories now. Her father was overbearing and strict but she welcomed the stability he was offering. She had no choice, what with no money and no husband and a baby on the way, and yet she knew she was a lot luckier than most girls in her position. She went back into the sitting room, opened the damaged drawer and slipped the shares certificates, along with the photographs of Henry and his friends into her pocket. Closing the drawer, she took a last look around.

Just as she was about to leave, she heard a soft knock on the front door. It was Mrs Holborn. Her face was grey and Annie knew instantly what had happened. Glancing back at Annie's parents, Mrs Holborn shook her head. They didn't need words. As their eyes locked, Annie opened her arms and Mrs Holborn went to her.

'I'm so sorry, Mrs Holborn,' said Annie.

Her neighbour had swallowed hard and nodded curtly. 'Thank you, my dear. In the end, he went peacefully and we were all there. All the best to you and the baby and I'm sure everything will all turn out fine.'

Annie had slept on the back seat of the car on the way back to Worthing. As she woke, her first drowsy thought was of Henry. She loved him and she couldn't bear the thought of being a lone parent. She would write to him. It wasn't over yet, was it? He was only on remand. The jury would find him innocent and they could start again. Maybe they could find a new place to live. Eastbourne was nice, or Bognor Regis. But the next day, after sleeping late and mooching around her parents' home all day, her thoughts were beaded on another string. It was going to be a long and unbearable three weeks until the trial. How was she going to survive without him?

Sarah worked hard to get the baby clothes finished. There were times when her eyes hurt and her back ached, but gradually the romper suits and dresses took shape. Life was a struggle. It seemed that no matter how hard she tried, she was still living hand to mouth. It had taken a while to recover from the loss of her purse and now a loaf of bread had gone up to fourpence h'penny. Everything seemed bleak until one afternoon after she'd collected Jenny from school, she'd found an envelope pushed through her letter box with a ten bob note inside. There was nothing written on the envelope but she knew where it had come from. Mrs Angel was such a dear and she certainly lived up to her name.

It was a lot quieter next door as well. Mrs Rivers had gone to stay with her sister, although the neighbour who told her didn't know her address.

Sarah's need to keep going was relentless. Cleaning the house, doing the washing, making sure her girls were clothed and fed, queuing at the shops, the walk to school and the walk back again, working in the pub and the big houses, and once the children were in bed, sewing, sewing, sewing. Sarah knew she was exhausted but she dared not stop. It didn't help matters much that the newspapers were full of gossip about the beautiful Princess Margaret. Whenever Sarah wiped the tables in the pub and someone had left their paper from the day before, she would see the princess smiling up at her from the *Daily Mirror* or the *Evening News*. Sometimes she was pictured doing the rumba or being welcomed by some dignitary somewhere. Eighteen years old, Sarah thought ruefully, and never done a day's work in her life. How the other half live…

She made plans. She would put some of the money Mr Lovett gave her by and save up for a sewing machine. She'd seen an advertisement for a Singer treadle for £23/18/6, way beyond her means of course, but she'd ask the rag-and-bone man to look out for a second-hand machine. She'd be methodical and stick to it. When she got the machine she would put a card in Mrs Angel's window, something like, *Seamstress, alterations and children's clothes at good prices*. If she worked hard she could start a little business. In the meantime, Lil Relland had plenty of second-hand clothes in her shop. It wouldn't take much to cut some of them down for baby clothes, and once she'd got a little capital behind her, she could buy some new material in the market. It might take a year or two, but with a bit of luck she need never be beholden to anyone again.

The police asked her to go back to the station to make a statement. It seemed to take a long time, but when it was over, she was glad it was done. Thankfully, Vera had dropped her a note to say she would look after the girls on the day of the trial.

Sarah had a sneaky feeling it was only for the money, but she said nothing. If she confronted Vera, she knew her sister would turn her back on her and she wouldn't be able to find anyone else. Sarah had had plenty of friends before she'd married Henry, but he'd never wanted her to continue friendships. 'You've got me now,' he'd say with that puppy-dog look of his. 'Why do you need anyone else?' So gradually she'd lost touch with her friends. It wasn't until he was out of the picture that she'd realised how isolated she'd become. Since then, there wasn't time for anything else except keeping her head above water. She had to keep going for the sake of the children. The thing she hated most was that she was becoming very short-tempered with them. If Lu-Lu messed about while Sarah struggled to get her dressed, they'd both end up in tears. It hurt her beyond words when Jenny brought a picture she'd painstakingly painted home from school called 'My Mummy'. It was the usual childish attempt with a big woman standing outside a red-brick house and smoke coming out of the chimney.

'That's my house,' said Jenny pointing, 'and that's you.'

'Oh, it's lovely, darling,' said Sarah, pinning it to the wardrobe door with a drawing pin, but she was disturbed by the picture. The woman staring back at her looked very cross, when all she wanted was for her children to have a happy childhood.

Sarah had heard on the grapevine that the old lady who had lived in the two rooms downstairs wasn't expected to live. With that news came more uncertainty. The housing shortage was so acute in the town that she knew she would have new tenants before long. What would they be like? Or worse still, what if the cottage was condemned and pulled down? The landlord had never bothered to repair the leak on the stairs, no matter how many times she'd asked, and it was obvious that he didn't care about the damp creeping up the walls in the kitchen. What would she do if he pulled the place down?

Peter Millward turned up at her door one early evening to say he had recommended her book-keeping skills to a couple of other friends. Once she'd sorted out the muddle he'd got himself into, it was easy enough to look them over once a month, but although Sarah would have welcomed the income, and she was grateful for his kindness, she had to explain that she would be hard put to find the time to do anything else.

'I hardly have a minute to myself as it is,' she explained.

'Are you sure?' he asked and Sarah hesitated. What if Mr Lovett couldn't sell any more of her things? Could she afford to turn down another source of income?

'Let me take you out,' he said suddenly.

Sarah's hand flew to her mouth. 'You're forgetting that I'm a married woman,' she began, her face colouring. What a stupid thing to say. She wasn't married at all.

'That doesn't stop you and the girls from having a treat,' he smiled. 'Come on. Nothing elaborate and no strings attached ... fish and chips in a café?'

Sarah hesitated. The girls had never been in a

café before and it would be so nice to have somebody else cook for her.

'Good,' said Peter, sensing his victory. 'I'll call for you on Friday at six,' and with that, he lifted his hat and was gone.

It turned out to be a lovely time. The café was noisy and crowded but the fish and chips were delicious and the children were as good as gold. Sarah watched her girls tucking in and, for the first time in months, she felt relaxed and happy.

'You look better already,' he told her.

Sarah smiled. 'This is very kind of you.'

'Not at all,' he said with a twinkle in his eye. 'I'm just looking after my own vested interests.'

Lu-Lu threw her spoon on the floor and they were distracted while Peter got a clean one.

'I'm getting another two lorries,' he went on once they were settled again. 'The business is expanding quite rapidly. Don't suppose you'd like a full-time job as a secretary?'

Sarah hesitated. It would be so much easier to have one job rather than racing about from one thing to another. Men always got far more money than women, she knew that, but she thought Peter would give her a fair wage. It would most likely be enough to cover the cost of living, but would it be enough to pay the rent? And what would she do with Lu-Lu? Jenny would be at school, but she knew without asking that Vera wouldn't have her. Besides, she'd have to get her all the way over to Lancing and then fetch her after work if she did. If she had to fork out on bus fares, she'd probably end up back where she'd started.

'If you're worried about the little one,' he said, pre-empting her protest, 'I know a really good woman who would look after her.'

Sarah frowned. A stranger looking after her baby all day? She wasn't sure about that ... but perhaps...

'Tell you what,' said Peter, 'think about it. I don't need an answer straight away.'

Sarah watched him as he went back to the counter to buy mugs of tea for them both, an ice cream for the girls and to pay for their meal. He was such a kind man. A lump formed in her throat. Oh Henry ... why? Why?

'We'll have to put in place a few ground rules about this.'

Malcolm Mitchell had gathered his wife and daughter in the sitting room of his comfortable home near the Thomas A Becket public house, about two miles from the centre of Worthing. He was anxious to regain control of a tricky situation. His good name was at stake. As a member of Worthing Borough Council, his reputation had to be squeaky clean, and as a Freemason even more so. They had let Annie sleep late as usual and now that breakfast was over and the maid was in the kitchen, where she could no longer eavesdrop on the conversation, he was anxious to decide on their next move. 'Your mother will arrange a place for your confinement and for the adoption society to take the baby as soon as it's born. You must stay indoors until the trial comes up. We don't want the neighbours or the gutter press making your predicament into a public spectacle. I think if you keep a low profile, there's no reason why you can't pick up the threads of your life again once the birth is over.'

Neither woman spoke. Annie sat on the edge of the sofa staring at her hands, while her mother sat in the armchair gazing somewhere into the middle distance. Her father stood by the fireplace.

'Of course,' said her father, slipping his thumbs either side of his waistcoat and thrusting out his generous stomach, 'if you had listened to me in the first place, you wouldn't have found yourself in this situation.'

Annie's face flamed. He just couldn't resist, could he? He had to keep reminding her that it was her own headstrong actions that had brought all this to pass.

'You seem to forget,' Annie mumbled, 'that I didn't know he was already married.'

'That's as maybe,' said her father, 'but *I* knew he was a thief and I'm going to make damn sure he pays for his crimes.'

Annie's head jerked up. 'You knew? But you never said anything!'

'I was trying to protect you,' said Malcolm. Already the atmosphere between them was heating up. 'He and I had words when that brooch went missing. Of course he denied it, but I knew it was him.'

So it was the brooch that had brought them to the police station, not his own daughter's desperate need. She'd been too miserable to ask why they were there. DS Hacker had said the brooch was stolen, but Annie didn't think for one minute that it had come from her father's shop. 'You should have said something in the first place,' she said.

'And would you have listened?' he challenged. 'No. You were too besotted with him to take any notice of anything I said. Well, from now on, my girl, things will have to change around here. If you are going to live under my roof,' he was wagging his finger now, 'I want you to promise that you will do as I say.'

Annie remained silent. Looking at his pompous face and wagging finger, it occurred to her that her father could be insufferable at times.

'I'm only doing this for your own good,' Malcolm Mitchell insisted. 'If you do as I say, when this has all blown over, and people have forgotten what happened, you'll probably be able to find a decent young man who will forgive your past and take you as a wife.'

Annie could feel her heartbeat quickening again. 'None of this was my fault!' she cried. 'And I wouldn't have run off with him if you'd given him a chance, Father.'

'Oh, I think you already knew something about his character,' her father spluttered. 'That's why you didn't invite your mother and me to the wedding.'

'You hated him from the word go,' she cried. 'And I did invite you. You chose not to come.'

'I never hated him,' Malcolm insisted. 'But I knew he was no good.'

Annie said nothing.

'If the chairman of the Borough Council gets to hear of all this...'

'You don't give a damn about me, do you?' Annie cried.

Judith's hand flew to her mouth. 'Annie,' she gasped. 'Language...'

But her daughter wasn't listening. 'All you can think about is how this looks to your snobby friends.'

'Don't be ridiculous,' Malcolm snapped.

'You never had time for Henry,' Annie blundered on. 'All those snide remarks.'

'And which one of us turned out to be right?' her father demanded. 'Eh? Which one?'

'Malcolm, dear,' Judith Mitchell interjected, 'I don't think this is helping.'

'Oh, here we go,' her husband bellowed. 'Somehow I thought you'd be sticking up for her before long.'

'I'm going to my room,' said Annie, getting to her feet.

'Sit down!' her father spat, but Annie ignored him. Calmly walking from the room, she closed the door. She could still hear him shouting, 'Annie? Annie, come back here this minute...' as she closed her bedroom door and lay on the bed. It was still a couple more weeks until the court hearing, but she'd made up her mind she wasn't going to get into any more arguments with her father until it was over. She'd give the baby up like they said. Not because her father wanted it but because it wasn't fair to bring a child into a world where its grandparents were warring with its mother and its father was in jail. To have it adopted was by far the best thing. That way the baby could have a mother and father who loved and wanted it.

'It's the best I can do for you,' she told him, as

she ran her hand wearily over her bump. But when the baby moved in response to her touch, she knew she could never do it.

Eight

The courtroom in Lewes was on the High Street. When Annie first saw it, she thought it an imposing building. It dated from Victorian times and was made of Portland stone with a portico of four pillars which covered the steps leading to the three doors at the top. Above the steps, a single Victorian lamp lit the way. Lewes had had its share of famous trials and most notably had gained notoriety as the place where Patrick Mahon was tried for the murder of Emily Kaye in the infamous Crumbles murder case, a case which had been handled by none other than the famous forensic pathologist, Sir Bernard Spilsbury. Annie only knew all this because there had been a lot in the paper about him when Spilsbury had died at the end of 1947.

With the castle itself as a backdrop, Annie wished she was here as a tourist rather than a wronged woman. Flanked by her parents, she was hustled through the doors and into a waiting area where she sat down. Her father prowled the corridors, jangling the coins in his pocket, and her mother, a bag of nerves, kept going to the toilet. Their drive to Lewes had been uneventful, and although she knew it really worried her mother,

Annie had little to say. She found her silence acted as a defence mechanism because talking only encouraged her father's constant ranting about Henry and how he knew all along that he was a bad lot who would eventually come to a sticky end. It took all her willpower not to react but she refused to kowtow, knowing that this was by far the best way. With only a month to go of her pregnancy, Annie no longer had the energy to argue or defend herself, but at least she had the satisfaction of knowing how much her refusal to respond irritated her father.

She had been there about ten minutes or so when she saw the woman who had come to her house on that fateful day and accused Henry of being her husband. This time, dressed in a brown suit with patchy velveteen cuffs, she was on her own. The two of them made eye contact and as the woman gave her a nod of recognition, Annie turned her head away before working her mouth into a thin half smile. They sat apart, the woman sitting primly with her handbag clutched tightly on her lap and Annie staring at the floor.

'You'd think they'd have a proper waiting room,' her father complained. 'How much longer have we got to hang around here?'

Annie didn't see Henry until she was in court about an hour later. As she stood in the witness box, he sat opposite the judge in the dock. He looked pale but he was smartly dressed in his best suit. Her heart lurched and as she looked at him he mouthed, 'I love you.' She felt slightly bewildered.

The inside of the courtroom was even more imposing than the outside, although the wood panelling behind the judge's seat and along the walls made it seem rather dark. The ornate vaulted ceiling gave the room a kind of conservatory feel. In the centre under the judge's bench was a large table where a woman stenographer sat listening to and recording the proceedings. The jury sat in front of her. Annie scanned their faces. They were all men and, judging from their dress, from all walks of life. Three of them seemed very old and one man sported a huge walrus moustache.

As she was sworn in, Annie recognised Mr West, but the man who spoke up for Henry was new to her. Somewhere along the line she had been told his name was Mr Collingwood, King's Counsel for the defence. She was asked to give her name and then before Mr Hounsome, the KC for the prosecution, began his questioning, the judge interrupted.

'If the jury are at times constrained to think that there might be an element of humour about bigamy, they should remember that there is another side to the case which is more important and has no humour whatsoever.'

Annie drew her grey and black swagger coat around herself and the members of the jury stared at her with concern. Turning to her, the judge said in a less severe tone of voice, 'Considering your condition, Mrs Royal, would you like to sit down?'

Annie nodded, but the moment they brought a chair was the moment she felt her greatest humiliation. She still wore her wedding ring and yet even as she put her right hand on the Bible, it felt as if she was telling lies. Her coat slipped open and her advanced pregnancy was obvious to all. Every eye in the courtroom was upon her. She could see the gentlemen of the press at the back of the court scribbling in their notepads and, worst of all, her father who had already given his evidence about the missing brooch and his toxic relationship with Henry, glowering from the public gallery. A woman in a fur coat and broad-brimmed black hat was sitting to the right of her father. Annie had never seen her before but she stared down at her in a way that made her feel uncomfortable. Could this be the other woman who had made a complaint against Henry?

Annie answered the questions put to her with dignity and truthfully. Yes, she had married a little over a year ago. Her marriage certificate was passed around. No, when she signed the certificate, she had no idea her husband was still married.

'He told me his first wife had died in the war,' Annie explained.

There was a murmur in the gallery and she glanced up to see her father shaking his head in disbelief. Her mother, sitting to the left of him, was dabbing her eyes.

'You met when the defendant worked in your father's jeweller's shop?'

'Yes.'

'You had a speedy courtship?'

'Yes. We met and married within three months,' Annie smiled.

'And you set up home in Horsham where your husband then got a job working for another local jeweller,' said Mr Hounsome, luring her on. His tone was gentle and concerned. Annie began to relax.

'Yes. He was very well respected,' she said proudly. 'Henry likes things done just so, and they gave him a promotion almost straight away.'

'In other words, you noticed that he brought home more money.'

'Yes.'

'Did your husband ever bring items from the shop back home?'

'Yes. There wasn't always time to finish what he was doing so he brought bits and pieces back home. He often worked late into the night.'

Mr Hounsome showed her a watch and some jewellery. 'Have you seen these before?'

'Yes. That was one of the watches he was cleaning, and the necklace had a broken clasp. My husband repaired both of them one evening.'

'He brought them home, but did he take them back the next day?'

'Of course.'

'How do you know?'

Annie chewed her lip thoughtfully. She had presumed the items were in his briefcase when he left in the morning.

'Mrs Royal, how do you know for sure that your husband took the items back to the shop?'

'I trusted him,' Annie said stoutly. 'I'm sure that's what he would have done.'

'But he didn't, did he? The watch and the necklace are here in the courtroom.'

Annie frowned.

'They were found in your home. Hidden in your husband's wardrobe.'

She began to realise that Henry was charged not only with the theft of the brooch from her father's shop but with other thefts too.

'Someone had broken into the drawer of the dresser, Mrs Royal.'

'That was me,' she said quickly.

'You broke into your own dresser?'

'Yes. I was looking for money,' said Annie. She glanced towards Henry and noted his look of disapproval. 'I wanted to go and visit my husband in prison and I knew he kept money in the drawer.'

'Why not use the key?'

'My husband had the key.'

'Were you looking for money, or perhaps you thought that with your husband in custody you could help yourself to a watch or a necklace or two?'

'No!' cried Annie desperately. In the public gallery her mother stood up to leave.

'M'lord,' Mr Collingwood protested. 'Mrs Royal isn't on trial here.'

'It is my client's contention that she drove him to steal, to satisfy her constant demands for more money.'

'That's not true!' Annie cried helplessly. 'I never did that.'

'Proceed with another line of questioning, Mr Hounsome,' said the judge.

Mr Hounsome pressed her on other matters; her negligible social life, the loss of friendships and her lack of contact with her parents; all, he suggested, was the result of Annie wanting to have Henry to herself. She protested heatedly that everything he'd said was so negative and blatantly untrue. Annie could hardly believe her ears and although she tried to keep ahead of what he was saying, the questions came so thick and fast it gave her no time to think. But one thing she understood all too clearly; he was implying that somehow Henry's plight was her fault.

When Mr Hounsome finally sat down, Annie had told the truth, but she had a sinking feeling that she had only made matters worse. In his defence, Mr Collingwood had her tell everyone what an excellent husband Henry was and how well he looked after her. She told them of her shock when meeting the first Mrs Royal and how she was convinced that there had been a ghastly mistake – but it was to no avail. She could tell from the stern faces of the jury that she had done little to help Henry and that she had probably sullied her own reputation to boot. She left the witness box with a heavy heart.

Sarah gave her evidence clearly and precisely, but there was a distinct wobble in her voice. Annie listened from the benches and heard how Henry had married Sarah on March 12th, 1939 and that they had two children. Soon after their second child was born in 1947, Sarah told the court, he had left town very suddenly.

'Have you been left destitute by the defendant?' Mr Hounsome asked.

Lifting her head defiantly, Sarah took in a deep breath. 'I have no financial support from my husband if that's what you mean,' she said, 'but my children are well cared for.'

'Have you experienced any change in your

circumstances since your husband left?'

'Without his income I had to leave our marital home and take up lodgings.'

Annie shifted her feet uncomfortably. She hated the idea that a mother and her children had been deserted in that way, but she was sure Henry would never be that callous. It wasn't her fault, yet somehow she felt responsible.

'What contact did you have with your husband?'

'None. Not until someone told me they'd seen him in Horsham and I went there to find him.'

'You took your children along,' Mr Hounsome went on. 'Was he pleased to see them?'

Shaking her head, Sarah dabbed her eyes. 'He threw us out of the house.'

Annie closed her eyes as in her head she could still hear Sarah's little girl, bewildered and frightened, calling for her daddy.

When Mr Collingwood, the KC for the defence, stood up, he persuaded Sarah to tell the members of the jury that up until the time he'd left, Henry had been a model husband, and reluctantly she had to agree.

'Is it possible that your husband's war experiences damaged him and led to this confusion?'

'I doubt it,' said Sarah stoutly. 'Because of his age, he was called up late and was only in the army pay corps.'

There was a ripple of laughter in the courtroom. Annie's jaw dropped. That wasn't true. Henry had told her he'd been a POW since Dunkirk. She leapt to her feet. 'That's a lie. My husband was a war hero.'

The court was suddenly filled with murmurings.

'Silence in court,' said the judge.

'But what she's saying isn't true,' Annie insisted.

The judge glowered and banged his gavel. 'Any more outbursts like that, young lady, and I'll have you removed.'

Annie sat down dejectedly and the counsel resumed.

'You say that your husband wasn't called up until the war was well advanced,' Mr Collingwood continued. 'What was his line of work before that?'

'He was in a jeweller's shop in Littlehampton,' said Sarah, 'until he was called up in 1943.'

'So if it wasn't a bad experience during the war, what do you think contributed to the change in your relationship?'

'The birth of our second daughter,' said Sarah. 'He was terribly disappointed that we didn't have a son.'

'Are you sure?' said Mr Collingwood. 'Didn't Mr Royale tell you that he was upset and had to leave you because he had just found out that his first wife hadn't properly divorced him? Isn't that was why your own relationship broke down?'

'When I married him, I had no idea he already had another wife,' Sarah gasped. She glanced at Henry in the dock. 'I always thought that *I* was his first wife!'

Up in the public gallery, Malcolm Mitchell let out, 'Good God!' The woman in the fur coat sitting next to him let out a sob as she pushed a handkerchief to her mouth and hurriedly left the courtroom.

When Sarah stepped down, they called Kaye

Geraldine Royale into the witness box. Annie remembered her instantly as the woman who had watched Henry going to work on the day of his birthday before darting behind the gate. She was the same woman who had tried to speak to her in the park. Sarah recognised her too. She was the elegant woman waiting in the car the night that Henry was arrested.

As soon as she was sworn in, Kaye told the court that she and Henry had been married in 1929. They had been very young, she eighteen and he twenty-five. They were unfortunately childless, but her husband had developed an obsession with having a son.

'He wanted to leave his mark in the world and to have a son to carry on his name,' she explained. 'He said he planned to do something amazing in his life, so amazing that he would make the front pages of the newspaper when he died.'

There was a muffled titter in the courtroom until the judge brought down his gavel. 'Carry on, Mr Collingwood.'

Kaye began to cough.

'Are you all right, Mrs Royale?' asked the judge.

'I'm sorry,' Kaye spluttered. 'I've got a tickle in my throat.'

The judge asked the usher to bring a glass of water and they waited as she settled down. With Mr Collingwood's encouragement, Kaye went on to say that when Henry had left their marital home she had made no attempt to find him. She had been content to leave things as they were. After the war, her personal circumstances had changed and she had traced him to Horsham where she had eventually discovered that he had gone through not one but two forms of false marriage.

'I planned to confront him, but when I saw that the girl he was living with was pregnant, I couldn't do it,' she said, sipping from the glass again. 'So instead I went to the police and made a formal complaint.'

After Kaye stepped down from the witness stand, it took a while to sum everything up and then the jury went out.

As the courtroom emptied, Kaye sat on the bench in the corridor to have a cigarette. If someone had asked her to put her feelings into words, she would have struggled to do it. Part of her felt numb. The whole messy proceeding seemed so unreal – like one of her own radio plays, only this time she was one of the main characters and Henry the villain. She hadn't seen him for ten years. He looked the same. Older of course, but he still had that suave, debonair look about him. He was still self-assured, although now that she was older and wiser herself it seemed more like cockiness. His face had a few more lines but the good-looking man she had loved after Bunny Warren died was still there. Even after all these years, her heart constricted when she saw him again, but the love was gone, most likely washed away with every tear she'd shed when he'd walked out on her. She'd made up her mind to make a new life for herself and so she had. Henry seemed like someone from a far country, occasionally in her thoughts but never close by. She'd fallen in love again eventually, but because it had taken so long to find Henry or even to discover if he'd survived the war, she hadn't been sure whether she was a widow or needed a divorce. In the meantime, her new love moved on and she lost her chance of happiness. That made her angry.

The usher called them back in and, quickly repairing her lipstick, Kaye went back into the courtroom. The sight of Annie and Sarah sitting dejectedly on the benches aroused another emotion. Poor kids. She wasn't the only one whose life had been ruined. How could Henry do this?

The jury returned and the court was silent as the verdict was given. Henry Royale was found not guilty on the charge of theft but guilty of bigamy. He was given six months.

Malcolm Mitchell said nothing as he took his wife and daughter to the Whispering Gallery tea rooms nearby. He had decided that they should have some sort of refreshment before beginning the journey back to Worthing and ordered tea and cake. Annie knew she would find it hard to swallow anything but she didn't argue. Her mother seemed to be in a daze, simply following her father and keeping her eyes downcast. Annie felt confused. She had wanted to believe that everything those women said in the witness box was all lies, but Henry hadn't told her the whole truth either. Everything was so jumbled up now. Henry was a lot older than she'd thought. He'd told her he was thirty-six but it turned out that he was forty-four, practically an old man. That whirlwind courtship which had been so romantic at the time seemed tawdry and cheap now. Gradually, lots of other things began to fall into place.

She understood at last why he hadn't wanted her parents to come to the wedding and perhaps he had even engineered everything to make sure they never got their invitation. He didn't want her writing letters either. Perhaps that was why he wasn't too keen that she should make new friends either. It hadn't occurred to her until now how isolated she had become. She looked down at her bump. With a father like that, what hope did her baby have? But then she remembered how he'd told her he loved her as she'd gone into the witness box and how he'd shouted out, 'Look after my son, Annie. I'm coming back,' as they'd taken him down. He'd looked so broken, yet so sincere, and now she didn't know what to think.

Looking up, Annie noticed there was a small commotion in the street outside. With a shock, she realised that Sarah Royal had stumbled on the pavement and fallen. As soon as she saw who it was, Annie leapt to her feet.

'Sit down,' her father growled.

Several people ran to help, including the first Mrs Royale. When they hauled Sarah to her feet and dusted her down, she looked pale and disoriented. The door of the café was pushed roughly open and the group of people staggered inside, helping Sarah to a table.

'Look away,' her father said again. 'Take no notice.'

Annie turned her head but she could still see what was happening on the other side of the room by looking at the reflection on the windowpane. She watched everybody settle Sarah into a chair as they fussed over her grazed knee, and all at once

Annie understood why the café had such a strange name. She could hear everything being said at the other table as if they, were sitting right next to her. It really was just like a whispering gallery.

'Could you bring us high tea please?' Kaye asked the waitress. 'Mrs Royal hasn't eaten all day and is feeling rather faint.'

'No, no,' said Sarah. 'I'm all right, really.'

'I insist,' said Kaye. 'This has been a ghastly day for all of us, and apart from the fact that you must be starving, I think you may have a touch of shock.'

Annie glanced back and saw Sarah looking at her through tear-filled eyes as she reached for a handkerchief. Malcolm thumped his daughter's arm to remind her not to look.

The tea came and Kaye poured her a cup, loading in two spoons of sugar before passing it to Sarah. 'How will you get home?' she asked.

'I came on the train. I have a return ticket.'

The waitress brought a plate of sandwiches and a cake stand. 'I am so sorry about all this,' Kaye said as she left. 'If there had been another way…'

'It's not your fault,' said Sarah. 'I had no idea he was still married to you. In fact, until I telephoned the police, I didn't know you even existed.' She sighed. 'I feel like my whole identity has been stripped away. I don't know who I am anymore.'

Annie's mother looked up. 'That's just how I feel,' Annie told her and her mother reached for her hand on the table to give it a squeeze.

'That's quite enough of all that mumbo-jumbo,' her father hissed.

'You said in court you're living in lodgings in

Worthing?' Kaye was saying to Sarah.

Sarah nodded.

'I live in Worthing too.'

Sarah regarded Kaye for a few seconds. 'What?'

'Oh, I'm sorry,' said Kaye, lighting up a du Maurier. 'That didn't come out well. It has to be a coincidence, but I live at Copper Beeches in Church Walk. That's East Worthing. You must come and visit me sometime.'

'What?' Sarah repeated.

'In fact,' said Kaye, 'why don't I take you home? My car is just outside.' The kindly tone of her voice prompted Annie to turn around and look at them directly.

'Annie,' her father hissed angrily. He stood up, scraping his chair noisily on the bare boards. 'Come on, we're going.'

When the three wives of Henry Royale looked at each other, it was as if the rest of the world faded into the distance. Sarah simply stared, while Kaye took a long drag on her cigarette as Annie blinked back at them both.

'Come along,' said her father, pulling at Annie's arm painfully and hauling her to her feet.

The waitress appeared with the bill. 'Please pay at the counter, sir.'

'Wait outside with your mother,' Malcolm Mitchell growled as he reluctantly let go of his daughter's arm and reached for his wallet. Annie gathered her things, her eyes still on Kaye and Sarah.

The three of them stared at each other as if in the frozen frame of a film until Annie's father, having paid the bill, dragged her towards the open café door.

'Good luck, darling,' Kaye called as Annie's father propelled her onto the street.

Bear had asked to see his Super.

'Good result, Truman,' said the Superintendent. He was taking his outer garments off and hanging them up. Outside, it was raining hard. 'Six months should cool his ardour a bit. Pity we couldn't have got him sent down for a bit longer. The man's a bloody menace.'

'Quite right, sir,' said Bear, 'and for that reason I should like to carry on doing a bit of digging.'

'On what grounds?' said the Superintendent, flopping down into his chair and wiping his wet face with his handkerchief.

Bear looked ahead, deliberately not meeting the Inspector's eye. 'My nose is itching.'

His superior grinned. 'I've heard about that nose of yours, Truman. All right, come and tell me when you've got something.'

Nine

Had the circumstances been different, Sarah would have enjoyed the drive back to Worthing with Kaye. Although she was far above her socially (she could tell that just by looking at her clothes), Kaye was ever so nice. She didn't put on airs or graces and she didn't talk down to Sarah either. She treated her as an equal. She was, Sarah guessed, about ten years older than herself, handsome rather than pretty, but very elegant. She was wearing a grey two-piece suit with a pink blouse, a plum-coloured hat and matching gloves, and she carried a black bag. Her court shoes were plain, but a glance at her legs convinced Sarah that she was wearing silk stockings. Her nails were well manicured and she wore some of that new Revlon pink nail varnish. Her hair under her hat was neatly coiffured and as she moved, Sarah caught the whiff of an expensive perfume.

On the journey, they talked as friends. 'So,' Kaye asked. 'What do you think about the new plans to revitalise Worthing?'

Sarah had to confess she hadn't really thought about it. 'I did catch a glimpse of the front page of the *Herald* in the newspaper shop,' she told Kaye, 'but I never buy papers.' It felt too personal to admit that she had little time for reading and that she didn't buy newspapers because money was tight. The picture on the front of the paper had showed some of the proposed, sweeping changes, with whole streets obliterated and wide boulevards taking their place. There was talk in the town of another bridge over the railway, but people couldn't see where the money was coming from to pay for all this. Even though the Allies had won the war, the country was on its knees and the most pressing need was housing.

'The one thing that worries me,' said Kaye, 'is that they'll sweep away everything that's old. I notice that the council is trying to get that lovely old Regency house on the seafront pulled down.'

'Are they?' said Sarah. There was a short pause

and Sarah guessed that Kaye knew she wasn't really interested. Who cared about run-down old buildings when people needed somewhere to live?

'What do you do?' Kaye asked, changing the subject.

'Most of my time is taken up with providing for my girls,' she said.

'Sadly I never had children,' said Kaye. 'How old are they?'

'Jenny is six and Lu-Lu is not yet two.'

'Lu-Lu?'

'It was what Jenny called her when she was born,' Sarah smiled fondly. 'Her name is Louise, but she couldn't manage to say that and it kind of stuck. They're very fond of each other.'

'They sound lovely,' said Kaye. She wriggled in her seat. 'Excuse me. My girdle is pinching.' Sarah was sympathetic. She'd had her own experience of pinching and badly fitted girdles. 'Why do we women put ourselves through all this?' said Kaye with a sigh.

'Why indeed,' Sarah smiled.

'How long were you with Henry?'

Sarah looked away. It was inevitable that the subject would come up, but she was embarrassed. 'We got together in 1938,' she said, 'but I would never have gone with him if I had known he was married.'

'I'm sure you wouldn't have,' said Kaye. 'We both know what a skilful liar Henry is.'

Sarah nodded. 'And how difficult to live with.'

'Oh yes,' said Kaye, gripping the steering wheel more firmly.

'So the bastard left you to bring up your girls

on your own?'

At first Sarah was a little shocked to hear Henry being called a bastard. It was strong language from an educated woman like Kaye. 'It's hard,' she acknowledged, 'but we manage and I wouldn't be without them for all the world.'

A bus pulled out onto the road, but Kaye didn't slow down. Sarah closed her eyes as she accelerated and overtook it. Pulling in front of the bus, Kaye ignored the driver's honking horn and sped on. 'What work do you do?'

'All sorts,' said Sarah, trying to sound casual, despite the hair-raising ride. 'Mostly I clean but I also sew baby clothes. Anything which will give me a bob or two.' She paused. 'And you?'

'I'm a writer,' Kaye went on. 'After Henry left, I hated being on my own, but in my line of work you get used to being solitary.'

'You've no relatives?'

'No, my mother was killed in the Norton Fitzwarren rail crash.'

'Oh, I'm sorry. I remember that,' Sarah remarked. 'The beginning of the war, wasn't it?'

'November 4th, 1940,' said Kaye bitterly. 'She'd been visiting an old school friend in Taunton. The wartime restrictions meant it was so dark the driver misread a signal and the train was derailed. Twenty-seven people died, including my mother.'

'I'm sorry,' said Sarah.

'It was pretty awful,' Kaye agreed, 'and I thought I was completely alone, but just recently I've discovered that I have a maiden aunt living near Chichester.'

'Strange how we lose touch,' Sarah observed.

'But you and I mustn't,' said Kaye. 'I know the circumstances are a little odd but it would be nice to keep in touch, don't you think?'

Sarah smiled. 'Yes,' she said uncertainly.

'It would certainly be one in the eye for Henry,' said Kaye, and they both laughed. 'That girl Henry was living with looked so young, didn't she? I felt a bit sorry for her.'

Sarah nodded. 'And that father of hers looked like a real tartar.'

Henry was livid. This should never have happened. How could he have miscalculated so badly? He knew Kaye was an intelligent woman, but he never dreamed she would follow him to the ends of the earth. She must have discovered where Sarah and the girls were living, but how on earth had she traced him to Horsham? He'd been so bloody careful. He should have moved right away. Perhaps if he'd gone to Leeds or Wales or somewhere like that it would have made it harder for her to come back into his life. He'd tried to blame Sarah and Kaye for the mess he was in but the jury didn't buy his story. The only bit of satisfaction he had was seeing that pompous ass Mitchell in the gallery. He almost wished he'd committed murder just for the satisfaction of seeing the look of affronted anger on his face.

When the judge sent him down they'd made him wait in the police cells, then he'd been transferred to Winchester. Why on earth they didn't leave him in Lewes he couldn't begin to understand. They'd strip-searched him when he'd arrived and he'd been told to submit to a doctor's examination. Full of indignation, he'd resisted until one of the prison officers had given him a clout on the side of his head and he'd caved in. Once he'd been kitted out with his prison garb, they'd marched him to his cell. It was little more than a box room, thirteen feet broad by seven deep, and nine feet high, with a rounded ceiling. The walls were painted mustard yellow, if you could call it that, with a dark green band about four feet from the floor. The floor was of shiny blackened bricks. On the left-hand side was a bucket toilet with a wooden seat and a packet of Izal toilet paper on the floor beside it. The barred window was close to the ceiling and in the middle of the end wall. The panes of glass were opaque with the exception of two which had been nailed up with board. Opposite the window was the narrow door through which he had come. He shivered. It was bloody cold.

There was a wooden bed with a mattress and bedding rolled up at one end. At a glance he could see that he had two grey blankets and one sheet. There was only one shelf, a quarter wedge of wood fixed to a corner on which he found a Bible. All his personal belongings had been left in his suitcase and locked away. The prison service had supplied him with a black hairbrush, a toothbrush, a tin mug and a bit of vile smelling soap. As soon as Henry walked in, the officer banged the door closed behind him and then looked at him through the spyhole before letting the cover fall. Henry froze as the sound of the key turning in the lock echoed through the cell and the full horror of his predicament burst into his mind.

This was to be his home for the next six months.

'Shall I take you to fetch your children?' Kaye asked. They were on the outskirts of the town with less than a mile to go until they arrived at Sarah's house.

Sarah hesitated. Jenny and Lu-Lu had never been in a car before. They would love it, but when she got to Vera's she knew they wouldn't be ready. Kaye would have to wait for them. 'I don't want to put you to any trouble.'

'It's no trouble and it'll be a lot quicker for you,' said Kaye.

'That would be very kind of you.'

'Not at all.'

When they pulled up outside her sister's house, Kaye tooted the horn and a face appeared at the window. Vera's eyes almost popped out of their sockets.

'Whose car is that?' she said, opening the door. The house smelled vaguely of cabbage and there were boxes in the hallway. Sarah had forgotten that Vera and Bill were moving to Lancing at the end of the week.

'One of Henry's wives,' she said mischievously.

'One of... Good God, how many has he got?'

'Mummy, Mummy...' Sarah's children threw themselves into her arms and she kissed them fondly. 'Have you been good?'

Having Kaye waiting for them in the car brought an element of haste. Sarah was grateful for that. It meant Vera had little time to do much probing, although when she was sure that Jenny wasn't eavesdropping on their conversation, she told Vera that Henry had been sent to prison. 'Please let's keep this to ourselves,' Sarah asked. 'I don't want Jenny upset.'

'How long for?' Vera wanted to know.

'Six months.'

Vera tut-tutted disapprovingly. 'A criminal. This is a first in the family. I don't know what Bill is going to say about it.'

Sarah held her tongue. She longed to remind Vera that she was the victim here and it wasn't her fault. Besides, who cared what bloody Bill thought about it? She gathered her children and their things and hurried them to Kaye's car. As they clambered in, Kaye pinched the end of her cigarette and flicked the stub into the road.

'It's not fair,' Carole grumbled. 'I want to have a ride in the car too.'

'Thanks Vera,' said Sarah as she put Jenny in the back seat and walked to the passenger door with Lu-Lu in her arms. 'I'll settle up with you later.'

Jenny sat as good as gold, her bright eyes dancing with excitement. Sarah glanced over her shoulder and saw her stroking the leather seats when she wasn't gazing wonderingly out of the window. Kaye asked her questions about school and Jenny answered politely.

'My goldfish died,' Jenny said eventually.

'Oh, I'm sorry to hear that,' said Kaye.

'We buried him in the garden. You can see him if you like.'

'I think Mrs Royale has to get home, darling,' said Sarah.

'Call me Auntie Kaye, please.'

'I'm hungry, Mummy.'

'Didn't you have tea with your auntie?' Kaye asked.

'Auntie Vera said Mummy was coming soon,' said Jenny. 'She said Mummy would give us tea.'

Sarah bristled with anger. The agreement had been that Vera would feed them when she and her family had their tea. She'd even given her a few coupons to help with the food.

She hated it when Kaye saw where she lived. Embarrassed and drained by the day, she thanked her profusely and bundled the children out of the car. To add to her fluster, she caught sight of one of her neighbours peeping out from behind the net curtain. A car in the street was unusual enough, but when it had a woman driver at the wheel, it was an object of curiosity. Kaye climbed out to help her.

'No, no. Don't get out,' Sarah protested at the same time dropping a glove and Jenny's school plimsolls. 'We'll be fine.'

'It won't take a minute to help you,' Kaye insisted, 'and besides, I have to see the goldfish grave, don't I?'

There was an envelope pinned on the doorframe. As she snatched it from its pin Sarah supposed it was another order from Mr Lovett. Today was his usual day to call into Mrs Angel's and he had promised to try and secure some more orders for her. Kaye had Lu-Lu in her arms as they walked into the house and Jenny was anxious to show her where Goldie was buried.

'We said prayers and everything,' Jenny was telling her proudly.

'I'm glad you did everything properly,' said

Kaye, winking at Sarah.

Now that she was actually in the house, Sarah felt obliged to say, 'Would you like a cup of tea before you go?'

'Love one,' said Kaye.

She put the kettle on while Kaye and the children went out into the small yard. As she waited for the water to boil, Sarah impatiently tore open the envelope. A second later, her whole world had crashed around her like a pack of cards. The headed notepaper said it all. Notice of Eviction. She slumped into the chair and pulled off her beret. No, no, after all that had happened today, this really was the last straw. She struggled to keep her composure, but she knew she couldn't do it anymore. After working all the hours God gave, after doing everything she could to keep the roof over their heads, now this had to happen. She felt a mixture of rage and pity for herself. Someone up there must have it in for her. What had she done to deserve all this? The sound of laughter filtered through the open back door, but Sarah could only put her head in her hands and burst into tears.

Ten

A couple of days later, Kaye set out for Chichester to meet her maiden aunt. This had been such a strange time. She had spent a lot of time reflecting on the past, something she'd deliberately avoided when Henry walked out on her all those years ago.

He had never been easy to live with, although given her condition when he had proposed to her, she had been glad to accept his offer of marriage. She'd been writing for women's magazines when she'd met him, but Henry was old-fashioned. He said he didn't want his wife to work. 'People will think I can't support you,' he said sulkily. So her passion for words had been shelved. Henry had been pernickety and had spent a fortune (money they didn't have) on his suits. He became angry if she questioned him, although he'd never been physically violent. When they'd first got married, she'd stood up to him, but over the almost ten years they were together, she'd found it easier to avoid conflict. When he finally left and she'd had to start all over again, she realised that her confidence was completely shot through. She had no friends either. Still, nothing was wasted. She'd drawn on her own experiences when writing her plays. Perhaps, she reflected as the spire of Chichester cathedral came into view, her own personal experiences might even help her aunt.

She had been excited to discover that Aunt Charlotte was so close, but what she hadn't told Sarah was that her aunt was in a mental institution. Just before the trial, Kaye had received a letter from the authorities telling her that '*although Charlotte wasn't cured, she was a great deal better, and in view of the present financial conditions, whenever possible, long-term patients are being re-homed with their families.*'

It had come as a shock to discover that she even had a relative. Her mother, who had died six years ago, had never mentioned a sister. As she drove the twenty miles to Chichester, she wondered what had happened to Aunt Charlotte and why she had been put away and apparently forgotten.

She found herself driving down a winding driveway overhung with thick rhododendron trees, and when she came upon the Home, it was a rather forbidding place. Put together in grey stone, the Victorian building was in a poor state of repair. The gutters were sprouting grass and the paintwork was peeling. Kaye rang the old-fashioned pull bell and eventually a junior member of staff came to the huge paint-starved front door. She seemed very nervous and as she put a basket of washing onto the hall table, Kaye couldn't help noticing her red, chapped hands. Kaye was asked to wait in the dark wood-panelled entrance hall. In the distance, she could hear voices, some in apparent distress. Eventually a man in a white coat appeared, his hand extended, 'Mrs Royale. I'm Doctor Smith. How good to see you.'

He invited her to his office and as they walked the dim echoing corridors, her shoes squeaked on the highly polished linoleum floor. Kaye was filled with a sense of foreboding. What a dreadful place. As she sat down in the office, he pulled a folder from a filing cabinet and sat on the other side of the desk.

'Miss Dawson came here in 1917,' said the doctor. 'She's been here ever since.'

'I had no idea,' Kaye began.

'Your grandmother left instructions that she should stay here for life,' said Doctor Smith, 'but we are more enlightened now. There is no reason why she should be kept here. There's nothing wrong with her.'

'So what happened to her?' said Kaye.

'She had a baby,' said Doctor Smith.

Kaye was horrified. 'She was put in a mental home because she had a baby!'

'Apparently,' said Doctor Smith. 'I've only been here a few months and it has taken me a while to get to grips with the system. It seems that she was homed here as a private patient, but the annuity ran out in 1936. When it came to my notice, I realised that your aunt had been done a great disservice. I think she was upset after the birth of her baby, maybe she had baby blues or depression, but most likely a few weeks' rest would have been sufficient to cure her.'

'I can hardly believe what you are saying,' said Kaye. 'If she came here as far back as 1917, that means she's spent almost all of her life in this place.'

The doctor nodded.

'Thirty years?' Kaye gasped.

'I am as appalled as you are, Mrs Royale,' Doctor Smith said. 'That's why I am keen to rehome people like her whenever I can.'

'I knew my grandmother was very strict,' said Kaye, still trying to get to grips with her discovery, 'but this is terrible. How could you let it happen?'

'It's not uncommon,' the doctor shrugged. 'Thank God we live in more enlightened times now.' Kaye could see that he was doing his best to help but she wanted to slap him. How could he be so matter-of-fact about something so terrible?

'So you're telling me that the only reason my

aunt is here is because my grandmother paid for her to stay?'

'I'm afraid so,' said Doctor Smith.

Kaye frowned. 'I don't understand why the rest of the family didn't do something. My mother, for instance.'

'It's possible she didn't even know,' he said. 'These things were all hushed up.'

'I'm taking her home straight away,' said Kaye stoutly.

'That wouldn't be advisable, Mrs Royale,' he said. 'Lottie, er, that's what we call her, is a nervous woman. She doesn't know you. I think it advisable that we take it one step at a time.'

Kaye could see the sense in what he was saying, but it pained her to think of anyone staying in a place like this any longer than was necessary, especially when there was no need.

'She has only ever been out as far as the hospital grounds,' he added. 'I think the big wide world would be a bit much all at once.'

'Yes,' Kaye conceded. 'You're right. But I should like to see her today if I may.'

'Of course,' he smiled. 'I'll take you to the ward now.'

As they stepped back into the echoing corridor, one thing was puzzling Kaye. 'If my grandmother's annuity ran out as far back as 1936,' she said, 'why didn't you contact me back then?'

'Apparently we did,' said Doctor Smith, 'and your husband set up another annuity which continued the payments until earlier this year.'

Kaye felt her face flame. She stopped walking and stared at the doctor in disbelief.

'I thought you knew,' he said.

'No,' said Kaye. She felt nauseous. 'I had no idea.' They began walking again, but her meeting with her aunt was spoiled. The only thought in her head was, *how could you do that Henry, you bloody sod.*

'Occklepep! Occklepep!' Lu-Lu pointed at the window and jumped up and down with excitement. Sarah smiled as she caught sight of Peter Millward pulling faces on the other side of the glass. 'Oh yes, it's Uncle Peter.' It was now Sunday and since that day in court, she had slipped back into her usual routine, including her weekly hospital visit to the old lady who had lived in the two downstairs rooms. She looked pretty dreadful these days, thin, wasted and barely able to hold a conversation. The nursing staff didn't even bother to put her teeth in because her gums had obviously shrunk so much. It didn't take a genius to know that she was never going to come back to the cottage, which was probably why the landlord had served an eviction order on the property.

She opened the door and Peter bent down to hug the girls. They had grown very fond of him and he of them. As he stood up, he held up a road map. 'Who would like a ride into the country?' he said, his bright eyes shining.

'Me, me,' cried Jenny, and Lu-Lu joined in, despite not having the faintest clue what it meant. Sarah began to protest but quickly saw that she was outnumbered.

She'd been lucky the day Kaye dropped her at the house. When she and the children came in from the backyard, Kaye had assumed she'd been crying with relief that the day was over. She'd made them both a cup of tea and while her back was turned, Sarah had slipped the eviction notice into the half-open drawer on the kitchen table so that Kaye was none the wiser.

She had just over a month to find a new place, but even before she set out, Sarah knew it was a tall order. Although Mr Lovett's money brought a little extra into the house, she still didn't have enough to pay two weeks' rent up front, something which was usually required in these days of acute housing shortage. Anyway, as soon as any prospective landlady discovered she was a single mother with two small children, the door was closed. It wasn't always that they didn't want children, but they knew that a woman alone would be a liability when it came to paying the rent. If she had no permanent job and no visible means of support, there was always the risk in their minds that she might be on the game. She had encountered the same problems when she'd moved into the little cottage. She had only got the place because of her promise to look after the old lady, which she'd done faithfully until she'd become too ill and had to go into hospital.

By the middle of the week, Sarah still had nothing and she was desperate. She had packed up what little she had and kept it in the lean-to shed in the garden just in case she had to make a quick dash for it. She told the children nothing. It was better that Jenny didn't have any more worries than she needed to have, and of course Lu-Lu was too young to understand anyway. Mrs Rivers had looked over the garden fence one afternoon. Which was a bit of a surprise because she hadn't realised her neighbour was back.

'They've locked him up.'

'Yes,' said Sarah. She didn't really want to discuss what had happened and she was still feeling a bit cross about the theft of her purse.

'I'm not sorry,' Mrs Rivers went on. Sarah was tempted to give her a mouthful until she added, 'He was always knocking me about.'

'You mean Nathan?'

Mrs Rivers nodded. 'They came for him while you were at the trial. Pinching coal he was.'

'I'm sorry for your troubles,' was all Sarah could say.

Peter drove them to a place a called Midhurst. The weather was becoming cooler but there was still enough warmth in the sun to make an enjoyable time, and as they drove through the Sussex countryside, the autumnal colours were stunning. They stopped near Benbow pond where the children fed the ducks and black swans, and from there Peter took them to the Queen Elizabeth oak, a massive tree reputedly a place where Queen Elizabeth I had once sheltered more than 350 years before.

Peter had come prepared. As the children played, he laid a plaid blanket on the ground and invited Sarah to sit down. The picnic basket he carried contained a green and cream coloured flask of hot tea and he had sandwiches and cake. They sat together, eating, talking and laughing, and at last Sarah began to relax.

'Can I go and play now Mummy?' Jenny had

put her face up so that Sarah could wipe the crumbs from her mouth.

'Stay where we can see you,' Sarah cautioned, as she wet the corner of her handkerchief and rubbed Jenny's mouth, 'and look after your sister.'

While Jenny went to look for daisies to make a daisy chain, Lu-Lu toddled after her big sister. Sarah leaned back on her elbows.

Peter was on his side, chewing a blade of grass. She tried to like his closeness, but every time she looked at him, her eye was drawn to his long and protruding nasal hair. 'So,' he smiled, 'are you going to tell me what happened in Lewes?'

By now the children were playing with the children of another family sitting closer to the wooden area. They were well out of earshot, so Sarah told him. He listened impassively and then leaned across the empty plates and took her hand.

'If he was already married to the first Mrs Royale when he married you,' he began, 'that means you were never married in the first place.'

Sarah lowered her eyes and nodded.

'You know what this means, don't you?' he said eagerly. 'You are free to marry again.'

Jenny shouted and waved, and her mother and Peter waved back.

'I know you don't have feelings for me,' he began again, 'but I am not a bad person, Sarah. If you would consent to marry me, we could have a good life together. I don't want to be on my own anymore. I'd be patient and I promise I would always look after you and the girls. I can offer you a nice home and you know for yourself that the business is expanding.'

She stared at him in amazement, not knowing what to say. Marrying Peter would certainly get her out of a hole, but she didn't love him. In fact, she'd never even thought of him in that way. She wasn't sure if she could bear him holding her close to him and that made her feel guilty. He was kind and reliable, but he wasn't her type ... what then was her type? A smooth-talking bigamist, she thought bitterly, who had deceived her so cruelly that she honestly felt she could never trust a man again. Not even a man like Peter.

'Don't say anything now,' he said, immediately sensing that she was going to turn him down. 'Just think about it, all right?'

She nodded. 'I will do the bookkeeping jobs though.'

'Good,' he said. 'Are you sure you'll have time?'

'I'll make time.'

Jenny wanted to sit on a tree branch, so he stood up to go and lift her. As she watched his receding back, Sarah's mind was racing. Would it be so bad being married to Peter? He was no oil painting but the girls would have a much better chance in life. He would provide for them all, she knew that, but was it fair to take up the offer? He deserved better than to be used in this way. And what about her wedding night? Could she give herself to Peter? As the thought crossed her mind, she found herself shuddering. She didn't want that ... not from him ... perhaps not from anyone ever again.

'Has she come down today?'

Judith Mitchell shook her head. 'I'm really worried. She doesn't talk and she doesn't want to come downstairs. She just sits in her bedroom looking out of the window.'

Malcolm Mitchell tut-tutted irritably. He had been struggling to control this situation for almost a week now. It was bad enough trying to keep a lid on it at the council offices. If anyone on the housing committee found out that his daughter was involved in a bigamy case, he'd lose any chance he had to stand for mayor. After all his hard work, it would be bloody unfair if this episode spoiled his chances. The doctors had told him his daughter was depressed, which was understandable, but Malcolm was from the old school. In his day when something bad happened, you didn't mope around, making yourself miserable about something you couldn't alter, you pulled yourself together and got on with it. He didn't understand why anyone would want to give up in the way she had. Granted, what had happened to her was awful. She'd been deceived by a rotten scoundrel and she was having a baby outside of marriage, but hadn't he protected her from the public gaze? Hadn't he kept the gutter press away? They'd told her old friends that she'd gone abroad for a while and, what's more, he'd even arranged for her confinement to be kept secret. That meant that once the baby was gone, after a few weeks of recuperation, she could resume her old life again and nobody would be any the wiser. He knew that whatever it took, he had to stop her from getting a reputation for being a 'bad girl'. What more did she want? Crying all day and refusing to talk to him and her mother wouldn't solve a damned thing.

Malcolm helped himself to a whisky and threw himself dejectedly into a chair. Didn't anybody in this family care about him? He was beginning to make his mark with his fellow councillors and had already impressed the current mayor, Leonard Bentall, by his suggestion that they should have a telegram already prepared for when the royal baby was born.

'Good thinking, Malcolm,' Leonard had said, giving him a hearty slap on the back. 'Splendid publicity for the town if we're the first.'

His suggestion for a public meeting about Beach House had also met with approval. Nobody would bother to come. Who cared about some old dump of a mansion when people needed houses? They could slap a demolition order on it and pull it down. It would cost a fortune to repair and the place was a bloody eyesore anyway.

He downed his drink, mounted the stairs two at a time, knocked on Annie's door and walked in. She was sitting in the chair knitting something. He walked over to her and planted a rough kiss on her forehead. To his surprise and delight, she looked up at him and smiled. 'Hello, Father.'

'How are you feeling?' he asked cautiously.

'Better.' She didn't say why and he didn't ask. They made small talk and then she promised to come downstairs for dinner when the gong went. Malcolm left the room happier than he'd felt in a long time. He really had sorted it out. She was all right now. With a bit of luck they could get through this and, providing she kept out of public view even at this late stage, they could still keep the baby a secret.

As he closed the door, Annie slid her hand back into her cardigan pocket and pulled out the re-addressed letter. In the moments before they'd said their last goodbye, she had given Mrs Holborn her parent's address and her old neighbour had kept her word. She had re-addressed a letter sent to her Horsham home and it had arrived with the second post. Her father had been playing golf and her mother was out shopping, so the maid had brought it up to her room straight away. She knew from the markings on the outside that it had come from Winchester prison – it was from Henry. In it he'd told her he hadn't forgotten her. He still loved her, in fact she was the only woman he had ever truly loved. He'd asked her to take care of his unborn son and he'd promised to fetch them both as soon as he got out of jail. Annie smiled. Henry went on to explain that what had happened had all been a ghastly mistake. Those other women had made up everything. They'd duped him and lied about him. But then she'd always known that, hadn't she?

There was a job advertised in the local paper. *Caretaker wanted for a group of people living in Alms Houses. Some light cleaning required and non-medical duties*. Sarah could hardly believe her eyes. This had to be an answer to her prayers. The wage was only 22/6 a week but the biggest perk of all was that the job came with free accommodation. Her heartbeat quickened. The residents were elderly but able to look after themselves. The charity running the scheme were looking for a young person – at twenty-eight she was that – and a caring individual – she was that too. A person in good health – she stepped up to the mark in that as well. Free accommodation. That would solve so many problems. She could easily get by on that wage. Hadn't she been living for some weeks on a lot less than that? She could manage to keep up the book-keeping and maybe even get that sewing machine a little quicker. The children didn't have grand-parents. Jenny and Lu-Lu would love having the residents fussing over them, and wouldn't the old people enjoy having young children living nearby? The more she thought about it, the better it sounded. There was a cut-off date for applications and she was in luck there as well. All she had to do was get references, but she was sure that would be no problem. The ladies she cleaned for were always praising her work and she knew the land-lord at the pub would give her a good reference. As soon as she could, Sarah dashed off a letter and posted it straight away. Perhaps her luck had changed at last.

Eleven

'If you've got money, you must have pinched it.'

'I never stole in my life!'

'Oh yes, you have. You used to steal from me.'

'For heaven's sake, you old battleaxe... I was six years old...'

Kaye Royale relaxed deep into her chair and took a long drag on her cigarette. This radio play was quite good, even if she did say so herself. She tried to imagine the housewives, the retired and the people who were for some reason unable to work, glued to their wireless sets up and down the country. She had enjoyed success with her one-off plays for some years now, but this was her fourth play in the Fear in the Afternoon series, one of the most popular dramas on the Home Service. The voices were excellent and each actor or actress chosen seemed perfectly suited to the people she had created.

'*I can't believe you just said that!*' the woman's voice went on. '*No son of mine would ever speak to his mother like that. I'm ashamed of you. All the grief you've caused me, I wish you'd never been born!*'

'*Shut up, shut up!*'

'*Don't you dare raise your hand to me!*'

'*No mother, don't ... don't...*'

The sound effects man recreated the sound of a violent blow, followed by a terrified scream.

'*Your father never raised a hand to me,*' said the mother, her voice as cold as ice, unflinching in a way which Kaye hoped would both thrill and surprise her audience who hopefully wouldn't have been expecting this turn of events, '*and I won't take it from you!*'

There was the sound of a fall and the audience would know the victim – not the mother but the son – was dead. Her cigarette finished, Kaye stubbed it out and reached for the packet. She listened to the rest of the play and kept the radio on until the credits had been aired. She liked to hear her name being read out just as it had at the beginning of the show. *Fear in the Afternoon presents* No Place for a Woman *by Kaye Hambledon, starring…*

As Kaye turned the wireless off, the telephone rang. It was her agent.

'Wonderful play, darling, and you certainly have the Midas touch. I've just had a call from the BBC. They want to meet you…'

Kaye had begun writing seriously in 1937. She had always enjoyed putting together the odd Sunday school play and knocking up something for the local amateur dramatic society, but as Henry's wife, she never dared to branch out any further. Henry had strong views about what women should and shouldn't do and didn't see the need for them to do anything else but housework. She'd given up her writing until things went sour in her marriage, after which she'd worked in secret, never even telling him when she had something accepted for publication. As war loomed and Henry deserted her, she turned her thoughts to more serious productions. Comedy was king during the war years and she'd managed to sell a whole raft of one-liners and some short comedy sketches to Charlie Chester (*Studio Stand Easy*), Eric Barker (*Merry Go Round*) and even the great Tommy Handley (*ITMA*). She had honed her craft and made a name for herself as Kaye Hambledon, using her maiden name, but her real love was writing crime thrillers. The radio series called *The Man in Black* which started way back in 1943, had brought Valentine Dyall to fame and she knew the BBC were on the lookout for new writers who could adapt some of the world's greatest horror stories into plays.

Whilst others recreated the works of Edgar Allen Poe and John Dickson Carr, Kaye's dream had always been to create her own stories and she began to make a name for herself with producers.

She and her agent discussed their meeting with the BBC and decided that she should come up to London on Thursday of the following week. As she put the telephone down, there was a sharp knock at the front door.

Her neighbour, Mrs Goodall, stood on the doorstep. 'Come in,' said Kaye with a smile, although she had no idea why the woman would be knocking on her door. Mrs Goodall was a large, matronly woman who had a reputation for being the local high-hat and made it her job to make sure everyone in Church Road conformed to her level of acceptance. Always immaculately dressed, today she was wearing a pale blue twinset and a grey pleated skirt. Her shoes, which always seemed too small for her feet, were of the black court variety. She put her hand up as she declined Kaye's invitation and took a deep breath. 'As you know,' she began, 'I am not one to complain…'

Inwardly, Kaye rolled her eyes. Mrs Goodall was always complaining.

'…but your radio was particularly loud this afternoon. I could hear it all the way into my lounge…'

Kaye loved the way she said lounge. It was more like 'le-awnge' and reminded her of the twang of the bow when she did her archery practice. 'Oh, I'm sorry,' Kaye began. 'Do forgive me, it's just that…'

'I hate to mention it,' Mrs Goodall interrupted,

as she waved the smoke from Kaye's cigarette away from her face, 'but loud noises lower the tone of the area, don't you know.' She tugged at her hand-knitted jumper and the pearls at her throat wobbled.

'I do apologise,' said Kaye pleasantly. 'And I promise to keep the noise down.'

Mrs Goodall gave her a triumphant nod and turned to go. As she watched her totter down the path in her all too small shoes, Kaye grinned. What a perfect character for her next play, and as a tribute to the one who inspired her, she would call the character Goody-Two-Shoes.

Mrs Goodall was a bit of a pain, but Kaye only had one really pressing problem – looking after Aunt Charlotte. Their first meeting had been a little strained but she had warmed to the forty-seven-year-old. She looked a bit like her mother. She had the same eyes and her mannerisms were similar, but whereas her mother was confident, Aunt Charlotte, or Lottie as they called her, was timid and unsure. Kaye had talked to her about Worthing, promising that she would soon be living with her. 'We'll take walks along the seafront,' she said. 'Maybe listen to the band…' and then realised with mounting horror that poor Lottie probably hadn't a clue what she was talking about. Kaye had left, promising to return the following week. What she needed to do was set up some sort of plan which meant that Lottie would be well looked after while she was working. She would have to employ some sort of live-in domestic. Kaye reached for *The Lady* magazine and turned to the agency pages. After she'd read a few advertisements, she reached for the telephone.

An interview! They wanted to see her next week. Sarah's first thought was what was she going to wear? She dashed to the bedroom and began sifting through her wardrobe. In the end she dragged out her utility suit, a navy pinstriped tailored jacket with a matching straight skirt once again. The next question was, did it still fit? She had lost a lot of weight and hadn't worn it for ages. When she put it on, it confirmed her worst fears. It was miles too big and looked baggy and shapeless. Thumbing through a *Woman* magazine she'd found in the ladies' snug at the pub, she found an article about alterations. If she made a dart here and shortened the jacket, on a dark night it could pass for one of those New Look suits. It wasn't as if she needed more material. Sarah felt a frisson of excitement. With her yellow spot blouse and a small brooch at her neck, she was sure she could impress the interview panel.

'Mummy, can I play outside?'

Jenny interrupted her thoughts, and instead of saying it was too cold, or that it was getting dark and it was almost teatime, Sarah found herself in a benevolent mood. She smiled down at her daughter.

'Of course you can, darling, but come straight in when I call you.'

She even pushed Lu-Lu's playpen next to the open door so that she could watch her big sister pushing her dolly's pram in the road. Then humming the Andrews sisters' song *Near You*, Sarah got to work.

Sarah's heart sank as she walked through the door a week later. There were at least sixteen other people waiting to be interviewed. Please God, she silently prayed, please let them like me the best. As they waited to be called, Sarah scanned the competition. Some were obviously unsuitable. One woman was riddled with arthritis and looked as if she'd be better off being an inmate rather than a carer. Another woman had difficulty in breathing. She was very large and was sweating profusely. Sarah guessed that, like her, they'd been attracted to the job by the promise of free accommodation. Other women looked very capable, some with warm, homely faces, whilst others had rather sour expressions. The wait seemed interminable, but eventually she was called.

There were five on the panel. One was a clergyman. Next to him sat a rather formidable woman with an expensive-looking felt hat and a fox fur thrown over one shoulder. At the other end of the table sat a military man with a large tobacco-stained moustache and next to him, a nurse. Surprisingly, a rather twittery man seated in the middle of them all, began the proceedings.

'Mrs Royal, what qualities do you have which would make you a suitable candidate for the job?'

Sarah answered crisply in what she hoped was an efficient, not too casual manner, listing her attributes.

The clergyman was sifting through her references. 'Your present employers speak very highly of you,' he remarked.

Sarah relaxed into the chair. Ah, so she had one

ally on the panel, she was sure of it. They asked her about her previous experience, her capabilities and her honesty. Everything seemed to be going her way. The panel seemed impressed by her answers.

There was a slight pause then the nurse asked, 'What would you do if you found one of the residents in a collapsed state?'

Sarah confessed that she had no medical knowledge before quickly adding, 'but I am more than willing to be taught.' She went on to tell them what she would do to get help and at the same time making sure the resident was comfortable and kept calm.

The military man nodded and played with his moustache. 'Excellent, very caring.'

The woman in the fox fur leaned forward. 'Royal ... Royal,' she mused. 'Don't I know that name?'

Sarah felt herself blush as the woman held her gaze.

'If you are the sole carer for your children,' the nurse went on sniffily, 'what would you do with them if you were suddenly called to help a resident?'

Sarah swallowed hard. She hadn't thought of that, but it was a reasonable question and she could see where it was leading. If she put her children first (and she would, of course), she wouldn't be totally committed to the residents.

'I would have to take them with me,' she said quietly.

'But supposing that resident was having a violent fit?' the nurse went on. 'Would you want your children exposed to such things?'

'I can't hide them from life.'

'Your smallest child is very young. What if she was frightened and upset?'

Sarah was stumped for an answer.

'Where is your husband, Mrs Royal?' said the woman with the fox fur, changing the subject.

Sarah could feel her heartbeat quickening.

'He's in prison, isn't he?' The woman leaned back in her chair with a slight curl of disdain on her lip. 'Isn't he the man recently convicted for bigamy?'

'Good God!' exclaimed the military man.

Sarah's head flew up and her eyes flashed. 'That may be the case, madam,' she said politely, 'but that is hardly my or my children's fault. You are not interviewing my husband. You are interviewing me.'

There was a slight pause while everyone digested what she had said. The clergyman spoke first. 'We understand perfectly, my dear,' he said, 'and you most certainly are not to blame, but you must understand that even the faintest whiff of scandal…' He shrugged. 'I'm sorry.'

'And as we've just seen,' said the nurse, 'as sole carer for your children, it would be difficult for you to give our residents your undivided attention.'

Sarah rose to her feet and walked from the room with as much dignity as she could muster. Outside in the fresh air, she leaned against the flint stone wall and tried to catch her breath. Everything had been going so well until that stuck-up old bag remembered where she'd heard

Sarah's name. Of all the rotten luck... She set off for home, walking briskly, and every now and then snatching a tear away from her cheek with the heel of her hand. Damn you, Henry. Damn you to hell.

'Sarah!'

Sarah was shaken from her angry thoughts by a well-cultured voice coming from a car which had drawn up beside her. It was Kaye Royale.

'How lovely to see you again,' Kaye cried. 'Can I give you a lift?'

'I don't have far to go,' said Sarah. She was in no mood for conversation, least of all with one of Henry's wives.

'Oh do come and have a bite of lunch with me,' said Kaye. 'My treat. I've got so much to tell you.'

Sarah hesitated. They weren't expecting her to turn up at the pub because she had told them about the interview and Lu-Lu was with Mrs Angel, so she really should spend the time looking for a place to live, but with Kaye looking at her so appealingly, and her own tummy rumbling, Sarah climbed into the passenger seat against her better judgement.

Annie was concentrating on a piece of knitting. She was by no means an expert, but she had to get this right. It was only a scarf in rib, but her progress was very slow. Knit one, purl one... She stuck her tongue out as she concentrated. Her head ached. The baby was almost due and she was enormous. Sitting down made her feel breathless at times. She couldn't quite believe that women went through all this to have a child. Knit one, purl one... It was imperative that she get this finished.

It was on the Thursday after school, three days after the interview, when Sarah got back home and found the cottage all boarded up. A man in a shabby raincoat with a greasy collar was waiting to collect her keys.

'Oh please,' she began. 'Give me just a little more time. You can't put me and my babies on the street ... please.'

The man couldn't look her in the face as he held his hand out and worked the fingers for the keys. Defeated, Sarah handed them over.

'Why?' she asked. 'Why has this happened? I've always paid my rent on time.'

'There's been complaints,' said the man.

'What complaints? Who has complained?'

'Nothing to do with me,' he sniffed. 'I'm just the bloke what collects the keys.' And with that, he climbed back into his van and started the engine. She had expected this might happen and had just spent a precious thirty bob on getting new keys cut from the old ones. Thank God she'd been one step ahead of them, but what was he talking about ... complaints.

The board the man had put over the front door covered the keyhole, so as soon as the van was out of sight, she took the children round the back and climbed over the gate. It was low enough for her to lift the pram over and having bashed the board to uncover the back door keyhole, she let them in. She knew they would eventually find out that they were still living in the property, but at least it gave her a bit more time to look for another place.

It was cold, so she was forced to light the fire (thank goodness for Peter Millward's bag of coal), and apart from the windows being boarded up, she was able to pretend that everything was perfectly normal.

'Why did the man do that to the window, Mummy?' Jenny was puzzled that they could no longer see out into the street.

'We have to be as quiet as pixies,' said Sarah, putting her finger on her lips. 'We don't want him to hear us, do we?'

'But why?'

'It's a game,' Sarah told her.

When she put the children in bed, she'd kissed them fiercely. Downstairs in the kitchen she allowed herself the luxury of a cry and she prayed to God for help as she sat at the table to consider her options. If she couldn't find somewhere to live, they'd take her kids away. She couldn't bear the thought of losing them. She should have told Kaye what was happening that day she'd stopped her and taken her for lunch, but Kaye was so full of what had happened to her aunt in the mental institution that they hadn't got round to talking about Sarah's problems.

'Lottie's a sweetie,' Kaye had told her. They were sitting in Hubbard's restaurant eating omelettes. 'But I'm going to have to take it one step at a time.'

'I can't imagine how awful it would be being stuck in one of those places,' Sarah had sympathised. 'Especially when there's nothing wrong with you.'

'I know,' Kaye had cried. 'And I can't let them chuck her out on the streets, can I?'

Sarah sighed. If only Kaye knew within a few days she would be in the same sort of predicament. She should have said something. Kaye might know of a decent landlord. She moved in those kinds of circles. As she went up to bed, she wondered again if she should marry Peter. It would certainly solve all her problems and yet she respected him too much to take advantage of him like that. If he ever found out that she'd only married him because she was homeless, it would hurt him deeply and she owed him more than that. And yet, as she toyed with the idea, she thought perhaps she could carry it off and he would never know. She closed her eyes and tried to imagine him in bed with her. Immediately his protruding nasal hairs took on enormous proportions. The thought made her shiver. No, she really couldn't marry Peter.

Over the next couple of days, she spent every spare minute looking for digs, moving out of town and towards the less desirable areas on the outskirts of Worthing, but to no avail. Every Nissen hut left over from the war and all the prefabs were already occupied. At the town hall, the woman in the housing department put her particulars onto a list and promised her that she would be considered for council housing when the time came.

'What does that mean? When the time comes?'

'We are going to build a whole new estate in the Durrington area,' she told her. 'The work should start soon.'

'But I need help now,' Sarah protested.

'And I'm not a magician,' the woman snapped. 'I can't conjure up a house out of a hat.'

Frustrated and upset, Sarah had left.

She had asked around her various jobs to see if anyone knew of lodgings.

'Fancy a bit of a change, do you?' Peter Millward asked when she'd quizzed him. They were sitting in his office at the coal yard. She was so desperate, even that was beginning to look attractive.

'Something like that,' Sarah smiled. Her heart was thumping in case he asked her more detailed questions, but thankfully he took her request at face value.

'I'll let you know if I hear of anything,' he promised.

The landlord in the pub shook his head when she'd asked him, and Mrs Angel had promised to put a card in the window for her. Sarah was coming to the end of her options. At the end of the week, she counted the money in her purse and in the sewing machine fund, and discovered it still wasn't quite enough for the two weeks' rent she would have to give as a deposit on a new home. She'd have to settle for something far smaller, but that was fine so long as she and the children could be together. But the next week she came back to the cottage to find a stout padlock on both the front and back doors. Oh God, now she was truly homeless.

Twelve

The weather in November was mild and still sunny. On November 15th, 1948, Malcolm Mitchell switched on his radio at ten o'clock in the morning and heard the BBC's John Snagge announce that at 9.14 p.m. the previous day, Her Royal Highness the Princess Elizabeth, Duchess of Edinburgh, had been safely delivered of a prince. 'Her Royal Highness and her son,' he told the nation in dulcet tones, 'are both doing well.' Having acted upon Malcolm's suggestion, among the first to send congratulatory telegrams to Buckingham Palace was Leonard Bentall, the mayor of Worthing, something which was worthy of a mention on the news on the Home Service. At roughly the same time, in Zachary Merton, a small maternity hospital in the village of Rustington about five miles from Worthing, Malcolm's daughter was safely delivered of her son. For the royal prince, there would be the traditional forty-one gun salute in Hyde Park and the bells of Westminster Abbey would ring out. For Malcolm's daughter, there would be no such celebration and from that moment on, at her father's insistence, no mention of her baby. The father of the prince had played squash during the birth of his son. Henry Royale had languished, quite rightly so Malcolm thought, in his prison cell.

For the past month, Annie had kept herself to

herself. To begin with, she'd spent a good deal of her time in her room, only coming downstairs for meals or when the doctor or the midwife called. She had perked up when she had received Henry's letters, and although she had to remain hidden from view, she spent time playing the piano. Since her marriage, her playing had become a little rusty, but she was a talented pianist and soon regained her abilities. The music had soothed and calmed her jangled nerves. The letters from Henry had kept her going during her isolation, but since her father found out about them, she hadn't received any more. However that didn't stop her writing to Henry every day and she bribed the maid with a couple of her old dresses to make sure she posted them on her way home. To make absolutely sure Henry got them, Annie would watch her cross the road and put them in the postbox on the corner from her bedroom window.

'My father is preventing me from getting your letters,' she told Henry, 'but I know you still write, my darling.'

She'd thought long and hard about Henry and relived their courting days and the memory of his passionate lovemaking. She understood that he was not perfect but she couldn't – nay, wouldn't – believe all the terrible things they said about him in that courtroom. The others might be quick to condemn him, but they obviously didn't love Henry the way she did. She still clung to the idea that this was all a terrible mistake. Perhaps he had a twin brother he didn't know about. But even if what they said was right, as far as she was concerned, she would forgive him. Henry was coming to get her and they would make a home together for the sake of their son.

All the decisions about her life were being made by others. The doctor, her father and her mother, had made all the arrangements for her confinement. She feigned obedience, but everything they'd said had floated over the top of her head, her only contribution being the occasional nod of assent. According to the doctor, she would have to spend the usual ten days after the birth in Zachary Merton and then she and the baby would go to a Mother and Baby Home until he was adopted. No one except the doctor knew of her situation and even her father's insistence that she revert back to her maiden name was designed to keep her away from the public gaze. She'd fought him over changing her name. In her eyes, she was Henry's wife and she still regarded herself as Mrs Royal, but in the end it was easier to give in. She had a private room in the maternity home and although her father was willing to engage a nurse to take care of the baby for her, the doctor persuaded him to follow the usual procedure.

'Let her nurse the child for six weeks,' he told Malcolm. 'It will make her face up to her responsibility. I realise that this situation is not her fault, but you don't want her making any more rash decisions.'

Malcolm could see the sense of that and when her father was around, Annie was compliant and cooperative to the point of slavishness. But when she was alone, Annie was busy making plans. Would she give up Henry's son? Never!

The day after the baby was born, the local press

came to the hospital to photograph any babies born at the same time as the new prince. Annie's child had been born at almost exactly the same time as little Prince Charles, but nobody dared to divulge that bit of information. They had to make do with baby Ian Sheppard who had been born a few hours before the prince.

Annie stayed quietly in her room, and for an hour in the afternoon, her mother would visit. After lunch, the nurses would close the curtains and make sure each mother was resting on her bed. The first day she came, Judith hadn't realised that this was part of the hospital routine and when the nurse said she would wake Annie, Judith wouldn't let her. Instead, she popped in to see the baby. He was awake but not crying. As she stood over his cot, he watched her with dark, intense eyes and her heart melted. She reached out and touched his hand and he automatically opened his fist and then closed it around her finger. From that moment Judith fell in love with her first grandchild, and all her visits were planned around the time when Annie was required to take her afternoon nap.

On day five, Annie, quiet and subdued, said to her mother, 'Take me home.'

'You have to stay for ten days,' said Judith.

'But why?' Annie protested. 'It's not as if there's anything wrong with me. I miss you and Father. I want to come home.'

Her mother was sympathetic, because once Annie went to the Mother and Baby Home, she would be forbidden to visit. Going to the Home meant she would be saying goodbye to her only grandchild forever. Up until that moment, Judith hadn't realised how hard that would be. 'I'll talk to your father,' she said.

'Can you give me some money and a few coupons?' Annie asked.

'Why do you need money?' her mother said, mildly curious.

'The trolley comes round in the morning and I'd like to buy a paper and some sweets,' said Annie.

Her daughter watched her mother dig into her purse and pull out ten bob. Annie smiled. She already had almost four pounds in her own purse, but that was for something else entirely. She leaned forward and rewarded her mother with a kiss.

The East Worthing Utopia Hotel was very run-down and Mrs Mumford the manager left a lot to be desired. A middle-aged woman with untidy grey hair, she wore a food-stained cardigan under her floral wrap-over apron. Her fingers were yellowed with nicotine stains and she smelled almost as bad as the hotel she ran.

Sarah felt ill at the thought of staying here, but what else could she do? It was all she could afford. She had worked out that if she eked out her money they could stay here for a couple of weeks.

The lino in the corridors was so dirty that her feet stuck to the floor when she stopped walking. They had to share the toilet with three other families. It was little better than a sewer and Sarah made it her job to clean it up. At first, she felt annoyed with the other tenants because they felt it beneath themselves to use a cleaning cloth. But on reflection, she understood that when you are at the bottom of the pecking order already, you'll take any chance you can get to be one notch above the rest. The toilet cleaner was truly at the bottom of the heap, but for now, Sarah didn't care. She did her best to keep her room clean and tidy, and having so little luggage was a distinct advantage. Sarah caught sight of one of the other tenant's room as she left the door open. She had four children and possibly the contents of a whole house in that one room. Bags and suitcases lined the walls in untidy heaps.

They all had to leave their rooms by ten in the morning and weren't allowed back until four in the afternoon. When Sarah complained, Mrs Mumford said, 'Them's the rules, like it or lump it.' The weather wasn't too cold as yet and she was grateful that it was dry. Each day after doing her cleaning jobs, Sarah looked for more permanent digs but there was nothing. She scoured the shop windows for vacancies and knocked on doors, but she was only met with disappointment.

Keeping the children clean wasn't too much of a major issue. Every couple of days, she booked into the Heene corporation baths. The children loved splashing in the water and when the attendant moved on, Sarah climbed in with them. They could have a clean towel and a little soap as part of the price and together they had a very happy time.

Her biggest worry was their clothes. Where could she wash them? To pay for them to be sent to a laundry was difficult. For a start, she was trying to keep what little money she had left for food, and besides, people who used the laundry usually had a laundry box which was collected from their address. The only sink in the Utopia was used by all the other tenants as well and it was difficult to find a time when somebody else wasn't washing, having a wash or washing up.

The few pounds she had saved for the sewing machine was fast being used up. She had just enough money for a couple more nights with Mrs Mumford when she decided she would have to swallow her pride and ask someone for help.

The next day Sarah realised that she had already left it too late. According to the note on the door, Mrs Angel had shut the shop and gone to stay with her sick sister, whilst Peter Millward was apparently in Wales. Sarah's heart sank. Because of her own stupidity, she was finally homeless. Before she'd left for her sister's, Mrs Angel had been pressing her for her new address in case Mr Lovett brought in another order, but her silly pride had made her fob her off. 'Isn't it silly?' she would laugh. 'I could take you there right now but I can't remember the name of the road. I'll tell you tomorrow. Can't stop. Must dash.' If only she had come clean, Mrs Angel might have even let her and the girls use her flat above the shop while she was at her sister's.

Finding that Peter wasn't at the yard was another blow. Before she'd been locked out of the cottage, by working late into the night, she'd finished the two lots of books he'd given her from his friends and was hoping to be paid. The money would have kept her and the girls at the hotel for a few more nights. The men at the yard told her that Peter was thinking of branching out again, this time with coaches. Day trips and holidays by the sea were becoming big business now and he wanted to be in on it from the start, so he'd gone to Wales to see some chap who had a coach for sale. She couldn't stop thinking about him and his offer of marriage. She felt terrible about the mess she'd got herself and the children into – at this rate they'd be sleeping rough on the street before the week was out. Marrying Peter was the most sensible option because it would give them a roof over their heads, but she still couldn't bear the thought of what she would have to do with him. She dreaded the welfare people finding out about her predicament, but every morning she woke with renewed hope that today would be the day she would find some rooms.

Sarah was well aware that they could soon end up on the streets. Luckily the nights were not yet terribly cold, so she would look for a shelter, a shop doorway or a space under the eaves of a bridge, and with all their things around them, surely she could manage to keep the cold night air at bay. Lu-Lu would be all right. She could still sleep in the pram, but Jenny was too big. Please God, she hoped it wouldn't come to that because she knew that was an absolutely last resort. If she was going to avoid sleeping rough, there was only one other course of action left. She would have to beg her sister for help. If Vera would take Jenny and Lu-Lu for the weekend, Sarah was sure she would find just the place.

She decided to go over to Lancing after school.

That would give the girls a whole weekend to settle down before Jenny had to go back to school on Monday and it would also give Sarah a couple of days without the children to concentrate on finding rooms. She would stress to Vera that it was only temporary and that if she helped her this time, she would never ask for help again. The more she rehearsed her little speech, the more convincing it sounded. All the same, at the back of her mind there was this niggling feeling that Vera would have none of it.

Annie's heart was thumping. At the other end of the phone, and to her utmost joy, she heard her father say, 'Worthing 253.'

She pressed button B and the coins dropped in the box with a clatter. 'Daddy?'

'Annie, how are you? How is the skiing going?'

She knew then that he had company and wasn't free to talk.

'I'm fine,' she said, willing her voice to stay strong.

'Good, good,' he said and then his voice became muffled as he added, 'that'll be all, thank you.' There was a short pause and then he added, 'Are they treating you well?'

'Yes, Daddy, I'm fine. Oh Daddy, he's lovely. You'd adore him. He's got your...'

'That's enough,' said her father, cutting her off. 'There's no point in talking about this. You know my views and that's an end to it.'

'But Daddy,' she tried again, 'if you just saw him I'm sure...'

'Annie,' he said curtly. 'No.' There was a short

pause while she struggled not to cry and he tried not to sound like the harsh parent. 'You hurry up and get on top form,' he said, his voice lightening up, 'and come home.'

'I want my son to come too,' she insisted.

'The subject is closed,' said Malcolm, hanging up and leaving his stunned daughter listening to the dialling tone.

Kaye put the phone down and stared into the middle distance. Her mother's younger sister had been living in her house for almost a week now and it hadn't been an easy transition. Apart from a couple of run-ins with Mrs Goodall who expressed her concern that Kaye was turning her home into a halfway house for the mentally ill, Lottie was still frail after her ordeal in the institution and could only cope with being on her own for short periods. Kaye had given Mrs Goodall short shrift and had devoted herself to taking Lottie on long walks by the sea and visiting local tea shops in an effort to help her get used to normal life, but she would cling grimly onto Kaye's arm and she froze every time someone spoke to her. To add to her present difficulties, Mrs Pearce, her new housekeeper, made no secret of the fact that she was nervous of Lottie and did her best to avoid being with her. Kaye had a shrewd suspicion that she and Mrs Goodall were in cahoots together and wanted to get rid of her aunt. Lottie might be nudging fifty but she still trailed around with a battered old teddy and constantly asked when she would be allowed to go back to her friends.

This should have been the most exciting time of

Kaye's life. The BBC wanted to see her and her agent again. With the promise of commissioned work, Kaye couldn't afford to let it pass, but she would need to be in London overnight and probably, if she was invited to have dinner with the producer, be prepared to stay a second night in a hotel. The difficulty was that Mrs Pearce was going on holiday to Paignton in Devon to be with her sister next week and it would be unfair to ask her to change her arrangements. What Kaye needed now was someone to help look after Lottie.

Several telephone calls to friends drew a blank and the enormity of what she had taken on began to dawn on her. In the end, she rang a nursing agency and provisionally arranged for Lottie to be looked after by a live-in nurse, but it was far from ideal. The cost wasn't the issue. Kaye was more worried about Lottie's reaction to having a nurse. She worried that she may be panicked by the uniform. It was only as she strolled in the garden before dusk that Kaye thought of Sarah. When she had gone to her little house, it was obvious that Henry's second wife was in dire straits, and when Kaye had taken her for lunch, she'd had the feeling that Sarah was a bit run down. She was a fiercely proud woman, but she might be amenable to looking after one middle-aged confused lady for a couple of nights, and she was sure the children would enjoy staying in her home. That one time when she had been to Sarah's house, Kaye couldn't help noticing that they didn't even have a proper bathroom. She'd guessed that the rather odd shelving in the kitchen probably meant that the only bath in the house was probably under the boards. On the other hand, her home, Copper Beeches, had a lovely big bath where the children could play in the water for as long as they wanted. There was plenty of food in the larder, and apart from her own bedroom, she would give Sarah the run of the house. The more Kaye thought about it, the better the idea sounded. Tomorrow, she would get the car out and go and see her.

Thirteen

'I'm looking for Mrs Royal.'

The man he had stopped looked blank and shrugged his shoulders. Detective Sergeant Truman, known affectionately as Bear had already knocked on several doors in the street before he found anyone at home. He felt sure Mrs Rivers next door was in but not answering and he couldn't blame her. Since her son had been locked up yet again, the woman had no time for the police. He'd been surprised and strangely upset to see the eviction notice on Sarah's door and the heavy padlocks across the handle. The windows were boarded up too. With everything else that had happened to her, hadn't the poor woman suffered enough?

'She left,' said another neighbour passing in the street. 'I don't know where she went, I'm sure, but she packed up the baby's pram and she left.'

'When did she go?' said Bear, tipping his hat.
'A couple of weeks ago.'
Damn, he thought. He'd only just missed her. 'Did you see which direction she went?'
'I mind my own business,' said the woman, shaking her head.

Annie's baby had acquired a reputation for being the perfect, contented child. He slept all night, which meant that the night nurses didn't come to the nursery, so it was four days before one of them realised that Annie was creeping into the nursery to feed the baby herself.
'Don't tell a soul,' she told the startled woman, 'and I'll make it worth your while.'
'Your father has left strict instructions...' she began.
'My father need never know,' said Annie. 'He is my baby and I will never give him up.'
'But they won't let you feed him yourself in the Mother and Baby Home,' said the nurse. 'You do know that, don't you?'
Annie tilted her head defiantly. 'I'll cross that bridge when I come to it.'
'I really should tell Sister,' said the nurse. 'If you've got milk coming in, they'll have to bind your breasts.'
'Oh please...' Annie pleaded. She kept it up until the nurse, worn down by her persistent pleas, agreed. As she left the nursery, Annie slipped one of her precious pound notes in the woman's pocket and put her finger to her lips. 'Don't tell a soul.'
Alone in her room, Annie had spent some time

composing a letter to her godmother. Auntie Phyllis was a bit of an eccentric who lived in a run-down property in Kent with her beloved dogs. The family hadn't seen her for some time, but Annie knew Auntie Phyllis had her father's disapproval because she was living in sin with an artist. Because they had never married, Annie hoped her godmother, unlike her father, would be broad-minded about letting her keep her baby. Perhaps in return for a little housework, she might consider giving them a roof over their heads until Henry came home. She reminded her of her childhood promise, 'Any time you need me, just holler,' and hoped she could find it in her heart to give them a lifeline. Once the letter was in the post, Annie looked for a reply. By the time she and her son were taken to the Mother and Baby Home on the tenth day, Annie still hadn't heard from Auntie Phyllis. It was a great disappointment. Judith looked a little puffy-eyed as she said her goodbyes, but she promised to pick Annie up in a month's time.

'It'll be almost Christmas by then,' Judith smiled. 'We'll put this behind us and have a wonderful time.'

Annie was cheerful and chatty, but the sinking feeling she now had was getting stronger by the minute. As they prepared her for the journey, the nurses bound her breasts.

'I can't understand why you still have milk,' said the sister. 'Your breasts are still quite full.'

When she had gone, Annie allowed herself a smile and eased the binding. Shutting herself in the toilet, she released herself from the bandages and expressed some of her milk over the sink with her hand. It seemed an awful waste but she had to keep her milk flowing for the sake of the baby. Someone came to the door and called out, 'Are you all right in there?'

'Yes,' Annie called back. She pushed her breast back under the binding and turned on the taps to flush the milk away. Her father may have refused her a home but this part of the plan was working well. All she needed was a reply from Auntie Phyllis.

The walk to Lancing took Sarah an hour. The weather was overcast and there was a definite drop in the temperature. The wind was coming off the sea, so it wasn't a pleasant experience. Sarah had put both children into the pram with the hood up and was making a game of pushing them. She knew Jenny was tired after school and they were both hungry, but she wanted to get to Vera's place before dark. All their stuff, not a lot now, was under the pram and it was starting to rain.

She was three shillings short for another night with Mrs Mumford. She was tempted to go back and weather the landlady's anger in the morning, but that would be like stealing. With all her troubles Sarah had never once stooped to thieving before. She had been a stupid fool. She should have asked for help earlier, but ever the optimist, she'd held out in the hope that something good would turn up the next day. She was determined not to let the children see her crying, so she had to keep swallowing the lump in her throat.

When Vera opened the door, the smell of frying

sausages wafted out. 'Sarah!'

'I'm sorry to drop in on you like this Vera,' Sarah began, her mouth salivating, 'but I'm in trouble.'

Vera kept her arm on the door, effectively barring her entry.

'I've been evicted,' said Sarah helplessly.

'Well, you can't stay here,' said Vera quickly. 'We haven't the room.'

'I just need somewhere for the kids for a couple of days...' Sarah began again.

'No!' said Vera, glancing anxiously up and down the street. 'I can't. You'll have to find somewhere else.'

'That's just the point,' said Sarah as the door began to close. 'There is nowhere else. You don't have to take me in, just the girls.'

Vera leaned out and hissed in her face. 'I've already told you there's no room here. If you've lost your place, that's your own fault.'

'Vera,' Sarah said hopelessly, 'please. They'll take my kids away.'

'Look, I'm sorry this has happened,' said Vera, 'but our place is far too small and I've just decorated. I want you to go now. Bill will be home from work soon and he won't want to see you on the doorstep looking like a tramp. You've got no right to come over here trying to spoil what I've got.'

With that, the door closed. Sarah stared at the glass for several seconds and cursed herself for coming. She'd known in her heart that this would happen, but she'd hoped against hope that Vera might at least be willing to take Jenny and Lu-Lu.

'Are we going home now, Mummy?'

Sarah choked back her tears and smiled at her

trusting little girl. 'Soon,' she said, picking up the bootie which had fallen from her dolly's foot, 'soon.'

'Have you any idea where Mrs Royal is?'

The woman across the road was putting her key into the front door. Kaye had come out to post a letter to Henry. Now that she knew exactly where he was, she had got her solicitor to draw up the divorce papers, citing two counts of bigamist marriage as proof tantamount to adultery. She didn't have to worry about reputations being ruined. Sarah and Annie's predicament was already in the public domain. As the letter hit the bottom of the pillar box, she felt a wonderful sense of release. All she wanted now was to find Sarah, so she'd gone straight round to her house and was puzzled to find it all boarded up.

The woman across the road shook her head.

'Do you know when she'll be back?'

'You're the second person asking me that today,' said the woman. 'Got slung out, didn't she.'

'What?' Kaye was horrified. 'But why? Where is she living now?'

The woman shrugged. Kaye chewed her lip anxiously. 'I need to find her.'

'Could try Mrs Angel.' Kaye recognised the name and the woman gave her directions, but Mrs Angel, who had already put her 'Closed' sign across the door, didn't know where Sarah was either. 'I've only just got back from my sister's. I haven't seen Sarah yet.'

Kaye told her about the boarded-up house and the eviction notice in the window. 'I had a feeling something wasn't quite right,' Mrs Angel said. 'She asked me if I knew of any lodgings, but she never breathed a word to me that she was actually homeless. I thought she just fancied a change of scene.'

'Do you think she could have found somewhere else that easily?'

Mrs Angel looked thoughtful. 'Come to think of it, she's never asked me to take the card out of the window.'

'Do you think she would have gone to stay with anyone else? Her sister, perhaps?'

'I doubt it,' said Mrs Angel. 'She and Vera don't get on.'

Kaye frowned anxiously. 'I'm really worried about her.'

'Now that you've told me,' Mrs Angel nodded, 'I am too.'

'Do you know her sister's address? I took her there once to pick up the girls, but I can't quite remember.'

'She moved to Annweir Avenue,' said Mrs Angel. 'That's in Lancing, but I don't remember the number.'

Kaye got back into her car and drove over to Lancing. It didn't take long to find the road, but it was quite long. Kaye knocked on every other door, but it wasn't until she stopped a woman with a shopping bag that she found out where Vera was living. She crossed the street and knocked on the door.

As she opened the door, Vera was saying, 'Look, I've already told you... Oh!'

'Is Sarah here?' Kaye asked.

Carole pushed in front of her mother and stared at Kaye.

'I'm afraid she isn't,' said Vera, putting on her poshest voice. 'I haven't seen her for days.'

'But Auntie Sarah was here just now, Mummy,' Carole piped up.

Vera gave her daughter a look to kill. 'Oh yes,' she flustered. 'Of course. How silly of me. I quite forgot.'

'She wanted to come in,' said Carole, 'but Mummy said no.'

'Carole,' Vera hissed. 'You don't interrupt adults when they are talking. Now go to your room.'

'But Mummy...' Carole protested.

'Now!' Vera snapped.

The child slunk away and Vera turned back to Kaye. 'I'm afraid I don't know where my sister is,' she said indignantly. 'I cannot be held responsible for her actions, but I have told the authorities about those children. It's not right for her to be trailing them around all over the place. They need a good home and a warm bed.'

Kaye opened her mouth, but before she could say another word Vera had closed the door.

Kaye frowned. Where would Sarah go? And what did her sister mean when she said she had told the authorities? If Sarah really did have nowhere to go, what on earth would she do with her children when it was cold and it was starting to rain? Kaye shuddered to think.

They were almost back on the outskirts of Worthing when the rain started to come down really hard. Sarah had both children in the pram.

They were very squashed, but at least she could put the hood up, and with the pram apron across their legs, it kept some of the cold and wet at bay. The springs were creaking all the time and Sarah worried that the one holding the back wheel might actually give way. The pram had been a hand-me-down when she got it and since then she had used it for two children and a couple of moves. Right now it groaned under the weight of all it carried. She was dog-tired and hungry. She had given the children her last piece of bread and emptied the jam pot. Not an ideal meal, but it was all she had. Having shared her meagre breakfast with the girls this morning, Sarah herself hadn't eaten a proper meal since the day before yesterday.

She knew her sister was ashamed and embarrassed by her poverty; but she hadn't counted on Vera actually turning the children away. She was fairly confident that she wouldn't be welcome, but she still couldn't quite believe that her own sister had turned her back on her two nieces. Although it would have stuck in her throat to say the words, she would have asked for a few bob to tide her over if Vera hadn't already slammed the door in her face. What galled Sarah even more was the knowledge that she and Bill had a three-bedroomed house. Angrily, she wiped a tear away from her face with the heel of her hand and pushed doggedly on.

There was a shelter up ahead. It was a Victorian structure and it faced out to sea, which wasn't ideal, but it had a seat and a roof. She pushed the pram up the slope from the road and headed for it. There was nobody around, although the shelter smelled vaguely of urine. She turned the pram away from the sea and took some stuff out of the hessian bags underneath. Using their clothing, she made a bed on the seat and pulled Jenny out of the pram.

'Are we going home now, Mummy?' she asked.

'Soon,' said Sarah, her voice choked with emotion and fear. 'Let's have a little rest here first, shall we?'

The child lay back without protest and Sarah covered her over. Lu-Lu was struggling to sit up in the pram. 'No, lay down darling,' Sarah said. 'Go to sleep, there's a good girl.'

With the whooshing of the waves in the background, it didn't take long before they both drifted off. Sarah sat hunched up on the bench and shivered with the cold. Everything warm was wrapped around her children. Think on the bright side, she told herself. The landlord at the pub would pay her again tomorrow. If they spent the night here, she could put her wage together with the six bob she had left and buy a couple of nights back at the hotel. They'd be together for one more day. After that, if she couldn't find anywhere for them to live, she would have to let the Welfare put them into a Home. Sarah shivered again. She was destined to spend a cold night sleeping rough, and the enormity of her situation hit home. She faced the sea and wept. She wept for Jenny and Lu-Lu because she had let them down. She wept for her mother because she missed her and wanted more than anything to have a hug. She wept angry, frustrated tears because of Vera and her heartlessness, and she wept for all the other homeless, cold and frightened people in the world. In 1946, there was a lot of talk in the town about the Vigilante group in Brighton who were 'vigilantly' scouring the streets of the town looking for empty buildings and giving them to the homeless. The landlords didn't like it of course, but it gave a needy person a roof over their heads. She wondered vaguely about trying her luck with them, but then the thought of dragging the girls for thirteen miles along the seafront for something which may or may not still be there, brought her back to her senses. She remembered how immediately after the war, people desperate for homes, took over old army camps and RAF stations. They mostly went to ex-servicemen and their families, but what about the empty huts the Canadians had vacated on their base in Shaftesbury Avenue not long after VE Day? Could it be possible that the rows and rows of Nissen huts were still there? Worthing Borough Council had built a lot of prefabs, especially in the Castle Road area, rabbit hutches some people called them, but what she wouldn't give for one right now.

'Sarah?' the voice was gentle. Seeing who it was, Sarah shot to her feet. She hadn't heard Kaye creeping up on her. She stared at Henry's wife. Was she having a dream or was she real?

'Oh Sarah, why didn't you tell me?'

Sarah felt a massive rush of emotion, but as Kaye came towards her she put up her hand and backed away. 'Please go away,' she said. 'Don't, just don't.'

'I came to look for you because I need your help,' said Kaye.

'You need my help?' Sarah choked. She laughed sardonically. 'And how exactly can I help you, Mrs Royale?'

'You remember my aunt?' said Kaye. 'She's living with me now, but the thing is, I have to go up to London and I wanted to ask if you would help me look after her.'

Sarah opened her mouth but nothing came out. There was a lump in her throat the size of an orange and she couldn't stop shaking. Standing in front of her children, she indicated her predicament.

'Then perhaps we could both help each other,' said Kaye, pulling her coat tightly around herself as the chilly sea air bit into her. 'I have some empty rooms in my house.'

'No,' said Sarah, shaking her head in belief, her eyes filling with tears. 'No. It's too much... I can't.'

'Why not?' said Kaye. 'Lottie isn't mad. She's been traumatised, but she's all right. She won't hurt the children, I promise.'

Sarah sat down on the edge of the seat again and, leaning forward, put her hand on her head. This wasn't happening. She must be dreaming.

'Look,' Kaye persisted, 'You come and work for me and you can all be together. I won't hold you to anything. Just until you can find something better.'

Sarah put her hand over her mouth to stop the cry of anguish she knew was coming and stared at her helplessly. What was the catch? There had to be a catch.

Lu-Lu sat-up and cried. Sarah took her out of

the pram and onto her hip. 'Shhh. Shhh. It's all right, darling.'

Then Jenny stirred. 'Mummy, I'm cold.'

Down by the road, they heard a car door slam and two people began walking up the embankment. The man carried an umbrella and the woman wore flat shoes and a mackintosh. Two policemen were walking towards them from the opposite direction and eventually the four of them merged as they came towards them.

'Oh God,' Sarah whispered anxiously. 'The welfare. They've come for my children.'

'Leave this to me,' said Kaye. She put out her hand and took Jenny's. At the same time she began to stuff everything back into the pram.

'Mrs Royal?' said the woman as she approached.

'Yes,' said Kaye, just a little ahead of Sarah. The woman seemed a little flummoxed.

'We've come for your children,' said the man. 'This is no place for little ones and I hope you are not going to make a fuss for their sakes.'

'Actually,' said Kaye stepping in front of him, still holding Jenny's hand. 'That's very kind of you, but I already have my car. In fact, you are parked right next to it.'

'Who are you?' the woman demanded.

'Mrs Royale,' said Kaye, striding down the grassy slope towards the road and her waiting car. 'Is that you, DC Harris? You know me, don't you? Copper Beeches. I can't think why you've chased after my cousin. This has all been a ghastly mistake, of course. I asked her to come and look after our aunt and somehow or other we've made an absolute muck-up of the plan. Still never mind, we found each other in the end, didn't we dear? All my fault of course, but let's get these children home and tucked up in bed.'

By now everyone had reached Kaye's car and she was busy bundling Jenny in the back. She opened the front passenger door for Sarah and almost manhandled Sarah, cradling Lu-Lu in her arms, inside.

'Now just a minute…' said the woman.

'DC Harris,' Kaye called, completely ignoring the woman as she walked around the car. 'I wonder if you would be an absolute sweetie and push the pram round to my place. I don't like the thought of leaving it there. You never know who might be around.'

As she slipped into the driver's seat, the woman opened the back passenger door.

'I wouldn't do that if I were you,' said Kaye coldly. She could see that the woman was about to make Jenny get out. Kaye smiled and in a slightly less hostile tone added, 'If you want to pop round tomorrow, we'll talk then. DC Harris knows my address, don't you?' She leaned over and pulled the rear door shut. 'Goodnight.'

And with a jerk on the accelerator pedal, she left them by the roadside.

Fourteen

As Kaye showed Sarah and her children into the hallway, an angry red-faced woman came out of the kitchen.

'Mrs Pearce,' Kaye began apologetically. 'I'm so very sorry. Everything took much longer than I thought.' Tight-lipped, Mrs Pearce reached for her coat on the hallstand while Kaye turned into a room which looked like an office and came back out with an envelope. 'Thank you so much for waiting. I hope you have a nice holiday. I have given you a little extra and once again I'm sorry. It won't happen again.'

Mrs Pearce stuffed the envelope into her handbag. 'No, it won't happen again, madam,' she said curtly, 'because I won't be coming back. I can't be doing with people crazy in the head and,' she added as she looked Sarah and her children up and down, 'vagrants.'

Sarah bristled with anger and shame. Jenny and Lu-Lu stared at the woman wide-eyed. Thank goodness they had no idea what the word meant, but Sarah felt that they could tell by the tone of her voice that it wasn't complimentary. Kaye stepped between them and opened the door. 'I'm sorry you feel that way,' she said stiffly. 'Goodbye.'

As soon as the door closed, Kaye turned around. 'Where's my aunt?' she said anxiously. She went from door to door calling, 'Lottie...' but to no avail.

'Come upstairs with me,' said Kaye as she put her hand onto the bannister. 'She must be in her room.'

The house was beautifully furnished. Sarah's glimpse into the office revealed book-lined walls and a leather-topped mahogany desk. Through the open door of the sitting room, Sarah saw cosy chairs with cushions and a cheerful fire behind the fireguard. The stairs were carpeted, although the brass stair rods could have done with a shine. At the top of the stairs they passed a large room, which was obviously the master bedroom, and turned to the right.

'Auntie...' Kaye called. 'Lottie...'

They came to another room and Kaye flung the door open without knocking. A woman sitting in an armchair jumped. She'd obviously been dozing and they'd woken her up. She suddenly put her hands over her head and drew her knees up into the foetal position as she turned away from them. 'I'm sorry, I'm sorry, I'm sorry...' she cried plaintively.

Kaye glanced back at Sarah in shocked surprise. 'Dear God,' murmured Kaye as she rushed to her aunt's side, 'what has that woman done?'

Sarah wasn't sure what to make of it. Kaye was clearly blaming Mrs Pearce for her aunt's distress, but what if ... what if... She couldn't bring herself to even think of the alternative. Her fears were immediately allayed as she watched Kaye put her arms around her aunt's shoulders, all the while talking to her in a soothing manner. Eventually the older woman relaxed and smiled. She seemed to be in her late forties or early fifties. Her hair was going grey and the style rather unflattering and flat. It was also very short, almost as if she'd once had her head shaved and her hair was growing back again. She wore good clothes, a pair of new slippers on her feet and a pair of black patent leather shoes stood next to the chair.

'We've got some visitors, Lottie dear,' Kaye told her gently. 'Would you like to help me make up the beds?'

The older woman dabbed her eyes with a handkerchief and stood up. 'Oh,' she beamed at the children. 'Aren't you lovely?' She walked towards Jenny and Lu-Lu in the doorway. 'Hello.'

'Say hello, Jenny,' said Sarah and shyly Jenny obliged.

'As we were driving here, it occurred to me that you and the children could have the rooms at the top of the stairs,' said Kaye, walking on. 'They're a bit sparse at the moment but we can soon fix that. There are two rooms together and it would be like having your own place.' She stopped off at the airing cupboard and pulled out some sheets and pillowcases. Giving half to Lottie, they made their way towards the back stairs.

To Sarah's surprise and delight, it really was like a small flat. Each of the two rooms had two beds and although it was sparsely furnished, it was clean and airy. A third door revealed a poky bathroom, but it had its own bath. Sarah was conscious that her chin had developed a constant wobble and her eyes brimmed with unshed tears.

'As you can see,' said Kaye matter-of-factly,

'now that Mrs Pearce has walked out on me, you would be doing me a great favour if you could stay for a while.'

'I don't know how to thank you,' said Sarah in a small voice.

'Lottie, dear,' said Kaye, dismissing Sarah's gratitude with a wave of her hand, 'do you think you could make up the beds while Sarah gets her children ready for bed?'

Sarah felt her face colour as she remembered her pram and all their belongings still sitting on the seafront, she supposed. 'I have no clothes to put them in.'

'Let me see what I can find,' said Kaye. As soon as she'd gone, the two women decided to make up the beds together. Sarah kept glancing at Lottie. The woman seemed childlike rather than simple. She didn't say much, but Lottie and Lu-Lu seemed to create a bond almost immediately. Every time Lottie shook out a sheet she would say 'Boo!' and Lu-Lu would laugh. Jenny was a little more reticent. 'Is this our new home, Mummy?' she whispered earnestly.

'It is for a while,' said Sarah. 'Nice, isn't it?'

Kaye reappeared with a vest and a chemise. She had tied a knot in each of the shoulder straps. 'Will these do for now?'

Sarah took them gratefully. This woman's generosity was unbelievable. How could she ever repay her?

'You can give them a bath if you want to,' she said. 'There's plenty of hot water, and when you've got them settled, come down to the kitchen and we'll talk.'

She and Lottie left them to it, although a few minutes later Kaye sent Lottie back with soft, fluffy towels and scented soap. In the distance, Sarah heard the doorbell ring and for a second wondered if the welfare people had come to take her children, but she needn't have worried. The children enjoyed their bath, and when they got back in the bedroom, two glasses of milk and some biscuits waited on the bedside locker. Sarah tucked them into bed, and although it wasn't her habit, this night, because they were in a strange house and a strange bed, she sat with them until they fell asleep.

Downstairs in the kitchen, Kaye had some sandwiches waiting. Sarah was so full of emotion as she sat down that she could hardly speak. Lottie appeared in the doorway and announced that she was going to bed. She kissed Kaye on the cheek. 'Can I play with the children in the morning?' she asked Sarah as she left the room.

'Of course you can,' Sarah smiled.

'She's perfectly harmless,' said Kaye as soon as she was sure Lottie was out of earshot. 'It's just that she wouldn't be able to look after herself. All her life, people have told her what to do and she's lost the ability to think for herself.'

As Sarah filled her growling stomach, Kaye explained about her trip to London the following week. 'If you decide to stay,' she said, lighting up a cigarette, 'I could offer you say, £2/10/- a week?'

Sarah's mouth dropped open.

'You and your children will live-in of course,' Kaye went on. 'All found.'

'Are you sure?' Sarah said. 'That's very generous.'

'I get the feeling that you won't take advantage,' Kaye smiled as she blew the smoke from her cigarette into the air above, them.

'Never,' Sarah breathed. 'So what are my duties?'

Kaye blew out her cheeks. 'I need a housekeeper,' she said. 'Now that I'm having more demands made on me for my work, I really can't concentrate on shopping and washing and stuff. And of course, there's Lottie. As I explained, she's been shut away from the world for so long. I want her to learn to be independent, but at the moment I don't want her left on her own for long periods. You don't have to mollycoddle her, she enjoys doing things, but you'll have to be prepared that she might get under your feet.'

'I understand,' Sarah nodded.

'She seems to love the children,' said Kaye. 'By the way, DC Harris brought back your pram. I've left it in the porch for now and your things are in the hall.'

'I saw them as I came downstairs,' said Sarah.

'Take the rest of the weekend to settle in,' said Kaye, 'and start first thing Monday morning.'

Sarah was tempted to fling her arms around Kaye and kiss her, but instead she whispered a heartfelt thank you. Later on, as she lay on her bed, Sarah felt as if she had died and gone to heaven. Whatever happened, she would make sure Kaye never regretted her kindness, and for as long as she was able, she would make this a happy move for her children.

The Mother and Baby Home was ten miles from Worthing. It was in a leafy suburb of Bognor Regis and quite close to the sea. The Matron was surprisingly kind and understanding, but straight away, Annie knew she would find it difficult to feed the baby in secret because all the mothers were kept together in the same room.

'Didn't they stop your milk?' Matron asked.

'They tried,' said Annie, rolling her eyes innocently, 'but then I thought it would be easier to carry on. After all, they say breast milk is best, don't they?'

Later, after feeding time was over, Annie was called to Matron's office.

'I know you want the best for your baby,' said Matron, trying some emotional blackmail, 'but you're upsetting the other girls, dear.'

'They were happy to let me feed him in the maternity hospital,' Annie lied.

'You will find it a lot harder when you have to let him go,' Matron cautioned.

'I know,' said Annie, 'but I don't mind that. It's the least I can do for him.'

'I don't know what your father will say about this.'

'Does he have to know?'

Matron pursed her lips and sighed. 'I can see that you're a very determined young lady,' she said.

'I've no wish to be disrespectful, Matron,' said Annie, 'but I'm not like the others. I genuinely thought I was married to my husband. It feels as if the baby and I are being punished for something beyond my control.'

'The adoption society is coming to see him next week,' said Matron. 'They have a lovely couple lined up.'

'That may not be necessary,' said Annie, her heart thumping. 'I have written to my godmother and she will give us a home for the time being.'

'You are a well-educated young woman,' Matron conceded, 'but I think you're deluding yourself. A baby is an enormous responsibility. Your godmother may not want a small child in her home. And besides, I don't want to encourage petty jealousies in the nursery.'

'Then send me to my room,' Annie insisted. 'Be angry with me in front of them if you like, but please let me do this one thing for my baby.'

Amazingly, Annie got her way, but even though she was the first in the hall every morning for the post, Auntie Phyllis didn't reply.

Malcolm Mitchell strode towards the thirteenth hole. Although there was a distinct chill in the air, it was a pleasant morning. They had driven off reasonably well and he had played a fairly consistent game, but at four over par he was no match for his opponent. Keith Martin, a retired Major, was having a blinder of a game, mainly pars with a few birdies and bogeys – definitely the best bit of golf Malcolm had seen in a long time. It was beginning to gall him a bit. Normally he could rely on thrashing Keith.

Malcolm had missed his golf during the war years. There had always been too much to do. Too old to be called up, Malcolm had found other ways of helping the war effort, mainly by joining the Observer Corps and spending many a cold night on High Salvington identifying incoming planes and plotting their course. Judith had done her bit by joining the Knitted Comforts Fund and holding meetings in their house, where the members collated hundreds of knitted items for the troops abroad.

He teed up for his next shot. The ball flew into the air and Malcolm rocked on his heels as he watched it go at least 350 yards uphill. It hit a rough patch, bounced and rolled onto the green. A short putt and he would be two under par for this hole.

'Good shot,' said Keith, and Malcolm suppressed a smug smile.

Now that peace had come, he had new horizons in his sights. His jewellery shops were doing well and since he'd joined Worthing Borough Council he had ambitions to become mayor. All this unsavoury business with Annie made it more difficult. He wasn't just thinking of himself. He needed to keep her reputation intact as well. People were prone to gossip and this sort of thing could do an awful lot of damage to a young girl. Annie had already made one ghastly mistake and it was down to him to stop her making another. Trouble was, she was so damned stubborn although where she got that from he didn't know. He cleared his throat noisily. He hated it when they rowed.

Keith was concentrating very hard as he prepared to tee-off. A second later the ball was heading straight for the green. Malcolm closed his eyes. It was a perfect shot, damn him, and with the game he was having there was every possibility of him getting a hole-in-one. He heard a sharp sounding 'whack' and Keith groaned out loud. Malcolm opened his eyes to see the ball, which had obviously hit a wall jutting out slightly onto the green, coming back towards them. Fortunately, Keith ducked as it made its return and landed a couple of yards behind him in the rough.

'Oh, bad luck,' said Malcolm. He turned his head quickly in case Keith saw the smirk on his face. Perhaps there was a God in heaven after all.

Monday morning, bright and early, Sarah began her new job. She had spent the weekend doing her own washing and she'd walked back to her old address with the pram to retrieve what she could from the coal bunker and the shed at the back. She had written letters to her two wealthy employers telling them of her new position and that she wouldn't be back. She called in to see Mrs Angel who was delighted for her and promised to send word of any new orders Mr Lovett might bring. Sarah said her goodbyes and headed off to the pub where the landlord told her she had been the best worker he'd ever had and wished her all the best.

Peter Millward was still in Wales. She wondered vaguely if he was looking for properties. Perhaps he was planning to move to a new area. She pushed a note through the office letter box and left. She was a little disappointed that he wasn't there and the thought that she might never see him again made her feel a bit sad. She would have liked to have thanked him in person and she still had some of his paperwork.

Her first job was to cook breakfast, but once Kaye went into her office, how Sarah planned the day was pretty much left up to her. When she suggested going out, Lottie trailed a few steps behind her pushing the pram. She discovered a school nearby in Lyndhurst Road and asked the head teacher if she could register Jenny. It would take her at least half an hour to walk to Jenny's old school and this one was only five minutes away. She was in luck. The Head took her daughter there and then. Sarah left Jenny happily sitting in her new classroom.

There were some nice shops in Coronation Buildings in Ham Road, between Copper Beeches and the school. Annie ordered fruit and veg from the grocer and meat from the butcher to be delivered before midday. The butcher thumbed his nose and grinned. 'The same arrangement as Mrs Pearce had?' he whispered confidentially.

Sarah's eyes flashed. Clearly Kaye's previous housekeeper had been up to something dodgy. 'I expect everything to be completely above board, Mr Carson,' she said haughtily. 'Mrs Royale likes top quality produce, but if that is a problem, I can always try elsewhere.'

'No, no,' the butcher protested quickly. 'You shall have only the best.'

'And at the proper price,' said Sarah stiffly.

'At the proper price,' the butcher agreed sheepishly.

Back at the house, she heard raised voices in the office. After a few minutes a pompous-looking woman with tightly permed hair came out into the hall with Kaye following.

'Sarah, show Mrs Goodall to the door, will you?' said Kaye.

Mrs Goodall looked Sarah up and down as if there were something evil-smelling on the bottom of her shoe. 'There's no need,' she said haughtily. 'I know the way.'

As the front door banged, Kaye let some air out of her mouth and muttering, 'Bloody woman…' went back into the office.

When Lu-Lu looked up with a confused expression, Sarah planted a kiss on the end of her nose. The little girl played within sight of her mother while she began a systematic spring clean of the whole house. As she got started, Sarah realised it would take her more than a week to clean each room properly. Mrs Pearce had only cleaned the centre of the room and the nether regions left a lot to be desired. Sarah was determined that before long she would have the house as shiny as a new pin. She made Lottie and Kaye a light fish dish for lunch and she and Lu-Lu ate alone in the kitchen. Having put Lu-Lu down for a nap, Sarah prepared the dinner, and later, with Lu-Lu sitting up in the pram, she collected Jenny after school. Sarah decided to have an hour alone with the children before getting the meal on the go. Lottie was a bit put out at first, but Sarah gently insisted.

'You can come back at five,' she told Lottie. 'Go and do some of your sewing for a bit, or look at a magazine.'

She had turned one of their two rooms into a sitting room where the children ate their tea. It was wonderful because now she had time to read stories and hear about Jenny's day. Right from the word go, Jenny loved her new school. It was Mrs Audus this and Mrs Audus that... Sarah listened and smiled.

'William Steel pushed me,' Jenny complained.

'I'm sure he didn't mean to,' said Sarah.

'He did,' Jenny insisted. 'He called me a silly fat bum-bum.'

'That wasn't very nice,' said Sarah mildly. 'If I was you, I wouldn't take any notice of people who called me names.' She hugged her daughter and ruffled her hair. 'Haven't you got anyone else you can be friends with?'

'Oh, Mummy,' Jenny beamed, 'I've got lots and lots and LOTS of friends. I've got eight hundred friends.'

'There you are then,' Sarah laughed. Was there ever a happier time in their lives?

While Kaye and Lottie ate their meal, Sarah put the children to bed and once the kitchen was cleared, she had the evening to herself. She settled down in the kitchen with her sewing.

'You don't have to be out here on your own,' Kaye told her as she came out to see where she was.

Sarah thanked her and promised to be with them sometimes, but she asked for the freedom to choose.

'Lottie is so much happier since you all came,' Kaye smiled as she left her to it.

Fifteen

By the middle of December, Kaye realised she didn't have time to go up to London to do her Christmas shopping so she made good use of Hubbard's department store and the other shops in Worthing. She enjoyed buying things for others, and with a house full of people, Christmas this year promised to be great fun. Employing Sarah had been an absolute godsend. She had been living with them for a couple of weeks now and was so efficient and yet completely unflustered by what was going on around her. Aunt Charlotte was putting on weight and several times Kaye had heard her singing as she worked around the house. Sarah seemed to have the knack of making Lottie feel indispensable and yet she was never overtaxed by what she was asked to do. Lottie loved the girls and they were such good children. When Kaye occasionally took them out for a ride in the car, they were always polite and well-mannered.

Sarah had already been busy with the Christmas preparations too. Kaye recalled seeing a cake and some mince pies going into storage tins in the larder. The butcher had promised them a chicken, a minor miracle in itself considering the shortages in the country, and Lottie and the children had been busy making paper chains out of some old rolls of wallpaper and some glue. How Sarah had done all this on far less money than Mrs Pearce had spent was a mystery. Kaye's grocer's and the butcher's bills had already dropped by a third and yet they were eating the best quality meat and a lot more vegetables.

They had already planned the day itself. St George's church in the morning, Christmas dinner, and then they would all open the presents around the tree together. After that, she would accept an invitation for herself and Lottie to have drinks and an evening with friends, leaving Sarah and her children to enjoy the rest of the day on their own. It was going to be the best Christmas she'd had in a long time and she felt like a silly schoolgirl every time she thought about it.

Having spent time in the toy department, Kaye bought a nice doll for Jenny and a cuddly rabbit for her sister. For Lottie she had bought a wrist-watch, a puzzle and some smellies for the bath. Buying for Sarah proved to be a little more difficult. It would be all too easy to overstep the mark. Sarah was turning out to be a dear girl, but she was still her employee. Kaye couldn't make up her mind between a day dress (Sarah had few nice things), or a coat (hers was threadbare), or something much smaller. Frustration got the better of her, so she decided to have a cup of tea instead.

She sat near the window and watched the crowds of shoppers down below. It was raining, but the crowds were sheltered by the huge canvas canopies in front of almost every shop. People hurried across the road and got on buses, their arms laden with parcels.

The restaurant was emptying. Another hour and the shop would close. The waitress brought her tea and as she looked up, Kaye saw someone she recognised across the room. She couldn't remember the name but she remembered her face.

'Good afternoon,' she smiled over the tables between them. 'I'm sorry, I don't recall your name but you're Annie's mother, aren't you?'

Judith Mitchell looked startled, but she was polite enough to return Kaye's greeting.

'Won't you please join me?'

The waitress had just arrived and, looking straight at Judith, pulled out the chair. Judith had it in mind to decline but thought better of it, and a second later, she was sitting at Kaye's table.

'Better make that tea and cakes for two,' said Kaye, and as the waitress left them, she put out her hand. 'Kaye Royale.'

'Judith Mitchell.' They shook hands and for a while they made only small talk.

Judith appeared to be troubled by something. 'Didn't I see you at the public inquiry?'

'Did you?' said Kaye. 'I was there but I must have missed you.' Kaye had gone to the meeting in the Assembly Hall where the Borough Council had put forward a proposal to pull down the large Regency house on the seafront. Under new government legislation, and the newly formed Town and Country Planning Act, the people of Worthing had to be consulted before Beach House, as it was called, was demolished and a swimming pool erected in its place. Having thought the outcome was a foregone conclusion, the councillors had been surprised to find that there was strong opposition to the proposal.

'I must say,' Judith smiled, 'it was a lively debate.

That woman with the fox fur got very angry, didn't she?'

Kaye nodded. 'My neighbour, Mrs Goodall,' she said. 'I fear I've made an enemy for life.'

'But at least Beach House was saved,' said Judith.

'It's all too easy to destroy these lovely buildings,' said Kaye, 'and once they're gone, they're gone.'

'I heartily agree,' said Judith. She warmed to this woman.

'Has Annie had her baby yet?' Kaye smiled. She spoke in hushed tones, anxious not to embarrass her guest, though there were few other customers.

Judith nodded. 'A little boy.'

The order for Judith came and the waitress busied herself arranging everything just so. While Kaye poured the tea, she offered Judith first choice of cake.

'Forgive me,' said Kaye as she dabbed her mouth with the snow-white napkin, 'perhaps I'm being a bit too nosy, but is she keeping him?'

'She wants to,' said Judith, 'but my husband is adamant that she give him up.'

'I'm sorry,' said Kaye. She couldn't imagine how awful it would be to be made to give up your baby. And how ironic that just as the baby came, Henry was in jail. He would have been delighted to have his son at last.

'I must say,' Judith remarked, 'you seem remarkably calm about all this. The whole experience must have been pretty awful for you as well.'

'Henry, you mean? It was all a very long time ago. He left me way back in 1938. I only decided to stir up the hornet's nest when I was thinking about getting a divorce.'

'So you were in Horsham to get a divorce?'

'That was the plan,' Kaye smiled. 'Unfortunately the man I thought I would marry once I obtained a divorce had a better offer.'

'I'm sorry,' said Judith.

'Don't be,' Kaye said nonchalantly. 'It was probably a lucky escape!'

The two women laughed.

'Have you seen your grandson?'

Judith's face lit up as she talked at length about the baby. 'He's so intelligent. He can focus his eyes and he listens quite intently when you speak. I think that's remarkable when you consider he's only a month old. Do you have any children, Mrs Royale?'

Kaye shook her head. 'I couldn't have children,' she said, her voice dropping. 'That's why Henry left me.'

Now it was Judith's turn to be sympathetic. 'Oh my dear...'

'It's all right,' said Kaye, lighting up a cigarette. 'I fill my life with other things.' She really liked Judith. Under different circumstances they could have been friends. They spent the rest of their time at the table talking about their Christmas plans and admired the girl employed as a mannequin as she paraded through the tea rooms in a fabulous, strapless, dark-green velvet gown with a bustle back.

As they stood to leave, Kaye said, 'If she kept the baby, would your daughter be able to support herself?'

Judith shook her head. 'That's her problem. She could only do it with her father's support.'

'Pity,' said Kaye. 'I could have offered her a room at my house.'

Judith grabbed her arm. 'You really would do that?'

'Why not? The poor girl deserves the chance to keep her baby, but I'm not in a position to support her unfortunately. I already have a dependant maiden aunt. Annie would be welcome to a room in my house if she had the means to pay for it.'

They were about to part company when Judith caught her arm again. 'Mrs Royale... Kaye,' she began. 'I hardly dare to ask, but my husband gives me a generous dress allowance. Could I pay for her room and board? He won't guess where the money's going. Men never notice things like that.'

Kaye agreed. 'But what will she do? It seems a bit unfair to prolong the agony if she's forced to give up the baby because she still can't support herself at a later date.'

Judith sighed and put her hand over her mouth. It was frustrating to be so near and yet so far from what Annie wanted. Come to that, she didn't want to give up her beautiful grandson and have him brought up by strangers. Given time, she felt sure she could persuade Malcolm to welcome the boy, but there was no guarantee of that and Kaye was right. It would be unfair to raise Annie's hopes.

The waitress came back. 'I'm sorry, madam, but we're closing,' she said, addressing Kaye.

They made their way to the till where Kaye

settled the bill. 'Has Annie got any skills we could exploit?'

Judith shook her head. 'She was good at tennis and she can play the piano.'

'I have a piano,' said Kaye. 'Could she give lessons?'

Judith took in her breath. 'I don't know ... well, yes I suppose she could. She'd have to practise and maybe take an exam, but if it were a means by which she could keep the baby...' Her eyes were bright with excitement.

'Then it's settled,' said Kaye. 'Don't wait until she's discharged from the Mother and Baby Home. Send her straight over to Copper Beeches.'

They walked through the almost deserted store discussing the rent and how it was to be paid.

'There's one small thing,' said Kaye as they stood together on the street, 'and I'm not sure how you are going to feel about it.'

Judith's joyous expression changed into an anxious frown.

'I already have another lodger,' Kaye went on. 'Sarah.'

'Sarah?' said Judith, not understanding.

'Henry's middle wife,' said Kaye. 'It looks like all three of us will be living under the same roof.'

Henry never walked around the exercise yard when he was let out of the cell, he jogged. They only had an hour a day and he knew that if he was to stay healthy, he had to make sure he kept fit. There was little time to talk to other prisoners, but he didn't care. Most of them were thick or stupid, and besides, he preferred his own company. He had read the Bible from cover to cover, something he'd never done before, and after that he'd requested other books. There was little choice but he'd managed to read a few that were interesting. He preferred real life rather than made-up stuff, but if it was a really good author, he could lose himself in the pages for a few hours. Occasionally he managed to get hold of a newspaper. It was usually a couple of days old, but it kept him abreast with the outside world. Prison life, he soon discovered, was mind-numbingly boring. It brightened his day no end when he got Annie's letter. A son … a baby boy. Henry smiled. He would leave his mark on the world after all. It had always bothered him that he had no son to carry on his name. Girls were all right but a son carried the seed. He didn't believe in God, so having a boy was his only chance of immortality. His head was full of plans. He'd go back to her and let Annie keep the boy for the first few months. Babies need their mother, plus he wasn't very enamoured with small children, but then he would take his son far away, as far as possible, and raise the boy himself. He would create a prince among men, a powerful leader, someone the world could respect and follow. He'd give him true values. Women should know their place; fathers should be respected and honoured for their wisdom and children should be brought up to know right from wrong. Hadn't his own father quoted 'spare the rod and spoil the child' often enough? He hadn't stinted his discipline on Henry and look what a fine example of manhood he had become.

Today it was raining, so his time for exercise was

cut short. Nonetheless it still gave the prison authorities time enough to change his life for the foreseeable future. When he got back to his cell, Henry's cast-iron single bed had been swapped for a wooden bunk bed and, what was even worse, he had a cellmate.

The man on the bottom bunk was a large mean-looking thug who had clearly been in one fight too many. Henry spotted a sweet wrapper on the bed beside him. The thieving bastard had been helping himself to his precious coffee crunches. They were Henry's only pleasure in life and he had to make each little bag Annie sent in by post last. He knew the screws helped themselves when they were 'checking' the contents of the bag, and if this man helped himself as well, Henry would have nothing left. He felt the rage well up within him, but one look at his fellow prisoner told him not to start a fight. His nose was crooked and he had cauliflower ears. He was almost as broad as he was tall and he made Charles Atlas himself look like he was the scrawny weakling.

As soon as he saw him, Henry turned to protest, but the door was already closing. He eyed his companion. The man put down the newspaper he was reading and glared at Henry. 'What you looking at?'

'Nothing,' said Henry.

The cell had been small enough when he was on his own, but now it seemed like a shoebox. Henry pulled the sheet from the top bunk and began to make up the bed. When he had finished, he climbed on top and lay staring at the ceiling. The two men said little for the first hour, but by the end of the day Henry had discovered that Big Frankie was in prison for GBH. It was a little disconcerting to discover the translation for that was Grievous Bodily Harm, but Big Frankie told him it was a long time ago and as long as Henry didn't 'get up his nose' he was perfectly safe.

Just before lights out, Big Frankie gave Henry his newspaper. It was only the *Daily Sketch*, but at least Henry could catch up on things. On the front page, the new prince was pictured with his mother and the King at his christening. On the sports page, he read how the up-and-coming boxer Rocky Marciano had floored Gilley Ferron three times and won on a technical knockout, but the story which interested him most was of a woman who had taken the world of radio by storm. Her plays were critically acclaimed and she had just been voted the nation's favourite playwright. When he looked at the picture of her next to the article, Henry took in his breath. It was Kaye. She was dressed in an evening gown and beautifully groomed with an expensive-looking brooch on her lapel. To be that successful, he knew she must be raking it in. Dear God, and he'd only just signed those divorce papers she'd sent. Not only that, but he'd also put them outside for posting. He had to get them back. It was imperative. He jumped off the bunk and began thumping the cell door. 'Open up. Guard, guard, open the door.'

'What's up with you?' said Big Frankie.

'I've put a letter out for posting and I want to get it back,' said Henry helplessly. The only thing between himself and all he'd ever wanted was those damned divorce papers.

'Got any money?' said Big Frankie.

'What's that got to do with anything?' Henry snapped. 'Guard, open this door.'

'I've got a contact in the post room,' said Big Frankie, looking at his fingernails. 'If you want something bringing back, it'll cost you.'

Henry turned towards him. 'You can have my tobacco allowance.'

'Done.' Big Frankie sat up and the two men shook hands. 'Who's the letter addressed to?'

'Dobbin and Son Solicitors,' said Henry. At the same moment the light snapped off and they were plunged into the dark. Henry groped for his bed and climbed back up. 'It's a London address.'

'It's as good as done.' Big Frankie's disembodied voice wafted towards him and Henry relaxed. A slow smile spread across his lips. When all this was over, his little boy would have all that money could buy. He'd changed his mind about the boy's mother. If he played his cards right, he could get rid of all three of the silly cows who had betrayed him and start all over again. Come to think of it, he could use the old hag's money. She had been there at the trial, hadn't she. If he worked on her, she could help him go somewhere like South Africa or California, and then, after he'd ditched her, he could sit in the sun with a drink in his hand and a pretty girl on his arm. He felt himself harden. Now that was a plan.

Sixteen

Peter Millward was back and he had asked Sarah if he could take her and the children out for a Christmas treat on her day off. The girls were very excited when she told them that they were going to the pantomime at the Connaught and then having a meal. Of course, they'd never been to a pantomime before and hadn't a clue what it was, but it was enough that Uncle Pete was taking them.

It was good to see Peter again, although he was upset that Sarah hadn't told him about her troubles.

'You were away,' she reminded him curtly, 'and I had no way of getting in touch with you.'

'My father lived in Wales,' he said. 'He was ill and then he died.'

Sarah was immediately filled with remorse. 'Oh Peter, I'm so sorry.'

'It's okay,' he said, 'you weren't to know. I stayed on to settle everything.'

'I thought you'd gone there to buy a coach or something. That's what the chap in the office told me.'

He shook his head. 'I don't think so,' he smiled, 'I've got enough on my plate with the lorries.'

'Is everything all right?' she asked anxiously.

'Yes,' he said cautiously, 'but you know what it's like when you leave other people in charge. They never do things the way you like it to be done. But enough about me, what about you? How are you liking your new position? The girls look well and happy.'

Sarah told him how she had almost spent a night sleeping rough and now she lived in a lovely home. She said that her employer was kindness itself and the children were looking forward to Christmas. She didn't mention that although she had nothing to complain about, she was strug-gling with her emotions. She had been content for a while, but as things became more settled in her life, she found herself brooding over the past. She had become angry ... very angry. What sort of man was Henry Royal? How could he have dumped her like that? How could he turn his back on his beautiful daughters without so much as a postcard to ask after their welfare? She remembered with bitterness that he hadn't even had the decency to look at her in the courtroom. He'd mooned over the silly bitch who was carrying his child. She'd even caught him mouthing 'I love you' a couple of times when Annie looked up at him, but he had no time at all for her. And when Sarah had sat in the witness box and given her evidence, he hadn't even acknowledged her presence. He'd stared up at the ceiling or down at his fingernails the whole time. She felt as if she had kept everything buttoned up for so long, but now it was hard to keep her feelings inside. Kaye had been extraordinarily kind and Sarah knew she was more than lucky to have a roof over her head, but she couldn't shake this feeling and the rage inside her gut was so strong, it was becoming more difficult to keep it in. She knew she shouldn't be thinking thoughts like this but they pushed their way uninvited into her mind. Why was Kaye doing this? What was her angle? She could have had any woman in Worthing to do her skivvying, so why did she choose her? Was it some perverse way of getting her own back on Henry? The bizarreness of the situation was beginning to dawn on her. With the two wives of one man living under the same roof with his children, it felt like a harem. It wasn't Christian. Sarah wanted to make the thing work, but the whole situation was beginning to make her feel ill.

During the day, she busied herself with everything she could think of to blot out the thoughts, but when she lay on her bed, as comfortable as it may be and as tired as she was, she couldn't sleep. Some days she thought that she couldn't stay a minute longer and that once Christmas was over, she would have to look for somewhere else to live. But then she would see how much her children had blossomed in the short time they'd been in the house. Lottie adored them and played with them all the time. Lu-Lu was talking now. She loved to sing little songs, and although she mixed up the words (*horsey, horsey don't ooh pop*), she sounded so sweet. And Jenny was confident enough to be in the school nativity play, although she still complained about William Steel. Sarah had made her a long dress out of an old piece of sheet she'd found in the attic so that she looked the part of the Innkeeper's wife, and Jenny practised and practised her lines. '*Can I help you?*' '*No, I'm sorry, there is no room in the Inn,*' and finally, '*Come into the stable...*' Could she risk unsettling them all over again? The answer was no, but the feelings of anger and betrayal simply wouldn't go away.

'Sarah?' She became aware that Peter was looking anxiously at her.

She laughed as if she'd been thinking of something else. 'Sorry, miles away. We're fine,' she assured him. 'Couldn't be better.'

When the panto was over and they came back to the house, the children were tired but happy. Jenny had loved everything, and although Lu-Lu had been scared of the villain when he first appeared on the stage with a drum roll from the orchestra pit, she soon recovered herself and was so relaxed she dropped off to sleep towards the end. Sarah had enjoyed herself too. Back home at last, Peter carried Lu-Lu to the door, fast asleep in his arms, but Sarah didn't ask him in. She could see the disappointment on his face, but somehow she couldn't bring herself to do it.

'Happy Christmas,' he said, putting the sleeping child into her arms.

'Happy Christmas to you too,' said Sarah. She reached up and pecked his cheek. 'And thank you for a wonderful time.'

'Have a nice time?' Kaye asked as she came through the door.

Sarah nodded and smiled.

'When you've put them to bed,' said Kaye, 'could I have a little word?'

Annie stared at her mother with her mouth open.

'You do see, don't you?' Judith went on. 'This is the most marvellous godsend. I can help you with the rent and once you've got the baby weaned, you can start giving piano lessons.'

'Wait a minute, wait a minute, Mother,' said Annie, putting her hand up to silence Judith. 'Let me get this right. You actually want me to go and live with Henry's first wife?'

'Oh darling, please don't be difficult,' said Judith. She was visiting her daughter and grandson in the Mother and Baby Home. They were alone in the main sitting room because all the other mums were still taking their afternoon naps. 'I know it sounds odd but...'

'Odd?' Annie practically shrieked. 'It's sick. It's not normal. Why would that woman even want me in her house?'

'I don't know,' said Judith. 'I didn't ask why, I was just grateful to have found a way of keeping you and the baby together.' They both looked down into the crib where Edward Henry Royal lay sleeping. 'You won't find many other landladies agreeing to take a small baby.'

'I shan't be needing a landlady,' said Annie resolutely. 'I'm going to stay with Auntie Phyllis. I've written her a letter explaining everything and as soon as I get a reply...'

'Auntie Phyllis,' said Judith. 'But you won't be able to stay with her.'

Annie tossed her head. 'And why not?'

'You obviously never listen to a word I say,' said her mother. 'I told you almost six months ago that Auntie Phyllis had had a stroke. She's in an old people's home.'

Sarah was furious. She sat in her small sitting

room, her heart thumping and hardly able to control her feelings. That settled it. She'd have to go. There was absolutely no way she would stay under the same roof as that damned woman. How could Kaye even think such a thing? She'd kept calm as the idea was mooted, but now she was hopping mad. 'The poor thing has nowhere to go…' Did Kaye really expect her to feel sorry for the girl? Why should she? She was nothing more than a cheap tramp. She had ruined her whole life and, what was far worse, the lives of her children. They'd been happy before that silly trollop came along. It wasn't right, the three of them under the same roof. No, she wouldn't be a part of it. Either she or Annie lived in the house. Not both of them. Half an hour later, as Sarah climbed wearily into her bed, the full import of the situation finally dawned. She had no choice. She'd have to put up with it because she had nowhere else to go. Careful not to let her children hear, for the first time in months, Sarah cried herself to sleep.

It hadn't been easy getting out of the Mother and Baby Home without being seen. Annie knew that Edward's prospective parents would be arriving at the end of the week, so she had to act quickly. To hear about Auntie Phyllis had been a bitter blow, but she couldn't give up yet. All she had to do was get from Bognor to the Thomas A Becket in Worthing. Her father had refused to discuss what she was going to do with the baby over the telephone and he had never once come to visit them either in the maternity hospital or at the Mother and Baby Home, but she was convinced that one look at his beautiful grandson would be enough.

It was a long walk to the railway station and Edward was heavy. She had left her suitcase in the left luggage department a couple of days before, sneaking out when she was supposed to be having a rest, and as soon as she'd collected it, she caught the train. At West Worthing she hailed a taxi using the last of the money she had squirrelled away, and in no time at all she was going up the drive of her childhood home. Her plan had worked. All she needed now was for her father to fall in love with his beautiful grandson. She paid the driver and he carried her case to the front door. Just as her mother opened the door, Edward woke up and cried.

'Oh Annie,' her mother said despairingly.

'Who is it?' Her father's voice was right behind her.

Judith leaned against the door saying, 'You'll have to come back later. Your father...'

'If he could see Edward...' Annie began. The door was yanked back and her father bellowed, 'What's he doing here?'

The taxi driver put the suitcase on the step and turned to go.

'Hang on a minute, my man,' said Malcolm. 'You can take them back to wherever you picked them up.'

'Daddy!' Annie cried desperately. 'Please. Please don't turn us away. This is your grandson.'

'I have no grandson,' said Malcolm. He pulled his wife back into the house and began closing the door.

'At least look at him,' Annie pleaded.

The taxi driver looked bewildered. 'Where to now, missus?'

'I don't have enough money for a return trip,' Annie shouted at the closing door. She had been so sure her father would relent as soon as he saw Edward, but what chance did they have when he wouldn't even look at him?

The taxi driver put his finger on the doorbell. After a minute or two, Judith reappeared with her handbag under her arm. 'Go to Kaye's house,' she told Annie. 'I'll ring her and tell her you're coming.' She handed the driver a pound note. 'Copper Beeches, Church Walk.'

'Judith!' Malcolm's angry voice boomed from inside. 'Come in and shut that door immediately.'

Copper Beeches looked wonderful. There were paper chains from the hall to the sitting room. Sarah had pinned holly and ivy trails along the picture rails and around some of the pictures. Christmas cards lined the mantelpiece and the dresser in the dining room. Centrepiece in the sitting room was the Christmas tree, decorated with edible gingerbread men and Christmas bells. There were candles too, although she and Kaye had agreed that for safety reasons they wouldn't actually light them. Lottie helped Jenny and Lu-Lu to hang their stockings by the fireside and an air of excitement pervaded the house.

Christmas was to fall on the Saturday this year, but it was the Monday before which changed all their lives forever. It was seven in the evening when they heard the sound of a taxi pulling into the drive and a few minutes later the doorbell rang. A tearful Annie stood on the doorstep with Edward in her arms. Kaye answered the door and took her straight into the sitting room. Sarah came down the stairs and saw Lottie fussing over the baby. Pulling the door closed behind her, Kaye came out into the hallway and smiled at Sarah.

'Would you take Annie's things upstairs for her,' she asked, 'and then please join us in the sitting room.'

Sarah, tight-lipped and pink with irritation, climbed the stairs with Annie's luggage and put everything in the front bedroom. The bed had a grey counterpane and a flowery eiderdown, although it would be hardly needed in this lovely warm centrally heated house. Kaye had found a low chair in the attic, and with a beige throw over it, you would never know that the fabric underneath was in desperate need of repair and attention. Sarah had a keen eye for detail, so there were flowers on the chest of drawers and a pretty runner across the bedside table. The baby would have to sleep in a deep drawer for the time being, until they could find a second-hand bassinet for him. When she'd prepared the drawer, Sarah had thought of cutting up an old blanket and making it into baby blankets, but that was a bridge too far. Although she had spent the past week preparing for the newcomers and everything looked really nice, now that Annie and her baby were here, she couldn't hide her resentment. She put the suitcases on the floor and went back downstairs.

'I was so sure my father would love him when he saw him,' Annie was saying as Sarah walked into the sitting room with a tray of tea. 'But he steadfastly refuses to see him.' She looked up and Annie's jaw dropped. 'You!'

'Yes me,' said Sarah coldly. 'We're all here.'

Annie dabbed her eyes and looked at Kaye. 'I don't understand. My mother never told me *she* would be here as well.'

Sarah felt herself bristle. Kaye busied herself with the teapot. 'Does it matter?' she said calmly.

'Of course it matters,' Annie spat. 'That woman ruined my life.'

Sarah had stuck her nose in the air and was on her way out of the room when she stopped in her tracks. 'I ruined *your* life,' she said, turning to face Annie. 'You were the one who made off with my husband.'

'I didn't know he was married,' Annie cried. 'He thought you'd divorced him. I'd known Henry for almost three months before we were married.'

'It takes longer than that to get a divorce, you silly cow.'

Lottie made a strange noise.

'Girls…' Kaye stood to her feet.

'That's not my fault,' Annie whined. 'And anyway, who are you calling a silly cow?'

'Me and my children were left destitute because of you,' said Sarah, her eyes blazing. She advanced towards Annie, her chin jutted forward. 'We ended up facing a night in a wayside shelter.'

'I can't help that!' Annie shouted. The baby woke up and started crying. 'Now look what you've done.'

'More to the point,' Sarah snarled, 'look what *you've* done. If you hadn't run off with my husband…'

'Girls, please…' said Kaye.

'That's rich coming from you,' Annie retorted as she bent to pick the baby up from the sofa. 'You did exactly the same thing to her.'

She jerked her head towards Kaye and Sarah froze. It was then that they all became aware of Lottie. She was acutely distressed, rocking herself backwards and forwards in the chair with her hands over her ears and making little grunting sounds. Kaye sat on the arm of her chair and put her hand around Lottie's shoulders. 'It's all right, darling,' she said soothingly. 'They've stopped now.' She looked up at the two women. 'She can't bear arguments. Sarah, show Annie to her room, and when you've settled the baby, I want you both down here. I'm taking Lottie up to bed.'

'You needn't think I'm staying here,' said Annie.

'And where do you think you're going at this time of night?' said Kaye, helping Lottie to her feet. 'You've just told me that your father won't hear of you going home.'

Annie pouted like a petulant child as Sarah led the way to her room and left her and the baby to it. She climbed the back stairs to her own little sitting room and threw herself into the chair. She was shaking, she felt hot and she was furious. Everything had been fine up until now. What on earth was Kaye thinking, having that silly schoolgirl in the house? She cried a little then washed her face. Thankfully, her children had heard nothing of their argument. They were asleep, Jenny with her face slightly flushed. Sarah picked up a toy and tucked the blanket around Lu-Lu's bare shoulders and then went back downstairs.

As she walked into the sitting room, Sarah gave Annie a frosty glare. Annie was warming herself by the fire. Although there were plenty of chairs and a sofa nearer the fire, Sarah sat stiffly on a high-backed chair next to the Chinese cabinet behind the door. She wanted to be as far away from Annie as she could.

'I just don't understand it,' said Annie over her shoulder. 'Why is she doing this?'

Sarah shrugged. The rage she'd felt a while ago had dissipated, but she was in no mood to be friendly. She didn't even want to look at Annie. Feeling snubbed, Annie turned her back.

A few minutes later, the door burst open and Kaye, a cigarette dangling from between her lips, reappeared with two bottles of red wine. 'Get us some glasses, will you Sarah,' she said. 'I have a feeling we're all going to need this.'

Seventeen

With the glasses in front of her, Kaye poured the wine and handed them around, then with a swish of her midnight-blue taffeta skirt, she sank into the armchair. Sarah moved back to the upright chair and Annie stared blankly ahead.

'I met Henry when I was seventeen,' Kaye began. As she spoke, she was looking deep into her glass and swirling the wine against the sides. 'He was so charming, so attentive. I hadn't met anyone like that before. We had a brief courtship and then we married. My folks weren't invited ... some mix-up with the invitations he said.'

Annie shifted herself uncomfortably in her seat.

'Sound familiar?' Kaye smiled. 'I remember your testimony in court being very similar.' Annie said nothing.

'I had a white wedding, although I wasn't a virgin.' Kaye's candour was a bit embarrassing, but already the atmosphere in the room was changing. Although Sarah and Annie remained silent, the angry tension of an hour ago was already slackening.

'I was already pregnant when we married and my baby was stillborn,' said Kaye. Her voice was toneless but somehow it didn't hide the agony of her loss. 'I was very ill, not expected to live at one point, but Henry was the model husband.'

'I'm so sorry,' Sarah murmured.

Kaye didn't acknowledge her concern. 'In the end,' she said, first dragging on her cigarette and then taking a great gulp of wine, 'I had to have a hysterectomy, so no more babies for me. Henry was very disappointed and I felt that I had let him down badly.'

It was Sarah's turn to feel a little uncomfortable. Hadn't she felt like that? By having two girls when he was so desperate for a son, she had let Henry down as well. 'Kaye…' Sarah began, but Kaye put her hand up.

'Henry only ever wanted three things. Bizarrely, his first love was a coffee crunch, the second, smart clothes, and thirdly, he'd always wanted a son,' she continued, 'but you both knew that, didn't you?'

Embarrassed, Sarah looked away as she put her wine glass to her lips. 'He was disappointed that we didn't have a son,' she said quietly.

'Well, he's got his son now,' Annie simpered and Sarah glared at her.

'We were happy for almost four years,' Kaye went on. 'When I found out that he had other women, I hated it, but I always prided myself that he came back to me.' She blew the smoke from her cigarette above her head. 'Henry wasn't easy to get along with, and after seeing him in that courtroom, he doesn't seem to have changed much. He always was very pernickety and spent a fortune on his suits, though where the money came from, I never knew. Everything had to be done just the way he wanted and he got very angry if I forgot something.'

Annie cleared her throat and took a mouthful of wine. She knew how that felt. Hadn't he been angry with her the day the police came? How could she forget it? She looked down at the glass in her hand. She'd never had wine before. It was heady and strong, but not an unpleasant taste.

'He started telling me what to wear,' Kaye continued. 'I didn't mind of course because I always thought Henry knew best.' She emptied her glass and walked around with the bottle topping up the others. She paused by the fireside to throw on another log. The fire crackled and spat as the flames took hold. Back in her chair, Kaye resumed her narrative. 'When he finally left me in November 1938 I was totally lost. I'm a strong woman, I know that now, but back then I didn't know what to do. I had no idea how to pay the bills or where

I would find the rent money. How was I going to survive? He'd left me with absolutely nothing, of course. I couldn't access the bank account even though it was a joint account. The bank would only accept his name on the cheque.'

November 1938, thought Sarah. That was around the time she'd met Henry and they'd married only four months later. Kaye's story was familiar, more than familiar. Kaye's story was her story.

'Of course, I had to get out of our marital home in Chichester,' Kaye went on with a sigh. 'I had to sell all my lovely things for a song and start all over again.'

Annie emptied her glass in one go. Sarah stared somewhere into the middle distance. It seemed that Henry was a serial husband. He had done exactly the same thing to each one of them.

'That,' said Kaye, breaking into their thoughts again, 'was when I had my first stroke of luck. The war came along and other people's misfortune became my good fortune. I joined the Women's Timber Corps. Lumber Jills they called us, and I loved it. I had a roof over my head and I could be outdoors, far away from falling bombs and air-raid shelters.' She smiled to herself. 'By that time I had my own place, but I moved from there to a hut in the forest. We worked mainly in the Forest of Dean and the New Forest cutting down twenty-five-year-old conifers. I was what they called a snedder. I had to chop all the bits off the trunk with a billhook so that it was ready to go to the sawmill. It was damned hard work, but it helped me to pull myself together and realise that I was perfectly capable of being without Henry.'

She stood up again to replenish their glasses. Both Sarah and Annie seemed more relaxed, but neither of them made eye contact with her.

'I'm sure my story is familiar,' said Kaye, sitting down. 'There's a pattern, d'you see? For people like Henry, it's all about control.'

'Not for me it isn't,' said Annie, lifting her head defiantly. 'When he gets out of prison, Henry is coming for me and we're going to make a proper life together for our son.'

Kaye smiled at her. 'He'll be glad you've given him a boy,' she conceded, 'but as for the rest, I'm not so sure. I hope you won't be disappointed because there's no telling with Henry.'

'All I can say is that you don't know Henry like I do,' Annie retorted.

Irritated, Sarah glared at her again. Silly little prig.

'You're probably right,' said Kaye, sounding far more gracious that Sarah felt. 'But then I never did manage to give him what he wanted.'

Nor did I, thought Sarah. They fell silent and sipped their wine.

'Okay, so you've made us face up to the fact that Henry does this all the time, but why are you doing this?' Sarah asked tetchily. 'Why have you got us all together? What's the point?'

'I can see that I've made you angry,' said Kaye. Embarrassed, Sarah looked away. 'Oh, it's all right to be angry,' Kaye went on. 'It was never my intention, but I think we're all going to have to deal with some very confused emotions.' She emptied the first bottle of wine. 'You see, I met someone during the war,' she began again. 'I loved him dearly, but it took me a long time to realise that I was too afraid to have another relationship. I suppose I kept worrying that he might turn out like Henry. I didn't realise it at the time but I was emotionally crippled.'

'There's nothing wrong with my emotions,' Annie snapped.

Sarah chewed the inside of her mouth anxiously. Was that why she couldn't allow herself to get too close to Peter Millward? Was she emotionally crippled too? Anyway, what on earth had that got to do with living together with Henry's two other wives?

'I let the man go,' Kaye went on, 'but then I had my second stroke of luck.' She waved her hand. 'This house and an unexpected legacy. It put me well and truly on my feet again and has given me the chance to carry on with my passion for writing.'

'Who do you write for?' asked Annie, suddenly interested.

'Plays, mainly,' said Kaye, 'but I've just been commissioned to write another one for the BBC.'

'The BBC?' cried Annie, clearly impressed. 'That's amazing.'

'The point is,' said Kaye, looking directly at Annie, 'when I saw the two of you in the courtroom that day, I wanted you to have the same chances.'

'Oh, I couldn't write a word,' said Annie.

'You misunderstand...' Kaye began.

'You mean you planned all this?' Sarah asked incredulously.

Kaye stood up to open the second bottle of wine. 'No, not at all. How could I, but when I saw you, I liked you. That drive back to Worthing put an idea into my head and when I realised that my aunt couldn't be left, I thought of you and, as it turned out, you needed a stroke of luck too.'

'You needn't worry about me,' said Annie. 'I shall only be here until Henry gets out of prison.'

Sarah pursed her lips angrily. She wanted to smack her one. Why did the silly girl keep banging on about it?

'I know it won't be easy,' said Kaye, filling each glass again, 'but if you stay here, Sarah, you'd be doing me a great favour, and Annie, you'd get to keep your baby.'

'So let me get this right,' said Sarah cynically. 'All you want is to give both of us the chance to gain our independence?' She didn't believe for one second that was the only reason. Kaye was setting herself up as Lady Bountiful, but there had to be a catch somewhere ... there always was.

'That's the whole idea,' said Kaye. 'Being alone would be difficult, but with the three of us working together it should be a lot easier. We'd help each other.' She sat back down and Sarah frowned, puzzled. 'Think of it as a sort of co-operative.'

'The Henry's wives co-op?' Sarah muttered. This was crazy, bizarre.

'As far as I'm concerned,' said Annie, 'living here is only temporary.'

'I didn't think for one minute that either of you would want to live with me for the rest of your lives,' Kaye chuckled. 'But each of us could help each other, you know, a bit like giving someone a leg up.'

'Henry will be out soon,' Annie tutted. 'He'll support Edward and me. I don't need to get a job.'

'It won't hurt for you to develop a skill,' Kaye said patiently. 'What about you, Sarah? How best could you support yourself and your children?'

Sarah was beginning to feel rather light-headed. Her anger was mellowing but her brain was still refusing to function. She shrugged. 'It would have to be something respectable.'

'A shop?' Kaye suggested.

'I have no capital,' said Sarah, gulping more wine.

Annie turned to face her. 'What are you good at?'

'Cooking,' Sarah said dully, 'sewing ... but there's not a lot of money in either of those.'

'You're good with people,' Kaye chipped in. 'How about nursing?'

'Fat chance,' Sarah scoffed. 'How on earth would I manage shift work with my children?'

'We'll help each other, remember?' said Kaye.

The full import of what she was proposing finally began to dawn on Sarah. She really meant it, didn't she? Help each other make a new start ... put the past well and truly behind them... 'You're actually saying that you would look after my children while I was learning some sort of skill?'

'Why not?' said Kaye.

Sarah sat up straight. If this was true, then Kaye was offering her a golden opportunity. This was more than a stroke of luck, this was a whole future. 'I don't know,' she said, her voice suddenly small. 'All my life I've sort of bumbled along. I've never even thought about being independent.'

'Would you like to be a nurse?'

Sarah shook her head. 'Married women aren't allowed to nurse anyway,' she said. 'I know I'm not married but I do have two children. They would never allow me to nurse under those circumstances and, to be honest, I'm far too squeamish.'

'My mother wants me to teach the piano,' Annie hiccupped.

'You have to take exams for that,' said Kaye.

'I won't really need it,' said Annie. 'Henry will be out before the summer and he's coming back for ush.'

'Oh, do shut up!' Sarah blurted out. There was a shocked silence and then she appealed to Kaye. 'Look, we both know that if she went back to him he'd never allow her to work.'

'You're probably right,' said Kaye, 'but how long before he moves on?'

'Henry would never leave me and the baby,' cried Annie.

'Then why not do it to please your mother?' Kaye suggested. 'She's going without her dress allowance to give you this chance to keep Edward.'

Annie sighed and pulled a face. 'I'm very rushty. I shall need a shedload of practice.' She closed her eyes as she spoke but didn't seem to notice that her speech was becoming slightly slurry.

'You practise and we'll take care of Edward,' said Kaye.

Annie rounded on her. 'Hang on a minute. What about you? What's in it for you?'

'I've just lost my independence again,' said Kaye, walking around with the wine bottle once more. 'I shall need someone to look after Lottie when I'm writing.'

Annie went to put her elbow on the arm of the chair and missed.

'Go steady with that wine, Kaye,' Sarah cautioned. 'Don't forget Annie is breastfeeding.'

'Hells bells,' said Kaye. 'I'm sorry. I never gave it a thought.'

They heard a distant baby cry. Edward was awake and hungry. Annie leaned forward. 'Are you saying it'll be in the milk?' She giggled. 'Oh dear.' She wobbled to the door and went upstairs.

Kaye smiled after her and then turned to look at Sarah, but before she could say anything, Sarah stood up abruptly. 'I need to go to bed. It's been a long day.'

'Sarah,' Kaye said to her receding back, 'I know you are angry, but it's really not her fault.'

Alone in her room, Sarah finally felt the heat draining from her cheeks, but she didn't want to stop feeling angry. Not yet. She had really been looking forward to Christmas, but everything was spoiled now. Miserably, she undressed and climbed into bed. As she heard the baby's reedy cry coming up the stairs, she turned her face to the wall. Kaye actually expected her to live in the same house as that silly girl. How was she going to cope? Talk about rubbing your nose in it, but she was in no position to do anything about it now, so until she could stand on her own two feet, she would have to put up with it.

Eighteen

Sarah spent the remaining days leading up to the big day finishing off the jobs in the kitchen. The first week after she'd arrived at Copper Beeches, she had found some spices in the pantry and, using her own coupons as well as Kaye's, she'd managed to get all the ingredients together to make a Christmas cake. She'd soaked a pound of mixed fruit overnight so that the currants and sultanas swelled, then she'd baked it and stored it away until now. It was ready to be decorated with a couple of snowmen and a chipped Father Christmas she'd found at the back of the drawer. When she'd finished, she felt quite chuffed about it In keeping with tradition, she'd made two cakes, but she rewrapped the second cake in greaseproof paper and put it in an airtight tin ready for Easter. Her mother had always said that fruit cakes improved with keeping. Because of lack of time, she'd bought the Christmas pudding at the school Christmas Fair which was held in the middle of December. It was ready for reheating on the day and all she had to remember was to push a silver threepenny bit deep inside. On Christmas Eve, she planned to make cheese straws and more mince pies (using her own home-made mincemeat laced with stout) and later in the evening, when her children were in bed, she would wrap up their presents.

Ever since the delivery man carried the Christmas tree into the house on December 22nd, a rich aroma of woodland forest had filled the sitting room. It stood in a bucket of sand and the children helped Kaye and Lottie to decorate it with some rather threadbare pieces of tinsel, edible gingerbread men and Christmas bells. Lottie climbed onto a chair to put the angel on the topmost branch, while Jenny held onto a piece of crêpe paper which Kaye tied onto the outside of the bucket, making an oversized bow. The children watched starry-eyed as the ruffled crêpe paper streamers were hung across the room crossing at the centre where several balloons hid the drawing pins from view. By the time they'd finished, the whole room looked very festive and Lottie clapped her hands, her button eyes shining with excitement. 'This is going to be my best Christmas ... ever.' Sarah couldn't resist putting her arm around her shoulder and giving her a hug.

The weather outside was damp and grey and every afternoon, a thick sea mist drifted across the driveway and lawn. The rest of the country was in the grip of fog as well. Trains were badly delayed and in some places the fog was so dense the authorities had to put detonator flares on the rails to help oncoming trains to see that they were on the line. Without flares the train drivers couldn't see a thing. In London, even in daylight, large oblong flares had been set up on the pavements to light the way, but already four people had been killed as a direct result of the terrible weather conditions. But all that didn't stop Kaye from gazing out of the window and saying, 'I wonder if it will be a white Christmas this year?'

Annie kept herself apart from the others. Most of her time was taken up with the baby anyway and she was becoming more and more concerned. Now that she had him all to herself, Edward didn't seem to like her. Every time she changed his nappy and wrapped him in his shawl he screamed. He cried in his cot until, hot and sweaty, he exhausted himself and finally went off to sleep. Annie tried everything to make him happy. She would rock him and talk soothingly, but it was no use. He resisted all her attentions and continued to cry and, what was even worse, he did it day and night. She was beginning to feel worn out herself and it didn't help matters when Mrs Goodall came round to complain that when she'd opened her bedroom window to give the baby some fresh air, Edward's crying had disturbed her afternoon soirée with friends.

When her mother turned up the day before Christmas Eve, Annie had every intention of asking her what to do, but instead they had rowed.

'If you really loved me,' she'd pouted angrily, 'you would have given me my independence. I shouldn't be forced to stay here with these women. Why can't I have a flat of my own somewhere?'

'Oh darling,' her mother protested, 'just think how dismal it would be being on your own.'

'I may as well be,' Annie grumbled. 'Nobody here talks to me anyway.'

Her mother raised an eyebrow. 'And have you bothered to talk to them?'

'That's not the point,' said Annie, raising her

voice. 'I want to come home with you and Father. How can you expect me to spend Christmas in this ... this hellhole?'

'You know perfectly well that your father won't have you back while you've still got Edward,' said Judith firmly. 'He has to be very careful about getting involved in even a whiff of scandal. People can be very unforgiving about those in the public eye.'

'Sometimes I think he cares more about his reputation than he does about his family,' Annie snapped.

Judith sighed. 'Annie, it's time you stopped moaning about what you haven't got and made the most of what you have got. I'm doing my best.'

'Oh yes, of course, I forgot,' said Annie cuttingly. 'You've given up your dress allowance, haven't you? Not much of a sacrifice for your only daughter, is it?'

Judith was cut to the quick but she managed to keep her cool. She told herself her daughter was overwrought. Looking after a tiny baby was a big responsibility and she was only young. She couldn't understand why Annie hated being here. Everyone seemed so nice and her room was really attractive. They sat drinking tea and making quiet conversation until the baby stopped crying and fell asleep.

As she left, Judith handed her daughter a couple of presents, one for her and the other for Edward. Annie, in turn, handed her a jar of Pond's cold cream wrapped in some of last year's Christmas paper for herself and a brown paper parcel for her father.

'Take care of yourself, darling, and I'll try to see

you again before the New Year.'

Her mother gone, Edward woke up and began to bawl again. Annie frowned dejectedly. 'Oh Edward, what am I going to do with you? I wish your daddy was here.'

Christmas promised to be a bleak time for Henry, stuck as he was in a place which reeked of bleach, cooked cabbage and pent-up testosterone. He had two presents. A tin of coffee crunch, riffled, and a light-hearted book called *Whisky Galore* by Compton MacKenzie. Both presents, reeking of her expensive perfume, were from the woman he called his 'guilty secret' and helped to while away a very tedious and boring day. There was the promise of the Salvation Army band coming to play in the prison grounds on Christmas Day, but apart from that, the prison routine was barely altered despite the season. There was little variety in his life now. The Criminal Justice Act passed by parliament in July meant that life in British prisons had changed. Hard labour had been abolished as had being whipped for violent crimes; but in its place the prison authorities expected the inmates to take part in other activities. Henry was given the choice of bookbinding or hand-sewing mailbags. He chose the bookbinding and it meant that once a day he was able to get out of his cell and go to the prison workshop.

One thing gave him great pleasure. Big Frankie had been true to his word and had retrieved the letter Henry had sent to Kaye's solicitor. A couple of days later, Henry sent it back again, but this time the papers inside had been ripped up, with his own signature heavily scratched out. He had also inserted a Christmas card he had procured from another inmate. It had cost him an extra slopping-out duty, but it was worth every stinking minute. Inside he'd written, 'Happy Christmas to my darling wife, Kaye. I can't wait to see you when I get out in April.' Next Christmas, he told himself, he would be well-off again, and with his son. He couldn't wait to see Kaye's face when he turned up on the doorstep. The only problem now was to find out exactly where she lived. He'd racked his brains to recall what she'd said when she'd climbed into the witness box. It took a couple of days before he remembered that the judge had allowed her to write down her address on a piece of paper. The court usher had handed it to him, so the judge was the only one who knew where she lived. Damn. That meant he had to work out another plan. It was obvious that the solicitor wouldn't pass on her address. The BBC would know where she was but getting the address out of them might prove to be a bit tricky.

Sarah woke up in the middle of the night. The baby was crying again. She lay on her back and waited for him to stop, but his angry protest seemed to go on forever. What on earth was his mother doing? Why didn't she pick him up? Sarah tutted to herself. If Annie didn't go and see to the child soon, she would have to. As soon as Peter Millward got back from Wales, she would accept his offer and marry him. He was right. He was a good man and the girls thought the world of him. She would learn to love him and forget his unattractive features. She suddenly felt relaxed. She should have made this decision months ago.

The door of her room opened slowly, and because Sarah slept with the curtains open, she could see Jenny standing there rubbing her eyes. 'Mummy, Edward is crying.'

I know, darling,' said Sarah, throwing off the covers. 'Go back to bed. I'll see to him.' She took her daughter back to her room and tucked her into bed. The night light on the saucer was guttering, so she found a new one before she left. Lu-Lu snored on peacefully. 'Don't worry,' she said, kissing Jenny's forehead. 'Mummy will sort it out. I guess Edward's mummy has fallen asleep.'

Pulling on her coat (she had no dressing gown), Sarah hurried downstairs. That girl had to be told to pull her socks up. This was the third night in a row everyone in the house had gone without sleep. As she neared Sarah's bedroom, she heard Annie say, 'It's no use. Whatever I do he cries. He hates me.'

Sarah knocked quietly and pushed the open door wider as Kaye was saying, 'All babies get fractious at times, dear. He'll settle down soon.'

'But I'm so tired,' Annie complained.

Sarah took in the scene. Annie was sitting dejectedly on the edge of her bed. Kaye sat with her arm around Annie's shoulder and Lottie was rocking the drawer while Edward screamed the house down.

'Ah,' said Kaye, relief in her voice. 'Here's Sarah. Sarah's a mother. She'll know what to do,'

They all looked up at her expectantly. Annie was as white as a sheet with large dark circles under her eyes. Kaye was in her dressing gown but Lottie was only in her nightie. 'My baby didn't cry,' Lottie told them quietly. 'My baby was a good baby.'

'I'm sure he was,' said Sarah, stopping to give Lottie an encouraging squeeze on her arm and a smile.

'He just won't stop,' Kaye appealed to Sarah.

'He doesn't like me,' Annie whinged.

'It's not you he hates,' Sarah said. 'It's that shawl. You need to take it off.'

As she advanced towards the drawer, Annie leapt to her feet. 'That's what they told me to do in the Mother and Baby Home,' she said defensively. 'Sister said...'

'All babies are different,' said Sarah, lifting the top blanket from Edward's shoulders. 'Can't you see he doesn't like being trussed up like that?'

'I've put him down exactly as the midwife showed me,' Annie insisted.

Their eyes met in a look of mutual animosity. 'Please yourself,' said Sarah huffily and turned to leave.

'No, wait!' cried Kaye. Sarah remained where she was but she didn't turn back. 'Annie,' Kaye continued, 'you've just admitted to me that you're desperate. I'm sure you've done everything possible to make Edward happy, but plainly he's not. Perhaps we should give Sarah the benefit of the doubt.'

'But...' Annie began again.

'It really wouldn't hurt to try, would it?' Kaye

insisted. 'And if it doesn't work, we'll send for the doctor.'

Annie swallowed hard and let her shoulders sag. 'Oh, all right then.'

Kaye turned to Sarah. 'Sarah?'

Sarah's heart was already thumping with indignation and she was sorely tempted to stalk out of the room, but for the sake of the baby she couldn't do it. It took every ounce of her strength to turn back to the cot where Edward was becoming very hot under the collar. His mother had wrapped his arms so firmly in the shawl that he couldn't move at all. With the hand of expertise, Sarah lifted him from under the covers and removed his cocoon. The baby flailed his arms angrily but almost immediately became a lot calmer. Sarah dabbed his sweaty head with the shawl and said gently, 'There, there, little man. That's better, isn't it?' She looked at Annie. 'Have you got a cold flannel somewhere?'

Lottie produced one and Sarah wiped the baby's forehead with it to cool him down, all the while talking softly to him. The three women watched as she lay him back down again. He protested for a few seconds but then lay quiet.

'So it was the shawl?' said Kaye incredulously.

Annie dabbed her eyes and looked into her baby's bed. 'Oh Eddie...' she said softly. 'I'm sorry.'

He moved his head slightly, his unfocussed eyes searching for her, then he lifted his hand and two fingers spread themselves involuntarily. It looked a little like Churchill's victory sign, but because his hand was facing the wrong way, it was more like the much ruder 'up yours' sign. Despite herself, Sarah giggled. Annie glanced at her and sniggered. Then Kaye chuckled, and without fully comprehending why everyone was laughing, Lottie joined in. It was a pivotal moment.

Back in her own bed, Sarah lay in the dark thinking about Peter again. Helping Annie out had changed a lot of things but not the one thing that mattered. As soon as Christmas was over she would tell Peter that if the offer was still there, she would marry him. The sooner the better.

Nineteen

A good night's sleep was what everybody needed and on December 23rd that's just what happened. The atmosphere in the house on Christmas Eve was totally different. It may have been because everyone was looking forward to the big day, but it felt so much more than that. Sarah began the day bright and early by cleaning out her pram and polishing the coachwork. When she saw Annie coming downstairs for breakfast, she said, 'If you want Edward to have a little bit of fresh air, you are welcome to use the pram.'

Annie hesitated for a second, so Sarah added, 'Look, we don't have to be bosom pals, but we are stuck in exactly the same position. I, for one, find it exhausting keeping up the hostility between us. Couldn't we agree on a truce?'

Annie's mouth formed a thin smile and she

nodded. 'Truce.' Sarah turned towards the kitchen. 'By the way,' Annie added, 'thanks for last night.'

'You're welcome,' said Sarah without looking back.

Later that morning, with Edward asleep in his pram in the back garden, there was a knock on the front door. When Sarah opened it, she was surprised to see the detective who had interviewed her before the trial standing there.

'Oh.' Her immediate thought was that something had happened to Henry.

'I don't know if you remember me?' he began.

'I do,' said Sarah. 'They called you Bear, but I'm afraid I can't remember your proper name.'

'Detective Inspector Truman,' he smiled. 'Please don't worry. There's nothing wrong, it's just that I wondered how you were getting along.'

'Come in, come in,' Sarah smiled. He seemed to fill the kitchen with his presence once he came through the door, but it was not an unpleasant feeling.

The room was warm and cosy, a hive of activity. Lottie sat at the table busily polishing the silver cutlery. She made a space for him and Sarah introduced her.

Annie came through the kitchen with a bucket of nappies. Jenny and Lu-Lu were playing shops under the kitchen table. The girls peeped out at him.

'Hello you two,' he said. 'Are you looking forward to Christmas?'

Jenny nodded shyly, but Lu-Lu went back under the table. 'My daughters,' Sarah explained.

'Can I get you some tea? A mince pie?'

'Sounds wonderful,' he said.

They made small talk and Bear – she couldn't think of him as Detective Inspector Truman – ended up rocking Jenny's dolly while he waited for the kettle to boil. He and Sarah sat opposite each other at the table with the tea.

'Lovely mince pie,' he commented. 'Have you heard from Henry?'

'No.' Sarah shook her head.

'I have,' Annie called from the scullery. 'When he gets out, we're going to find a place of our own.'

'That's nice,' said Bear, smiling across the table at Sarah with a quizzical expression.

'That is Mrs *Annie* Royal,' said Sarah. 'Henry's third wife.' She suddenly frowned. 'How did you know I was here?'

Bear looked slightly uncomfortable as he told her he'd known where she was ever since she'd been brought to the attention of the welfare people.

'You came to check up on me?' said Sarah defensively.

'Not at all, but I'm glad you're settled now,' he smiled. 'Actually, there is something you may be able to help me with. Did you or your husband know a Mrs Grenville Hartley?'

Sarah shook her head. 'No, I didn't, but I can't answer for Henry. He had a lot of acquaintances mostly connected with his work he never introduced me to. Why?'

With the nappies rinsed and boiling away in the copper in the scullery, Annie reappeared. 'Perhaps Annie knows the lady.'

Bear asked the question again, but Annie had never heard of Mrs Grenville Hartley either.

'Can I borrow Jenny and Lu-Lu for a minute?' said Annie, clearly anxious to get away. Sarah nodded uncertainly and they went upstairs.

Bear studied Sarah's face. 'You live together?'

Sarah nodded. 'We *all* live here. Lottie is the first Mrs Royale's aunt.'

'Do you know where my baby is?' Lottie said and Bear gave Sarah another quizzical look.

'They made her give him up when she had him because she wasn't married,' she explained. 'Lottie gets upset because she doesn't know what happened to him.'

'I'm sorry to hear that, madam,' said Bear sympathetically, 'but rest assured, he must be happy where he is. The police would have found out if something was wrong.'

Lottie smiled. 'Yes, of course,' she said. 'You're right. He would have had a happy childhood.'

Bear stood to go.

'You never did say why you think Henry knew Mrs Hartley,' said Sarah. 'Who is she anyway?'

'Who was she,' corrected Bear. 'Mrs Grenville Hartley was found dead on the beach near the pier. She had apparently taken her own life.'

'I remember hearing about that,' said Sarah, her hand automatically going to her throat. 'Poor woman, but that was ages ago and what's it got to do with Henry?'

'It's taken us a while to formally identify her,' said Bear. 'We don't think Henry was directly involved in her death, but it appears that he spent quite a bit of time with her.'

'I don't understand,' said Sarah.

'I can't say anything for definite,' Bear went on, 'but certain allegations have been made and we are duty-bound to investigate.' He could see that she was upset by the revelation so he added, 'Please don't concern yourself unduly, Mrs Royal. There is absolutely no suspicion on your good self.'

'I'm pleased to hear it,' said Sarah stiffly.

He stood to go but then paused. 'I wonder,' he began again cautiously. 'I shouldn't really say this when I'm on duty, but there's a good film on at the Rivoli...'

'Oh, I'm already spoken for,' said Sarah quickly.

'I see,' Bear smiled. 'Then I wish you a very happy Christmas and all the very best for 1949.'

'Thank you,' said Sarah, and then he was gone.

The children didn't reappear until three quarters of an hour later when Annie took them into the sitting room.

'What have you been up to?' Sarah asked as Kaye and Annie brought them back into the kitchen for their mid-morning break.

'Nothing,' said Jenny, giving her sister a hefty nudge. 'It's a secret.'

'See-ret,' Lu-Lu agreed.

For the first time since they all came to Copper Beeches, the three wives of Henry Royale, Lottie, Jenny and Lu-Lu shared coffee and milk and ate one of Sarah's newly baked mince pies at the kitchen table. Conversation was a little awkward, but they all agreed to start Christmas Day by taking the children to the midnight service at St

George's, just down the road.

By 4.30 p.m. everything was ready. Sarah and Lottie had prepared the vegetables and Annie had laid the table. Kaye spent the afternoon with friends, arriving back home at 5 p.m. laden down with more brightly coloured packages, which she put around the base of the tree. At the same time, Sarah was filling the log basket in the sitting room. As she rose to her feet, she couldn't help noticing two envelopes on the tree with 'Mummy' written on the outside. For a second or two, her eyes smarted. So that's what Annie was doing with the girls. She glanced at the clock. 5.15 p.m. The shops closed at 5.30 p.m. It was too late to get something for Annie and Edward. Her heart sank. Not to buy them anything had been quite deliberate, but now she felt terrible. She was being petty and unkind. The girl had put out an olive branch, but she had done nothing in return. Then she remembered a half-finished romper suit for Mr Lovett. Sarah hadn't been back to see Mrs Angel for a couple of weeks. She had meant to pop round, but somehow she'd always been too busy. There was still a lot to do to it, and maybe it didn't smell so good. After all, her things had got very damp when she was homeless, but, with a bit of luck, she might get it finished before tomorrow afternoon, which was the time they had all agreed to open the presents under the tree.

'I have a suggestion to make,' Sarah said as Kaye poured them all a sherry later that evening. The children were in bed and all surprisingly asleep, Edward included. 'Why don't I babysit while you three enjoy the Christmas Eve service together?

There may be a few late-night stragglers from the Half Brick in there and I'd rather not expose my girls to drunkenness.'

It sounded reasonable and everyone thought it a great idea, which left Sarah an uninterrupted hour and a half to finish the romper suit. It wasn't enough. It was 3.20 in the morning before Sarah finally switched out the light.

It seemed an awful lot of work for one day, but when the holidays were over, all three wives thought it had been worth it. Christmas 1948 would go down in everybody's diary, in Lottie's words, as the best Christmas ever! There had been tears along the way; Annie's when she unwrapped the romper suit from Sarah, and Sarah's when she opened the cards from her children. Lu-Lu's was a scribble of course, but Jenny had made her a paper bookmark and in her best writing, had written 'To Mummy from Jenny' on the back. Sarah imagined her sitting at the table, her tongue protruding as she concentrated, and she knew how much effort the little girl had put into getting her letters right. Kaye wiped her moist eyes when Lottie gave her a box of homemade sweets. Sarah had helped her to make them one afternoon in the week leading up to Christmas. It had been a learning curve for Lottie, but she had risen to the occasion with childlike enthusiasm. The girls were overjoyed to get their presents from Kaye and it seemed that Lu-Lu never wanted to be parted from the rabbit. There was one small hiccup when Jenny took the shoes off her new dolly and replaced them with the booties she kept on her old doll. Sarah thought she saw a glimpse of irritation on Kaye's face, but it soon passed. Lottie loved her watch, while Annie and Sarah had some scented bath salts. Kaye had the most gifts. A box of 200 cigarettes, boxed handkerchiefs, perfume, things for the bath and several hand-knitted items, and although Sarah's embroidered tray cloth and Annie's caddy of tea (a gift her mother had brought for Kaye) seemed to get lost in the pile, she was most appreciative. They had all eaten until they were stuffed and in the evening, as soon as the children were in bed, Kaye and Lottie went out, while Sarah and Annie managed to listen to the radio together before having an early night.

On Boxing Day everyone went out for a walk. They walked as far as the pier, with Annie pushing Edward in the pram and Lu-Lu, still holding onto the rabbit, managing to walk most of the way. They passed Beach House which was in a bit of a state, although the council had made a start on the repairs or at least got as far as putting a fence all around it. Further along the seafront, they bumped into Bear strolling along the beach with some friends. Sarah felt her face flush as he wished them all a happy Christmas and an even better New Year. As they returned his greeting, she wished she hadn't been quite so hasty. Bear was really nice. On the way back Lu-Lu had to sit at the end of the pram with her legs dangling over because she was tired. Monday was an extra day's holiday because Boxing Day fell on the Sunday and then it was all over until next year.

They brought in the New Year separately. Kaye motored to East Sussex to spend the evening with friends. The lavish New Year party was given by Kaye's old school chum, Norah Durbridge, whose husband Francis was enjoying a notable success with the BBC himself.

'It's an absolute age since I saw you two,' Kaye complained as Francis lit her cigarette with an onyx table lighter. Kaye was wearing a black and cream silk cocktail dress with a heavily beaded bodice. It had cap sleeves and was ruched at the waist. The hemline was just below the knee. She also had elbow-length black silk gloves and a small ostrich-feathered headband. 'What have you been up to?'

'I've been busy with the children,' said Norah, 'and Francis has been getting to grips with a certain radio detective.'

'You must be so proud of Paul Temple,' Kaye told Norah's husband. 'It seems that the listeners can't get enough of him.' Francis smiled shyly. 'They tell me the BBC had 7,000 telephone calls after the first episode.'

'Thank you, darling.' Someone had handed Kaye a drink. 'Any more in the pipeline?'

'Plenty,' Francis chuckled. 'But tell me about your success. We were delighted to see that you've been voted the nation's top playwright.'

'It was a bit of a surprise.'

'Nonsense,' said Francis. 'It's about time you were recognised for your achievements. It was much deserved, my dear.'

'Thank you,' said Kaye modestly.

'And now I'm told that you're sitting very close to a new contract,' said Francis. 'Perhaps after that, who knows…' He moved closer and whispered conspiratorially, 'Hollywood?'

Kaye laughed softly. 'It's not quite as exotic as that,' said Kaye, 'and you know the score, everyone's favourite today and tomorrow's fish 'n' chip paper.'

'How true,' said Francis sagely.

Kaye sipped her wine. 'I believe I may have poached one of your favourite actors ... Boney Crawford?'

'Good Lord,' cried Francis. 'The last I heard of him, he was playing Holmes in *The Adventure of the Speckled Band*.'

'That's enough of you two talking shop,' said Norah, slipping her arm through Kaye's. 'Darling, there's somebody here I want you to meet.'

Her cream-coloured full-length evening dress rustled as she led Kaye to a sofa where a man was deep in conversation with a blonde actress.

Francis introduced Kaye to Percy Granger and then encouraged the actress to another part of the room. Kaye and Percy stood together indulging in a little small talk. She liked him. He was younger than her, and seemed more like an overgrown schoolboy, but he knew her work and seemed very interested in what she was doing.

'Are you a writer?' she asked.

'Television producer,' he smiled.

Kaye nodded sagely. She knew little about the workings of a television studio, but she wasn't about to admit to that.

'Now that the war is over, this is a whole new world,' he said. 'I've long admired your work and when Francis said you were coming, I asked to meet you. Tell me Miss Hambledon, would you be interested in working in television?'

'You're asking me to write for television?' Kaye gasped. 'Do you think there is a future in it?' She sat down, crossed her legs and took one of the cigarettes he had offered her from the tortoise-shell cigarette box on the table in front of them. 'It sounds like a nice idea, but who in the world can afford to buy one?'

'We think it will really catch on,' Percy said, lighting both their cigarettes. 'Now that the Sutton Coldfield transmitter is up and running, we can already reach the Midlands and central Wales. It won't be long before programmes are available in the whole country.'

Kaye gave him an unconvinced smile and took a long drag on her cigarette. 'You've still got some way to go,' she said. 'The last I heard less than a third of the population even own a television. Somehow or other, you're going to have to appeal to the masses.'

'You are absolutely right,' he said, 'but all it needs is for one really exciting project to turn the whole nation into television viewers. The real question is, are you one of our pioneers?'

A maid drifted by with a drinks tray and Percy grabbed a glass. He gestured to Kaye, but her glass was still half full. She was still sceptical about what he was saying, but she was also beginning to feel a small frisson of excitement. 'I'd like to believe what you're saying, but even if people have a television, will they have the time to watch it?'

Percy leaned back on the sofa. 'I'll say this for the BBC,' he said. 'They have a very clear vision for the future. The feeling is that we can appeal to the family audience. Instead of going out to the pictures, people can gather around their television screens in the home. The nation needs families. We want to make television time, family time.'

'But television sets are awfully expensive,' Kaye mused.

'True,' said Percy, 'but already there are firms looking into a rental market. The point is, Kaye, we need to be ready. We shall need programmes, plays and ideas of the highest quality. The world of broadcasting is about to undergo a radical change. As well as informing people, it's becoming a mode of entertainment. What I am asking you is, are you in or out?'

'That's a stark choice…'

'We love your radio plays, but this would be the making of a new career.'

'I presume I'll only get paid on broadcast?'

'And at the moment we can only transmit pre-recorded programmes,' Percy nodded. 'It may take a while to filter through, but you'll get a far larger rate of pay than you do for radio. I'm sure your agent would look into the possibility of securing you an advance.'

Kaye could feel herself beginning to tremble with excitement. He was right. This was a fantastic opportunity and one she'd be a fool to let slip. 'Let me submit a few ideas,' she said, doing her best to sound nonchalant. 'Would you accept a cast list and a synopsis?'

'From someone of your calibre and reputation, that would be fine,' he said. 'I have to warn you that the wheels will move very slowly in this business. We're sitting here at the beginning of 1949 but it may be the beginning of the fifties and beyond before you'll see your work being broadcast.'

'That's all right,' Kaye smiled. 'I have time.' A wisp of smoke caught in her throat and she coughed.

'That's a nasty cough,' said Norah reappearing. 'Are you taking something for it?'

'I'm fine,' said Kaye, regaining her composure. 'I'm not ill or anything, but I can't seem to shake it off.'

'Cut down on the weed, darling,' Francis joked.

'I know, I know,' Kaye laughed, 'but it helps me concentrate when I'm writing, and if I don't smoke, I'll be eating all the time.'

Percy patted his slightly rounded stomach. 'Tell me about it,' he chuckled and, spotting an old friend, excused himself.

'You seemed deep in conversation,' said Francis, clearly fishing.

'He's looking for television writers,' said Kaye, 'but you knew that, didn't you?'

'Interested?'

'You bet,' she laughed. 'I certainly wasn't expecting that!'

'Life is always full of surprises,' Francis chuckled. 'By the way, how's Henry?'

'In prison,' said Kaye, picking a piece of tobacco from her bottom lip with her gloved hand, 'for bigamy.'

Malcolm Mitchell stared at the brown paper parcel in front of him. Judith had given it to him just before Christmas but he still hadn't opened it. He poured himself a whisky and turned the key in the lock of his study door. They were off to a New Year's Eve party and Judith was still getting ready, but he didn't want her bursting in on him. Taking a large mouthful of his drink, he sat at his desk with the parcel in front of him for some while before he undid the string. It was a navy scarf, hand-knitted and even his inexpert eye could see it wasn't very well done. On the top there was a postcard with a picture of Bognor pier before the war on it. On the reverse he read, '*To Granddad with love from Edward.*' Malcolm took a deep breath before pushing the scarf, paper and postcard into the bin. His chest was tight and he had a lump in his throat.

He wept silently until he heard Judith calling as she came downstairs, 'Are you ready, Malcolm?'

Blowing his nose heartily, he stood up and downed the rest of his drink. 'Coming.'

She tried the door handle. 'Why have you locked the door? What are you doing? Come on, we'll be late.'

Taking Annie's gift out of the bin, he opened the desk drawer and shoved everything inside. 'Coming.'

Sarah, Annie and Lottie celebrated at home. When the children were tucked into bed and sleeping, Sarah's thoughts turned to Bear. Why had she said she was spoken for? It was a stupid, old-fashioned expression and she hadn't exactly given Peter any firm promises. Bear seemed such a kind man. When he'd come to the house that day, he had a small gift for the girls, a bar of Cadbury's chocolate each. To make it last, Sarah allowed them one square each at teatime.

In the end, Lottie was the first footer. After knocking enthusiastically, she came back into the house on the stroke of midnight with the traditional gifts of a silver sixpence to bring financial prosperity, a slice of bread to represent daily food, some salt for honesty, and a knob of coal for good cheer for the following year.

It seemed like a good start, but in January the whole country was plunged into mourning when Tommy Handley, the man whose comedy show *ITMA* had got them through the awful war years, suddenly died of a brain haemorrhage. In the shops there was little other conversation and the grief so openly displayed took the powers-that-be by surprise. Kaye went to the funeral, of course. *ITMA* had taken a lot of her short sketches in the early days. The day after they'd buried him at Golders Green cemetery, Kaye had a surprise visit from her solicitor.

Mr Dobbin was an efficient-looking man but very near retirement age. He had known the family for years but only became Kaye's solicitor after her mother died. Smartly turned out in his pinstriped suit with matching waistcoat, the expression on his pinched grey face told her that he hadn't come with good news. Sarah had shown him into Kaye's writing room where she sat at her typewriter, a cigarette dangling from her lips, working towards a deadline and trying to plan something for her first television play. Until she saw who it was, she didn't welcome the intrusion.

'Shall I get you both some coffee?' Sarah asked.

With a cough, Kaye crushed her cigarette into

the already overflowing ashtray and stretched her body. 'We'll go into the sitting room, Sarah.'

'I hate to disturb you, my dear,' Mr Dobbin apologised. 'I can see that you are very busy.'

Kaye rolled her right shoulder and rubbed it. 'It's fine,' she said. 'I've been sat at the desk for too long. My shoulder is killing me. I need to change position.'

He followed her into the sitting room and they watched Sarah as she held a newspaper over the front of the fire to help it draw.

'I've had a communication from Mr Royale,' he said as Sarah left the room and they sat close to the dancing flames. He took an envelope from his briefcase and handed it to her. 'I'm afraid it's regarding the divorce. In short, he's refusing to allow it.'

'Refusing to allow it?' Kaye repeated. She coughed and tipped the contents of the envelope onto her lap. The solicitor's papers requesting his signature had been torn up. Mr Dobbin waited until she had opened the Christmas card and read Henry's accompanying letter which began with *My dearest Kaye…*

I know I have treated you shabbily and you have every right to be angry, but I have changed. I know now that I believe in the indissolubility of Christian marriage. The Church gave us its blessing and since I've been here it has served to make me understand that we should not break our marriage vows. This is why I cannot agree to the divorce. I loathe the thought of defeat in anything which is why I am asking you for a second chance. Please don't do this, my darling. We can work it out and have a good marriage once again.

May I offer you my heartfelt congratulations on your splendid achievements at the BBC.

Your ever loving Henry.

Kaye got up from her chair and, standing with her back to Mr Dobbin, gazed angrily into the fire. Her chest was tight with indignation. 'I don't understand,' she said eventually when she had calmed down and composed herself again. 'Half the country is getting divorced, but he has to dig his heels in. Why?'

'I get the feeling that he thinks he has more to lose by letting you go, my dear.'

'But he doesn't want me,' said Kaye, sitting back down and dabbing her eyes with a handkerchief. 'He never had a good word to say about me when we were together.' She looked up helplessly. 'What's he playing at?'

'He mentions the BBC,' said Mr Dobbin cautiously.

'It's the money, isn't it,' she sighed. 'He thinks I'm rolling in it and that's why he wants to come back.'

'That is my considered opinion,' Mr Dobbin nodded. The door opened and Lottie came in with a tray of coffee. She hovered for a second or two then put it down. Kaye thanked her and gently ushered her from the room.

She turned back to Mr Dobbin. 'What can I do? If I let him come back here, he's just as likely to take everything.'

Mr Dobbin nodded again. 'And he'd have every right to. The wife's property is her husband's. Our laws are still quite archaic when it comes to marriage.'

'But doesn't the bigamy case prove his adultery?'

'You would have to do it all over again in a divorce court,' said Mr Dobbin. 'It means names and places. And if as he says, he doesn't agree with divorce, he could drag it out for years.'

'But I don't want him back in my life!' Kaye lowered herself into a chair. She felt sick. Five minutes ago she felt fulfilled and contented with life. Now there was a huge threatening cloud hanging over her. She couldn't go back to being Henry's wife, she just couldn't. 'I've finally got something together for myself and my family.'

'I can see that, my dear,' said Mr Dobbin, 'which is why I came down from London to see you in person. We have to discuss what to do for your protection.'

Kaye took a deep breath. He was right. As unpleasant as it was, she had to lay aside her own feelings and deal with it.

'First and foremost I have to protect my aunt,' she said, reaching for the cigarette case. 'She is happy. For the first time in her life, she feels safe and loved. Oh, I know she still grieves for her child, but apart from that, she is content. I can't allow Henry to disturb that.'

'He is your next of kin,' Mr Dobbin reminded her, 'and as head of the house…'

'I won't turn her out,' Kaye cried. 'There is no way she could face going back into that awful place and she's incapable of taking care of herself.' Kaye shook her head in frustration. 'She wouldn't last five minutes on her own.'

'You could put some sort of settlement on her,' said Mr Dobbin. 'Something legally binding which would make sure she'd never lack for anything, should, God forbid, anything happen to you, and your husband did decide to come back and take over.' He took the cup of coffee she held out in front of him. 'Or we could offer him a sum of money to stay away…'

'Do you think that would work?'

'Knowing Henry,' said Mr Dobbin, shooting out his bottom lip, 'frankly I don't. He'd be back for more in no time, but you could try.'

'What do you think I should offer to keep him away?'

'I think perhaps £2,000 would give him a good enough reason,' said Mr Dobbin with a casual shrug as Kaye spluttered. 'I can draw up some papers for him to sign ... to make sure that he agrees not to come back if he takes the money.'

'£2,000 is an awful lot of money,' said Kaye.

Mr Dobbin nodded in agreement. 'But if it brings you peace of mind…'

'It's going to be very awkward with the others here as well,' Kaye mused.

'Others?'

'His two bigamist wives are living in this house,' and seeing Mr Dobbin's jaw drop she added, 'long story but it works for us. Thank God he doesn't know where we are all living.'

Twenty

While Kaye was talking with her solicitor, Sarah took the opportunity to go and see Mrs Angel. She'd dressed carefully, wearing a hand-knitted Fair Isle jumper under her winter coat. Her coat was new ... well, new to her. She'd bought it at Lil Relland's shop in North Street for 10/6. A scarf around her neck kept the cold wind at bay. She was going to see her old friend because she needed to replace the material she had used for Edward's Christmas present and make another romper suit for Mr Lovett. She was dying to see if Mrs Angel had any more orders. Mrs Angel was so delighted to see her that she turned the open sign on the door to 'closed' and they went out into the living quarters at the back of the shop.

'Where are the children?' Mrs Angel asked as she put the kettle on.

'Jenny is at school,' Sarah said, 'and Lu-Lu is being looked after by Kaye's aunt Lottie. It's the first time I've let her do it and she's so excited, but I don't want to stay away too long. I've got to pop round to the yard to see Peter Millward when I leave here.'

'So tell me what you've been doing since you left the fisherman's cottage.'

Sarah told her old friend all about Christmas and how she and the girls were getting along in their new home. She left out the bits about how much Annie irritated her and that she was planning to marry Peter Millward if he would still have her. Instead, the picture she painted was rather rosy.

'I wish I could have helped you more,' Mrs Angel sighed.

'What more could you have done?' said Sarah. 'Besides, you had enough on your plate with your sister being ill. How is she, by the way?'

'Recovered, but it has shaken her up a bit,' said Mrs Angel. 'She's talking about retiring. Oh my dear, you should have said. You and the girls could have stayed here for a while. It would have been a bit of a squeeze but we would have managed.'

'You've already been more than a friend to me,' said Sarah. She went on to explain about the romper suit.

'I'm so sorry, my dear,' said Mrs Angel, pushing a cup of tea in front of her. 'I'm afraid Mr Lovett won't be taking any more orders and he's obviously forgotten you still had one to make. He retired. I have a new representative now.' She leaned forward and put her hand beside her mouth in a conspiratorial way, 'He's not nearly as nice as Mr Lovett.' And Sarah laughed.

'Perhaps it's just as well,' said Sarah, doing her best to hide her disappointment. 'I have little time for sewing now.'

'I'm glad things have worked out so well,' said Mrs Angel. 'I had high hopes that you and Peter might get together one day.'

Sarah looked away and changed the subject. Peter's letter had been brief and to the point. *'I hope you and the girls had a wonderful Christmas. If it's all right, could you pop by the yard this afternoon? I can't wait to see you and I have something very special to ask you.'*

She'd been thinking a lot about him since the holidays began. She'd missed him being around and Lu-Lu talked incessantly about Occklepep. The urgency to leave the house had long gone and she and Annie rubbed along together fairly well. She knew they would never be close friends, but at least they had stopped being enemies. Sarah enjoyed working at Copper Beeches. She never thought she would, but she enjoyed giving Kaye and Lottie a high level of care and attention. She had not only made it a home but she'd put her own feminine touches around the place and, funnily enough, in doing so she didn't feel one bit like a servant. But if she married Peter Millward, she could make a home of her own, a permanent place for the girls and somewhere safe and secure. The time they'd been apart had served to crystallise her feelings. She still didn't love him, but she was willing to give this relationship her very best shot. She would grow to love him, she was sure of that, and perhaps once she got used to it, even that tuft of hair at the end of his nose wouldn't seem so bad. He obviously had feelings for her. After all, he wouldn't have said, '*I can't wait to see you*' if he hadn't.

As she hurried towards Peter's coal yard, Sarah could feel her nervousness returning. She patted her hair in place and climbed the fire escape steps two at a time. As she pulled the door open, Peter was just coming out of the little kitchen at the rear. When he saw Sarah, his face broke into a wide smile.

'Sarah,' he cried. 'Come in, come in. It's so good to see you again. Did you have a nice Christmas?'

Sarah closed the door and began to unwind her scarf from around her neck. The little office was stuffy and the smell from the paraffin heater overwhelming. 'We did,' she smiled. 'It was the best we've had for a long time.'

'I'm glad,' he said, returning her smile. 'So was mine.' He turned his head and called over his shoulder, 'Better make that three teas, darling. Sarah's here.'

Sarah was conscious that her jaw had dropped but she quickly recovered herself.

'Sit down,' he invited. 'We've got a lot to talk about.'

Her mind was in a whirl. Darling? Who was darling? Her cheeks were flaming with embarrassment. Thank God he couldn't read her thoughts.

'I can't stay long,' she blurted out. 'I have to collect Jenny from school.'

The kitchen door creaked slightly and Peter jumped to his feet to hold it open wide. A small dark-haired woman entered the room carrying two cups of tea. She was older than Sarah, homely rather than pretty, with small features and smiley eyes. She was wearing a hand-knitted lemon twinset which was so beautifully done it would have easily won a WI competition. She wore lipstick but no jewellery. Sarah cupped her hands around her tea as the woman nipped back for a third cup and joined them at the desk.

'This is Nancy,' said Peter proudly. 'Nancy is my fiancée.' They gazed lovingly at each other as she sat down. 'I asked her to marry me on New Year's Eve and to my utter amazement, she said yes.'

Sarah swallowed hard. All those trips to Wales – they were nothing to do with expanding his business interests, were they. He must have been seeing Nancy for some time. How could she have got this so wrong? A knot had formed in the pit of her stomach.

'Congratulations,' she said heartily. 'I wish you both every happiness. You deserve it.'

Leaning forwards, Peter kissed Nancy's hands.

Sarah cleared her throat. 'What was it you wanted to ask me?'

'Um? Oh yes,' said Peter. 'I know you're very good with a needle and we wondered if you would mind giving Nancy a hand with her dress.'

'It's a bit of a cheek,' said Nancy when Sarah didn't answer straight away. 'I mean I don't know you, but Peter says you've been a real brick to him.'

Sarah was struck dumb. What could she say? This wasn't Nancy's fault. Now she understood how desperate Peter had been to get married. As an older man, he wanted to settle down before it was too late.

'Perhaps we shouldn't have asked,' said Nancy uncertainly.

'No, no, it's fine,' Sarah protested. 'You just took me by surprise, that's all.'

'I already have some material,' said Nancy, a Welsh lilt in her soft voice, 'and of course we shall pay you.'

'I wouldn't hear of it,' said Sarah. 'Consider it

my present to you both.'

As they discussed the dress and when Nancy would need fittings, Sarah struggled not to give way to tears. It was ridiculous being so upset because she didn't love Peter, but when she'd read his letter, it never once occurred to her that he had something else in mind. Thank God she hadn't said anything to Mrs Angel. That would have been too embarrassing.

'I'm afraid there's something else,' said Peter sheepishly. 'Now that I've got my Nancy, I shan't be needing a bookkeeper anymore.'

Sarah swallowed hard. She hadn't done his books for a while and was rather hoping he would give them to her today so that she could update them. 'I wouldn't expect anything else,' she said brightly. 'As a matter of fact, I was going to tell you that now that I've got a housekeeping job, it would be a bit difficult to find the time anyway.'

Peter looked relieved. 'So it all worked out in the end.'

'Yes,' she smiled. 'It all worked out in the end.'

Henry sat in his cell with a self-satisfied grin on his face. Halfway through his sentence and everything was going so well. He knew he was the envy of half the prison because he had already had his regular visitor, his guilty secret. Many of the prisoners thought she was his rich mother. Henry wouldn't be drawn as to her identity. Instead, he would smile mysteriously and tap the side of his nose. He preferred to play his cards close to his chest and today he would have another visitor; Annie was coming with the baby. That would get them all talking about him. He would see his son for the very first time. He'd been waiting for the visitor's bell ever since lunchtime and now, at last, the cell doors were being opened.

They didn't have long. Visiting times were only an hour and it wouldn't be private. The room was filled with other prisoners waiting to see their wives and girlfriends. He sat at a table and watched the door. She was one of the last ones to come in. She was wearing a brown coat with a knitted scarf about her neck. Her hair was covered by a headscarf and she was carrying the baby in her arms. His heart lurched. She sat down in front of him and smiled.

'Let me look at him then,' he said.

She pulled back the shawl and turned so that he could see the baby. He was asleep, and contrary to what his guilty secret had said about newborn babies, he wasn't a screwed up little thing with a wizen face. Edward had a peachy-coloured little round face, with slightly flushed cheeks. He looked almost cherubic, and although his eyes stayed firmly shut, his hand came up and his fingers moved as if in salute to his father. Suppressing a smile, Henry let a little air escape from his mouth. So this was his son. His boy. After all this time, he could show the world what he was made of. They wouldn't look down on him now. He was a man and he'd proved it. He had a son. His name would go on for another generation. This boy was a Royale. He became aware that she was talking.

'You won't believe the time I've had getting here,' she was saying. 'I brought him in the pram and I've had to ride in the guard's van all the way. It was a bit of a trial when I got to Southampton because I had to change platforms, but the porters were very kind and I made it in time. It was a bit lonely in the van all by myself, but at least I was able to feed Edward.'

He glanced up at the boy's mother, a look of disapproval on his face. 'You didn't go exposing yourself in public, did you?'

'Not exactly,' she laughed.

'I won't have it,' he said, screwing his hands into a fist. 'No wife of mine should do ... that in public.' He curled his lip.

'Oh Henry,' she smiled. 'How else am I going to feed him? He can't go all day without milk.' She looked up at him and was alarmed by the expression on his face.

'It's disgusting,' he hissed.

'I'm very discreet,' she said anxiously. 'No one can see a thing. I put the shawl over my shoulder like this...'

'Shut up,' he snapped, his eyes flashing with anger. He spun his head around to make sure no one was listening. A warder came towards him.

'Everything all right here?'

'Everything's fine, Mr Chambers,' said Henry cheerily.

'Madam?'

'Yes,' said Annie somewhat shakily. 'Everything's fine.' Mr Chambers moved on. 'I'm sorry, Henry.' Her voice was thick with emotion. 'Please don't let's fight. There's so little time.'

He looked at his son again. She should have the kid on the bottle. It wasn't right, his boy suckling her breast like that ... and in public. He shuddered at the thought, but aware that Mr Chambers was still watching them, he changed the subject. 'So what have you been doing with yourself?'

She prattled on, telling him about nothing in particular. Her mother, the Mother and Baby Home... God, he'd forgotten how irritating she was. In the end, he switched off and filled his head with his own thoughts. Kaye would have had his letter by now. He wondered whether to send another one, but he resented the fact that that pompous old twit Dobbin would read it first. If only he had her address.

'I told Mother I wouldn't stay,' Annie was saying, 'but she wouldn't hear of my having a flat on my own. Surprisingly though it's turned out to be all right.'

'What has?' he said dully.

'Oh Henry,' she protested. 'You haven't heard a word I've said. I said I don't really mind living with Sarah and Kaye.'

He started. 'Wait a minute, wait a minute ... you're living with Kaye?'

The baby stirred and began to protest. She lifted him onto her shoulder and rubbed his back gently. 'Yes,' she smiled. 'And Sarah and Jenny and Lu-Lu as well.'

Henry blinked. 'Well, I'm damned.'

'Of course, we can't stay there once you get out of prison,' she said. 'It wouldn't be right, would it, all three of us under the same roof as you, but I'm saving every penny I can. When I've passed my piano examination I'll be able to charge the proper price for lessons, but even now I can get a few shillings, and there's no shortage of mothers wanting their little darlings to play the piano.'

Henry wanted to laugh out loud. For weeks, he'd been sizing up just about every inmate in the prison before he confided in someone who might be able to trace where Kaye was living. He'd written to the BBC, but just as he'd thought, his letter had been ignored, and now, here was the silly female telling him that they were all together in the same house!

Edward began to wail. 'He needs his nappy changing,' she said, 'and I have to feed him.'

'You're not doing that here,' said Henry, looking around anxiously.

'Of course not, silly,' she said. 'I'll have to go to the Ladies somewhere.'

Silly? He felt his anger rising. Silly. For two pins he would have bellowed at her for talking to him like that, but he had to stay controlled. He had to be the model prisoner if he was going to get out on time.

'I may not be able to come again,' she was saying. 'It's very expensive and we want a bit of money behind us for when you come out.'

'I quite understand, my dear,' he said, relieved. 'Take care of yourself.' He watched her as she walked to the door and lifted his hand in a wave as she left.

Back in his cell, Henry got out his prison-issue writing paper. He could write all three of them a letter now if he wanted to. He knew exactly where they all were. One of Annie's letters fell on the floor. He opened it and looked at the address, Copper Beeches, Church Walk, Worthing. He put the letter back. No need to write to any of them just yet. He had other fish to fry ... much wealthier fish.

'Blimey,' said Big Frankie, 'only just seen her and you're writing to the missus already. It must be love...'

Henry grinned. 'Something like that,' he said as he penned the words. It was time to reel his guilty secret in. 'My dearest, I hardly know how to put this down on paper, but I need your help...'

Twenty-One

Peter's wedding was only a couple of weeks away. It had put pressure on Sarah to get the wedding dress done, but luckily Nancy had chosen a fairly plain design. The material was a white floral brocade and the dress itself was sleeveless, with a wide empire-line band fitted to the waist. The slightly pleated skirt was short and the only other shaping came from two darts at the bust. Nancy was going to wear a tulle head-dress with a short veil and carry spring flowers. Now that she was able to use Kaye's treadle sewing machine, Sarah had been confident that it wouldn't take long to do, and she was right.

The dashing of her plans concerning Peter left Sarah with a bit of a dilemma. It was obvious that she couldn't stay in the house forever, but what was she going to do? She'd toyed with the idea of becoming a Spirella corsetière, which was a respectable job she could do from her own home. She had looked into it and discovered that she would need three weeks' training in Letchworth, near to London, and then she could set up her own franchise. Money was the problem. She would have to save hard if she was going to do it. There was no money to be made in dressmaking, so where on earth did her future lie? She may have lost Peter Millward's books, but based on his recommendations, a couple of other businesses had retained her services. Sadly they only brought in pennies. She needed to think of something a little more lucrative.

Downstairs in the kitchen, Lottie was peeling the potatoes ready for dinner. She was good at routine and Sarah didn't have to remind her anymore about when to do things.

'You're busy.'

'You know me,' said Lottie chirpily, 'I don't let the feet grow under my grass.'

Sarah turned her back so that she wouldn't see her laugh. Lottie still didn't talk very much and she sometimes got everything round the wrong way, but if she saw Sarah laughing at her it might destroy her confidence. It was obvious that she enjoyed living at Copper Beeches. As Sarah prepared the cabbage, they could hear Kaye coughing. Lottie looked up and they shared a look of concern. When the coughing reached choking proportions, Sarah left the kitchen and hurried to the study. Kaye was on her feet desperately trying to catch her breath. Her eyes were watering and she was very red in the face.

'Ring for Doctor Bradley,' Sarah called over her

shoulder as she heard Lottie's footfall right behind her. She closed the door, anxious that Lottie shouldn't see her niece in such a state.

Kaye was panicking. She spluttered into her hand, retching and throwing herself about as she desperately tried to catch her breath. Sarah snatched a handkerchief from her own pocket and handed it to her.

'Kaye, you need to move into another position,' she said, helping Kaye to bend over towards her knees. 'Try and control the cough and concentrate on your breathing. Breathe through your nose, that's right, that right…'

After a few seconds, Kaye began to breathe normally, but she was clearly exhausted by the episode.

'Lift your head now,' Sarah said. Kaye wiped her nose with her handkerchief and as Lottie opened the door, Sarah looked up. 'Can you get Kaye a glass of water, Lottie?'

'I feel dizzy,' said Kaye hoarsely, 'and my head is banging like a drum.'

'I'll get you to bed in a minute,' said Sarah, 'but you need to calm down a little first. Lottie has rung for Doctor Bradley, but I think he will only tell you what you don't want to hear.'

'Cut down on the cigarettes,' said Kaye dolefully.

''Fraid so,' said Sarah. The two of them exchanged small smiles. Lottie reappeared with the water and Sarah steadied Kaye's trembling hand as she took a gulp. 'Take it slowly,' she advised.

They didn't have to wait long before the doctor put in an appearance. The National Health Service had begun in July of the previous year, bringing free health care to everyone in the country, but some patients had continued as before. Kaye was one of them and Doctor Bradley always found time for his private patients.

Having shooed Sarah and Lottie from the room, he gave Kaye a thorough examination. 'Any other symptoms?'

'I've got a terrible headache,' Kaye admitted. 'And I do feel a bit worn out these days.'

'Any muscular pain?'

'Whenever I work too hard, I get a pain in my right shoulder.'

'When did you last have a holiday?' said Doctor Bradley, a neat little man with a moustache designed to make him look older. He'd taken over from his father when he retired from the practice and was the second generation who had cared for Kaye and the family. He put his stethoscope back into his bag.

Kaye shrugged. 'It's been a while. I've been very busy.'

He smiled. 'I know, I heard your latest play on the radio the other day. Very good, in fact I would go so far as to say brilliant.'

Kaye basked in a pink glow of pleasure. 'Thank you.'

'How many cigarettes do you smoke a day?'

He'd caught her off guard. 'Um...'

'That tells me it's too many,' he said, 'and judging by the look of that overflowing ashtray, I should say far too many.'

'They say they're good for you,' said Kaye feebly. 'They calm your nerves.'

'There's a new school of thought now,' said Doctor Bradley. 'Smoking is not as beneficial as we first thought. In fact, cigarettes have been linked to getting other diseases.'

'All right,' she said grudgingly. 'I'll cut down.'

'I should like to run a few tests,' Doctor Bradley went on. 'I'll arrange for you to see a colleague of mine in Harley Street. The next time you're in town, make an appointment and pop along to see him.' Kaye nodded dully. 'In the meantime,' Doctor Bradley continued, 'get someone to put a bowl of water near the fireplace. The air is very dry in this room and that won't help with your breathing.'

As he left, Kaye gathered her things. She was in desperate need of some sleep. Sarah followed her up to her room and closed the curtains. Kaye undressed as far as her petticoat and slid under the eiderdown. It was chilly in the bedroom so she was grateful for the hot-water bottle Sarah had already put there. As she closed the door, Sarah glanced at her employer. Kaye really didn't look well at all.

'*Until we can find a place of our own*,' Henry wrote, '*I shall be staying with an old family friend.*'

Annie was furious. She had already written to explain that she was sure Kaye wouldn't mind him being in the house with her and the baby, although she hadn't actually broached the subject with Kaye herself yet. She was confident that however she felt about Henry, Kaye would never turn Edward out of his only home. She'd explained to Henry that she wasn't the least bit embarrassed about being with the other wives, but now he'd written this! Didn't he want to be with his son? She banged her thigh in frustration. She had been looking forward to having Henry back. It was proving desperately difficult to find somewhere else to live and nothing was a patch on the room she and Edward shared at Copper Beeches. It was quite big and another person could easily fit in with them. It wasn't as if Henry had much stuff, and besides, as soon as he got another job, they could find a place of their own.

She had hoped that she would have plenty of piano students by now but a chance remark by one of the mothers had put paid to that. Mrs Riley had asked Annie if she was related to Kaye. It seemed like a simple request from an adoring fan and without thinking Annie had laughed out loud, 'Well, we share the same husband, but that's all.' Mrs Riley had been visibly appalled. Gathering her child's things and grabbing Oliver by the arm, she'd made for the door. Annie tried to explain that it was nothing untoward, but her client was in no mood to listen. Oliver didn't come back for his Tuesday lesson and before long Annie noticed that some of her other clients had dropped away as well.

'Perhaps you should try and get some other job,' Sarah suggested when Annie told her.

'There isn't a lot of point,' said Annie. 'Henry will be here soon.'

Sarah sighed audibly but said nothing.

With nothing much to do, Annie was bored. Oh, she had Edward of course, but Kaye had been laid up for a couple of days with exhaustion and Sarah was making a wedding dress in her spare time. The only other person in the house, apart from the children, was Lottie, and quite frankly Annie didn't have much to do with her. She was a funny little woman and could be a bit embarrassing at times, not the sort you had as a friend. As soon as Kaye felt better she would be too busy for idle chit-chat. She would be back at her desk.

Annie hadn't been back home since before Christmas, but she knew her parents were away. Her mother took her to Hubbard's for afternoon tea now and then, but at the moment they were in York visiting Granny. Annie pouted. Everybody got to do things except for her. It wasn't fair.

'Why don't you take yourself off to the pictures,' Sarah suggested when Annie grumbled about being fed up. 'I'll look after Edward.'

Annie's eyes lit up. 'I'd sooner go to the dance at the Plaza ballroom,' she said.

'Then go and enjoy yourself,' said Sarah.

Annie hesitated. 'Do you mean it?'

'Of course,' smiled Sarah. 'We'll take care of Edward.'

Dizzy with excitement, Annie telephoned an old friend and agreed to meet her at the entrance, before spending the rest of the afternoon going through her clothes. This was the first time she'd actually met up with anyone from Worthing. She knew her father wouldn't approve and up to now she had always hesitated in case he found out, but all at once she felt her old defiant self coming back. She had some beautiful dresses, and although it was a bit of a struggle, she still fitted into them. In the end, she chose a pale lemon dress with a navy zigzag pattern across the skirt. Its sweetheart neckline was flattering, especially when she put on the two-strand pearl necklace her mother had given her on her sixteenth birthday. She fed Edward and had put him down in his cot by six thirty. He played for a while with his teddy and the bell she had tied across the cot with a ribbon and then fell asleep. On her way out, Annie stopped by the sitting room to give everyone a twirl. Kaye was reading a story to Jenny and Lu-Lu and all three agreed that she looked lovely.

'See you later,' Annie cried as she hurried out. 'I'll be back in time to feed him.'

As she turned into the street, she glanced towards Mrs Goodall's house and saw her watching from the sitting room window. Annie stopped and, looking right at her, she leaned forward and stuck out her tongue. With a shocked expression, Mrs Goodall dropped the net curtain.

'That was nice of you to babysit,' said Kaye as she and Sarah sat together in the sitting room. She had persuaded Sarah to join her once the girls were in bed, using her recent illness as leverage. Lottie was sitting under the standard lamp having a go at sewing a button onto a cardigan while they all listened to the radio. The programme was *Twenty Questions* in which the members of the team had to discover a mystery word using only twenty questions. 'And the mystery word is bicarbonate of soda ... bicarbonate of soda.' In a hidden studio, Norman Hackforth had just given the radio audience the word the team were struggling to find. Stewart MacPherson, the chairman, told the team it was mineral.

'She's young,' Sarah shrugged. 'The girl needed a bit of fun.'

'You're a very caring person,' Kaye remarked as they worked on a jigsaw puzzle together. 'Have you given any more thought to a career?'

On the radio, Daphne Padel squeaked, 'Can you drink it?'

Sarah shook her head. 'I've thought about it but I can't make up my mind what to do.' She explained about Spirella and its drawbacks. 'I'd like to do something with people, like running a tea rooms or something. Does that piece go there?'

There was a round of applause on the radio when Jack Train asked, 'Is it medicinal?'

'Bicarbonate of soda.'

The radio audience applauded. 'She's very clever that Anona Winn,' said Kaye.

'I'm just going to the toilet,' Lottie suddenly announced. 'I'm busting.'

'You've done amazing things with her,' Kaye remarked as soon as Lottie had gone. 'She's hardly the same person anymore.'

'She still doesn't say much,' said Sarah, 'you know, express an opinion on anything, but she's getting there.'

They worked quietly, picking up pieces and putting them down, sometimes finding a place to fit. 'Henry will be out soon,' said Kaye as the programme came to an end. She switched the radio off.

'But he doesn't know where we are, does he?' said Sarah cautiously.

Kaye shook her head and raised her glass of

wine. 'Thank God for that.' And they laughed. 'I sometimes wonder why I put up with him for so long. He was always so pedantic about everything.'

'In my house I had to fold the laundry a certain way, I could serve nothing from a tin for the main course, and he would only allow three more knobs of coal on the fire after nine thirty,' Sarah grinned. 'Oh look, that red bit belongs there.'

'Heavens above,' Kaye laughed. 'Did you have all that too?'

'I was so in love with him, I didn't mind,' Sarah said. 'Now that I've tasted my independence, I couldn't go back to that.'

Lottie came back into the room and Sarah decided to go and check on the children. They were all asleep, and when she came back, Lottie presented her with her work. 'I knew the top button was the most important,' she said.

'Very good,' said Sarah. 'Well done.'

Glowing with pride, Lottie excused herself and went to bed.

'What did she do?' said Kaye as soon as she was sure her aunt was on her way upstairs and out of earshot. 'You didn't say anything but I could tell she'd done something funny.'

'She moved every single button up one and then put the new button at the bottom of the cardigan,' said Sarah, suppressing a sympathetic smile.

The dance floor was crowded. Annie hadn't sat down all evening and she was worn out. She had just bought a lime cordial and kicked off her shoes. Her old school friend, Madge, threw herself into the chair beside her and put her feet on the chair next to them.

'My feet are killing me,' she laughed.

'Mine too,' said Annie. For the first time in weeks she was truly enjoying herself. She hadn't given Edward or Henry or Copper Beeches a moment's thought since she'd arrived.

'I thought you were abroad,' said Madge. 'Mummy said your mother told her you were in the South of France.'

'I wish,' sighed Annie.

'So where were you?' said Madge, coming closer.

Annie hesitated for a moment and then scuffed her chair towards her friend. 'If I tell you, will you swear to keep it a secret?'

Madge's eyes lit up. 'Of course,'

'You won't tell a living soul?'

Madge leaned forward eagerly. 'I swear.'

'I got married and had a baby,' said Annie.

Madge's chin dropped. 'You're married?'

'Well, not exactly,' said Annie.

A young man came to the table, but both girls shook their heads dismissively. 'What do you mean, not exactly?' Madge said as he left.

Annie explained about Henry.

'You don't mean you were the other wife in that awful bigamy case?' Madge gasped.

'Shh,' said Annie. 'Keep your voice down.'

'I'm sorry, I'm sorry,' said Madge, 'but this is unbelievable.'

'Promise me you won't tell,' said Annie, suddenly anxious.

'My lips are sealed,' said Madge, edging forward again. 'So tell me, what was it like ... being a married woman?'

Kaye fitted another piece into the jigsaw and yawned. 'Annie should be home soon. I gave her money for a taxi.'

'When he comes out, where do you think Henry will go?' said Sarah.

'I don't know and I don't care,' said Kaye. She glanced up at the clock.

'I don't want him back in my life and yet I can't stop thinking about him,' said Sarah. 'There was so much I didn't like. My pet hate was when he used my flannel in the bathroom.'

'Oh, that didn't bother me too much,' said Kaye, emptying her glass of wine. 'I just thought about the last part of my body I'd washed before he'd used it on his face.'

For a second Sarah seemed puzzled, but then she roared with laughter. They hadn't noticed that Annie had walked into the room. 'How could you?' she demanded.

'Oh, hello,' said Kaye. 'Did you have a lovely time?'

'That was horrible, what you just said about Henry,' Annie cried. 'You hated him, didn't you?'

'No, we didn't hate him,' said Sarah, her face slightly pink. 'We wouldn't have stayed as long as we did if we'd hated him. Given time, Annie, you'll begin to see what he's really like.'

'Well I think he's wonderful,' she said. 'You just don't understand him. When I was with him, we had a lovely home and he was always loving and caring. Everyone makes mistakes. Anyway, now I know why he left the both of you to live with me. You're thoughtless and cruel and you may as well know that as soon as he comes out, we're going to get married. Properly married.'

Sarah began packing the loose pieces of the jigsaw back into the box. She said nothing.

'Annie, I didn't want to tell you this,' said Kaye, 'but I have asked Henry for a divorce.'

'Good,' said Annie. She turned to leave. 'And about time too.'

'The trouble is,' Kaye called after her. 'He doesn't want one.'

Annie stopped in her tracks and turned back, her eyes blazing with indignation. 'What do you mean he doesn't want one? Of course he wants one.'

'When my solicitor came the other day, he brought a letter from Henry,' Kaye went on patiently. 'Henry has refused to sign the divorce papers and he says he wants to give our marriage another try.'

Annie stared at her, her face wreathed in disbelief. 'I don't believe you,' she cried. 'You're just saying that to upset me. Henry loves me and we're going to be properly married.'

'Oh Annie,' Kaye sighed. 'Don't you see? All Henry wants is for us all to dance to his tune. I don't want to stay married to him – you're welcome to him – but he loves playing these cat-and-mouse games. Henry is no good and the sooner you realise that, the better.'

Annie covered her ears with her hands. 'Stop it, stop it! It's not true. You're lying. Anyway, I don't care if we never get married. I'll live in sin with him forever if I have to!' and with that, she flounced out of the room.

Kaye flopped back into her chair.

'Is all that true?' Sarah gasped.

'I'll show you his letter if you like,' said Kaye. 'It's full of his usual holier than thou drivel. You and I know that Henry uses people, especially women. The trouble is, they just can't see it. It took me years to work out why he did what he did. Somehow or other, he gets gullible people to do things they would never have normally done ... and I should know, I was one of them for far too long.'

They sat for a minute or two, the only sound in the room that of the dying fire.

'Kaye, I need to confess something to you,' said Sarah. The wine had gone to her head, but she was thinking clearly. 'I pawned your cigarette case.'

'My cigarette case?'

'A lovely silver filigree one. Henry had it in the back of the kitchen drawer,' said Sarah. 'I was desperate for money. The girls were hungry so I pawned it.'

'Oh, I remember that,' Kaye shrugged. 'If it helped, then I'm glad.'

They both stood up ready to go to bed then Kaye added, 'Funny though. He told me it had been pinched.'

Sarah frowned. 'I'm sure it was yours. It was engraved *Kaye from Henry*.'

'Then it would have been,' said Kaye. 'Henry told me one of the nurses took it when I was in hospital. In fact, he was adamant.'

'What happened to her?'

'She got the sack.'

Twenty-Two

'Sarah, forgive me for asking,' Kaye began, 'but they are looking for someone to make the teas at the new Labour Hall.' She had come out of her office and accosted Sarah as she walked downstairs with the dirty sheets. 'I was wondering if Lottie could do it, but I don't think she'd be brave enough to go on her own ... not at first anyway. Could you help her? They say they'll pay.'

Sarah thought it would do Lottie good to get out of the house and if she got a small wage, so much the better. 'When do they want her?'

'They have a whist drive every Tuesday afternoon, two till four and the amateur dramatic society meet on a Friday night for rehearsal. That's seven until ten, but she doesn't have to stay that long. Once the teas are done she can go home.'

'I'd like to help,' said Sarah, 'but it's a bad time for me. What about my children?'

'They'd be in bed by seven, wouldn't they?' said Kaye, flicking ash from her skirt. 'I don't mind looking after them once a week.'

'Tuesday afternoon won't be so easy,' said Sarah, 'I have to collect Jenny from school at three.'

'I hadn't thought of that,' said Kaye, 'but if you could do the evening with her for a few weeks, she might manage the Tuesday afternoon on her own.'

'Will the job still be open after a few weeks?'

Sarah asked. She knew only too well that there were plenty of women desperate to earn a few shillings who would snap up a nice little job like that.

Kaye tapped the side of her nose. 'I've called in a favour,' she smiled, 'and I gave the am-dram a free play.'

'In that case,' said Sarah, 'I think Lottie would love it.'

The first evening they set off for the Labour Hall, it was dark and cold, but the snow which looked as if it might fall, held off. Sarah and Lottie walked along arm in arm, the closeness of their bodies keeping some of the cold out, even though the wind bit their cheeks. The job was simple enough. The actors in rehearsal had a break at around eight fifteen. Lottie had to have the tea ready and serve it from a hatch which opened out from the kitchen. When everyone had finished, she had to wash up the cups and saucers and put them away. Once the kitchen was tidy, she was free to go, and for all that she would be paid a very generous five bob.

The two of them set out the cups and saucers and put the urn on to boil. They knew they weren't supposed to open the hatch until break time, but listening to the play taking shape in the hall was too much of a temptation to miss. They pushed the hatch slightly and watched the actors through the crack.

The Coach Party was a comedy, and a very funny one at that. A group of holidaymakers had been forced to spend the night in a haunted hotel after their coach had broken down. There was a lot of slamming of doors and people in various states of undress, although there was nothing indecent. Sarah was fascinated by the timing. They had to be so careful to be in the right place to deliver a line or exit before someone else came on stage. If a line came too quickly, the joke was lost, but if the timing was right, it was hilarious.

When 8.15 p.m. came, Lottie opened the hatch and served the piping hot teas. Sarah stayed in the background as much as possible. After all, it was to be Lottie's job. The actors were a bit over the top in their praise of Lottie, and Sarah had a shrewd idea that they had either waited a long time for someone to fill the post or that Kaye had had a word with them. Whatever the reason, Lottie loved it.

'About time, Bear,' a flamboyant actor named Sebastian called out. 'You must have smelled the tea.'

Sarah's heart skipped a beat as Bear Truman came into the room. He was not as big as she remembered, but he still had a commanding presence. 'Sorry folks,' he said. 'I had to deal with something that couldn't wait.'

'What could be more important than our new play?' said Sebastian.

'What indeed,' said Bear, shaking his hand vigorously. He handed him a sort of mousetrap contraption and a box. 'Here are your props.'

Sebastian fiddled with the mousetrap until it made a loud snapping noise. It looked as if his hand must have been caught in it, but instead of crying out in pain, he laughed and said, 'That's terrific, Bear. Thank you.'

'Careful with the other one,' Bear cautioned as he handed him the box.

Sebastian put his hand inside and when he drew it out, it was covered in fake blood. 'Perfect,' he cried, slapping Bear on the back.

When Bear came to the hatch, he was surprised to see Lottie. 'Hello, what are you doing here?'

'Lottie is our tea lady,' said Sebastian, 'so you'd better be nice to her.' He hurried away and Bear took the cup and saucer Lottie offered him.

'Ah,' said Bear. 'That hits the spot. You're looking very nice tonight, Lottie. What have you done to your hair?'

'Sarah did it for me,' said Lottie. She stepped back so that he could see Sarah at the sink.

'Is there no end to Sarah's talents,' he teased. Sarah kept her back to him. She felt ridiculously self-conscious and she could feel her face heating up. She'd forgotten, or maybe she'd never noticed before, how good-looking and attractive he was. 'Nothing to say, Sarah?'

In another part of the room, Sebastian clapped his hands. 'Right everybody, back to work.'

Wiping her hands on the tea towel, Sarah turned with a smile. 'Are you in this play?'

'No, I just help out with the scenery,' he said.

Sebastian pushed in front of him. 'Excuse me folks, sorry, it's time to crack on,' he said shutting the hatch. Then Sarah heard his muffled voice calling, 'Right, stage places everybody, chop, chop.'

All at once, Bear had hopped into the kitchen and was beside her, putting more teacups into the water. He grabbed a tea towel to help with the drying up and made small talk. Although Sarah replied as normally as possible, he still had her knocking the milk over and dropping teaspoons.

When they were all done by quarter past nine, Bear offered to walk them home. Sarah said, 'Oh we'll be fine, thanks,' but at the same time Lottie said, 'Thank you, that would be very nice.'

Bear beamed. It was a lot colder now. Sarah and Lottie linked arms again. Bear walked on the edge of the pavement next to Lottie but Sarah was ridiculously aware of his presence.

'See you next week,' he said cheerily as they walked into the gate.

Over the next few weeks, Sarah looked forward to Thursday evenings in the Labour Hall, although the weather took a turn for the worse in March when there was some late snow. As the play rehearsals advanced, Bear was more active. Dressed all in black, he moved the scenery quickly and silently between scenes. For such a big man, Sarah was amazed at his agility. The times she loved most were when he walked them home. In the weeks since he'd been doing it, she'd discovered that he'd been brought up in Canada. His mother was English and had gone out there as a governess to some British Embassy children. His father was a Canadian and when he died, she had returned to her roots, bringing her young son with her.

'The boys at school never teased me about my accent,' he joked. 'Even at ten years old, I was head and shoulders above all of them.'

Sarah laughed, wishing with all her heart she had known him back then as well.

The beginning of the week brought the snow. It was late for the time of year. At first it looked pretty, but once it had partially thawed and then snowed again, the roads were treacherous.

'Don't you miss all that lovely sunshine?' Lottie asked one evening as they crunched home in the icy weather.

'Sometimes,' smiled Bear and, looking directly at Sarah, added, 'but some things over here make up for it and they have a lot of snow in Canada.'

'Are you married?' Lottie asked bluntly.

'Lottie…' Sarah scolded in an embarrassed whisper.

Bear roared with laughter. 'No, I'm not married, Lottie.'

'Why not?'

'Perhaps I never met the right girl,' said Bear.

Sarah knew he was still looking at her, so she pushed her head further down into her thick scarf. Thank goodness the darkness hid her crimson face. As they reached the gate, Lottie walked on, but Bear tugged at Sarah's arm. 'You said you were only coming with Lottie for a few weeks.'

'Next week is my last one,' said Sarah, glancing up at Mrs Goodall's window in time to see the curtain drop. 'I only agreed to do it for six weeks, just to get Lottie started.'

'The company are meeting on Highdown on Sunday,' he smiled. 'Would you and the children like to come up with us for a bit of fun in the snow?'

Sarah smiled shyly. 'The girls would love that. If you think the snow will last that long.'

Lottie turned back enthusiastically. 'Can I

come too?'

'Of course you can,' Bear said quickly. 'We can get the bus to Goring and walk from there. I've got a toboggan, so the children won't have to do too much walking.'

'Sounds fun,' said Sarah, her heart already racing.

'Then I'll see you next Sunday,' he said, saluting her with his gloved hand. 'Ten thirty at the bus station.'

It took her ages to get to sleep that night. Every time she closed her eyes, Bear's smiling face swam before her.

Kaye's next-door neighbour, Mrs Goodall, lay in her bed looking up at the ceiling. She wasn't a person of nervous disposition but all these comings and goings next door were making her so. She'd seen yet another person down there tonight. He hadn't stayed long, but he'd seen her watching him as he skulked about in the shrubbery. He'd made a rude sign as he'd gone past her window. He wasn't the only one because there was that other shifty-looking man she'd seen creeping about the garden the other day. She'd seen him a day or so later leaning against the wall of the twitten when she'd gone to post a letter. He tried to pretend he was reading a newspaper, but she didn't like the look of him, and she certainly didn't like the idea of his hanging about. She tut-tutted to herself. Ever since those girls had arrived next door, they had lowered the tone of the place.

Sunday dawned crisp and cold. The snow was

still around, although they hadn't had any more since Friday. The air was clear and bright. Sarah wrapped the children up warmly and they couldn't wait to get started.

Bear rang the doorbell at ten, looking very pleased with himself. 'I've got a car,' he beamed. 'It's a bit of an old banger, but it'll get us up the hill in one go.'

He stepped aside and they all admired the 1930s Morris Ten which stood on the driveway. With Lottie and the children in the back seat, they set off in high spirits.

The theatre group was already on the hill having an impromptu snowball fight when they arrived. Sebastian was getting the worst of it. No one could resist the chance to get some good-natured revenge for all the times he'd shouted at them in rehearsals.

They walked to the top of the hill and joined the other revellers with sledges. Bear had pulled Jenny up the hill on his toboggan, but as he turned it round, he sat behind her with his feet either side of her to go down the hill. Sarah watched as Jenny squealed with delight as they raced away. A little while later, Bear did the same with Lottie, the older woman clearly having the time of her life. Of course, it wasn't long before Lu-Lu was begging for a turn. She seemed to have grown up all of a sudden and had moved from baby to toddler in just a few short months. After trudging up the hill a couple more times with Jenny, Bear suggested that Sarah sit on the toboggan with him, and hold Lu-Lu in front of her. With Bear and his strong arms wrapped around her as he steered the toboggan downhill, Sarah could hardly breathe for the closeness of him. She loved it. The cold winter air rushing by her cheeks was exhilarating, but Lu-Lu wasn't quite so sure about the ride and refused to get back on again once she'd reached the bottom of the hill. Bear seemed disappointed.

'I'll look after the girls if you both want to go,' Lottie offered as they reached the top.

'Race you to the bottom,' shouted Sebastian.

'Come on Sarah,' cried Bear, and before she knew where she was, they were back on the toboggan, flying down the hill. They beat Sebastian and his co-rider by a fag paper and rolled off the sledge onto the snow, laughing. After another trudge back up the hill, someone produced a flask or two of hot tea and they stood around warming their gloved hands on the cups. By four, she, Lottie, Bear and the children were all arriving back at Copper Beeches. It was all over far too quickly, but Sarah had never enjoyed a day so much.

'Thank you for a wonderful day,' she said as he helped her with the children.

'Sarah, you told me once that you were spoken for,' he said just as she was about to close the door. 'Was that true?'

'Not exactly,' said Sarah. She smiled up at him, keenly aware that she was blushing like some silly schoolgirl.

'I should like to ask you out, but a man in the police force has to ask permission to court a girl first.'

Sarah was surprised. 'Really?'

'They would want to check your background,'

he went on. 'It can sometimes take a while. Would it be worth my while asking to court you?'

'You know my past,' she said quietly.

'I know none of this was your fault,' he said.

'It won't harm your career in any way ... going out with the wife of a bigamist?'

'No.'

'Then I'd like that,' she said shyly, and he smiled. But as she closed the door, she worried that it might not be as simple as that.

A small gaggle of people gathered in untidy groups outside the prison gates. It was early on a cold spring morning, the first week in April, exactly six months since Henry Royale began his sentence. Nobody spoke or even acknowledged one another. Embarrassed to be in such a place, each person deliberately ignored the other people waiting in the road by looking in the opposite direction. The door opened bang on eight and the first of the newly released prisoners walked out onto the street. There were five in all and Henry was the last to leave the prison. As the door closed behind him, he stood on the pavement savouring the moment, and as the bolts shot back into place behind him he looked up at the sky. He was free. It was over. What was going to happen next he didn't know, but one thing was for sure, he would never allow himself to set foot in a godawful place like that again. Of the other four prisoners, two were hugging their wife or girlfriend. One lifted a wriggling child with a mass of blonde curls in the air and kissed her on the cheek before leaning down to kiss the woman beside him. The fourth had no one waiting. He turned abruptly and with his hands thrust deeply into his pockets and his bundle tucked under his arm, he hurried away without looking back.

Across the road, a sleek black four-door chauffeur-driven Bentley Saloon waited, its engine purring. Henry smiled as the rear door slowly opened and, saying a polite, 'Good morning, Constable,' to a passing bobby on the beat, he walked across the cobbles and grasped the door handle. The chauffeur hadn't moved and Henry could sense that he was doing his best to appear invisible.

'Morning Matthews,' Henry said cheerfully.

He saw the man's back stiffen. Without turning to look, Matthews touched the peak of his cap. 'Good morning, sir.'

Henry bent his head and looked at the woman on the back seat of the car. 'How nice of you to meet me.' She offered him her gloved hand. Henry grasped her fingers and allowed himself to be pulled inside the car. As he closed the door behind him, he was surrounded by the smell of her heady perfume. The car moved off.

'Ada,' he sighed. 'My guilty little secret.' Smiling, he ran his finger down the side of her wrinkled face, then tilting her head back with his forefinger, he pressed his mouth over her lips.

'Oh Henry,' she sighed as he released her. 'I've missed you so much.'

Twenty-Three

'Mrs Royale?'

Kaye looked up as the nurse called her name. She followed her into the X-ray department where she slipped the hospital dressing gown from her shoulders and stood in front of the machine. Once positioned, the girl, who was wearing a heavy apron, went behind a screen and asked Kaye to take a deep breath and hold it. It was difficult because immediately she felt the need to cough, but eventually the girl was satisfied.

'When will I get the results?'

'In about a week,' said the girl. 'I believe you have an appointment to see Mr Young in Harley Street? Your results will be on his desk when you see him.'

Kaye nodded and went back to the cubicle. She blanked everything out except getting dressed. She'd only come because Doctor Bradley had insisted and because he had actually made the appointment for her. Her breathing was a lot easier now that spring was in the air and with a decent summer, or perhaps a short holiday in the sun, she'd be back to normal in no time. One thing was for sure. She had no time to be ill. Life was too full, too exciting. Fully dressed, Kaye hurried out into the street and hailed a taxi. Once inside, she lit up and relaxed.

Henry was coming out today. She had half

wondered if he would want to meet her, but Dobbin had promised that he wouldn't divulge her address. She didn't suppose that would stop him from finding her though. Henry was tenacious when it came to getting what he wanted.

The taxi dropped her right outside the door of Broadcasting House at the junction of Oxford Street and Regents Park. Kaye looked up at the imposing building made of Portland stone, and with only a careless glance at Eric Gill's massive statue of Shakespeare's Prospero and Ariel above the door, she went inside. Percy Granger, the producer, who met her in the foyer, looked younger than ever, and just as he had been at the Durbridges' party, he was very complimentary about her work. The year before, the BBC had launched what was proving to be a very successful programme called *Mrs Dale's Diary* and as Percy explained, he was eager to capitalise on the idea by producing another long-running series, perhaps with a little more grit.

Once they reached his office, Percy introduced her to Alistair Levin, a BBC lawyer. Twenty minutes later, Kaye walked out of his office with the contract of her dreams. Bursting with excitement, she hurried, already late, for her appointment with Dobbin.

'I can tell you've had a wonderful morning,' he said as he kissed her cheeks.

'I have,' she smiled. 'Life is wonderful and I'm on top of the world.'

'I'm so glad, my dear,' he smiled. 'No one deserves it more than you.'

They were sitting in his office, a rather cluttered and drab little room off the Edgware Road. The noise from the traffic outside was reduced to a dull rumble as they closed the door.

'Have you drawn up the papers?' she asked.

'All I need is your signature, my dear.' He called his secretary and another woman working in the office, to come in while Kaye signed the bottom line and then the two women signed below her signature as witnesses.

When it was done, Kaye flopped into the wide chesterfield chair and sipped the gin and tonic Dobbin handed to her. Yes, everything was looking good. She had agreed to send Percy some ideas involving a fishing family living on the South coast of England, but at the same time, she would work on another mystery story. So long as Sarah stayed to look after Lottie and she knew her aunt was happy, everything would work out fine. She would up Sarah's wages, and should she ever leave Copper Beeches, Kaye had just put everything in place to guarantee Lottie's future, ensuring that she would be well looked after. Henry might huff and puff to get her money, but thanks to what she and Dobbin had just done, it would only be over her dead body.

Detective Constable Harris threw the lean folder across Detective Inspector Bear Truman's desk. 'He's out. Got released first thing this morning.'

Bear looked up. 'Who met him? One of the wives?'

Harris shook his head. 'Better than that,' he smiled. 'He went off in a chauffeur-driven Bentley. The copper couldn't see the back-seat passenger but he was sure it was a woman.'

'Registration number?'

'LLD 732.'

'Gotcha,' smiled Bear.

'What exactly is he up to?' asked Harris. 'You've been digging around ever since he got locked up. I get the feeling you think he's up to no good in a big way.'

'I'm not sure,' said Bear. 'But several things didn't add up when we looked at the bigamy case.'

DC Harris gave him a quizzical look. 'Like what?'

'Like how come an ordinary family man could afford such expensive suits for one thing?' said Bear. 'He didn't have a job when we nicked him and yet his little wife thought he did because the money was still coming in. And if he wasn't working, what was he doing all day?' He rubbed his nose vigorously. 'My nose keeps itching. I'm sure the man is a villain.'

'You think he's got something to do with Mrs Hartley's death, don't you?'

'Mrs Hartley was seeing a younger man,' said Bear. 'According to her son, they fell out because she stopped giving the fellow money. I know she probably took her own life by jumping off the end of the pier, but I have a gut feeling Henry Royale's actions drove her to it. It seems to me that the man might be responsible for the loss of her fortune.'

'But if that's the case,' said Harris. 'What's he done with it?'

'What indeed,' said Bear.

'So what do we do now?' laughed Harris.

'Check out who this car belongs to for a start

and then we'll keep a close eye on Henry Royale. He's bound to trip up before long, you mark my words.'

When Harris had gone, Bear sighed deeply. There were times when the job got in the way and changed everything. He had been planning to ask Sarah out, but until he was able to do something about Henry Royale, he would have to wait. Even though they were in the twentieth century, there were times when the police force was positively Dickensian. As he'd told Sarah, if a serving police officer wanted to go out with a girl, he had to get permission from the Chief Superintendent. That girl had to be vetted and approved. He didn't think for one minute that Sarah had ever put a foot wrong, but now that Henry was out of jail, the powers that be had made it plain that Henry Royale was still a person of interest. The Super had advised him that it wasn't a good idea to start courting a girl who might be involved with somebody who was up to no good. Bear had stood smartly to attention and said 'Yes sir,' but back in his own office, he had thumped his desk with his fist. He really liked her, damn it, but for now his feelings had to stay on hold. Life was bloody unfair sometimes.

Now that her mother was back from Granny's, Annie decided to catch the train to West Worthing station and then walk to Thomas A Becket to see her parents. She had left Edward at home with Sarah and Lottie. She'd had no reaction about the scarf she'd given her father at Christmas, so she guessed he still didn't want to acknowledge his grandson. That being the case, she reasoned that if he saw the pram outside, he probably wouldn't even open the door. In the event, only her mother was in.

They sat at opposite ends of the sofa in the sitting room. Judith was pleased to see her, but she wished her daughter wasn't quite so impulsive. If only she would leave things to settle down. She was sure Malcolm would come around eventually, but she also knew that he would dig his heels in even harder if he thought Annie was trying to manipulate the situation. She was dismayed to hear that the piano lessons hadn't worked out. 'What are you going to do?' she said. 'In view of the way your father feels, I had hoped that if you were doing something respectable for a living he might come around.'

'I'm not unduly worried,' said Annie. 'Henry is out of prison now, and as soon as he has a job, he'll send for me.'

'He's not with you then?' Judith said cautiously. Her daughter shook her head. 'Any idea when he is coming back?'

Annie felt her face colouring. 'I don't know where he is, Mummy. He forgot to send me his forwarding address.' And seeing the look on her mother's face, she added, 'I'm sure he meant to. He promised me he'd be back for Edward and me.'

'Oh Annie, are you sure?'

'Yes, of course I am...' Annie began and then burst into tears. Judith moved to sit beside her daughter and put her arm around her. 'Oh Mummy, I'm so frightened. The other girls think he's a rotter and that he doesn't care about anyone except himself, but I don't want to believe that. Henry is a good man. He explained all about pretending to have a job when he'd been sacked. He was trying to protect me. He was working. He told me he even did the washing up for a hotel kitchen so that we wouldn't starve. I know he's not perfect, but he needs me to look after him.'

Judith handed her daughter a handkerchief. 'I hope you're right, darling, but you have to be sensible.'

'He will come back,' Annie insisted. 'He's always wanted a son, d'you see? If he doesn't come back for me, he'll come back for Edward.'

They heard the front door slam as her father came in. The two women looked anxiously at each other and a moment later the sitting room door creaked open.

Annie jumped to her feet. 'Daddy.'

Malcolm didn't move. Judith held her breath.

'Oh Daddy,' said Annie, flinging her arms around her stiff parent, 'I've missed you so much.'

Still Malcolm hadn't moved an inch. 'Is he back?'

'He's out of prison, if that's what you mean,' said Annie.

'Malcolm dear,' said Judith. 'He hasn't come back for Annie or the baby.'

'Where is the baby?' said Malcolm coldly.

'I left him with a friend,' said Annie. 'Oh Daddy, you'd love him. He's nearly five months old and you've never once come to see him. You don't know what you're missing, Daddy. He's such a sweet little boy.'

Malcolm put up his hand in protest. 'I don't want to hear,' he said stiffly, 'and I think you should leave.'

'Daddy, why are you doing this to me?' her voice already tearful again.

'How many more times must I tell you, Annie?' Malcolm's voice was cold. 'You are not married!'

'But I genuinely thought I was!' she protested. Her face flamed and she felt a rush of adrenalin. 'You seem to forget that *I* am the victim here. What am I supposed to do? I had a wedding day and I have a marriage certificate. I never went to bed with Henry before I was married.' She saw her father open his mouth but she gave him no chance to speak. 'You have no idea how this feels,' she went on, her voice moving up an octave as the anger and frustration rose inside. 'I feel totally humiliated. I feel like I've lost my identity.'

'Oh, don't be so bloody melodramatic,' he scowled.

'I'm not being melodramatic, Daddy.' Annie blew her nose. 'You tell me who I am? Go on, tell me. I'm not Henry's wife. And I'm not a tart and yet you tell me I'm not your daughter because I've had an illegitimate son.'

'I gave you a way out,' Malcolm retorted, 'and you threw it back in my face.'

'Malcolm,' Judith interjected.

'You could have had a good marriage,' said Malcolm. 'What about that Tim whats-his-name? He was nuts about you. Now there's someone who is going places.'

'Malcolm...' said Judith again.

'You can keep out of this and all,' Malcolm

snapped. 'I've worked all my life to give you a respectable life and standing in this town and the pair of you go behind my back and ruin it all.'

'I gave birth to that little boy, Daddy, and I can't give him up,' said Annie. 'I won't have him brought up by strangers either. He's my son, my responsibility.'

'And what about his father's responsibility?' Malcolm demanded. 'Why should it be laid on my doorstep?'

'It won't be,' said Annie. 'All I'm asking is for a little help until Henry comes for me. There's nowhere to go, Daddy. I'm not a widow, so I don't get a widow's pension. The government talk about provision for the children of single mothers, but I can't find any. I can't work because I have no one to look after Edward...'

'I'll look after him,' said Judith. Malcolm and Annie stared at her in amazement. 'You get a job and I'll look after him.'

'I give up,' said Malcolm with a sigh and rolling his eyes. 'Does my opinion count for nothing in this house?'

'Of course it does,' said Judith, 'but she's our daughter. Our child, Malcolm, and she needs help. To hell with respectability when it comes between us all. I'm sorry, but I can't turn my back on her.'

Malcolm glared angrily at them both and left the room, slamming the door behind him.

Annie lowered herself back into the chair and in a wave of relief whispered, 'Oh Mummy... I will try and make it work. I promise. Thank you.'

'Darling, you've not eaten a thing.'

Ada Browning stared at Henry's plate in dismay. They were sitting in her conservatory watching the latest April shower running down the glass. Behind them, Billy, her budgerigar, swayed on his perch and made newly acquired rude noises. Ada still couldn't quite believe that Henry had agreed to come and live with her. 'Think of your reputation,' he'd cautioned when she'd first suggested the idea. But she'd begged and pleaded with him and to her absolute delight he'd finally agreed. He was such an attractive man. She knew she was no spring chicken, but it didn't seem to matter to Henry. He told her time and again that she was beautiful, that he loved her big breasts and her big tummy. He'd told her that he'd never experienced a woman like her before and he didn't seem to notice her wrinkly skin or her flabby arms. Of course, she had tried hard to maintain her youth, but it was a losing battle. Her weight had ballooned with her advancing years and now, no matter how expensive the cream, it did little to keep the wrinkles at bay. She still enjoyed sex, especially with Henry, and he was an energetic lover.

They had met almost a year ago. She had taken some jewellery into a little jeweller's shop in Horsham to be mended and Henry had served her. It only took a brush against his hand for her to feel such a surge of desire that she'd asked him if he would come back to her house and inspect some other pieces. He'd agreed reluctantly and furtively, telling her under his breath that if the manager found out, he'd be for the high jump.

That's what she'd liked about him. He was so sweet – willing to go out of his way, even if it caused difficulties for him.

The first time he'd come, he'd looked at some pieces, drunk some whisky and that was all. He didn't seem to understand what she really wanted, but then Ada was fully aware that he was a bit of an innocent. The second time he came, she'd taken the initiative, leading him to her bedroom, and before long, they were making passionate love. Afterwards, he'd apologised profusely as if it was all his fault, and begged her not to say anything because he'd get the sack. She didn't see him for a week, and when she spotted him near one of her regular walks with the dog, she discovered that he was indeed out of a job. He was desolate and she was very consoling. Instead of going into work, he'd come to the house and they'd made love almost every day. He wasn't married to the girl he was living with, he'd told her that, but it came as a shock to her when Henry had ended up in prison for bigamy.

She hurried to his side and put her heavily bejewelled hand onto his shoulder. Henry lowered his head and rubbed his forehead wearily. 'I'm sorry,' he said. 'I'm afraid I've completely lost my appetite. I'm so worried about my son. I can't think of anything else.'

'It may not be as bad as you think, darling.'

'What time did you say Nelson will be here?'

'At ten,' she said. She slid onto his lap, and when she put her arms around his neck, he looked up and kissed her. His hand went to the fold of her dressing gown and sought her breast. He toyed with her nipple and already her heartbeat had quickened. She was nudging sixty-two, but she felt like a silly schoolgirl. She was drunk ... that's what it was. She was drunk on Henry Royale.

'You are so good to me,' he murmured. 'If you hadn't paid for this private detective, I couldn't have done it.' He looked up at her forlornly. 'What can I do to repay you?'

'You don't have to repay me, my darling,' she cooed. 'I'd do anything for you, you know that.'

He laid his head on her chest and she felt him shudder with emotion.

'Er-um,' Matthews stood in the doorway clearing his throat. 'Mr Nelson is here, madam.'

She rearranged her gown and got shakily to her feet. 'Show him in, Matthews,' and with as dignified an air as she could manage, she went back to her seat. Henry grinned and blew her a kiss.

Dennis Nelson, private detective, was a weaselly-looking man with a constant dewdrop on the end of his nose. Thankfully it never fell – he either sniffed it back or rubbed it with his handkerchief – but she was wary of accepting a handshake. Quite frankly, he revolted Ada, but she deemed him a necessary evil if she was to get this business sorted out.

'I have kept a weather eye on the young lady in question,' said Nelson, consulting a grubby-looking notebook, 'and I can report that she has left the child on several occasions.' He went on to list several days when Annie had been shopping or to the library, but Henry was most interested to hear that she had gone to the dance at the Assembly Rooms. In fact, he was visibly shocked.

'She went dancing?'

'Presumably she left the baby with somebody?' said Ada.

'That's not the point, Ada,' Henry snapped. 'The mother of my child should not be cavorting about in the dance hall, especially not the dance halls of Worthing.'

'No, no, of course not, my dear,' Ada agreed hastily.

'What about her morals?' said Henry high-handedly. 'Have you seen her in the company of men?'

'Afraid not, sir,' said Nelson. He was quite aware that Henry wanted to dish the dirt on his wife if possible and it frustrated him no end that he hadn't been able to find any ... so far. 'I've seen two of the other ladies in the company of a man, but not your wife.'

'If they are entertaining men in that house,' Henry snapped, 'who knows what my son is being exposed to?'

'I shall step up my vigilance,' said Nelson, 'and I am sure we shall find out what the young lady is up to.'

Ada wrote another cheque and the man hurried on his way. Henry was desolate. 'What am I to do, Ada? I am stuck here all day. I have no money, no transport. I can't get to Worthing to see my son and I can only imagine the horrors of the place he's living in. Oh Ada, my heart is broken ... broken.'

She was at his side in an instant. 'That settles it. I'm going to give you your own bank account.'

Henry looked up at her with tears in his eyes.

'No, no, I can't allow you to do such a thing.'
'Henry,' she said firmly. 'I insist. Now let's hear no more about it. As soon as I get dressed, we'll go to the bank and set it up.'
'Oh Ada, my darling,' he whispered. 'You're wonderful.'
'After we've been to the bank,' she continued, 'we'll take a walk around to Motors of Mayfair and get a car... No, no,' she put her hand up in protest, 'I won't hear another word. You need a car to get to Worthing and you shall have one.'
'Oh Ada,' said Henry, slipping his hand under her dressing gown and drawing her onto his lap again. 'Perhaps you could get dressed a bit later on, my love. There's something I'd like to show you first.'
Ada's eyes glistened with excited anticipation. 'Oh Henry...' she sighed.

Twenty-Four

'Mummy, William Steel hit me.' Jenny was sitting up in bed with wide eyes and in telltale mood.
Sarah was getting ready to read her a story before tucking her up for the night. 'Was he the boy who wanted to speak to you in the playground yesterday? Why did he do that?'
Jenny shrugged. When William had come over to her, she had run off.
'There must have been something,' Sarah insisted.

'No, Mummy.'
'Did you do something to annoy him?'
'I told him I didn't want to do country dancing with him,' Jenny admitted.
'Why ever not?'
'Connie Jackson says nobody wants to dance with him because he smells.'
'Well, Connie shouldn't say things like that,' said Sarah. 'And you shouldn't be unkind to a person just because someone else doesn't like them.'
Jenny lowered her eyes.
'It was wrong of William to hit you,' said Sarah, 'but perhaps you really upset him.'
Jenny nodded. 'Sorry, Mummy.'
Sarah hugged her daughter. 'If William hits you again, tell Mrs Audus, but I want you to promise me that you won't join in when people say nasty things about him, okay?'
Jenny nodded miserably.

It didn't take long to set up an account in Henry's name, and although the bank manager seemed a little surprised at the amount she put into it, knowing how frugal she had always been up until her husband's death, he did exactly as Ada had asked.
Motors of Mayfair were delighted to see Mrs Browning again so soon. It wasn't long since she'd bought her Bentley, and although they'd let it go at a knock-down £3,500, it wasn't every day that their clients spent so freely. Mr Slade was assigned to her, and Henry took an immediate dislike to the fellow. Slick in his pale grey suit, Mr Slade was far

too smarmy for Henry's liking. They wandered along the rows of cars mostly waiting to be exported abroad. Henry asked what he thought were pertinent questions, but it seemed that although he answered politely, Mr Slade couldn't hide his disapproval of Henry.

'So do you think this one is the car I should choose?' Henry asked.

'I'm sure that's up to you, sir,' Mr Slade said snootily. 'I really cannot say.'

It took some time, but eventually Henry settled for a delightful Riley Drophead Coupe in a glossy evergreen. It had been made for the North American market and was therefore a left-hand drive. It was a two door car and best of all, it was a convertible. Mr Slade held his head on one side and said apologetically, 'I'm afraid that one is £1,200, madam.'

To his delight Ada didn't even blink.

Henry ran his fingers across the pale leather seats and laughed. 'My goodness, it's a beautiful car but I don't think we should spend that much do you, darling?'

Twenty minutes later, the car was his.

He drove her out of town and she loved every minute with the wind in her hair and a handsome man by her side. They stopped in nearby Richmond Park for tea and on the way back into London they had a meal in Fleet Street.

'I've had such a wonderful day, darling,' Ada sighed when they reached her flat in Mayfair.

'So have I,' said Henry.

There were three letters waiting for him. He'd had to inform the authorities where he would be and so they had forwarded them. He was still getting letters from Annie, but quite frankly she bored him so he hadn't bothered to read any of them for ages. He had obviously left one behind in his cell and the prison authorities had re-addressed it. While Ada went upstairs to get ready for bed, Henry helped himself to a malt whisky and ripped the first letter open. It was from Dobbin, Kaye's solicitor.

My client, Mrs Kaye Royale, was somewhat disappointed that you thought it necessary to rip up the documents sent from this office. She had instructed me to inform you that she will be suing you for divorce on the grounds of serial adultery. You will be hearing from us in due course.

In the meantime, I must insist that you do not harass my client or attempt to contact her in any way.

Henry swore as he screwed the paper up and lobbed it into the wastepaper basket. Damn the man. Did the interfering old goat really think he could tell him what to do? He threw himself sulkily into a chair. The second letter was from Annie.

I can't wait to see you again and I've been telling Edward all about his wonderful daddy. I can't wait to move out of this house. Have you found a place of our own yet, darling?

The silly spoiled bitch had no idea. Where did she think he was going to conjure up digs for them with a small baby? Henry's eyes narrowed and a slow smile moved across his mouth. What did he care about her opinion? All that mattered now was getting hold of Kaye's money and his son. The rest of them could go to hell. The third letter was from an estate agent. He read it quickly.

Everything was going to plan. Henry smiled then downed his drink, enjoying the burning sensation as it slid down his throat. In the bedroom Ada was sitting up in eager anticipation.

'I must leave you tomorrow.'

She panicked. 'Oh Henry, why?'

'I have to see my wife's solicitor.'

'But darling,' said Ada, 'if he's your *wife's* solicitor, he won't see you.'

Henry sat dejectedly on the edge of the bed. 'Don't you see, Ada, I have to try,' he said brokenly. 'Dobbin is more than just a solicitor. He's an old friend, and besides, he's retired now. I have to make him see my side of the story and then I can get my son back.'

Ada gathered him in her arms and he wept on her shoulder. 'Oh my poor darling,' she whispered onto the top of his head.

'All I want is to see my son,' he said, his voice muffled by her frilly nightdress.

'Of course you do,' Ada soothed. 'We'll get onto *my* solicitor tomorrow.'

He lifted his head and, cupping her face in his hands, breathed on her lips as he brushed them against his. 'What would I do without you, my darling?' Seconds later she was putty in his hands once again.

In the event, it didn't take Annie long to find a job. She decided to begin with the small shops nearer home, cold-calling and asking if they had any vacancies. In the early afternoon she went into a tobacconist and sweet shop in Steyne Gardens and asked if there might be a possibility of a position as a counter assistant.

'There might be,' said the man behind the counter, who had introduced himself as Mr Richardson, the shop's owner. 'Next week it's the end of sweet rationing and they're saying that there will be a high demand. It'll be hard work and I'm looking for a capable girl with good references.'

'I am both of those things,' said Annie, exuding a confidence she didn't really have. Kaye would give her a reference, she was sure, and she'd made up her mind to prove her worth. She had to if she was to keep Edward.

Mr Richardson, a wiry man with a bald head and glasses, looked her up and down. 'Very well Miss... Miss...?'

'Mrs Royal,' said Annie.

'Mrs,' Mr Richardson frowned. 'Do you have children?'

'I have a son, but my mother takes care of him.'

'I see,' said Mr Richardson, and from the change in the tone of his voice, he was clearly thinking that Annie must be a war widow. 'In that case, my dear, I should be pleased to offer you a trial run.'

Annie could have kissed him, but she restrained herself and agreed to start first thing the next morning. It only took her about twelve minutes to walk from home, so she'd be able to come back to Copper Beeches for lunch, which meant she wouldn't have to spend a whole day without seeing Edward.

'That was quick,' said Sarah when she told her. 'Congratulations.'

'I have to work from 8.45 a.m. till 5.45 p.m. Monday to Saturday with a half-day off on Wednesday,' said Annie.

'Sounds reasonable enough,' said Sarah.

'My wage will be £2/18/- for the first month rising to £3/1/6,' Annie went on. 'That's if I'm deemed to be suitable for the job.'

'Let's hope you like it then,' Sarah smiled.

'Oh, I'm determined to,' said Annie, sweeping her son up in her arms. 'I have to, for Edward's sake.'

The morning of Annie's first day in the shop, it began to rain. Sarah grabbed the basket and ran outside to collect the washing. April showers were seldom heavy and soon passed but she was anxious to get the baby's washing inside. Annie didn't have many things, and now that Edward was becoming more active, it was harder to keep him clean. His grandmother had arrived early that morning to look after him and taken him away in the pram. Sarah had no idea where she was going, but she supposed it was somewhere to show him off to her friends. She obviously adored the little boy.

Sarah pulled the washing carelessly away from the line, not bothering to fold them neatly as they went into the basket. She glanced up and saw that Mrs Goodall was watching her from the bedroom window. Didn't the woman have anything better to do with her life than constantly keeping an eye on what was happening next door? Since Kaye sent her packing that time, she'd stopped coming round to complain, but her disapproving glares were a constant. The soft, warm rain trickled into Sarah's eyes as she looked up at the washing and already her shoulders were damp, but when she reached the end of the line and the last item, Sarah froze. Her apron had been slashed. She held the pieces and stared in disbelief. It had been cut with something very sharp. There were no frayed edges or jagged tears. Whatever had been used to cut the apron had sliced through the material like a knife through butter.

Her heart began to pound. She spun around anxiously, but although she had the feeling she was being watched, Mrs Goodall was gone and she was quite alone in the garden. Snatching the apron down and rolling it into a ball, she hurried to the house. What could this mean? It had to be Henry's doing – after all, he'd been out of prison for almost ten days, even though he hadn't put in an appearance. But why was he doing this? Did he think she had been the one who had brought the police to his house the night he was arrested? He'd been very angry when he'd seen her in Annie's kitchen and she couldn't forget the rough way he had manhandled her and the children through the back door, but cutting up washing somehow didn't seem his style. True, he had lost his temper that night, but normally he was very controlled. He had never seemed a vengeful man either. Henry did things for the moment and when he'd got what he'd wanted, he moved on. Perhaps prison life had changed him more than most.

'Are you all right?' Lottie cut across her thoughts and she realised she was still standing by the back door with the basket of washing on her hip.

'Yes,' said Sarah, 'but the washing is back to

square one.'

'I'll get the clothes horse,' Lottie smiled.

While she was gone, Sarah threw the cut up apron into the ragbag. No point in worrying anyone else. Together, they put everything onto the clothes horse and by then the rain had stopped.

'We'd better not chance it again,' said Lottie. 'I'll put it in the lean-to.'

Sarah watched her go. Dear Lottie. She was much more confident and even beginning to take the initiative now and then. She wished she could confide in her, but that was probably a step too far just yet. Sarah chewed her bottom lip anxiously. What should she do about Henry? If only she had someone to talk to.

Henry slid along the bench and looked towards the counter. 'Two teas, love.'

The woman behind the huge British Rail teapot reached for two chipped cups and set them on the counter. 'This ain't a bleedin' waitress service.'

Outside on the concourse, they could hear a train working up steam and the announcer telling everyone that the train just about to leave Platform 8 was heading for Basingstoke. 'Well?' he said, looking at Dennis Nelson.

Nelson shook his head. 'I've been watching that house morning, noon and night, but she hasn't put a foot wrong.'

'That'll be fourpence,' said the woman.

Henry stood up and collected the teas, leaving the right money on the counter. He plonked them down on the table, slopping a little in the saucers as he did so. 'Is she still going to dances?'

'No, sir,' said Nelson, pulling the cup towards him.

'What about men?' said Henry irritably.

'I tell you, sir, that girl is as pure as the driven snow. In my opinion…'

'Nobody asked you for your opinion,' Henry snapped. He was in no mood to hear what a good woman Annie was. His future lay with Ada and her fortune right now, but he didn't want to leave the country without his son. A man carrying a large suitcase bumped Henry's arm and apologised as he walked by. Henry didn't even seem to notice. 'So what does she do all day?'

'Since I last saw you at Mrs Browning's place,' Nelson went on, 'she's got herself a job.'

'Got a job?' said Henry, spitting feathers. 'I'm not having any wife of mine going out to work. What sort of job?'

'She works in a sweet shop.'

'What about my son? Who's taking care of him?'

'Cllr Mitchell's wife,' said Nelson, spooning two sugars into his tea. 'I believe she's the young lady's mother.'

Henry's face darkened. 'I'm perfectly well aware of who she is,' he snapped. So she was back in cahoots with her mother. Damn and blast it. He sipped his tea. It was strong enough to strip varnish.

'Did my wife see you watching her?'

'I'm pretty sure none of them realise they've been watched. I am very discreet.'

'You sure?' Henry demanded. 'Because she's bound to be on her best behaviour if she thinks she's being watched.'

'With my raincoat on, nobody in that street has ever noticed me,' said Nelson. 'I will admit the old biddy who lives next door spotted me a couple of times, but there's no love lost between them so you've no need to worry on that score.'

'It doesn't matter,' said Henry. 'When I've finished with her, everybody in town will know what sort of a woman she is.' There was no disguising the look of triumph on his face. Nelson must have looked puzzled because Henry leaned back and took his wallet from his back pocket. He laid three photographs onto the oilcloth between them, then turned them around for Nelson to see. 'Good, aren't they?'

Nelson picked one up and looked at it more closely. Now he could see that the woman in the photograph wasn't Annie Royal but a clever look-alike.

'That's enough,' said Henry, snatching it back. 'My old mother used to say if you look at things like that, you'll go daft in the head.'

'But...' Nelson began.

'Once I send these around Worthing, no one will think she's a fit mother,' said Henry. He laughed maliciously. 'And Daddy can kiss being the next mayor goodbye.'

Nelson felt his stomach churn. His mind was working overtime but he had to keep everything businesslike.

Henry put the photographs back into his wallet. 'Now tell me about the others.'

'As I already explained, it appears that Mrs Sarah is housekeeper to the older Mrs Royale,' said Nelson. 'She's something big with the BBC, so the local gossips tell me. She's up in town again next week.'

'Where's she staying?'

'That I can't say for sure,' said Nelson.

Henry ground his teeth angrily. 'You're not a lot of use then, are you,' he said bitterly. It was important that he get all the loose ends tied up before his next move.

'But the local butcher reckons she likes to stay at the Langham,' said Nelson. He was beginning to feel very uncomfortable. The man seemed to be conducting some sort of vendetta. His mind was in a whirl. He didn't like the tone of Royale's voice and what he was going to do with those pictures. That young woman didn't deserve this. Nelson was well acquainted with the nastier side of life, but Henry Royale had stooped to a new low.

'How the devil would the butcher know?' Henry demanded.

Dennis Nelson thumbed his nose. 'Her housekeeper mentioned it when she cancelled an order.'

Henry grunted.

'Shall I continue my observations?' Nelson said pleasantly. Perhaps while he was down there, he could take the opportunity to have a word with Mrs Royal.

Henry reached for his wallet and pulled out two pounds. 'That should be enough to cover what you've done since we last met.'

'Two quid?' spluttered Nelson. 'Now hang on a minute...'

Henry rose to his feet. 'I shan't be needing you again.'

'But what about my expenses,' Nelson protested. 'A return trip to Worthing, five nights' bed and board, and then there's…'

'That's all you're getting from me,' said Henry, swiping the back of his coat with his glove as he stood up. 'I paid you to find out what she was up to and all you've come back with is the life and times of Snow bloody White.'

'I can't manufacture sin,' Nelson protested. 'I run a respectable agency. Besides, you didn't employ me. Let's see what Mrs Browning thinks.'

Henry pushed his face up close to Nelson. 'You keep away from Mrs Browning. Or else…'

Dennis Nelson's eyes grew wide. 'Are you threatening me, Mr Royale?'

'I don't know,' said Henry. 'You're the detective. You work it out.' With that, he swept out of the tea rooms, leaving Nelson with an uneasy feeling that all three of those women were in real danger.

Annie spent her first week in the shop preparing for the big event. Sweets had been rationed since July 1942 and the allowance had remained at 3 oz a week, although at the height of the war it did drop to 2 oz a week. All that was to end on Monday. There was great excitement at the thought of unlimited sweets and hordes of children gathered outside the shop to choose what they would buy once the shop opened. The first thing Mr Richardson asked Annie to do was make a poster.

To celebrate the end of rationing The Sweetbox will give away 250 bags of sweets to the first 250 children under the age of 14 years. Monday, 25th April at 9 a.m.

It took her most of the morning but she quite enjoyed doing it. The shop had a steady stream of customers who bought cigarettes, tobacco and the occasional pipe, but few people were buying sweets. Everyone was waiting for Monday. Whenever they had a spare five minutes she made up the giveaway bags. They were more like twists with a few sweets inside, but, nonetheless, to a child who was only used to a few sweets a week, they would seem like gold dust. The business kept Annie's mind away from the fact that Henry still hadn't been in touch, and as they worked together, she and Mr Richardson were settled in each other's company.

Kaye wasn't feeling too good again. Her chest was tight and even though she craved a cigarette, she often found it hard to draw on it. Her cough was troublesome too and Sarah would tut crossly whenever she emptied the ashtray, but she still hadn't told anyone about her X-ray examination. Thank God she had another appointment to see her Harley Street specialist on Tuesday.

With Kaye away in London, Sarah decided to go and see Vera. She hadn't seen her sister since that night in December when she'd refused to help her. Sarah had mixed feelings; one part of her said good riddance, but another part of her kept saying whatever she's done, she's still your sister ... blood is thicker than water. After the way Vera had treated her, Sarah had at first vowed never to speak to her again, but as time went on, she couldn't stop thinking about her. The day her mother died, they had both promised her that they would look after each other, and as angry as she was with Vera, Sarah took that promise very seriously. Since Jenny had moved to her new school and Vera didn't know where she was living, there was little chance of them bumping into each other, so it was up to her to make the first move.

Jenny was off on a school trip to Lancing where they were going on a nature walk. The children were very excited and it had been agreed that the whole class would take a short bus ride to the seafront and then walk back. Sarah hadn't been asked to be a helper, but Mrs Audus was grateful when she saw her at the bus stop. They got the children aboard without incident. As the journey progressed, some of the children had to give up their seats and stand in the aisle to let fare-paying adults sit down. Sarah got off the bus before the rest of the class and Lu-Lu waved a cheery goodbye to her big sister.

Vera was kneeling, planting a few things in the front garden when they arrived. She jumped to her feet when she saw Sarah and Lu-Lu.

'Where the devil have you been?' she cried crossly. 'I've been worried sick about you.'

Sarah kissed her proffered cheek and Vera looked down at Lu-Lu. 'My, you have grown, haven't you? Come and give your auntie a kiss.'

But Lu-Lu was reluctant and hid behind her mother's skirt.

'I suppose you want a cup of tea,' said Vera grudgingly as she wiped her hands down the sides of her apron. 'Take off your shoes before you come in.'

She led the way into the house, complaining, 'When you didn't even bother to send a Christmas card I went round to your place,' she said wrinkling her nose, 'but it was all boarded up. Even that Mrs Rivers had gone. It proper upset me, I can tell you. I thought I'd never see any of you again. My nerves were so bad I was under the doctor for weeks.'

Sarah found herself apologising.

As usual, Vera's place was immaculate. It was like a show house. Everything in her spotless kitchen matched or blended. The walls were canary yellow and she had yellow gingham curtains. The kitchen chairs had matching cushions and there was absolutely nothing on the work surfaces.

'Sit still, Lu-Lu,' Vera said pulling out a chair, then looking at Sarah she said, 'does she need to go to the toilet?'

Inwardly, Sarah sighed. This was going to be a trying visit.

Although the doctor's office was plush, it bordered on the old-fashioned. Furnished with heavy, dark furniture, there was little light coming through windows which were badly in need of a window cleaner. Kaye perched herself slightly sideways and was almost swallowed up by the leather seat in the waiting area. She flicked an imaginary piece of fluff from her grey pencil skirt.

'Mr Young will only be a minute,' the receptionist told her. She was a plain-looking woman with a severe bun and round-rimmed glasses. 'Can I get you anything?'

Kaye shook her head and at the same moment

Mr Young opened the door to his office and came out with a middle-aged man. 'Book another appointment,' he smiled, 'and I'll see you in a month.'

The two men shook hands and the doctor went back into his office. Kaye watched the patient make his appointment, and as he turned to leave, the man raised his hat to her. 'Top rate man,' he smiled encouragingly.

Kaye nodded and relaxed.

As the street door closed, the doctor came out to fetch her. He shook hands and steered her towards the office but not before he'd mouthed something to the receptionist. The room was panelled and clearly from a bygone age. The windows were small and there was a couch against one wall. Kaye sat on a more formal chair on one side of his desk while Mr Young went around the other side.

'Your results are all back now, Mrs Royale,' he began. 'How are you feeling?'

'A bit breathless at times,' Kaye admitted. She took off her gloves and unbuttoned her jacket. 'I do get rather tired. I'm hoping you might prescribe a tonic.' She smiled encouragingly but the doctor's face remained serious.

'I'm afraid I have some rather bad news,' he said, coming around the desk again. He perched on the corner and reached for her hand. 'Mrs Royale ... Kaye ... my dear, the results are not good.'

'You mean I'm going to need an operation?' Kaye was already focussing her mind on a possible delay of her deadline. It would be a bit inconvenient but not insurmountable.

'Kaye, I'm afraid you have lung cancer. It's

pretty advanced and there's not a lot we can do.' Mr Young paused to let her digest what he had just said.

She searched his face desperately. 'A friend of mine said she had radiotherapy,' she began.

'It's far too late for that, my dear,' said Mr Young. 'In fact, I'm afraid I can't offer you any treatment.'

She became aware that he was still holding her hand and snatched it back. There was a soft knock on the door and the receptionist came in with a tea tray. Kaye fiddled with her gloves. Mr Young waited until his receptionist had gone and then poured his patient a cup. He put in two large spoons of sugar and, opening his desk drawer, took out a small silver flask. 'You've just had one hell of a shock,' he said, 'but one thing I can promise you. When the time comes, we will make you as comfortable as possible.'

Her brain refused to function. She felt as if she was watching a film or a play on stage. It didn't seem real. When the time came? She watched him lace the tea with brandy, or perhaps it was whisky, and took the cup. Her hand trembled slightly and her chest was tight. She could feel tears pricking the backs of her eyes. 'How long?' she whispered. 'How long have I got?'

He looked her straight in the eye. 'Three to six months.'

Kaye gulped the tea. Six months, was that all? But she'd only just got her success. All those years struggling to be independent and recognised and all she'd got was six months. It wasn't fair. It wasn't real. This was a horrible dream and she'd

wake up in a minute. 'Are you sure?'
Mr Young nodded. 'I'm sorry, my dear.'
Kaye rose unsteadily to her feet.
'It's a pity you didn't bring someone with you,' Mr Young was saying, 'but if you would like to take a seat in the waiting room, I've arranged for a nurse to escort you home.' They'd reached the big leather chair again. 'My receptionist has telephoned her and she will be here shortly.'
Kaye wasn't really listening. 'I'm sorry... Who will be here?'
'The nurse who will take you home,' said Mr Young.
'But I live in Worthing.'
'Fine,' said the doctor. 'She will go with you all the way.'
'I'm not going back until tomorrow.' She felt irritated. She didn't want this silly conversation. She didn't want a nurse either.
'She'll do whatever you want.' He patted Kaye's shoulder. 'I'm so sorry, my dear.'
She was suddenly filled with anger. She wanted to smack his patronising, condescending face and was glad when he left her settled in the waiting area. Her half-drunk cup of tea was placed on the low table beside her, and when she looked up, Mr Young was already showing his next patient into his office. The receptionist went back to her typing, and when she turned to the filing cabinet for something, Kaye slipped out onto the street.

Twenty-Five

'What have you done to your hair?'

Sarah and Jenny were in the kitchen where Jenny was helping her mother to lay the table. Sarah moved some books from the table so that they could put on the tablecloth. She'd been curious about the silver salver she polished every week, so she'd been looking at some old books about antiques. She found them fascinating and even identified the painting of a springer spaniel in the hallway as a William Albert Clark. She hadn't realised before but quite a lot of Kaye's things were very valuable.

She and Jenny had been talking about the school trip. The children had been along the shoreline collecting things for the classroom nature table and then they had sat on the green near the war-time shelters to eat their lunch. Jenny had talked excitedly about the different seaweeds she had found and she and her mother had hung a piece she'd brought home with her outside the back door.

'Mrs Audus says it will tell us what the weather will be like,' Jenny said.

'I'm sure it will,' Sarah agreed. 'If it's wet, it's raining, and if it's all dried up, it'll be sunny.'

Jenny had looked at her mother with a puzzled expression before they both laughed out loud. 'Oh, Mummy...'

Jenny had turned her head and that's when Sarah noticed her pigtails. 'Oh Jenny!' Sarah cried. 'You've cut one of your plaits right off.'

'I didn't, Mummy.'

'Don't lie to me, Jenny,' said Sarah. 'You know I don't like it when you tell porky-pies. I can see that you have and it's very naughty.'

'But I didn't,' Jenny protested.

'Then who did?' Sarah challenged.

Jenny shrugged her shoulders.

'So why did you do it?'

Her daughter stared miserably at the floor. 'I didn't.'

'Go to your room.'

Her voice was sharp and Jenny burst into tears. She ran from the room, her thundering footsteps crashing up to her bedroom as she continued to protest her innocence. 'I didn't do it. I didn't, I didn't.'

Sarah lowered herself onto a chair. It had been a long and trying day. Her visit with Vera had been unbearable; in fact, she hadn't even once asked Sarah how she was.

The evening paper was in front of her. Usually Kaye kept it until the next morning, reading every inch of it, but today Kaye was in London and staying overnight. Sarah pulled the paper towards her and thumbed idly through the pages until she came to the accommodation section. There were some houses available, but the rents were more than her wage. The flats were a tad better, but she would still struggle to feed and clothe the children on what Kaye paid her. When she first came to Copper Beeches, she had been angry, resentful and upset. Over the months she had found happiness again, but it was becoming a constant fear that with Lottie capable enough to look after the running of the house, Kaye would no longer have a need for her. In case the worse came to the worst, Sarah felt she had to have a plan for her future. She had almost saved enough money to pay the deposit on a place, but she would have to have a better-paid job to cover a higher rent. She glanced down the situations vacant column. Housekeeper, chambermaid, secretary in a dairy, counter assistant and telephonist ... they all sounded tempting, but she had two little girls to look after as well. What if one of them was ill? Who would take care of them?

The door opened and Lottie came into the room with Lu-Lu.

'We've had a lovely bath,' said Lottie. Lu-Lu looked tired and sleepy as Lottie strapped her into her highchair. 'What's up with Jenny?'

'She's cut her hair,' said Sarah crossly, 'and now she's only got one plait.'

'Oh dear,' Lottie grinned. 'I remember doing something like that when I was a child. I took a huge lump out of my fringe and even though my mother caught me with the scissors still in my hand and the hair in my lap, I denied it.'

Sarah felt herself soften. Lottie was right, and thinking about it, she'd done something similar herself when she was about Jenny's age. It was a shame the plait was gone, but perhaps it was an opportunity to give Jenny a new hairstyle. She'd give her a few more minutes alone in her room and then call her downstairs and give her a trim after their meal.

Lottie finished laying the table. As Sarah dished up the meal, she reflected on how much Lottie had changed. The timid mouse too frightened to say anything had gone. Now that she felt safe and secure, Lottie was proving herself to be an intelligent woman with opinions of her own. True, she still leaned on Sarah quite a bit, but she was no longer downtrodden and scared. She had gained her confidence and she was trustworthy. As Lottie tousled Lu-Lu's hair to keep her awake, she could see that the pair of them truly loved each other. How tragic that Lottie had been in her late forties before Kaye came along. There must be other people just like her out there who only needed a helping hand to be able to live productive lives. Kaye had done a remarkable thing by bringing Lottie into the house, but she'd only been able to do it because she had the money.

Thinking of money gave Sarah an idea. She enjoyed bookkeeping, and although his new wife Nancy now did his books, the two businesses Peter Millward had put her way wanted to retain her services. If she could manage to take on a few more local businesses and save the money, she could put it towards a new career. How much money would it take to become an expert on antiques, she wondered?

The post was late this morning. Usually it was on the mat at seven thirty sharp, but Sarah didn't pick it up until gone ten. She'd been cleaning the bathrooms and now it was time for a break. Annie had gone to work and her mother had taken Edward out. Jenny was at school and Lu-Lu was playing with a little friend for the morning. Lottie was in the kitchen cleaning Kaye's gloves. She'd found an old newspaper in the bottom of a drawer and read in it that using stale bread was an excellent way of cleaning kid gloves. They had been pondering what to do with the gloves because they knew that they would shrink if washed in water, and yet they were so dirty inside that if something wasn't done soon, they would have to be thrown out. That would have been a pity. Kaye absolutely loved them. As soon as she saw the newspaper cutting, Lottie was a woman on a mission.

Sarah made the tea and got out some shortbread fingers.

'It's working,' said Lottie, showing her one of the gloves.

'Well done you,' Sarah smiled.

Most of the letters were for Kaye of course, but surprisingly Sarah had one today too. It was a bit bulky, although whatever was inside was soft. As she opened it, she cried out in shocked surprise as she saw what was inside.

'What is it?' cried Lottie.

'Nothing, it's nothing,' said Sarah, stuffing the envelope into her apron pocket.

'But it is,' Lottie insisted. 'You've gone as white as a sheet.'

Sarah looked away. Lottie stood up and went to her. 'What is it, Sarah? Show me. I'm not a child. You can trust me.'

Sarah put the envelope onto the table and Lottie's hand flew to the side of her face as she gasped. 'But that's Jenny's plait. How did it get there? Who sent it?'

'It must have been Henry.'

'But why? Was there a note? Why would he do that?'

'Because he thinks I told the police about him and that's why he ended up in jail.' Sarah was trying to stay calm, but her hands were trembling as she tried to pour the tea.

'You must go to the police,' said Lottie. She put her arm around Sarah's shoulders. 'Do it now.'

'What good will it do?' said Sarah. 'He hasn't even written on the envelope, so how can I prove it was him?'

'Go and talk to Bear,' said Lottie. She glanced at the clock. 'You took Lu-Lu over to little Alfie's place to play this morning, didn't you?'

Sarah nodded dully. 'I've got to fetch her at eleven forty-five.'

'I'll pick her up,' said Lottie. 'You don't have to be back here until it's time to pick Jenny up from school. Go, go.'

Sarah flung her arms around Lottie and they hugged each other.

'Go,' said Lottie again.

Putting the envelope and Jenny's hair into her shopping bag, Sarah hurried out of the house. A moment or two she was back again rummaging in the ragbag until she found the slashed apron. Her heart was thumping and her mind was in a whirl. As soon as she was out of the gate, she began to run. Supposing Henry was watching the house, suppose he could see her now? The street was empty apart from a passing cat. And when she got to the police station, what would she do if Bear wasn't there? She didn't really want to explain everything to somebody else. Think, she told her panicking brain, think...

'Kaye?'

As soon as she heard his voice, Kaye froze. She had been stumbling along the street in a sort of a daze. Her jacket was still undone and she had a thumping headache. Even though the hotel was in a quiet mews, she'd slept badly.

'Kaye, darling...' As she heard his voice, her stomach tightened and her heartbeat quickened. His footfall was right behind her. 'Kaye, is it really you? Oh darling, I'm so pleased to see you.'

She turned slowly. This was the first time she'd been this close to Henry in years. In the courtroom, although he seemed to fill the room, there was a fair amount of space between the witness box and the dock. Now he was only an arm's length away from her. He was smiling and he looked very dapper in a beautifully cut, expensive suit, with his hair slicked down and the flash of a large gold ring on his finger. He was carrying a slim black case.

'You look wonderful,' he said, taking her hands in his. 'This is such a marvellous coincidence.'

She snatched her hands back. 'What are you doing here, Henry?' Her voice was cold.

'Looking for you, darling,' he said smoothly. 'I bumped into your producer at the BBC. He told me you were in town and I guessed you might be staying close by.'

She frowned crossly. 'What were you doing

there? Are you checking up on me or something? Leave me alone, Henry.'

'My only concern is that you are all right,' he smiled. 'Percy Granger said some lovely things about you.'

Was it only a day since she'd seen Percy? Only one day since that wonderful contract and then that terrible news in the doctor's office. After what Mr Young had told her, she'd stumbled out onto the street and walked for hours. It was only as the sun was going down that she'd realised what she'd been doing. She was exhausted and had to get a taxi back to her hotel. She'd rested on the bed for a while and then telephoned the girlfriend she was supposed to be meeting in the evening. She'd pleaded a terrible headache and asked for a dinner date another time. Another time ... would there even be another time? She'd often played a party game where you had to decide what you would do if you only had four minutes to live. Real life wasn't a bit like a game. She'd never realised how much death would dominate her thoughts. She felt emotionally crippled. It was impossible to make plans because she couldn't think of anything else.

'Are you all right, old thing?'

Kaye snapped herself back into the here and now and frowned crossly. 'How did you find me?'

He wasn't about to tell her about Dennis Nelson and her neighbourhood butcher. 'Let's go for a meal or something and we'll talk.'

He looked so suave, so well dressed and wealthy. She wanted to scream at him, beat his chest with her fists, and tell him that life was bloody unfair and she hated the fact that people like him did horrible things and always came out smelling of roses, but she felt too weary, too beaten to bother. 'No,' she said dully.

'Oh, please darling,' he said, taking her elbow.

'Stop calling me that,' she snapped. 'I don't want a meal. I'm just about to catch the train back home.'

'Let me take you home,' he said, taking her suitcase from her.

'Give that back!' she snapped. She didn't want him coming home with her. She couldn't bear his probing questions they were bound to come before long. 'No, Henry,' she snapped as she reached for her case. 'I'm catching the train.'

'I could easily drive you to Copper Beeches,' he said. 'It's only a couple of hours and it's such a lovely afternoon. We could stop on the way.'

Copper Beeches... Kaye's jaw dropped and she felt sick. 'How did...' she began.

'How did I know where you live?' he said in that same cocky know-it-all way she remembered from when they were together. 'Annie told me the address, of course. I was planning to come and surprise you all anyway, but I wanted to see you first.'

Kaye frowned crossly. 'What horrid little plan are you hatching now, Henry?'

'Kaye!' he cried in an injured tone, his hand flying to his chest. 'Can't I do a little favour for my dear wife now that I've found her again?'

'All I want from you is a divorce,' she murmured. *Not that it matters now* ... she thought bitterly.

'That's what I want to talk to you about,' he said. 'Let me drive you back and we can have a chat about it. Look, I want to do the right thing by you, Kaye. I know I've treated you shabbily and I want to make amends.'

Coming from anyone else but Henry, Kaye might have believed him, but she knew him better than that. 'Pooh.'

'I want to explain,' he was saying. 'I want you to forgive me.'

'Saying sorry might go some way towards that,' she snapped.

'And I am, darling,' he said. 'I am so sorry.'

No, he wasn't. She could tell from the tone of his voice that he was playing games again. She wasn't daft. He was up to something, but somehow she allowed herself to be led by the arm and after a few minutes they had walked into a small mews where a rather flashy car was parked.

'Here we are,' he said, opening the front passenger door. 'Hop in and I'll have you back home in no time.'

She was suspicious. 'Who does this belong to?'

'It's mine,' he laughed. 'I'll show you the logbook if you like.'

'It's a left-hand drive,' she remarked.

'They're supposed to be for the North American market,' he said, 'but with the top rolled back, who could resist it?'

Kaye frowned and, against her better judgement, climbed in the car.

Henry came round to the driver's seat and threw her case into the back. It landed on top of his own. He started up the engine and they began to move. Just before he pulled out onto the road, he patted her knee. 'I'm going to enjoy this, darling. It'll be just like old times.'

Twenty-Six

The entrance to the police station was quiet. The building was fairly new, only opened in 1939 and in Union Place, not too far for her to walk from East Worthing. She was out of breath, having run most of the way, and as luck would have it, Bear was in the reception area as she burst through the door.

'Can I help you, madam?' said the desk sergeant, and at the same time, Bear looked up and said her name. 'Sarah?'

She felt her knees buckle and made a grab at the desk.

'All right, madam,' said the desk sergeant. 'Take your time.'

'I'll take care of this, Sergeant,' said Bear, lifting the flap on the top of the desk. He came to her side and put his strong arm about her waist. Immediately Sarah felt a wave of relief. She and Bear had met several times since that day in the snow. He had put in the paperwork to ask for permission to court her, but things were moving very slowly. She allowed him to steer her in the direction of a small room leading from the entrance, at the same time calling for some tea. She was trembling uncontrollably as she lowered herself into the chair, but he remained businesslike and calm. As the door closed behind them, his presence filled the room. He hadn't said a word as yet, but she felt that now she was with him, everything was going to be all right.

'Oh Bear, I wanted to ask for you,' she blurted out. 'I so much wanted to talk to you ... but I thought perhaps it wasn't the done thing.'

'Well, I'm here now,' he said, his voice as gentle as a whisper. 'You look very upset. Whatever's happened?'

So she told him. She told him about the cut up apron and now the incident with Jenny. He examined the plait and the envelope that had contained it carefully, but didn't interrupt what she had to say. She told him that she often had the feeling she was being watched, and not just by Mrs Goodall. Eventually she was all talked out, spent and exhausted and struggling not to cry. Someone had brought a cup of tea in for her. She picked it up, her hand still trembling, and gulped a mouthful. Why did the English always think everything would be all right after they'd had a cup of tea? It was a ridiculous thought but somehow it worked. She was thinking more clearly now.

'No address on the envelope,' he mused.

'That means that he must have pushed it through the letter box himself,' she said, staring at him helplessly.

'What makes you think Henry has done this?'

'He thinks I was the one who reported him to the police.'

'But Jenny is his daughter,' said Bear.

'And he was really horrible to her the last time

he saw her.' She explained how Henry had hustled them all out of the house and how upset Jenny had been.

His face darkened as he twirled the plait in his fingers. He was angry. Angry because this would put his request to court Sarah firmly on the back burner, and more importantly, angry because no man should treat the mother of his children, or indeed his children, in such a way. He frowned. Something else was niggling at him.

'You don't believe me,' she challenged. 'You think I'm imagining it?'

'I didn't say that, Sarah,' he said, shaking his head, 'but something doesn't quite add up.' He held the plait next to his own shoulder. 'If Henry was this close to Jenny, why didn't she tell you she'd seen her father?'

Sarah gulped. He was right. She hadn't thought of that. Jenny adored Henry and of course she would have said if she had seen him. 'But who else could have got that close...' She felt a chill run through her body even as she said the words.

'Somebody so ordinary that nobody noticed him,' Bear mused, 'or her. Jenny was probably distracted, talking to her friends. It wouldn't have taken more than a second or two.'

'But how could it have happened?' Sarah protested. 'She was on the beach with all the teachers. Surely they would have seen something as dreadful as this?'

'You say the whole class travelled together to Lancing?'

Sarah nodded. 'Oh God, it happened on the bus, didn't it?'

'Probably,' said Bear.

'I got off *one* stop before her,' said Sarah. 'One stop! He must have moved like greased lightning.'

Bear looked thoughtful. 'Did you see anyone on the bus you knew? Someone who might have a grudge against you?'

'No,' she said helplessly. 'Like I told you, we've had some trouble with the next-door neighbour, Mrs Goodall, but I can't imagine she would have anything to do with this. She's not the sort of person to catch buses, if you know what I mean.'

'What sort of trouble?'

Sarah gave him a brief résumé of the various times they had had a run-in with Mrs Goodall. There was the complaint about noise from the radio (when Kaye was listening to her play). She'd complained about the police coming at the dead of night (that was when DC Harris brought her pram back from the seafront). She'd complained about Annie being rude (apparently she'd stuck out her tongue at her) and the number of callers to the house (including, would you believe, Lottie's first footing on New Year's Eve!). She'd rung the doorbell when Edward was crying in his pram or when Jenny shouted in the garden... Funnily enough, when Sarah added them all up, there were a lot more than she'd thought. 'She can be a bit of a pain,' she told Bear. 'Kaye thinks it's because they crossed swords at the public meeting about Beach House. Mrs Goodall thought it was an ugly eyesore and needed to be pulled down, but Kaye and her friends got a preservation order slapped on it. She can be difficult, but being responsible for something as vindictive as this... I can't believe she'd do it.'

Bear nodded and Sarah remembered how sharp she had been with her daughter when she'd found the cut plait. 'When I told Jenny off,' she said brokenly, 'she told me she didn't know when it had happened and I didn't believe her. I feel terrible now.' The tears rolled down her face and she searched her pocket for a handkerchief. 'I was so cross with her and it wasn't even her fault.'

He looked sympathetic but made no comment. Little did she know how much this was hurting him too. Picking up the apron, he said, 'He most likely used something like a Stanley knife, probably a 199, which is very sharp. I reckon it would have cut through the hair very quickly. And you can't think of anyone else who might have done this?'

Sarah shook her head.

'Have you any enemies? Someone from the past maybe?'

A cold chill ran through her body. 'Nat Rivers,' she said. 'We used to live next door to him and his mother. He hates me.'

Bear raised an eyebrow and wrote the name in his notebook, which was resting on the table between them.

'He used to knock his mother about,' Sarah went on. 'I could hear him through the walls. He got sent to prison and then Mrs Rivers moved away. I bumped into him once. He accused me of knowing where she was, even though I didn't.'

Bear carried on scribbling. 'If it wasn't Nat, can you think of anyone else?'

Sarah leaned forward. 'Could Henry have persuaded someone he met in prison to do it?'

'It's possible,' Bear frowned. 'But why would he do that?'

'I don't know... I guess you're right,' she conceded.

They fell silent, Bear examining the apron again and Sarah drinking the rest of the tea. 'So where do we go from here?'

'What I'll do is get you to say all this again while somebody takes it down,' he said. 'Now that this has been flagged up, I'll make sure an officer goes around Church Walk to check that there's no one loitering about.'

'Should I tell Jenny?'

'Personally, I wouldn't,' said Bear. 'You'll only frighten her, but make sure you are the one who picks her up from school and keep an eye on her.'

'I will,' said Sarah, blowing her nose.

'Stay for a few minutes and finish your tea.' He stood to his feet and as he moved from the room, his hand briefly covered her shoulder. 'Try not to worry.'

The door closed and Sarah sighed. She could still feel the warmth from his touch. She had longed to sink into his arms and for him to hold her, but he couldn't do that, could he. He was the policeman and right now she was just another member of the public. She brushed a tear away from her cheek and stood up. Oh, why did life have to be so complicated, and if not Henry, or Nat Rivers, who else would have done such a terrible thing?

Henry was in full swing. Ever since Kaye climbed into the car, he hadn't stopped talking. She was enjoying the feel of the wind in her hair, blowing it into an untidy mop of curls. She turned her face towards the oncoming road and blanked out most of what he was saying, only mumbling an occasional reply. Her conversation with Mr Young was constantly going round and round her head. '*It's pretty advanced and there's not a lot we can do.*' He must have meant there was nothing they could do, and yet she'd heard that some people had an operation to cut out the diseased part. Why wouldn't Mr Young do the same for her? Surely she could walk around with half a lung ... it certainly beat the alternative. She made up her mind to ring him as soon as she got home. She would demand a second opinion.

'You have no idea how dreadful it was,' Henry was saying. 'I honestly thought I would never survive…'

Lung cancer ... hadn't George VI got the same thing? He smoked a lot as well. Perhaps there really was a link between smoking and cancer. She'd hardly given it much attention and there were denials in the press, but everybody knew that the King had spent time in hospital having an operation earlier in the year. Of course, nobody actually said what it was for, but everybody thought the same thing.

'She wants me to cruise around the Rock of Gibraltar,' Henry prattled on. 'I know it was reckless of me to promise, but I really can't get out of it.'

Kaye leaned her arm on the car door and turned away from him. What on earth was he talking about? Her mind drifted back to her own problem. Should she tell Sarah and Annie? And what was going to happen to Lottie? Thank God she'd had Dobbin draw up those papers. Had she signed them all? Yes, yes she had.

Henry interrupted her thoughts again. 'Kaye, we've been stuck behind this blessed lorry for the past mile,' he said petulantly. 'Can you see if anything is coming the other way?'

'Now you see the disadvantage of having a left-hand drive,' she remarked, but he didn't laugh.

Henry pulled out slightly and Kaye looked ahead. There was a clear stretch of road. 'Pull out now,' she said, and Henry motored past the lorry. As soon as they were back on the right side of the road, he went on with his discourse and Kaye went back to her thoughts. She'd forgotten how self-centred and arrogant he could be. Oh, he could be charm itself when he wanted something, but if he didn't get it, another Henry emerged.

'So I fully intend to come and live with you as soon as I get back,' he said casually. He reached over to the glove compartment and took a coffee crunch from a small paper bag.

Kaye's head spun round. 'Pardon? Come and live with me? What are you talking about?'

'Sweetheart,' Henry scolded, 'you haven't been listening.'

'So tell me again,' she said irritably.

Unwinding the paper with his teeth, he popped a sweet into his mouth. 'After I've done this cruise, I'm coming to live with you.'

Kaye felt a rush of adrenalin. 'There's no room,' she said crossly.

'It's a big house,' he smiled.

'Apart from my own rooms,' Kaye spat, 'Sarah and her children have a space in the attic, Annie is in one of the bedrooms with Edward, and of course Lottie has the second bedroom. There are no other rooms so, no, you can't stay with me, and besides, why would I want you living with me? I want to divorce you, Henry!'

He changed gear as they began a hill climb. 'Who is Lottie?'

'My Aunt Charlotte,' she said bitterly. She paused, remembering. 'The one you made sure stayed in the mental home. And while we're on the subject, why did you do that Henry? Why did you keep Granny's arrangement going?'

Henry shrugged his shoulders in an innocent expression. 'I thought that was what you wanted, darling.'

Kaye bristled. 'But you never even spoke to me about it. How could you possibly know what I wanted? Anyway, she's living with us now.'

'Can't someone else look after her?'

'I don't want anyone else looking after her,' Kaye snapped. 'She's my aunt and she lives with me.'

'I don't fancy being in the same house as some batty old woman who ought to be locked up,' said Henry.

'Henry let's get this straight once and for all – you are not coming to live with me,' Kaye shrieked. 'And I'll thank you to keep your opinions to yourself. Lottie is not batty!'

She could hear him crunching his sweet as Henry accelerated the car angrily.

Annie enjoyed working in the shop, especially first thing in the morning. At times she and Mr Richardson had a job to keep up with the numbers of customers coming into his shop. He was obviously glad of his decision to employ an assistant, especially one as capable as she was. At first, the children were patient but excitable and noisy as they waited to be served, but when it came close to the time when they should be in school, they became fractious. Annie could control them far better than he could because they could sense his discomfort and messed him about.

'Come along now, young man,' he said sharply to one small boy with rather dirty hands. 'Don't touch anything and hurry up and make up your mind. There are other people waiting.'

'I'll have a Mintola,' the boy said, pointing to the shelf, but when Mr Richardson got the jar down he said, 'no, hang on a minute, I'll have some Spangles and a Punch.'

'You don't have enough coupons for that, me laddo,' said Mr Richardson.

The area behind the counter was small and Annie and Mr Richardson kept bumping each other as they rushed to serve the customers. Once they both bent down at the same time and nudged each other. The children giggled, and someone said in a loud voice, 'Whoops-a-daisy. Looks like the meeting of the big four,' which made several customers laugh out loud. Mr Richardson blushed a deep crimson.

As school time loomed, the shop emptied. 'Mr Richardson,' said Annie as Mrs Richardson produced a large mug of tea from the flat upstairs, 'may I make a suggestion?'

He looked a little cautious but told her to go ahead.

'I am very new here and you understand the tobacco labels far better than I do,' she said, blinking for effect. 'Would it help if I stayed behind the sweet counter when the rush is on, then I wouldn't get in your way?'

She could see at once that he liked the idea and she imagined his inner thoughts. The children played him up. It would be far better to let Mrs Royal do it.

'If you think you could manage the sweets on your own,' he said pompously.

'If I get stuck,' she smiled affably, 'I can always call to you.'

Mrs Goodall couldn't believe her eyes. Yes, yes she was right. The woman wheeling that baby away from Copper Beeches this morning was none other than Cllr Mitchell's wife. She had seen her a couple of days ago and hadn't been too sure, but now that she had the woman's photograph right in front of her, she was positive. She glanced again at the article headed 'Cllr Mitchell and his wife, Judith, visit spring flower show' and raised a satisfied eyebrow. What was Judith Mitchell doing with that baby? There could only be one answer. The child had to be a relative and what relative could it be other than her own grandchild. So the little minx who had put her tongue out wasn't married. Mrs Goodall smiled to herself. She had been right all along. That Kaye woman was bringing the area into disrepute. Could it be that Mrs Royale was running a home for unmarried women? If she didn't do something about it, before long they'd end up with men prowling around the streets looking for loose women all day long. She'd seen one already. That weaselly man in the buff-coloured raincoat for a start. Dearie me, given time, she wouldn't even be able to walk to church safely. Come to think about it, there were four women living alone in that house and none of them appeared to go out to work, so how were they making their money? Her hand flew to her mouth in horror. She wasn't one to gossip of course, but could that house already be a ... a brothel? If this was so, then the children she saw in the garden were being exposed to goodness knows what. Mrs Goodall shuddered to think. It was her duty as a law-abiding citizen to do something about it. She didn't want to make trouble, but it couldn't be helped. With a deep sigh of regret, she reached for the telephone.

Twenty-Seven

Judith was enjoying looking after Edward. The weather for the time of year had been glorious, with temperatures reaching 84°F in some parts of the country. As always with the coastal areas, Worthing was a few degrees lower, but until today, every day had been beautiful. Judith made the most of it, playing with her grandson in the beach chalet she and Malcolm owned under the arches by Splashpoint. Built in the 1930s, they were made of brick with steel-framed Crittall windows and French doors. The roofs doubled as a walkway and each chalet had its own frontage, which was separated from the public footpath by a rail. From the footpath, you could walk straight onto the beach.

Over the years, Judith had made her chalet very comfortable. It was tastefully decorated and she and Malcolm kept a table and deckchairs inside. There were pictures hanging on the wall and they had a small Primus stove to make tea. There was a public tap at the end of the row of chalets, so they had plenty of water, but of course she had to bring the milk and sugar from home. There were no toilet facilities, but the public toilets in the gardens behind were quite sufficient.

During the war years everything had been boarded up, but now she could use the chalet to enjoy time with her grandson. He was such a good baby and at five months was already able to focus his eyes on his toys, of which there were precious few until Judith came along. He had a ready smile and she discovered that if she tickled him he had an infectious chuckle. In her eyes he was the most perfect little boy in the whole world.

She had been looking after him for nearly three weeks now. At first she kept well out of the public eye, but Edward was so delightful that most of the chalet neighbours had already popped along to chuckle him under the chin and invite themselves for a drink. Eventually that gave her the idea of using the place to hold informal gatherings with her friends. She would invite some for a light lunch and others for afternoon tea. Her housekeeper, Mrs Lang, made sandwiches and cakes, which Judith brought down in a tin, so it didn't take long for the chalet to become the 'in' place to be among her set.

Although her friends had come that afternoon, they hadn't stayed quite as long as they normally did. It wasn't cold but the sky was overcast and there was a definite feel of rain in the air. Judith had just put Edward back in his pram and was packing up his toys in an orange box, when someone stood in the doorway and blocked the sunlight. She straightened up to see Malcolm. Her heart began to race. Oh dear, he wasn't going to make a scene was he?

'Oh! You surprised me,' she said, doing her best to sound casual. 'I was just leaving ... but I can make us some tea if you want.'

He was staring at the pram.

Now Judith felt nervous. What was he going to do? He didn't seem angry, but there was no telling with Malcolm. 'Yes, he's in there,' she said cautiously. 'He's awake but quite content.' She poured some water into the kettle and lit the stove. 'Shouldn't take long. How did you know I was here?'

He normally never bothered about what she was doing. They led fairly separate lives and it suited them both. Malcolm said nothing and he still hadn't moved.

'He won't bite, you know,' said Judith. She went to her husband's side and slipped her arm through his. Slowly and falteringly, Malcolm allowed himself to be guided to the pram. Edward was playing with his own foot, but as his grandfather peered in at him, he fixed his gaze on Malcolm. 'Isn't he lovely?' Judith coaxed. 'He reminds me so much of Annie when she was a baby.'

Malcolm still hadn't said a word when the kettle whistled. Judith made some tea and reopened the cake tin as if it were the most natural thing in the world. She re-set the deckchair she had just put away and offered her husband a cup and saucer.

'I had a phone call from the *Worthing Gazette*,' he said dully. 'Someone saw you with the pram.'

'I'm not surprised,' said Judith, carefully avoiding the accusation that she was ruining his reputation. 'I've been coming here every day.'

'And now I hear it's the talk of the golf club,' he said, sitting down. His voice was emotionless, as if he were a newsreader on the radio. 'The chaps tell me you've been inviting their wives for tea.'

'Yes,' said Judith, sitting back down herself, 'and it's been quite pleasant.' They sipped tea together until Edward began to complain, so Judith got back up and took him from the pram. They sat opposite Malcolm and Edward fixed his big eyes on his grandfather once again. Judith watched her husband's hard expression begin to soften.

'I only wanted to protect her,' said Malcolm gruffly, 'to give her a new start in life.'

'I know, dear.' Less is more, she told herself. Don't say too much and don't get into an argument about it.

'It's going to be bloody hard for her to find a halfway decent husband now,' he said bitterly.

'I know, dear,' Judith said again.

They drank their tea and Edward played with a

rattle. The third time he dropped it onto the floor, Malcolm was the one who picked it up and gave it back to him. He still wasn't smiling, but she'd been married to him for long enough to recognise a change of heart when she saw it.

Judith looked at her watch. 'I have to go,' she told him. 'Annie finishes work soon and I have to get Edward back to the house for her return.'

'What does she do?'

'She works in a sweet shop,' said Judith.

Malcolm screwed up his face disapprovingly. 'A sweet shop?'

'That girl would scrub floors to keep her baby,' said Judith stoutly. She stood up with Edward on her hip and tried to straighten the pram sheet with her one free hand. Without thinking, she plonked Edward in Malcolm's arms and used both hands on the sheet. When she turned to take the baby back, her husband's eyes were moist.

'Times are changing, Malcolm,' she said quietly. 'And now that she's gained her independence I don't think she'd even want to come back home again.'

Malcolm put out his hand and Edward patted it happily.

'But we can help to support her, can't we?' she said, reading his thoughts.

Malcolm grunted, but Judith noted that he was in no hurry to hand the baby back.

'Henry, I can't be doing with all this,' said Kaye crossly. They'd been arguing about him coming to live at Copper Beeches for the past ten minutes. 'You've heard from my solicitors and I want a divorce.'

Little point now, she thought grimly, but at least it would free him to marry Annie. Her stomach fell away as she realised that if the cancer was as serious as Mr Young intimated, he'd soon be a widower anyway. *'When the time comes, we will make you as comfortable as possible.'* As comfortable as possible ... what did that mean? Was she going to be in a lot of pain?

'Now I can't see if I can pass this damned car,' said Henry. 'Is it safe?'

'No,' she said as he pulled out slightly. A bus going in the opposite direction came over the brow of the hill.

'We could have a second honeymoon,' Henry said, grabbing her hand, which was resting on her lap, and squeezing it.

She snatched it away and began to cough. 'Henry, you've got a son to take care of. You can't leave Annie to bring him up on her own. Pull out now.'

'Don't you worry about her,' said Henry; his tone changing out of all recognition as he pulled around the car. 'There's no way I'm letting that silly bitch bring up my son.'

Kaye turned to look at him. His jawline was set and his nostrils flared with anger. 'What did you call her?'

'You heard,' he said coldly. 'The woman was a brood mare, nothing more. I wanted a son and she gave me one. I've no more use for her now.'

'Henry!' Kaye was genuinely shocked. She knew he was selfish and self-seeking, but she'd never heard him use that tone of voice before.

'I've got plans,' he said, helping himself to another coffee crunch. 'I'm bringing my boy up myself.'

'But Annie is doing a perfectly fine job,' said Kaye. 'She adores that baby. In fact, you couldn't wish for a better mother.'

Henry crashed the gears and the car jerked forward. 'And I say she's no fit mother for my son.'

'Annie has fought tooth and nail to keep that child,' Kaye cried angrily. 'Henry, you can't do this. She loves him. Annie would die if she lost him.'

Henry glared at her. 'She'll get over it.'

Kaye began another coughing fit. The coldness in his voice sent a chill through her whole body. He was doing his best to wreck everybody's life, wasn't he? Not only hers but Lottie's, and now poor Annie's as well. Some of the old feelings came rushing back; the helplessness, the frustration when trying to make him see another point of view and, worst of all, the fear of him. For years she had lived on a knife-edge while trying to please someone who refused to be pleased. It had crippled her and stifled her creativity and now she felt as if everything was creeping back to the way it had been before. And in that moment, Kaye hated him.

'You ought to do something about that cough,' he said as she finished gasping for breath and fought the pain in her side. 'Here, have a sweet.'

She shook her head. 'Listen Henry, don't do this. We've all made a life for ourselves,' she said, trying to lighten the atmosphere between them. She had to cool the heat of the moment if she was to get through to him. 'I have a nice house and a steady income. Sarah is excellent with Lottie, and Annie has settled into a good routine. All the children are happy. You want your children to be happy, don't you?'

'Don't lecture me on what's best,' Henry snapped. 'Don't forget, woman, I am still your husband!'

'But I don't want you back!' she cried. 'You are not coming back to disrupt all our lives.' Kaye's head was thumping and she was beginning to feel really ill. 'No Henry, it's not going to happen.'

'Kaye,' he said, his tone suddenly softening, 'sweetheart ... let's not quarrel.'

He had accelerated and they were now stuck behind a removal lorry. She wished she hadn't agreed to this journey. The train would have been far less traumatic. Her skin felt clammy and the pleasure of the wind in her face was turning into a need to get out of the cold. What was even worse, she was close to tears. She couldn't bear it if Henry saw her being weak again.

'I'm sorry, darling,' he went on soothingly. 'Put all this down to my clumsy attempt to win back your affections.'

Kaye closed her eyes as the bile rose in her throat. 'I can't let you do this to us,' she said. 'In fact, I think it would be better if you put me down at the nearest bus stop and I'll make my own way home.'

He said nothing but she saw his fingers tighten around the steering wheel. The removal lorry had turned off and the car had picked up speed, travelling at dangerous rates which meant that they barely managed the corners on the narrow road. Kaye gripped the edge of her seat with her left hand and the handle of the door with her right until, much to her relief, they came up behind another slow-moving vehicle.

'Tell me when it's all clear for me to pass,' he said, pulling out slightly.

Kaye could see a lorry disappearing into the dip of the hill. 'Not yet... Henry, please think about this,' she tried again. 'I could give you some money. Give you a new start...'

'Like I said,' he said, 'I have plans for my son and that doesn't include his mother. That's why I'm coming to Worthing.'

'But she won't...'

'I'm not arguing with you, Kaye,' he said firmly. 'I'm going to fetch him right now.' He leaned over and patted her hand again. 'Annie will be fine. You got over it when you had your baby, didn't you?'

'My baby died at birth,' she said quietly. 'I never even saw him.'

He turned his attention back to the road. 'You could have done.'

Her head jerked up. 'What?'

'It lived for three days,' he said matter-of-factly.

Kaye gasped in horror. 'What! But why didn't you tell me?'

'The nurses told me there was nothing they could do,' he went on. 'It was deformed, d'you see. I thought it best.'

'It,' she spat. 'It... You didn't even think to tell me if I'd had a boy or a girl.'

'It was a girl.'

Kaye shuddered with an overwhelming feeling of grief and loss. Her baby had lived. She could have held her, kissed her downy head, told her she was beautiful. Even if she wasn't quite right, she would have been beautiful to her. 'How could you?' she choked. 'How could you be so cruel?'

'Me? Cruel?' he said. 'I wasn't cruel. I did what I thought was best.'

Kaye could barely contain her rage. 'Who do you think you are, Henry? God?'

'Perhaps I am,' he said, his voice measured. 'Anyway, it was all very quick. A pillow, a couple of seconds and it was all over.'

She stared at him in disbelief. Who was this man? Dear God, Henry was a monster.

'Anyway,' he continued, 'it wasn't mine, was it.'

'I never made a secret of it,' she said defensively. 'You promised you would bring the baby up as yours.'

'I didn't count on it being deformed,' said Henry. 'And a girl...'

And that's when it all became clear. It only took a split second but all at once everything fell into place. If he pulled out, they would hit the lorry head-on. There was no going back, but if she did this thing, she could save them all. Annie and her son, Lottie, and even Sarah and her girls. Sarah would take care of Lottie, she felt sure of that. Sarah was a level-headed woman and they were good friends. *When the time comes*, Mr Young had told her, *we will make you as comfortable as possible*. She didn't want to dwell on it but dying could take a long and painful time. This way it would all be over in a matter of seconds. The lorry was coming over the brow of the hill and straight towards them. 'Pull out now,' she said calmly.

The lorry driver had seen them and was standing on his horn. In the split second before Henry realised what she'd done, he tried to pull back, but there was nowhere to go. 'You bitch!' he shouted and as the tree came up to meet them, there was an almighty bang.

Twenty-Eight

Everyone was in a good mood and there had been a lot of laughter around the kitchen table at Copper Beeches. Annie was excited because she had spotted her mother and father walking home together with Edward. She'd hung back when she saw them reach the gate, afraid that her presence might spoil everything, but she did see her father kiss her mother on the cheek and hurry away, presumably to wherever he'd parked his car. Her mother didn't mention the fact that they'd been together when they met in the hallway, so Annie didn't mention it either. Even so, she felt sure it was a good omen.

'Does that mean you'll be leaving us and going back home?' Lottie asked as they ate their evening meal later on.

I don't want to,' said Annie. 'I know I've been a bit of a pain in the past, but I like my life right now. It's been wonderful having a bit of independence, but if I stay here, I still can't support Edward on my wages.'

'We will miss you,' said Sarah, passing the vegetable dish.

She meant it sincerely and hoped Annie understood that.

'I don't want you to go,' Jenny wailed, her eyes already filling with tears. 'Lu-Lu and me like playing with Edward.'

'Lu-Lu and I,' her mother gently corrected.

Annie grasped the little girl's hand. 'I'm not going just yet,' she said. 'Not for a long, long time. And if I do, Edward and I will have you over to our house to play. You might even be able to sleep over.'

'At your house?' said Jenny, brightening up.

'Maybe,' said Annie, glancing across the table at Sarah and giving her a shrug. She looked down. 'What's that you've got in your hand?'

Jenny climbed onto her mother's lap and showed her a piece of sewing. It was a tray cloth with some simple embroidery done on a large hole fabric. 'Oh, that's lovely darling,' Sarah beamed. The stitches were big and she'd obviously worked the thread using a crewel needle, but the vivid reds and blues brought a splash of colour to the table.

'I did it at school,' said Jenny, 'and Mrs Audus says it was the best in the class.'

'Isn't she clever!' cried Lottie. 'It's beautiful.'

'William Steel thought it was silly,' said Jenny.

William Steel, William Steel, Sarah thought angrily. He was beginning to be a real thorn in Jenny's side. She would have to have a word with Jenny's teacher.

'Do you know what I think,' said Sarah, holding

the little tray cloth up. 'I think Mr Lovett would want to buy this for his rich ladies in London.'

Jenny's heart was bursting with pride. 'But it's a present for you, Mummy.'

Sarah swallowed the lump in her throat and put it proudly under her plate as they ate the meal. As she looked around the table, she reflected on the changes in all their lives. She and Annie hadn't had a tetchy conversation for ages; Annie had grown up an awful lot since she'd arrived. Lottie was a completely different woman too. Confident and happy, she had a keen eye when it came to home furnishings and decorating. Even though the war had been over for four years, and things were getting slightly better, the country still had to make do and mend to some degree, but given a tin of paint or a few embroidery silks, Lottie could transform a broken-down chair or a clapped-out fire screen in no time. She'd taught herself a lot of new skills and particularly enjoyed inventing new dishes in the kitchen. Since her successful stint at the Labour Hall, in the past month, Lottie had even joined the WRVS, making quite a few new friends at the tea bar in Worthing Hospital, and she was a member of the Barnardo's Helpers League, where she was able to sell some of her crafts to raise funds for orphaned children.

Kaye wasn't with them tonight. Sarah knew that yesterday she was meeting an old friend in London and she hoped that the reason Kaye wasn't with them was because she had decided to stay an extra night. Sarah hoped she was having a good time. She deserved it. The only fly in the proverbial ointment was that awful cough of hers.

Kaye had cut down on her cigarettes since that choking fit of hers, but she hadn't given them up altogether because she said they calmed her nerves. Now that the better weather was here, she was taking walks along the seafront again, so Sarah had high hopes that her health would improve.

The children were thriving and happy. Lu-Lu loved her dollies, and apart from her run-ins with William Steel, Jenny was doing well at school. Edward, propped in the baby chair, was melting everyone's hearts with his gummy lopsided grins. Sarah had never seen such a placid baby.

As for her own life, if she was honest, at times it felt as if it had stalled a little. She still kept in touch with Mrs Angel and she still had the occasional order for baby clothes from her customers, although Mr Lovett had never come back to the shop. The two women would sit out in the back among the bags of 'put-by' wool customers left in the shop until they had the money to buy it. They'd have a quick cup of tea and talk over old times. Sarah had been to look at her old house, which had been done up and sold. The house next door where Mrs Rivers had lived had also been sold. Mrs Angel said she had left in a hurry, and just in time by all accounts.

'She'd left no forwarding address,' said Mrs Angel. 'She'd had enough of that son of hers, I suppose.'

'I don't blame her,' Sarah agreed, nodding her head sagely.

The gossip around the town was that when her son got out of prison, no one knew where his mother was, so he'd got roaring drunk, put a brick through the pub window and was arrested again.

And then there was Bear. Dear Bear. Her feelings for him were unlike anything she'd ever felt for any man. She thought of him constantly. She'd thought she'd loved Henry, but what she felt for him was nothing in comparison to what she felt for Bear. It was the difference between night and day, or a night light and a lighthouse. She wished the police would hurry up and give him permission to court her. They still met with others present, but she longed to be alone with him. The girls enjoyed his company and as she thought back to that day on the hillside when they had all ridden the toboggan together, she smiled happily.

Now that the house was clean and well run, Sarah found herself worrying about her next step. She did the books for three more local businesses and her burgeoning interest in antiques was gathering momentum. Yonks ago she had found an old book in a jumble sale called *The Encyclopaedia of Antiques*. It had only cost her a penny, but it was worth its weight in gold. She'd read it from cover to cover and had just discovered the soup tureen with salver she regularly cleaned twice a month was in fact from the late eighteenth century. Kaye had told them to throw it out and it had only been saved from the dustbin because Sarah had asked to keep it. 'Take it,' Kaye had laughed. 'Ugly old thing. You're welcome to it.'

She would do the decent thing and tell Kaye how much it was worth and if Kaye let her keep it, as she strongly suspected she would, she would sell it. She could use the money to pay for lessons with an auctioneer or an antique dealer.

'You're miles away.' Annie's comment brought her back to the present. 'Can you pass the custard, please?'

'What are you smiling about?' asked Lottie.

'Choices,' said Sarah, passing the custard jug. 'Something I never thought I'd have.'

Henry stared at the open car door trying to gather his thoughts. He stood shakily and painfully to his feet but saw at once that there was nothing he could do for Kaye. Served her right, the bloody bitch. She'd tried to kill them both. He could hear shouting, and just over the low hedge he could see somebody's head bobbing along as they ran down the road to the telephone box by the crossroads. By now, a couple of other cars had stopped and the drivers were helping the lorry driver down from his cab. Any minute they would be coming his way. The car had careered across the road as the lorry hit it broadside. He'd been unable to stop it ploughing through a hedge and on into a field where it had finally come into collision with a tree. Kaye had been thrown forward and lay partway across the dashboard. The windscreen was shattered. His car door must have burst open on impact, or maybe a bit before, because somehow or other, he had been thrown out onto the ground. Both suitcases had burst open on impact.

Her clothes were strewn across the grass. His papers fluttered everywhere. Painfully, he bent to pick them up, stuffing them any old how back into the case. The brooch he'd intended to give Kaye when he moved back in was still in its box.

A sudden thought hit him. If the police came, they might lock him up again while they found out what happened. Worse still, if they discovered he was an ex-jailbird they might not find the key in a hurry. He didn't want to be locked up again. He checked himself and discovered that apart from a pain in his side and a bit of blood when he took his hand away, he was none the worse for the accident. There was a wooded area nearby. If he kept close to the hedge, he could hide in the woods until everybody had gone home. If he could get back to London before nightfall, he could report the car stolen and no one would be any the wiser, or better still, he could hitch a lift to Worthing and fetch his son before anyone could put two and two together.

The voices were getting nearer – it was now or never. Keeping his body low, Henry ran along the edge of the hedge and ducked down in the dry ditch as the people from the road appeared in the field. He was hampered by the stitch in his side, which seemed to be getting worse, but from where he was he could see when the ambulance, and then the police arrived. He saw the ambulance take Kaye and the police took the lorry driver. There was one heart-stopping moment when a policeman looked across the field as if he was looking for someone else, but nobody came. Now Henry was quite alone. Years of neglect meant that the edges of the field were already very overgrown, but there was a gap between the bramble bushes and the road which was wide enough for him to move along without being seen. Safe in the woods, Henry leaned back on a reasonably soft spot and closed his eyes. He would rest here for a while and then hitch a lift down south. Everything was in place and he couldn't allow her to mess up his plans, not at this late stage. By this time tomorrow, he and his son would be out of everybody's reach.

After their meal, the children were put to bed and Lottie got the cards out. The three of them were playing a game of rummy when the telephone rang.

'Ah,' said a familiar voice. 'You're in.'

'Bear!' cried Sarah. 'How lovely to hear from you.'

'Can I come round?' he said, the seriousness of his voice making her feel uncertain.

'Yes, of course,' she said. 'Is everything all right?'

'I'll tell you when I see you,' he said, leaving her with the dialling tone.

About fifteen minutes later the doorbell rang. His face was grey and Sarah looked at him anxiously. Had the police authority told him they couldn't date? Her stomach fell away with disappointment. She really liked him, but she knew he loved his job. He would probably tell her he would give up being a policeman if it was the only way they could be together, but she couldn't let him do that, could she? How could she expect him to be happy in some other job? He was a copper through and through.

She showed him to the sitting room and as Lottie made to leave he asked her to stay. 'Where's Annie?'

'Putting Edward to bed,' said Sarah.

'I'd like you all to be here,' said Bear.

Sarah frowned. 'I'm afraid Kaye is in town but I'll call Annie if you like.'

Something must have happened to Henry, she thought as she called Annie's name up the stairs. He's married another woman or something. Annie came down a few minutes later and joined them in the sitting room.

'There's been an accident,' Bear said as they all looked at him anxiously. Sarah's hand went to her mouth, and Lottie let out a small cry. Annie stared blankly ahead. 'It's Kaye, I'm afraid. She's in hospital.'

Twenty-Nine

The street light was right outside the house, which meant it was difficult to slip unnoticed into the garden. He took his time until he was sure nobody was around, but as soon as he turned by the hedge, he caught his coat on a rose bush. The bloody thorns were about an inch long and he snagged his fingers a couple of times trying to release himself. He must be mad doing this. Why didn't he just forget it? Creeping along the flower border, he found a spot behind a large buddleia where he could see right into the kitchen. They hadn't drawn the curtains, so he could see a woman he didn't know and the two little girls sitting at the table eating a meal. His stomach rumbled, but by far the strongest emotion was the anxiety which had brought him here. His nose was dripping. He sniffed but it wasn't enough, so he pinched the end of it with his fingers and wiped his hand on his trouser leg. Then he saw the car coming into the drive. He only just managed to duck down behind the buddleia before the headlights would have picked him out. A man got out and rang the doorbell. As soon as the bloke went inside, he'd decided to leg it. She was safe for the moment, but he had to see her before it was too late. He'd played the waiting game long enough. It was time to put his plan into action. One last look at the house, but as he turned away, he had the feeling that he was being watched. His heart began to quicken as he scoured the garden. It was then that he saw the woman at the window. As soon as she realised he was looking, she let the curtain drop, but he knew full well that she was still there.

Mrs Goodall stepped back into the room. There! She'd been right all along. That man in the car knew exactly where to come and now there was another one lurking around in the shrubbery. She could tell he was a lowlife. What decent man would be hanging around the garden at this time of night? She ran downstairs to check that her front and back doors were locked. It really was too bad. Summer was on the way and she would have to keep her windows shut at all times. She was trembling, but she wasn't sure whether it was in fear or anger. The police had listened to what she had to say, but apart from making a note of her complaint, they hadn't even bothered to check her story. The newspaper reporter was a lot more interested, but the article she'd spotted in the *Gazette* only mentioned the fact that Judith Mitchell had cancelled most of her official engagements while she looked after her grandchild. It all sounded very cosy and the reporter had clearly missed the whole point. Those women were lowering the tone of the area. She'd have to go to the house tomorrow and give them a piece of her mind.

She was just washing up a few things from her simple supper when she suddenly had a new thought. What she needed was irrefutable proof of lewd goings-on. Putting the plate away quickly, she found a small notebook in her bureau and glanced up at the clock. It was coming up for eight o'clock. Then she wrote the date followed by, *7.10 p.m., man lurking in driveway,* on the first page. Her eyes weren't as good as they used to be, but then she remembered her late husband's opera glasses and spent the next ten minutes searching for them. Then, taking a glass of sherry upstairs, she positioned her chair by the bay window and waited.

Once they'd got over the initial shock, it was decided that Sarah should go to Kaye's bedside straight away. Apparently she had been asking for her. Lottie was too upset to go and Annie had elected herself in charge of the children and the house. Bear promised to make sure Sarah got home before the morning when she would have to take Jenny to school. After whizzing around the house to collect her coat and handbag, she was ready.

Bear had a car waiting in the driveway and took her arm as they went outside.

'Have you any idea how bad this is?' she asked as they began the journey to Horsham Hospital.

'It's serious,' he said simply. They drove in silence, each left to their own thoughts.

Bear was wondering if the woman next door was satisfied now that she'd seen Sarah being taken away in a police car. If she didn't stop phoning the station with her malicious stories, he'd have to go and have a word with her. He'd seen the gossip column in the *Gazette* and he had a shrewd idea she was the source. What did it matter that Cllr Mitchell's daughter had had a baby? It was nobody else's business but theirs. According to the police radio, Mrs Goodall had been ringing in again to say that she'd seen another prowler. The local bobby had been detailed to keep an eye out, but her call was regarded as more of a nuisance than anything else.

He was also chewing over something else. Someone in the Met had contacted Sussex police about the theft of a valuable diamond brooch from a Bond Street jeweller. The memo also mentioned a certain Henry Royale, late of Horsham and Winchester prison because there was a suspicion that he may be in the Worthing area. Bear had already checked every hotel and boarding house, but no one of that name was staying in the town. Bear couldn't forget the unsolved case of Mrs Hartley, the body on the beach. Henry's name had come up then. What was it about this man? Persuasive, unscrupulous, cool under pressure, he had a complete lack of regard when it came to the way his plans and schemes affected others. He had already wrecked Kaye's life and Sarah's and Annie's. True, the three of them had picked up the pieces in an admirable way, but no woman deserved to be treated the way they had been. Even the thought of it made him feel angry. How he longed to throw caution to the wind and tell Sarah how he felt about her. Feeling as he did about her and having her so close and yet untouchable was tearing him to ribbons. She knew he couldn't court her without police permission, but if the powers that be kept him waiting much longer, he'd have to resign. He had never felt like this about a woman and he wanted to spend the rest of his life with her. As for Henry, had he simply run off or was there something more sinister afoot? He had to protect Sarah and the girls and his gut feeling was that Henry should be back behind bars. And how much of this should he divulge to Sarah? He glanced over at her. Even in the dimly lit car, he could see she was pale and anxious. Right now he didn't want to add to her misery. She was upset about her friend and he was afraid that the outcome might not be good.

Sarah was worried about what she might find when she saw Kaye. Bear had said it was serious. What did that mean? Serious in that she was going to die or serious in that she was going to need a lot of help to recover? There was no doubt in Sarah's mind that if Kaye needed looking after, she would be there for her every step of the way.

'What was she doing driving a car?' said Sarah, suddenly remembering that Kaye had bought a rail ticket to travel.

'There was someone else with her,' said Bear. His tone was measured. 'She wasn't the driver.'

Sarah's chest tightened. It must have been the friend Kaye was staying with in London. 'Who was it? Do you know?'

Bear took a deep breath. 'The car belonged to Henry.'

'Henry!' cried Sarah. She turned her head sharply. 'Henry was driving the car?' A mixture of anger and disbelief surged through her body. Henry was supposed to be coming back for Annie and Edward. What the hell was he doing in a car with Kaye as a passenger? Then she realised. Of course. Henry was on his way back to Worthing to fetch Annie and Edward. He must have seen Kaye and offered her a lift. She'd squared the circle but somehow it still didn't feel right. 'Is Henry hurt as well?'

'We're not absolutely sure that she was with Henry,' said Bear, keen to qualify his assumptions, 'but the driver of the car is missing,' and the turmoil inside Sarah began all over again.

'I'm sorry. I don't understand.'

'To be honest, neither do I,' said Bear. 'Kaye has been drifting in and out of consciousness. We have a policewoman by her bedside and, as soon as we can, we'll try to piece together what happened.'

Sarah wiped her eyes. 'If you're not sure who the driver was, does that mean he ran off when the accident happened? He didn't stay and help her? How could he do that?'

The brokenness in her voice tore at Bear's heart. He longed to reach over and squeeze her hand, but for the moment he had to be the professional.

Bugger. He'd planned to do it tonight but now it would have to wait. Just his bad luck that some bloke in a car was there on the very day he'd decided to talk to her. He didn't bother to hang around. It was cold and he had to get home before he was missed. He walked back up the drive and, looking up, he saw an old woman up in the bedroom of the next-door house watching him through binoculars. Putting up two fingers, he walked away.

Horsham Hospital was an attractive building. It was built in the Arts and Crafts style and the main entrance faced the gateway. To the left and right, there were trees and shrubs and the single-storey buildings were on three sides, giving it a cottage feel.

'We need you to find out as much as you can, Sarah,' said Bear as he parked the car. 'Whoever was in that car is responsible for Kaye's injuries and we need to catch him.'

'Surely you're not suggesting that he tried to kill her?'

'Not at this stage,' said Bear, 'but the fact that he ran away from the scene of an accident is a criminal offence.'

Sarah nodded. 'I understand.' Her throat was as tight as a drum and she could feel her whole body trembling inside. Kaye, oh Kaye…

As they hurried through the entrance, Sarah caught a whiff of disinfectant and floor polish.

The soles of their shoes squeaked on the highly polished linoleum floor and as they passed the children's ward she could hear a child crying for her mother. The sister in charge of the ward was sympathetic. Sarah's heart sank as she told them about Kaye's condition. 'Her pelvis is broken and she has internal bleeding,' she said. 'I'm afraid she's far too unstable for anything more than bed rest at the moment. We are doing the best we can, but quite frankly, the cancer is so advanced, there seems little point in trying to prolong her life.'

'Cancer?' Sarah gasped.

'Didn't you know?' said the sister, her face reddening. 'Even before the accident, your friend had only weeks to live at best.'

Sarah staggered and she was aware that Bear had put his hand against her back to support her. Everything seemed so unreal she didn't know how to react. Yesterday everything was perfectly normal, but now she was being told Kaye already knew she was going to die. It seemed grossly unfair. It couldn't be true. She had no idea Kaye was so ill. She recalled that coughing fit a couple of months ago and she knew that sometimes Kaye was breathless, but cancer... Kaye must have gone to the doctor, but she'd never said a word. Could that have been why she was up in London?

'Mrs Royal, Mrs Royal?' The sister had touched Sarah's arm. 'Are you ready for me to take you to her now?'

Sarah nodded dully and turning to Bear, she said, 'Will you come with me?'

Kaye was in a room on her own. She looked as white as the sheet which covered her and they were giving her a blood transfusion. A policewoman rose from the chair next to the bed and picked up her cap from the locker as they walked in.

'Anything?' Bear whispered as she brushed passed them both. The policewoman shook her head and moved out of the way so that Sarah could get near. Sarah went to the bed and, sitting in the chair, she slipped off her coat and picked up Kaye's limp hand.

'Kaye,' she said gently, 'Kaye, it's Sarah.' Kaye's eyelids moved slightly as if she was struggling to wake up. 'I'm here now. It's Sarah.'

It seemed daft repeating the same thing over and over again, but Sarah had no real idea if that movement meant anything or if Kaye could hear her or even if she was aware of her presence. She saw her lips move but there was hardly a sound. She stood up and leaned over putting her ear close to Kaye's mouth. 'I didn't hear what you said. Tell me again.'

'My baby was born ... and he killed her...'

Sarah frowned. She was rambling. She didn't know what she was saying. Kaye didn't have any children.

'What are you talking about, darling?' Sarah had never used such a familiar term before but it slipped out easily. The lump in her throat was a mile wide. 'Your baby died, Kaye. That's what you told us.'

Kaye's eyes opened wide but she seemed to have difficulty in focusing. 'Henry…' It was an effort to get the words out. 'She was alive. A pillow...'

Sarah frowned. 'I'm sorry. I don't understand.'

'He told me...' Kaye gasped. 'He killed Bunny Warren's baby.'

Sarah glanced up at Bear. His expression was set in stone. Kaye suddenly looked at Sarah as if seeing her for the first time. Her otherwise limp hand seemed to find a strength of its own as she grabbed hold of Sarah's cardigan. Her eyes were wide with panic. 'Keep him away,' she rasped painfully, 'from Edward.'

Kaye fell back to the pillow and closed her eyes. She was still breathing, but Sarah looked up helplessly at Bear. He met her gaze then opened the door and shouted, 'Can we have some help in here please?'

'She will be all right, won't she?'

Lottie and Annie were back in the kitchen where Annie was making them both a cup of cocoa. Lottie had spent most of the evening quietly crying.

Annie put her arms around her shoulders. 'Of course. She'll be fine. You know Kaye. She's as tough as old boots.' Lottie gave her a wan smile.

Annie had never been in such close proximity to Lottie for so long before, but they were united in their overwhelming concern for Kaye. For the first time, it occurred to Annie how much they all owed her. If she hadn't thrown open her doors, where would they all be? Speaking for herself, she would most likely have been forced to give Edward up. She certainly wouldn't have a nice little job and her mother wouldn't have the grandson she adored. Lottie might still be in that terrible institution. From what Kaye had told them, the place where she was living was meant for people who were mentally ill. Annie couldn't imagine how dreadful it would be to be locked up all day with no hope of release ... and Lottie had been there for years and years. No wonder she had seemed a little odd at first. And as for Sarah, she had actually been homeless. Kaye had found her sleeping in a shelter overlooking the sea. Annie felt ashamed that she had turned her nose up at Sarah for that very reason. She shouldn't have done it. It wasn't Sarah's fault, and there but for the grace of God... The more Annie thought of it, the more she realised her debt of gratitude. She decided that in the morning she would buy Kaye a big bunch of flowers. She would write her a note as well, thanking her for everything, and when she got out of hospital, she would go out of her way to be helpful.

The milk boiled and Lottie blew her nose. Annie poured the milk over the cocoa powder and stirred vigorously, but when Lottie reached out to take her cup, Annie screamed and dropped it. It smashed on the flagstone floor, but neither woman paid it much attention. The man staring into the window had scared them half to death. They were both too busy running from the room in terror.

Thirty

Lottie and Annie huddled beside the radio in the sitting room early the next morning. After seeing the face at the window, even though they'd telephoned the police and the local bobby had come and checked the garden, neither of them had slept well and they were exhausted.

Last night, when he'd come with the awful news about Kaye's accident, Bear had told them that he'd arranged for an SOS message to go out on the Home Service of the BBC.

'And here is a message for Henry Royale of Horsham. Will Henry Royale, last known to be living in Horsham in Sussex, please go to Horsham Cottage Hospital where his wife Kaye Royale, also known as Kaye Hambledon, the well-known writer, is dangerously ill.'

By the time the pips began to herald the news bulletin, Annie had switched the wireless off.

'I don't understand why Sarah hasn't telephoned us,' said Annie. 'She must have known we would worry.'

'Poor Kaye,' said Lottie. 'I do hope she's going to be all right.'

'I'd better get a move on,' said Annie, glancing up at the clock. 'Are you sure you'll be all right looking after the girls on your own?'

'I'll be fine,' said Lottie.

Annie hurried from the room, calling over her

shoulder as she went. 'You will let me know if you have any more news?'

'I'll ring the hospital at nine and then send a message with your mother,' Lottie called after her.

Lottie didn't get to the telephone until after she'd taken Jenny to school. By the time she got back to Copper Beeches with Edward in the pram and Lu-Lu walking beside it, Mrs Mitchell had arrived.

'In view of what's happened,' she said, after Lottie had briefed her, 'would you like me to take Lu-Lu with me? It's not warm enough to go into the sea, but she might enjoy a paddle and there are other children playing nearby.'

'Are you sure?' said Lottie, secretly relieved. She not only wanted to contact the hospital but she also wanted to ring the police and ask them if anyone else had reported seeing the man they'd seen peering into the kitchen window after Bear and Sarah had gone. 'What about her lunch? Will you be bringing her back?'

'I could do,' said Judith, 'but I could easily stretch my own lunch for her.'

'Or I can stop by with a sandwich,' Lottie offered.

'Yes, why don't you,' said Judith.

With Lu-Lu 'helping' Judith get Edward into the pram, Lottie rang the hospital. 'Detective Truman and Sarah are on their way back home,' she said as she put the receiver back on its rest.

'I'll pop in on the way and tell Annie,' said Judith. Lu-Lu was quite happy to go with Mrs Mitchell, but they put on her walking reins, 'just in case'. There was a lot of waving and blowing of kisses but the three of them were soon on their way. They were so taken up with playing a game of peek-a-boo that Mrs Mitchell didn't notice the solitary black Bentley following her at a distance.

The journey back to Worthing had been difficult. Bear longed to comfort Sarah, but under the circumstances he could do little more than squeeze her hand. He knew the moment he touched her romantically he would never be able to hold himself in check. She sat next to him, dry-eyed. It's the shock, he thought to himself. There were still questions to be asked. Kaye hadn't told them anything about the accident: why she was with Henry or how the car came to crash. The Horsham police had ascertained that the car was brand spanking new. It had been frustrating that she had lost consciousness after she had spoken to Sarah. She hadn't been able to tell him anything of significance. The sister had explained it was because she was so weak. The accident itself, her underlying illness and the fact that she had lost so much blood; everything conspired against her. Kaye never stood a chance. In the early hours of the morning, she had died.

As they neared Worthing, although she was visibly upset, Sarah began asking questions. 'I still can't believe what she said about her daughter.'

'Did you know she had a child?'

'No ... well, yes,' said Sarah. 'We were having a heart to heart once and she told me she'd had a baby.'

'Henry's?'

'As a matter of fact, no,' said Sarah. 'She told me

she was already pregnant when she married Henry, but she told us that the baby was stillborn.'

'But Henry told her that the baby hadn't died,' said Bear.

'He must have done,' Sarah frowned. 'She once told me that she'd almost died herself, but surely they would have told her if the baby had lived?'

'She could have been confused,' said Bear.

'She didn't seem confused to me,' said Sarah. 'Desperate yes, but not confused.' She glanced across at him. 'Didn't you think she sounded very scared when she told us to keep Henry away from Edward?'

'As a matter of fact, I did,' said Bear.

'I still don't understand what happened all those years ago,' said Sarah. 'Kaye told me that she'd had a Caesarean birth and was out of it for a few days. If she was right about Henry, he must have done it because he didn't want the baby.'

'In that case, he's a very dangerous man.'

They fell silent. Bear was more anxious than ever to get Henry into custody. He was a man out of control. Who knew what he'd do next? Sarah was remembering the man she had married and comparing it to his behaviour towards Jenny that night when they'd gone to Annie's place in Horsham. Then there was what he'd done to Jenny's plait. Dear God ... it was like something out of a horror movie. It was like he was two different people.

'I've got Kaye's suitcase in the back,' said Bear. 'I'm going to have to go through it. The local bobbies said she had some paperwork with her.'

Sarah nodded. After a little while she said, 'Kaye and Henry married in 1930. The baby was born a few months later. Is it possible to find out if what she said was true ... that the baby lived? I know where her marriage certificate is kept. There may be other personal papers.'

'It's possible,' said Bear. 'Leave it with me and I'll see what I can do.'

Sarah nodded, satisfied.

'Sarah,' said Bear cautiously, 'you do realise that with Henry missing and Kaye dead, we're going to have to treat this accident as suspicious. The police will want to search the house.'

Sarah was silent for a while and then she said, 'I have no right to object anyway. I'm only a lodger and now that this has happened, when it's all over, we'll all be homeless again, I guess.'

'Don't do anything until the Will is read,' said Bear. 'Sit tight for as long as you can.'

'Whatever happens,' said Sarah quietly, 'would I be allowed to arrange her funeral?'

'That's up to the next of kin,' said Bear.

'As far as we know, Henry and Lottie are her only living relatives,' said Sarah.

The shop was crowded when Judith arrived. The queue was out of the door. Judith could see Annie busy serving customers with sweets. Today was the day sweet rationing officially ended. At this rate, the shopkeepers would be hard put to keep up with the demand. She put the pram brake on and left Edward with Lu-Lu tied to the pram handle by her walking reins outside while she pushed her way into the shop.

''Ere,' a fat woman complained. 'Get back in the queue and wait yer turn.'

'I'm not buying,' said Judith irritably. 'I just want to give someone a message.'

The crowd didn't like it, probably because they didn't believe her. 'Oi, stop her, will you,' someone cried and people began to push and shove.

Judith protested and fought back until a man grabbed at her coat and pulled her back towards the door. 'Unhand me at once,' she cried. 'How dare you!'

'Then get to the back of the queue.'

'I'm not here to buy sweets. I need to talk to someone.'

'Well, you can wait yer turn like everybody else,' said the man indignantly.

'I have to give my daughter a very important message.'

The noise inside and out of the shop was escalating. Children were being trampled on as adults pushed and shoved each other in the crush by the doorway.

'Now, now, there's no need to push.' Mr Richardson came from behind the tobacco counter with his hands in the air. 'Calm down everybody please. You'll all get your…' He was cut off in mid-sentence when somebody accidentally smacked him on the nose and knocked off his glasses.

Annie was trapped behind her counter and could do nothing about it, except shout up the stairs for Mrs Richardson to come and help them.

''Ere, I was before you.'

'Ow! That was my foot you trod on.'

Her employer's wife seldom came into the shop but she was an able-bodied woman with a commanding voice. 'Form an orderly queue or we're shutting the shop,' she bellowed. It did little to help.

'Get your elbow out of my ear.'

'Quarter of pear drops, please.'

'Watch what you're doing with that umbrella, mate.'

Judith managed to get far enough inside to catch her daughter's eye. 'Annie.'

'Mum!'

'It's all right, darling. Sarah and the policeman are on their way back,' Judith cried as she was propelled back through the door again.

The angry crowd continued to berate her as Judith walked to the pram. Lu-Lu was standing there, frightened and crying. Judith knelt down to comfort her and wiped her tear-stained cheeks with her own handkerchief. Once the child was calm again, she got to her feet and looked inside the pram. Her heart almost stopped. The pram was empty. Edward was gone.

Mrs Goodall put the finishing touches of lipstick on her mouth and rubbed her lips together. She patted her hair and slipped her feet into her best court shoes. It didn't take long to go from her house to the door of Copper Beeches, and almost as soon as she rang the bell, Lottie snatched open the door.

'Oh,' she said as soon as she saw her neighbour. 'Sorry, but we were expecting someone else.'

'My dear,' gushed Mrs Goodall. 'As soon as I heard the SOS on the radio, I just had to come over to say how sorry I am that dear Kaye is in hospital.'

Lottie blinked in surprise. Mrs Goodall being nice? This was a turn-up for the books.

'How is she?' Mrs Goodall went on. 'Can I come in for a minute?' There was little point in Lottie telling her it wasn't convenient. Mrs Goodall had already pushed her way into the hallway. She gave Lottie a polite nod and patted her hair again. 'When did she go into hospital? I had no idea she was ill.'

The silence hung between them until Lottie said, 'Actually, she was in a motor car accident.'

'Oh my dear!' said Mrs Goodall, putting her hand to her cheek. 'How terrible. Poor girl.'

Lottie frowned crossly. Something wasn't quite right. Mrs Goodall had nothing but complaints about them, and now here she was, behaving as if she was Kaye's best friend.

'I had no idea Mrs Royale's husband was around,' Mrs Goodall went on. 'I rather assumed he'd been killed in the war. Well, you live and learn, don't you? I was shocked when I heard it on the radio...'

'Mrs Goodall...' said Lottie, taking a deep breath.

'Now you mustn't be upset, my dear,' Mrs Goodall butted in. 'These things happen. You know I had no idea she's really Kaye Hambledon, the famous writer. I have admired her plays on the radio for some time.'

They heard the key go in the door, and when it opened, Sarah and Bear came in. They both looked tired, but Sarah looked awful. Her eyes were red and puffy and her face was pale.

'Detective Truman,' said Mrs Goodall. 'I was

just saying to Lottie that I was so upset to hear about Mrs Royale that I had to come straight over. Have you any more news?'

'Mrs Goodall, could you come back later? It's not very convenient right now,' said Sarah stiffly.

'Oh, don't mind me,' said Mrs Goodall. 'I'll be as quiet as a mouse.'

Lottie put her hand to her mouth. Bear sensed the problem at once. Now was not the time to cope with a nosy neighbour. 'I think it best if you go, madam, if you don't mind,' he said politely. 'I'm afraid I shall be here for some time.'

'You'll want to hear what I've got to say about that man I saw creeping around the garden last night,' Mrs Goodall insisted.

'I shall send a constable around to take a statement,' said Bear. He opened the door wide, making it impossible for Mrs Goodall to stay. 'Goodbye Mrs Goodall,' he said pointedly.

'Well, I'm glad that you are looking into it,' she said haughtily. 'I must say, that if you had acted when I first called, you might have caught the wretched man by now.'

As the door closed behind her, Sarah and Lottie exchanged a nervous smile.

'It's bad, isn't it?'

Sarah nodded. 'Kaye died at about five o'clock this morning.'

'Oh...' said Lottie.

They stood together, the silence between them hanging heavily in the air, then Sarah reached out and Lottie went into her arms. As they cried together softly, Bear made his way into the kitchen to make tea.

Judith felt her knees buckle as she looked up and down the street. Everything around her seemed normal. Fifty yards up the road, a road sweeper scooped some dirt onto his shovel and lobbed it into his handcart. Several women wandered by, heading in the direction of the town. By Warnes Hotel, a man with a suitcase was getting out of a taxi and giving the driver the fare. Judith scanned the area wildly but she couldn't see anybody with a baby in their arms.

She crouched down to Lu-Lu. 'Where's Edward?' She was doing her best not to let her highly anxious state frighten the child. 'Did you see who took him?'

Tears filled the child's eyes.

'I'm not cross with you, darling,' said Judith, 'but you must tell me if you saw someone taking the baby.'

Lu-Lu's chin quivered.

'Where's the baby?' Judith's voice was shrill.

'You all right, love?' One of the customers had come out of the sweet shop and was looking at her.

'The baby,' said Judith. 'Someone has taken the baby.'

The woman stared at the crumpled sheet with a blank expression. 'Who?'

A couple of other passers-by stopped next to the pram.

'Edward,' cried Judith. She was beginning to sound hysterical now. 'My grandson. He's gone. I left him for one minute while I gave my daughter an urgent message and when I got back to the pram ... he was gone!'

'Perhaps the little girl saw what happened,' said one of the women bending down to the child. 'Did you see the nasty stranger what took your little brother?'

Lu-Lu began to cry. Judith picked Lu-Lu up and let her straddle her hip. She couldn't stand around talking about it. She had to go and look for him. She had to find Edward. She raced along the Steyne, calling to everyone she saw, 'Did you see someone carrying a small baby? My grandson has been snatched. Have you seen someone with a small baby? My grandson has been taken. Have you seen anyone with a little baby?' By the time Judith came back up the other side of the Steyne, a small crowd had gathered by the pram.

'Any luck?' asked the first woman.

Pale and breathless, Judith shook her head. 'I'll have to tell my daughter. I don't know what she's going to say.'

'If you want my opinion,' someone said, 'you'd better call the police.'

'Is Lottie all right?' Bear was still sitting at the kitchen table when Sarah came back downstairs.

'She's resting on her bed,' said Sarah, taking her coat off at last. 'It's been a bitter blow.'

'I'd better report in,' said Bear, picking up the telephone. 'Tell them where I am.'

Sarah left him to speak to his superiors in private.

'It's a bit of a waiting game,' he said when he'd finished. 'We've got people searching for Henry, and the local bobby is checking outhouses and barns in the area in case he's holed up somewhere. We're also keeping an eye out at the station and on the buses.'

Sarah nodded dully. She lowered herself into a chair and put her head in her hands.

'The police came here last night,' he went on. 'Somebody reported a man hanging about in the gardens.'

'Mrs Goodall?' said Sarah.

'The call came from this house,' said Bear.

'Lottie never mentioned it,' Sarah said looking up.

'Other things on her mind,' said Bear. 'Apparently the local bobby found a footprint in the flower bed under the kitchen window. I don't suppose you can remember Henry's shoe size?'

'Nine.'

Bear nodded. 'The shoe print was a man's shoe size nine.'

'This is getting scary,' said Sarah.

'There will be extra patrols in the area tonight and all this week,' he said reassuringly. 'Please don't worry. We will get him.'

'I'd better go and check on Lottie,' said Sarah, rising to her feet.

'Before you go, Sarah,' said Bear. 'Men like Henry are trophy hunters. I'm told that they like to keep mementoes of what they've done. I think it gives them a feeling of power ... a sort of "I know something you don't know." Did Henry leave behind any strange things when he walked out on you?'

Sarah recalled Kaye's cigarette case, the one she'd been forced to sell to feed the children. She sat back down and explained what had happened.

'You've had it really tough, haven't you,' said Bear sympathetically.

She looked away. Bear stirred a spoon of sugar into his tea. 'Was there anything else?'

Sarah shook her head. 'Only an old suit of his, oh, and some baby's booties.' The words died on Sarah's lips as they came out and Bear gave her a puzzled look.

'Jenny put them on her old dolly.' She put her hand to her lips and the colour drained from her face. 'Do you know what, I think they belonged to her.'

'Sorry,' he said, 'you've lost me.'

'Those booties,' said Sarah, her eyes filling with tears. 'They belonged to Kaye. Now that we're talking about them, I remember a funny look she gave Jenny when she put them on the new dolly on Christmas Day. I thought at the time it was just that the dolly already had lovely shoes and that Kaye was offended.' She put her head in her hands again. 'Now I've got a horrible feeling they had belonged to her baby. Henry left them in the wardrobe for me to find.' Sarah looked up helplessly at Lottie. 'Oh my Lord, how much that must have hurt her.'

'It wasn't your fault,' said Bear gruffly.

'I know,' said Sarah, silent tears running down her cheeks, 'but all the same...'

Bear cleared his throat noisily. 'Did Kaye have anything belonging to another woman?'

Sarah wiped her eyes with her handkerchief. 'She never said.'

'What about Annie?'

'I can ask her when she gets back home,' said Sarah. 'She's at work. Mrs Mitchell has taken Edward and Lu-Lu to the beach chalet.'

Bear nodded. 'In that case, when I've finished my tea, I'll get to work in Kaye's office.'

Thirty-One

Once it became apparent that Edward was really gone, Annie had to be told. Her first reaction was disbelief, followed by anger and then blind panic. Mr Richardson was forced to close the shop.

Annie and her mother ran around the Steyne again, pushing the pram with Lu-Lu inside, choking back huge silent sobs as they looked from one to the other in bewilderment.

'I never should have trusted you with him.'

'It was only a second. Whoever did it was so quick.'

'You shouldn't have left him.'

'I didn't know it was going to take so long to get into the shop.'

The recriminations and accusations became more and more heated. When she got back to the shop empty-handed, Judith did her best to comfort her but she was distraught herself. 'I'm so sorry, darling. I'm so sorry.'

Mrs Richardson, who had come downstairs to take charge of the unruly customers who had been squabbling before they knew Edward was missing, was doing her best to comfort Lu-Lu who by now was very distressed.

'I'll never let you look after him again,' said Annie, shaking away her mother's comforting arm.

'It's no good taking lumps out of each other,' Mrs Richardson said sternly. 'You both need to pull together if you're going to find him. The police are on their way.'

A man in the crowd stepped forward. 'My name is James,' he said. 'I work at the hospital. I'll organise a search around the streets.' They heard him telling some of the bystanders to 'try Library Place and Marine Place ... you go the other way. York Road and Albert Place... I'll go along Warwick Gardens and Wyke Avenue. Ask everyone you see if they've seen someone carrying a baby.' People eager to help hurried away with anxious expressions.

'He can't just have vanished into thin air,' Annie wailed.

'I'm wondering if someone took him in a car or a taxi,' said Judith. 'I saw a taxi outside the hotel.'

Annie's face blanched. By the time the police arrived, the queue of people who had been waiting for sweets had largely gone, but when the constable asked the few of them left, it became apparent that because of the rumpus over Judith pushing in front of the queue, no one had actually seen the little boy being taken.

'But he was strapped in,' Judith sobbed. 'Surely someone must have seen them undoing the straps.'

The constable left them to go to the nearest police box. 'Sarge,' he said as he called in, 'we've got a major incident at the Steyne. Someone's kidnapped a baby.'

Bear answered the telephone in Kaye's hallway. As he listened, his face grew grave.

'What is it?' asked Sarah. 'Have they found Henry?'

'Edward has been snatched.'

'Oh my Lord,' cried Sarah. 'He's done it. Kaye was right, wasn't she? He's actually done it.'

'Done what?' said Lottie.

'Kaye's last words to me were, "Keep Henry away from Edward." She knew he was going to do something bad and it looks like he's kidnapped him.'

Lottie was horrified. 'What?'

'I have to get down to the Steyne,' said Bear.

'What about Lu-Lu?' said Sarah. 'Where's Lu-Lu?'

'The report was only about a baby,' said Bear, grabbing his coat from the hallstand. 'I have to go.'

'I'm coming too,' said Sarah. 'Lu-Lu needs me.'

'Well, I can't stay here and do nothing,' cried Lottie. 'I'm coming too.'

When they all arrived at the shop, it was a nightmare. While everybody panicked, tried to restore calm or generally talked over one another, Sarah picked up her distraught child and crossed over the road into Steyne Gardens. She found an empty park bench and pulled Lu-Lu onto her lap. She cuddled the child, rocking her gently and stroking her hair. She felt torn because of poor

Annie, but her priority was to comfort her badly frightened daughter. What had she seen? Had Henry tried to take her as well? She would have to take this slowly, one step at a time, if she was going to find out exactly what had happened. She hummed gently, her mouth on Lu-Lu's hair, and after a while her daughter dropped off to sleep, although her body still shuddered with a deep-seated sob every now and then. She was going to take a long time to get over this.

In Sarah's mind, it dawned on her that Edward's kidnapper must be Henry. Hadn't he told Annie he was coming for his son? At first, she comforted herself, if Henry had taken Edward, no harm would come to the boy, but Kaye's revelation about what happened to her own child added a frightening dimension to everything. Of course, nobody had expected him to take the boy without Annie's consent, but then Henry always was unpredictable.

'Is she all right?'

Sarah looked up to find Bear standing next to her. She nodded and he lowered himself onto the bench beside her. He was close ... close enough for her to feel the warmth of his body. She longed for him to put his arm around her and comfort her too, but he was ever the professional policeman.

'Has she said anything?' His voice was both calm and gentle.

Sarah shook her head. 'I haven't asked. She was too upset.' They were talking in whispers.

He nodded. 'It seems that there was some sort of commotion going on over the sweets in the shop and nobody saw what happened.'

'Do you think it was Henry?'

'Bearing in mind what Kaye said, who else?' Bear nodded. 'I've got everybody watching ports and airports and all patrol cars in Sussex will be on the lookout. We're doing house-to-house calls in the area but it's going to be a bit like looking for a needle in the proverbial haystack.'

'How is Annie?'

'The doctor is with her now,' he said. 'Once he's checked her out, we'll get her home.'

'Oh Bear,' said Sarah brokenly. 'What an awful day. Poor Annie doesn't even know about Kaye yet.'

'If I was you I'd leave that until she asks,' he said gently. 'She's got enough on her plate right now.'

She nodded. 'What are they doing now?' Several people had converged on the sweet shop again.

'Some chap from the hospital organised a search of the locality, but it doesn't look as if it's come to much,' said Bear. 'Still, good of him to do it. People need to do something.' He stood up. 'Are you all right to get home? I'm going to be here for some time.'

Sarah nodded and managed a brave smile as he hurried back to the shop.

A car pulled up and Cllr Mitchell got out. As soon as Annie saw her father, she rushed at him, hitting his chest with her fists. 'It was you, wasn't it? You took him. What have you done with him? Where is he?'

Malcolm seized her wrists. 'What is this? What are you talking about?'

'You never wanted me to keep him, did you,' Annie challenged. 'What are you doing here if you didn't have something to do with it?'

'Do with what?' Malcolm snapped. 'I was on my way to the beach chalet when I saw you all standing around in the street.'

'Edward has been kidnapped,' Judith explained.

Annie turned to her mother. 'Make him give Edward back,' she sobbed. 'I don't want him to be adopted. I won't sign the papers, I won't!'

Malcolm had gone as white as a sheet. 'Kidnapped? When? How?'

Judith gave him a brief résumé and his face blanched with fury. 'What were you thinking about, woman? Didn't you have him strapped in?'

'Excuse me for saying so,' Lottie began, 'but this isn't helping.'

They stared at her for a second. 'No. No, you're quite right,' said Malcolm, deflating like a balloon. 'Has anyone ordered a search of the area? Where are the press? Did anyone think to call them? Get it in the paper and whoever took my grandson will have no place to hide.'

Sarah sniffed back a tear. Poor Annie. What on earth was happening in their lives? When was it all going to end? Amazingly, Lottie had risen to the occasion. She could see her standing across the road with her arm around Annie's shoulders.

Dear Lottie. What enormous strides she'd made since coming to live with Kaye. Poor Annie was completely distraught. Whilst Sarah was lost in thought, Lu-Lu gulped down an enormous internal sob. Sarah tightened her grip slightly and her daughter relaxed. Sarah was searching her mind to think of a way to ask Lu-Lu what happened without upsetting her again, but then her daughter said, 'Can I eat it now?'

'Eat what?'

Lu-Lu opened her hand and there on her palm was a coffee crunch.

Thirty-Two

Annie refused to go home. They kept telling her that she should get some rest, but she felt compelled to stay. Judith seemed to have withdrawn into herself, the consequences of what had happened too horrible to think about, and yet her mind constantly travelled the same path. What if Henry harmed the child? What if he took him abroad? If Annie wasn't married to him, did he have the right to do that? Had Annie put his name on Edward's birth certificate? She stood by the pram picking at the covers and rubbing the handle as she desperately tried to remember something ... anything which seemed out of the ordinary. Lottie and Mrs Richardson had organised drinks for the people searching and in the process they had struck up a bit of a friendship.

By lunchtime, it seemed that half of Worthing was out looking for the baby. Someone went to the Town Hall and brought back an official who opened up the defunct air-raid shelter. It didn't seem to occur to anyone that if a padlock and key had to be used to open the door, then it was highly unlikely that Edward was there. But the shelter was searched anyway, along with the public toilets, including those by the pier. The beach was combed as well, but there was no clue to the whereabouts of the baby, not so much as a dropped bootie. The houses and small gardens in the immediate vicinity, the Methodist church and even the Egremont public house were all targeted by enthusiastic helpers.

'What am I going to do?' Annie wailed as she fell into her mother's arms.

The police had been to the bus station, asking drivers and conductors alike if they had seen a man carrying a small baby but everywhere they drew a blank.

'Annie, you must come home,' said Lottie gently. 'There's nothing more we can do here. Come home and get some rest.'

There wasn't much peace when they all got back to Copper Beeches. News had got out about Kaye's demise and people from the world of show business were ringing with their condolences. It was another bitter blow for Annie, so much so that her parents called for the doctor again. He gave her some sedation and left them to it once Annie had calmed down and was settled in bed.

Bear came to the house at about three. As soon as they opened the front door to him, they could tell by the grim expression on his face that Edward was still missing. Lottie showed him into the sitting room and Sarah arrived back home shortly after, having just picked Jenny up from school. She took the children upstairs to their playroom and as soon as she returned downstairs they all congregated together; the Mitchells (Annie was asleep upstairs), Lottie and Sarah. Bear told them that the police believed that Henry, for reasons best known to himself, had taken Edward away from Annie and he asked everyone to rack their brains for anything, no matter how trivial, which might throw some light on the problem.

Sarah told them about the coffee crunch Lu-Lu had been holding. 'They are his favourite sweet,' she explained. 'He eats them by the bucketload.'

'I think that more or less proves that we are looking for Henry,' said Bear. He turned to Lottie. 'Can you think of anything, Lottie?' His tone was gentle. 'Something we may not know?'

Lottie shook her head. She had never met Henry, but she remembered Kaye saying how glad she had been to be free of him. She'd likened him to a spider. 'She told me you got trapped into his web of deceit and you couldn't get out,' Lottie explained. 'She said when he'd played with you and got bored, he moved on, leaving behind broken hearts and a wrecked life,' Lottie dabbed her eyes with a handkerchief. 'Kaye told me that if she could do something with her life after Henry, I could pick up the threads of my own life after the mental home.' Her chin quivered and she blew her nose. Judith leaned over and rubbed Lottie's arm comfortingly.

'Sarah?' said Bear.

'I gave up trying to understand Henry a long time ago,' she said angrily. 'All I know is that he is selfish beyond words and everything he does is done because of what he wants. I refuse to be bitter about him anymore. I don't even want to think about him. The thing about Henry is that it doesn't matter how the other person feels, he always gets his own way.'

'Mr Mitchell?' said Bear.

'It's no secret, I never liked the man,' said Malcolm stiffly. 'He worked in my shop for a while and was charm itself, but I long suspected him of theft. He seduced my daughter behind my back and then ran off with her. The next thing we knew, he'd married her and she was having a baby. At first I didn't want the child and refused to acknowledge him as my grandson, but now ... now...' He broke off and, standing to his feet, went to the window, putting his back to them.

Bear looked at Mrs Mitchell. 'And you Mrs Mitchell,' he said kindly. 'I know this has been a terrible trauma for you, but can you remember anything, any small detail which might help us.'

Judith shook her head miserably. 'I've gone over and over everything,' she said, 'but there's nothing.'

'Go back to when you first looked into the pram,' said Bear. 'Was there anyone else around?'

Judith frowned. 'The shop was quite full but the street was empty ... apart from a man getting out of a taxi to go into Warnes Hotel.'

Bear wrote something in his notebook. Judith looked thoughtful. 'I stopped a couple of passers-by and then I ran around the Steyne looking for him. The only other person I saw was a road sweeper.'

'Road sweeper?' Bear repeated.

'He was sweeping near the Methodist church,' said Judith miserably.

Sarah excused herself and went to make some tea and do some sandwiches for the girls.

'Have you got any family nearby?' Bear asked her. He had followed Sarah out to the kitchen after speaking to Judith and could see she was on the point of exhaustion.

'My sister Vera,' she said,'

'Couldn't she come and give you a hand?'

Sarah laughed sardonically. 'I've given up asking Vera for help,' she said. 'She's always too busy.'

'Where does she live?'

Sarah told him, adding, 'But you're wasting your time.'

The doorbell rang and a florist turned up with yet another bunch of flowers. The shrill sound brought Annie to the top of the stairs. 'Any news?'

Sarah shook her head sadly and Annie shuffled miserably back to her room.

Bear left hurriedly and, about twenty minutes later, he came back with Vera and Mrs Goodall. 'These two ladies are happy to do some official police business,' he announced and Sarah blinked in surprise as Mrs Goodall took over answering the door and putting the flowers into vases while Vera sat in Kaye's office taking the constant phone calls.

'*Official* police business?' Sarah smiled as Bear closed the office door.

'Don't mock it,' Bear cautioned with a grin. 'Everybody likes to feel important.'

Somehow or other they got through the rest of the day. Sarah cooked a meal, but everybody except the girls had lost their appetite. They did a puzzle together until it was time for bed.

'Mummy, where's Edward?' Jenny asked as Sarah pulled the covers up.

'He's gone for a little holiday,' said Sarah. She put a bright smile on her face so that everything would seem perfectly normal.

'But why is Auntie Annie crying?'

'She misses him a bit, that's all.'

Lu-Lu was a bit clingy, but after all the stress of the day it didn't take long for her to sleep. Frustratingly, she had refused to talk about what happened to Edward, becoming more withdrawn every time Sarah or Lottie tried to coax something out of her. Downstairs, the phone stopped ringing at around eight, but it was hard to relax. They all went to bed at around nine, but it was a long, long night.

Henry had woken up during the night. It was still dark but he could hear movement all around him. He felt stiff and there was an odd-looking light in the corner of the room. His bed felt uncomfortable and a bit damp. Where was he? It was hard to focus in this half-light. He could hear a cry in the distance. He tried to call out but his tongue stuck to the roof of his mouth. He could really do with a nice coffee crunch. Never mind, he'd get up in a minute. All he needed was a couple more minutes to give himself time to thoroughly wake up. He put his hand out to feel for the sheet but he couldn't find it. He was tired. So tired. Just a short snooze and then he'd get up and see to his son.

'Wicked witch come back?' Lu-Lu had had a nightmare. She'd woken up screaming and Sarah had rushed to her bedroom. The child was covered in perspiration and clearly terrified. Jenny yawned sleepily and turned over when her mother came into the room, so Sarah carried Lu-Lu into her bed.

Sarah caught her breath. At all costs she mustn't frighten Lu-Lu or she'd clam up again. Mustering every bit of acting strength she had, she said casually, 'What witch is that, darling?'

'She took Edward.'

Sarah held her breath.

'No darling, she won't come back.'

Sarah's mind went into overdrive. A witch took Edward? Not a bad man? Lu-Lu had only been a few months old when Henry left. Apart from that time when she'd seen him at Annie's place, she didn't know her father. Could it be that the kidnapper wasn't Henry after all and that Edward had been snatched by a woman? Stay calm, she told herself. Sound casual when you speak. It was imperative that she didn't frighten Lu-Lu.

'Did you see her take Edward?'

Lu-Lu nodded.

'That was very naughty, wasn't it?'

The child began to cry again.

'Shh, shh, I'm sure you did everything you could, darling,' said Sarah, stroking her hair and kissing the top of her head. 'It's not your fault. She was a very, very bad witch.'

She let Lu-Lu calm down and then she said, 'How did you know she was a witch?'

'Shh, shhh, Mummy,' said Lu-Lu, wide-eyed.

She looked around nervously. 'She will gobble me up.'

Anger rushed through every vein in Sarah's body. How dare she? What sort of a woman frightens a little girl with something like that?

'No one is going to hurt you, darling,' Sarah said fiercely. 'I won't let them.'

Lu-Lu looked up at her mother and Sarah snapped a bright smile on her face. 'And Mummy, she had black hands.'

Black hands ... black hands...? All at once it dawned on Sarah what she meant. 'How did she take Edward away without anybody seeing, darling? Was she on her broomstick?'

Lu-Lu sat up on her elbow and looked her in the face. 'Oh Mummy,' she said with an expression which said Sarah should know these things. Sitting up properly, she spread her arms wide apart and said, 'She had a BIG black car.'

'How silly of me,' said Sarah, her heart rate going up. This was dynamite. She'd have to tell Bear first thing in the morning. He was looking for Henry, but the kidnapper was a woman.

Thirty-Three

Morning brought more heartache. Edward had been gone for twenty-four hours and they were no nearer finding him. As soon as she was up, Sarah telephoned the station to tell Bear that according to Lu-Lu, the kidnapper was a woman. He wasn't there, so she left a message. After breakfast Sarah took Jenny to school and, anxious to protect her eldest daughter from the worry they were all going through, she had a quiet word with her teacher. 'We'll do our best to keep it quiet if that's what you want, Mrs Royal,' Mrs Audus promised, 'but I think you'll find that everybody already knows about the kidnap. It's in all the papers, and some of the children are bound to have heard their parents talking about it.'

'Perhaps I should have told her then,' said Sarah.

'It would be better coming from you,' Mrs Audus agreed sympathetically.

She called Jenny from the classroom and together they explained that Edward's daddy had taken him on holiday for a while. Auntie Annie was upset because he hadn't asked her first, but everyone hoped Edward would be home soon. Jenny accepted the explanation without a word. As Jenny went back to her classroom, Sarah lingered to go to the office and speak to the Headmistress about her concerns over William Steel.

'We'll keep a weather eye on the boy,' said the Head. 'I don't tolerate bullying at this school.'

When she got back home, Vera and Mrs Goodall were back.

'I'm so grateful for your help, Mrs Goodall,' said Sarah. They were in the kitchen where Mrs Goodall was dealing with yet another bunch of flowers. Sarah was making a pot of tea.

'That's what neighbours are for, dear,' she said. Sarah blinked in surprise. 'I had no idea Kaye was so popular. I shall have to go back home and get some of my own vases. We're running out of them.'

'I'm sure Lottie would be happy for you to take some of the flowers too,' said Sarah, pouring Mrs Goodall a cup of tea.

'Do you think so?'

'Like you say,' said Sarah. 'We do seem to have rather a lot.'

She took another cup of tea to the office. 'Thanks for doing this, Vera,' said Sarah.

'That's all right,' said Vera. 'I had no idea you were living with someone so famous.'

'Neither did I,' said Sarah. 'She was a very unassuming person,'

'Do you know what?' Vera said, her eyes sparkling. 'I spoke to Jack Train on the telephone yesterday ... you know, *the* Jack Train.'

Sarah hesitated.

'What?' said Vera crossly.

'I don't want to seem ungrateful…' Sarah began, but they were interrupted as the telephone rang again.

'Miss Hambledon's residence,' said Vera in a posh telephone voice Sarah didn't recognise.

She left her sister to it.

By late morning, several Fleet Street reporters had turned up. Lottie took Lu-Lu upstairs when they started knocking on the door. Sarah got Vera to ring the police station.

'Mrs Royal,' one of the reporters shouted through the letter box.

'I can't sit here all day and do nothing,' said Annie, wringing her hands. 'I should be out there looking for him.'

'Where would you look?' said Sarah. 'We've no

idea where he could be. Henry could have taken him anywhere.'

'I know you all insist Henry took him,' said Annie tetchily. 'But why would he do such a thing? Edward is my baby too. Henry loves us both.'

Sarah squeezed Annie's hand affectionately. 'We can't understand it either,' she said. 'But I told you what Kaye said and it's too much of a coincidence.'

'I can't believe he would harm Edward,' said Annie stubbornly. 'I won't believe it.'

Sarah went out into the hallway and slipped her hand into her coat pocket.

'Mrs Royal.' The man shouted through the letter box again.

'Oh, I do wish they would go away,' said Annie as Sarah came back.

'Bear is sending a constable to stand by the gate,' she said. 'Hold out your hand.'

When Annie had done so, Sarah said, 'The person who took Edward gave this to Lu-Lu.' She dropped the coffee crunch into Annie's hand. Annie's face went white.

'Mrs Royal,' the reporter was back at the letter box. 'Did you know that a baby was found abandoned on the steps of St Mary's Convent this morning?'

The two women looked at each other and gasped. Annie jumped to her feet and rushed to open the door. As she did so, a photographer's flashbulb went off and everybody started talking at once.

'Mrs Royal how do you feel?' 'When did you notice the baby was missing?' 'Do you think your husband took the baby?' 'Are you breastfeeding your baby?'

'What's this about an abandoned baby?' Sarah shrieked over the noise.

'The child was found early this morning,' someone said. 'They've taken it to Worthing Hospital.'

Annie didn't wait a second longer. With Sarah shouting, 'Vera, tell Lottie where we've gone and phone the Mitchells. Annie, wait, I'll come with you,' and a bevy of reporters hard on her heels, Sarah ran down the drive after her.

As soon as he'd got the message from Sarah that Lu-Lu had described a witch with a black car and black hands, Bear had gone straight into the office to talk with his colleagues. Everyone agreed that the kidnapper must have been a woman wearing gloves. Taking into consideration what Judith had told him last night, he spent the morning tracking down the road sweeper and what he had said only confirmed Sarah's version of events.

Fred Pickles lived in a prefab in Castle Road in the Tarring area. He was about fifty-five and apart from having few teeth left, he was in good health. He proudly told Bear he walked to work each day, and after working an eight-hour shift in all weathers, he walked back home.

Bear asked him about the previous day.

'Yes, I heard the commotion,' said Fred, 'but I didn't see 'owt.'

'Did you see anyone carrying a baby?'

Fred shook his head. 'The only person I saw with a baby was an older woman in a big black 'at,' he said. 'She looked more like she belonged at Royal flippin' Ascot than Worthing.'

'Have you ever seen her before?' said Bear.

'Na,' said Fred. 'She got into a big car ... Bentley I think, but I don't think it would have been 'er what took the little-un. She looked too well-off.'

Now Bear knew for sure that Henry had had an accomplice.

'Did you see who was driving the car?'

Fred looked surprised. 'She was, o' course. She put the nipper in one of them wicker baskets on the back seat.'

Back in his office, Bear contacted Scotland Yard.

'DI Garfield,' said a voice.

'This is Detective Inspector Truman of Worthing police,' said Bear. 'I'm trying to trace an ex-con, Henry Royale. He came out of the nick about two weeks ago.'

DI Garfield snorted. 'Now there's a funny thing,' he said. 'We're looking for the same villain. What's your interest in him?'

'I've got nothing on him yet, but wherever he goes he leaves a trail of damage behind him,' said Bear. 'What about you?'

'Seems that our chum is wanted in connection with a distraction burglary in a Bond Street jeweller.'

'Tell me,' said Bear, smiling to himself.

'He was with an older woman, a Mrs Ada Browning,' said Garfield. 'She's the innocent party, I think. Jeweller has known her for years. She wanted a watch repaired and they asked to see some brooches. When they'd gone, so had one of the brooches.'

'So where is Ada Browning now?'

'Missing,' came the reply. 'I was rather hoping you were going to tell me you'd found her.'

'Why? Has Mrs Browning got any contacts in Worthing?' Bear was beginning to feel excited. Was Ada Henry's accomplice?

'Not that I know of.'

'Who reported her missing?'

'Her butler-cum-handyman. He noticed her car was gone.'

'Is that odd?'

'Mrs Browning doesn't usually drive,' said Garfield. 'Apparently she's been acting strangely for some time. Matthews is a sort of old family retainer. He's worked for her for nineteen or twenty years but he's known her a lot longer.'

'And this is out of character?'

'Totally. She opened a bank account for Royale,' said Garfield. 'And she even bought him a car. I only wish I knew how he did it. Lucky sod.'

'I'm afraid that car was involved in a serious accident near Horsham,' said Bear. 'The passenger died and the driver is missing.'

'Good God,' said Garfield. 'So the poor old duck is dead.'

'The dead woman was Kaye Royale, Henry Royale's only legitimate wife,' said Bear.

'*Only* legitimate wife?' Garfield repeated. 'How many has the man got?'

'Three,' said Bear.

'Blimey!' said Garfield. 'So where is she? Mrs Browning, I mean.'

'I don't know,' said Bear, 'but the evidence is quite compelling that she and Henry Royale may be involved in a kidnapping. We've got a five-month-old baby missing down here.'

Bear could hear Garfield relaying the message to somebody else. 'We'll clear it with our Super and come down to Worthing,' he said.

'Before you come, sir,' Bear managed to say before Garfield put down the phone again, 'would you check if Ada has made any other large purchases? Tickets to go abroad for instance. We have an airport nearby. Or has she hired a cottage or booked into a hotel around here? It may help us locate her.'

'Consider it done,' said Garfield.

Annie went straight to the children's ward but was stopped at the door by the sister. 'Visiting hours are from two till four,' she said sternly.

'You don't understand,' cried Annie desperately. 'That baby they found on the convent steps. It's mine.'

The sister took a step backwards. 'Yours?' she said coldly.

'Please, I've been going out of my mind with worry.'

'You're lucky the baby didn't die,' said the sister tartly.

'Oh thank God,' Annie cried. 'Thank God they found him in time. Can I go in now?'

The sister barred the way into the ward with her arm on the door. 'Have you any idea how cold it was last night?' she said crossly. By this time, Sarah had caught up with Annie.

'And have you seen a doctor? If you ask me, running down the corridor like that is a bit stupid in your condition.'

'Is it him?' cried Sarah. 'Is it Edward?'

'Edward?' said the sister, her tone softening, and then turning back to Annie she said gently, 'You're the mother of that kidnapped baby, aren't you?'

'Yes, can I see him now?'

The sister didn't move. 'I'm sorry dear, this baby is a newborn baby girl.'

As she heard the words, Annie fainted clean away.

Bear sat at his kitchen table with a sheaf of papers. Garfield was eating his fish 'n' chips. It was still quite early, but from the moment he had arrived in Worthing, Garfield had complained that he was starving. He was a studious-looking man with slicked-down hair and round-rimmed glasses. He was in plain clothes. He had a brown pinstriped suit and wore a white shirt with a brown diagonal striped tie.

Bear had gone to Worley's on North Street, which had the reputation of being the best fish 'n' chips in town.

They hadn't bothered with the niceties. The two men ate with their fingers out of the chip paper and each drank beer from a bottle.

'So Ada met Royale when he came out of Lewes prison,' said Garfield.

'In a black Bentley,' said Bear. 'And the road sweeper said he saw a large black car and the driver, a woman, was putting a child on the back seat.'

'That makes the main suspect Ada Browning.'

Bear nodded.

'What beats me,' said Garfield, 'is how this normally law-abiding woman could be persuaded to aid and abet him in taking his child.'

'When it comes to charm,' said Bear, 'Henry Royale's got it by the bucketload.'

'Next question, where would the pair be going?'

'Did you find out if she was splashing the cash?'

Garfield shook his head. 'Not since she bought him the car.'

'No tickets to go abroad?' said Bear hopefully. 'Hotel booking?'

Garfield licked the end of his fingers then wiped them on the newspaper before screwing it into a ball. 'No, nothing.'

Kaye's suitcase rested on the dresser. Bear wiped his fingers on a tea towel and placed it on the table between them. 'This belonged to the victim of the motor accident. The case had burst open on impact. Bits everywhere. Apparently it took them ages to pick everything up.'

At first, the contents stuffed untidily inside seemed disappointing. Apart from a change of clothes, some underwear and a nightdress, the only thing of interest was a large envelope. Bear opened it, but it only contained a signed copy of a contract for the BBC. It was muddy and had clearly been fished out of water.

Bear whistled as he read it. 'She was destined for great things. This is a television contract for a series of six murder mystery plays, each lasting for an hour.'

Garfield looked impressed. He was smoothing out a crumpled sheet of paper which had been in the case but not in the envelope.

'What's that?' asked Bear.

'Not sure,' Garfield frowned. 'It looks like some sort of property sale.'

They scrutinised it together. It was hard to make head or tail of it because it was only the second sheet of what must have been a two-page letter. It was signed M. Frantzen, solicitor.

'No address,' said Garfield, 'but look at the name at the top.'

'Henry Royale,' said Garfield. He shrugged. 'So how did she get hold of it...?'

'Beats me,' said Bear, 'but it looks as if he's been instructed to sell a property. 'Who would have thought it? I often wondered how a so-called ordinary family man who didn't have a job could afford such expensive suits. Maybe this is the answer.'

'How do you mean?'

'He fleeces women for their money and buys property,' he said. 'The crafty devil was empire-building.'

'You could be right,' said Garfield. 'But where the devil is the house?'

'I have a feeling the answer might lie with his other wives,' said Bear.

Thirty-Four

Ada stared anxiously out of the cottage window. Where was Henry? He was supposed to have been here by now but there was still no sign of him. Surely the car hadn't broken down? She shook her head. Impossible. Motors of Mayfair were one of the most reliable dealers in the country. Had he hit traffic? Yes, that must be it. He was supposed to have been here the night before last. Where was he? At least the baby was quiet now. She had prepared herself well, but there was so much to remember and it was years since she'd dealt with small babies. She'd made sure she had everything before she took the baby. Bottles, boiling pan, teats, nappies, nightdresses and day clothes, cardigans and bedding ... it had cost a small fortune and the shop assistant's glowing opinion of her was embarrassing to say the least.

'Your daughter is so lucky to have someone like you,' she said again and again. 'You are so generous, madam.'

She'd been a bit worried that the cottage might be damp, but the rental agent had arranged for some cleaning woman to come and lay the fire. Once it was lit, the place was quite cosy.

She'd watched the house in Worthing for a couple of days. Nobody noticed a well-to-do woman strolling in the area, and as luck would have it, the grandmother had made it so easy when she left the pram outside the sweet shop. She'd parked up and hurried along the pavement. There was a crowd outside the shop, probably getting their off-ration sweets, and she'd hesitated. But then there was a bit of a to-do because somebody had jumped the queue and Ada seized her chance. The little girl standing next to the pram had given her a puzzled look when she'd undone the pram straps.

'Why are you doing that?' she'd asked.

'I'm taking him to live with me.'

The child had stared at her. 'His mummy won't like that.'

Ada put her finger to her lips and hissed. 'Be quiet or I will eat you up.'

'Are you a wicked witch?' The child's voice was small and frightened.

'Yes, I am,' Ada snapped and the child's eyes had grown wide with fear. She felt a bit guilty about that, so she'd left her with one of Henry's sweets. 'Don't eat it until Mummy says,' she said as she slipped away without anyone seeing.

She'd laid the baby on the back seat and hoped he wouldn't roll off. Luckily he didn't, but he was upset when she'd got him back to the cottage. His nappy was rank and she struggled to get him clean. She couldn't face washing it, so she'd put it into a galvanised bucket and left it outside the back door.

She didn't even know the baby's name. Had Henry told her? She couldn't remember. Probably he had, but it was always difficult to concentrate when Henry was around. She longed to feel his strong arms around her and his mouth covering her with kisses. He never noticed the wrinkles. With Henry, she was young again.

Once at the cottage, she'd made up the feeds, careful to boil the glass bottles thoroughly first. He was difficult to feed but eventually she'd managed to coax him. He stared at her with rather puzzled wide eyes, so she'd kissed his forehead because he was Henry's baby. He couldn't finish the bottle, only managing four ounces, and when she sat him up he burped, but then he cried when she wrapped him in a shawl and laid him down. The noise gave her a headache and it was ages before he finally dropped off to sleep, sweaty and breathless.

She put on the radio but couldn't concentrate. Suddenly, with a start, she heard the announcer say, '*Here is a repeat of an SOS message for Henry Royale of Horsham. Will Henry Royale, last known to be living in Horsham in Sussex, please go to Horsham Cottage Hospital where his wife Kaye Royale, also known as Kaye Hambledon, the well-known writer, is dangerously ill.*'

Ada switched off the radio. What did this mean? She would have to tell him of course. This would alter their plans. They only put out an SOS message if someone was dying. It puzzled her that Henry had never mentioned that his wife was a well-known writer. She racked her brains, trying to remember exactly what he had said. She'd listened to some of the evidence in that awful courtroom, so she must have seen Kaye, but she couldn't remember what she looked like. It was hardly surprising. When Henry was around, there was no other light in the room. But now Kaye was 'dangerously ill'. She didn't fancy upsetting him the minute he walked through the door, but he'd have to know. Oh, where was he? She didn't like being alone with a baby she didn't know. She'd only agreed to take the boy because Henry was so desperate to be reunited with his child. He had told her how awful Annie was, her lifestyle and the way she had dominated him. Before his exquisite lovemaking, Henry could be so persuasive. In the cold, hard light of day, she'd kidnapped him, and if Henry wasn't here to vouch for her, she'd be in serious trouble. She wiped a tear from her cheek. Oh Henry...

Ada stayed by the window watching for him until night fell.

It was decided that Annie should go home with her parents. She'd protested a little because she wanted to be at Copper Beeches when Edward came home, but everyone agreed that what she needed most was peace and quiet.

Bear had put a solitary policeman by the gate at Copper Beeches, which meant the reporters turned their attention to others in the town.

Mr Dobbin arrived late that afternoon and waited in Kaye's office until Sarah came downstairs. 'I'm Mrs Royale's solicitor,' he explained as she came in. 'I think we met once before.'

'Yes,' said Sarah. 'And I know that as well as being her solicitor, you were a dear friend of Kaye's. I'm sorry for your loss.'

'And I yours, my dear,' said Dobbin. The doorbell rang for the second time since he arrived.

'You'll be wanting to talk to Lottie,' said Sarah.

'She's taken my youngest daughter out for a walk.'

Dobbin nodded. 'You were with Kaye when she died?' he said.

'I was.' She searched his face. He seemed to be desperately trying to control his emotions. She didn't want to add to his sorrow. 'The end was peaceful,' she said quietly.

He nodded again and blew his nose loudly into a large white handkerchief. The doorbell rang again. 'What on earth is going on here?' he asked.

'We think Henry has snatched his son,' said Sarah. 'As you can imagine, the baby's mother is distraught. The press and the telegram boy haven't left us alone since it happened.'

'Good God!' said Dobbin.

There was a slight pause before Sarah began again. 'Mr Dobbin, could I ask you something? Did Kaye ever mention having a child?'

'Her baby died at birth,' he said, 'but whether it was a boy or a girl, I have no idea. Why do you ask?'

Sarah explained briefly what Kaye had said. 'She was very anxious at the time,' said Sarah. 'She said, and I quote... "He killed Bunny Warren's baby."'

'Bunny Warren?' said Dobbin. 'She was engaged to a Bunny Warren before she met Henry, but he was killed.'

'I think he was the father of her baby,' said Sarah. 'Kaye was convinced that Henry murdered the child.'

Mr Dobbin looked startled. 'Perhaps she was delirious,' he said, busying himself with some papers in his briefcase.

Sarah sensed he didn't want to be drawn in. 'I expect you're right.' He was clearly disturbed by what she had said and Sarah regretted adding to the old man's grief.

'Mrs Royal,' he said stiffly, 'I am here because Mrs Royale directed me to take charge of her affairs should she die prematurely. I wish to go through some of her papers and I can see that with the baby missing everything could so easily get on top of you.'

'We're doing the best we can,' Sarah said defensively.

'Oh please don't think I'm implying any criticism,' said Dobbin quickly. 'I'm here to lighten the load. Kaye left instructions about her funeral and my staff will see to any notifications and arrangements which have to be made. That should leave you free to deal with the repercussions concerning the baby.'

Leaving him to it, Sarah found yet another telegram of condolence on the hall table. When Mr Dobbin said he would make all the arrangements for the funeral, Sarah was so relieved she could have kissed him. She was beginning to feel snowed under with all the telephone calls and letters which had come in the short while since Kaye had been gone. Although she and Vera had buried their mother, that had been a very quiet family affair. Kaye's funeral was obviously going to have to be a lot, lot bigger and far more than she could have coped with. With one sentence Mr Dobbin had lifted a ten-ton weight from her shoulders.

They tried to make the rest of the day as normal as possible. When Jenny came home from school, they all had tea. Vera had left early afternoon because she had to catch the bus back to Lancing in time to collect Carole from school. Mrs Goodall was just about to go when Bear turned up on the doorstep again.

'Tell me Detective, did you ever find those people who were running around the garden?' Mrs Goodall said rather pointedly.

'What people?' said Bear, clearly puzzled.

'The prowlers,' said Mrs Goodall. 'I've written it down.'

'You mean there was more than one of them?' Bear was surprised. 'Can you describe them?'

Mrs Goodall gave an exaggerated sigh. 'I already told your colleague, but it looks like nobody listened. What is the point of having a police force if they don't do joined-up writing?'

'Tell me.'

'One was a rather sneaky sort of a person. He wore a raincoat about two sizes too big for him. I saw him sitting on the wall a couple of times. Of course he was trying to look as if he wasn't there, but I saw him.'

'And the other?'

'Younger,' said Mrs Goodall. 'Much younger.'

'If I send a constable round to your house...' Bear began.

'That's what you policemen always say,' Mrs Goodall snapped, 'but nothing seems to get done.'

'I promise I will look into it,' Bear said.

'Huh,' said Mrs Goodall, tossing her head in the air.

'Any news?' Sarah asked him as her neighbour walked huffily back down the drive.

'I'm afraid not,' said Bear, crossing the threshold. 'How are you coping?'

Sarah shrugged. 'Annie has gone home with her parents, which is no bad thing.' She told him about the abandoned baby.

'Oh no,' he said. 'I could kick myself. I didn't mention it because I knew it was a girl. I didn't think about those damn reporters. I'm sorry. I should have told you.'

She smiled. 'We're all doing our best,' she sighed. 'I just wish it was over.'

'You and me both,' he said.

'Do you want to come in for some tea?'

'I'd better go,' he said. 'I came to give Annie an update, not that there's much to say. I didn't realise she'd gone back to her parents. Garfield and I have been looking through those papers we found in Kaye's suitcase. Tell me, where did you and Henry used to live?'

'We had a house in Littlehampton,' said Sarah. '42 Pier Road. I loved it there. It overlooked the River Arun.'

Bear felt a frisson of excitement but he kept his face serious. The address on the piece of screwed-up paper in the case was Pier Road. 'Did you own the house?' he asked casually.

'Lord, no,' she laughed. 'We rented it and when Henry left me, the landlord put the rent up so much that I couldn't afford it.'

There was a movement behind her and Mr Dobbin came out of the house. 'I'd best be off now, Mrs Royal,' he said, raising his hat politely. 'I've taken the few things I need for now; her birth certificate and Identity Card so that I can register the death, but if it's all right with you, I'll come back tomorrow.'

'Can I give you a lift somewhere?' said Bear.

'That would be most kind, Detective Inspector Truman,' said Dobbin. 'I'm staying at the Ardington Hotel. It's the Edwardian terrace by the gardens.'

'I know,' Bear smiled.

They said their goodbyes and left. Sarah went back indoors. The girls played together nicely until eventually she told them to get ready for their bath. There was an argument about which book they should have for their bedtime story. 'I want *Babar the Elephant*,' said Lu-Lu.

'You had that one last night,' said Jenny. 'I want *Millions of Cats*.'

'Tell you what,' said Sarah. 'As a special treat, you can have both.'

In the end she didn't have to read both books. Lu-Lu fell asleep half way through *Millions of Cats* and by the time she'd finished the story, Jenny was asleep as well. Sarah put out their clothes ready for the morning and crept out of their room.

After he'd dropped Mr Dobbin at his hotel, Bear had gone to see Annie straight away to apologise for the distress she had suffered because he hadn't mentioned the abandoned baby and to give her an update on the progress, or more to the point, the lack of it. The Mitchells invited him in but he declined the tea they offered. 'Being a policeman is a bit like being a vicar,' he grinned. 'We're both awash with tea.'

Judith smiled thinly and Bear made his apology.

'No news?' said Malcolm. They all looked exhausted. Annie was pale and had dark circles under her eyes. Her hair was greasy and badly in need of a wash. She wore an old baggy cardigan with frayed sleeves and a skirt which looked far too big for her. Judith didn't look much better. Malcolm, who was already hugging a glass of whisky, had a five o'clock shadow.

Bear shook his head. 'Afraid not,' he said. He paused. 'Are you planning to stay here now, Annie? I just need to know where I can contact you at all times.'

She was picking at the frayed edge of her handkerchief and nodded dully.

'No chance you might be thinking of returning to the home you shared with Henry?' She looked puzzled, so he added, 'The house in Horsham?'

'Number 7? I had to give it up,' Annie shrugged. 'I haven't been there since the trial. My old neighbour tells me it's got new people there now.'

'Why did you give it up?' Bear asked.

Annie glanced at her parents. 'After Edward was born, I was saving every penny I got in the hope that I could carry on with the rent, but without a regular income it was impossible.'

'I see,' said Bear.

Annie sat up as a sudden thought crossed her mind. 'You don't think Henry has gone back there, do you?'

'No, no,' said Bear. 'Nothing like that.'

'We could drive over there tomorrow and see, if you like,' Malcolm said eagerly.

Bear was alarmed to see that the hope that Edward might be in Horsham had brought the family back to life. 'Please let me assure you,' he said quickly. 'My colleagues in Horsham have already checked that avenue of investigation and, like you say, there's a new family living there.'

Their defeated, despairing expressions returned. Bear left, promising to keep them informed. After his conversation with Mr Dobbin and his visit to Annie and her parents, there was only one other thing he needed to do tonight. Something he wished he'd thought about earlier.

During the day, the wind had got up and several items had been blown from the washing line. Sarah looked around the garden. Everything was in its place, but she had an uneasy feeling that she was being watched again. Snatching the washing from the line, she bent to pick up a couple of table napkins and one of Jenny's socks. The feeling wouldn't go away. Someone was there, in the shadows. 'Who's there?'

She saw something out of the corner of her eye and approached the shed with caution, but no one was there. She went back to the washing but she felt jumpy ... scared almost. She paused as she pulled a blouse from the line and turned around slowly. The curtain in the upstairs bedroom of Mrs Goodall's house dropped. 'Oh it was you, you nosy old bat,' Sarah whispered good-naturedly. 'Back to your old tricks again.'

Mrs Goodall had decided to have an early bath and a long soak. The water was running and she decided to draw the bedroom curtains before undressing when she'd seen Sarah in the garden.

She hadn't wanted the girl to think she was spying on her like she used to, but as she went to draw the second curtain, Mrs Goodall saw something else. She nearly fainted with the shock. The prowler! He was back there ... in the garden.

It was only as Sarah walked back into the kitchen that she noticed a petticoat in the flower bed. It was dirty and would have to be washed again, but as she bent to pick it up, she saw footprints and a cluster of cigarette butts under the window. Immediately, her spine began to tingle and the hairs on the back of her neck stood up. Someone had been spying on them through the kitchen window again.

Oh God, it was Henry. He must have come back again. What did he want this time? Surely he hadn't come for her children as well?

'Mrs Royal?'

She straightened up quickly and came face to face with a man dressed in a shabby raincoat. Sarah took a sharp intake of breath. He was standing in the shadows, but she could just make out his stubbly chin. He had a trilby hat, which he took off as he came towards her. She was rooted to the spot and trying not to panic.

'I've been trying to catch one of you alone for days,' he said. 'I really wanted the other one but you'll do.'

They both stood staring at each other. Sarah's heart was pounding with fear. Who was this man and what did he want? She could see he was muscular and obviously very fit. 'Are you a reporter?' she squeaked.

He shook his head. 'What I have to say is for your ears only.'

Mrs Goodall was still watching them from her bedroom window. What should she do? She had to help, but she was only half dressed. If she stopped to put her corsets back on, the poor girl wouldn't have a chance. Pulling her dressing gown around her shoulders, she ran downstairs as fast as she could. Stopping only to grab something, she tore out into the garden.

Sarah felt trapped. She was standing in the flower bed and the only way she could get back into the house was to go past him. She had to keep him talking and hope against hope that someone, anyone, would walk by.

'You see, I know all about your Henry,' he said, coming closer.

Sarah backed away. 'Keep away,' she cried helplessly as she put her hand up. She could feel the wall of the house coming up behind her. She had nowhere to run. He put his hands up in supplication, but she misunderstood his motives. 'No. No!' she cried.

'I just want to talk,' he said.

'Then stay there,' she quaked. 'Stay where you are. I only have to call out and someone will telephone the police.'

'If I was you, Mrs Royal,' he said, leaning towards her and dropping his voice, 'I really wouldn't do that until you've heard what I have to say. Believe me, it's for your own good.'

They both heard a slight footfall and then a

voice behind him said, 'Oh no you don't,' as Mrs Goodall pressed her weapon into the middle of his back. 'I'll have you know that when I was young I was a crack shot.'

The man's hands shot into the air. 'Don't shoot, don't shoot!'

Sarah's relief was palpable because, at the same time, she saw Bear's car draw into Kaye's driveway. Bear and Garfield got out smartly and ran across the grass.

'Right, me laddo,' Bear was saying as he put handcuffs on the man, 'I'm arresting you on suspicion of trespassing on private property.'

Sobbing with fright, Sarah fell into Mrs Goodall's arms.

Thirty-Five

'I ain't done nothing! I was only talking to the lady. Look in me wallet. You'll see my identification there.' As he and Garfield were frogmarching the struggling intruder towards his car, Bear hesitated. 'I meant no harm,' their prisoner insisted. 'I came to warn them about Henry Royale. I'm a private detective.'

'This is the man I've seen hanging around the garden,' said Mrs Goodall triumphantly. She pulled her dressing gown closer to her body, suddenly embarrassed by her state of undress.

By now Garfield and Bear had their prisoner, still handcuffed with his hands behind his back, leaning across the bonnet.

Lottie had come into the garden and was doing her best to comfort Sarah. Bear went to her. 'Are you all right?' he said, gently taking her hands in his.

She nodded but her body still juddered.

He took a clean handkerchief from his pocket and shook it out before giving it to her. 'What's this all about?'

Lottie looked at the prisoner and gasped. 'He's the man I saw looking into the window last night.'

'It's not what you think, lady,' said the man. 'I was trying to talk to the other one. Annie Royal. She's in danger.'

All eyes were on the prisoner.

'My name is Dennis Nelson,' he said, looking nervously from one to the other. 'I was employed by Henry Royale to spy on her.'

'You what?' cried Sarah.

'Mr Royale wanted to bring up his son on his own so he wanted to prove that Annie was an unfit mother,' Nelson went on. 'I've been down here on and off for weeks, but I couldn't find a thing wrong with the young lady. Mr Royale was very angry and sacked me.'

'So what are you doing back here again?' asked Garfield.

Nelson told them about his final meeting with Henry, where he'd revealed his plan.

'Why didn't you go to the police straight away if you thought he was up to no good?'

'I've got a wife and kid,' said Nelson. 'I don't trust him. He knows where I live and he's quite capable of taking it out on them if I went to the rozzers. He never even paid me what he owed. Look Gov, I'm on the level. I just wanted to warn the girl, that's all. It cost me money to come down here.'

'Do you think Henry Royale is going to attack Annie?' Bear asked. He was searching through Nelson's pockets.

Nelson shook his head. 'Worse than that,' he said. 'He's got photographs.' He suddenly felt awkward to be talking about things like this in present company. These were respectable people.

'What sort of photographs?' Garfield pressed.

Bear was going through Nelson's wallet.

'The woman in the picture looks like Mrs Royal,' said Nelson, carefully avoiding Mrs Goodall's eye. 'She's posing like ... you know.'

'Posing?' said Mrs Goodall. 'What's wrong with that?'

Bear put the wallet back in Nelson's pocket and patted his chest.

'There's nothing wrong with that,' Nelson agreed quickly, 'except she's ... she's got no clothes on.'

Mrs Goodall gasped. Lottie looked puzzled. 'But why would she do that?'

'I don't believe it,' said Sarah stoutly. 'Annie is not that sort of girl.'

'I know, I know,' said Nelson. 'Like I said, the girl in the pictures *looks* like Mrs Royal.'

'I don't understand,' said Lottie.

'He's going to release them here, in Worthing,' said Nelson.

'But that will ruin her reputation,' said Mrs Goodall.

'Exactly,' said Bear. 'Then she would lose her good name and her child. You should have come to us sooner.' He jerked his head towards Garfield.

'And what would you have done?' said Nelson. 'Would you have arrested a man for having photographs of his wife?'

Garfield uncuffed the prisoner. 'What did you hope to achieve by seeing Mrs Royal?'

'I dunno,' said Nelson, rubbing his wrists. 'I just wanted her to know.'

While she was listening, Sarah had been going over some other things in her mind. There were other oddities they'd never solved. Was it possible that this was the man who had cut Jenny's hair? It didn't make sense if he was simply trying to warn Annie about some photographs, but what with everything else that had been going on, the assault on her daughter had been all but forgotten.

'What about my daughter's plait?' said Sarah. 'Was that your doing, and if so, why did you cut it off?'

'Cut off her plait?' said Mrs Goodall faintly.

'What plait?' Nelson protested loudly. 'I don't know nothing about no plait.'

'We're going to check your story before we let you go,' said Garfield.

'Nah,' said Bear, 'let him go.'

Garfield looked a tad surprised, but Nelson didn't hang around for him to change his mind. Picking up his fallen trilby, he hurried down the path. 'Thanks mate,' he called over his shoulder, 'I owe you one. Watch out for them photographs.'

'Was that wise?' Mrs Goodall asked. 'Shouldn't you have taken a statement, given what he's just said about Mr Royale?'

'We know where to find him if we want him,' said Bear. 'I searched his wallet, remember?'

Sarah moved closer to Mrs Goodall. 'Thank you,' she said. 'You were amazing.'

'I was a fool,' said Mrs Goodall modestly. 'It's a good job Detective Truman and his colleague turned up when they did. If that man had turned around and seen that I only had my late husband's walking stick poking in his back, we might both have been in trouble.'

'Well, thank you anyway,' Sarah insisted. 'You came just in time.'

All at once Mrs Goodall let out a gasp. 'My bath! Heavens above, I left the taps running.' And with, that she hurried away.

Once she was gone Bear turned to Sarah. 'Look, I know this is an awful lot for you to cope with at the same time, but we've come back here because we have a shrewd idea where Henry and his accomplice are.'

Sarah seemed surprised.

'We want to have another look through the stuff in Kaye's office again,' said Bear, by way of explanation. 'We're looking for something specific.'

As they went inside, Bear told them about the address on the scrap of paper found in Kaye's suitcase. 'It's a bit of a mystery how it got there, but we know she wasn't the only one in that car. We think that some papers must have been spilled when the car crashed. Henry must have grabbed most of them, but this one was missed.'

'What did it say?' asked Lottie.

'When we showed it to Mr Dobbin,' said

Garfield, 'he agreed that it was a solicitor's paper instructing the sale of a property. 42 Pier Road, Littlehampton.'

'But that was my old home,' Sarah gasped. 'I had to give it up when Henry left. I couldn't afford the rent.'

'The house belonged to Henry,' said Bear quietly.

'No,' said Sarah shaking her head. 'I had a rent book.'

'The house *belonged* to your husband,' Bear repeated more emphatically.

Sarah stared at him in disbelief. 'Then why did the landlord put the rent up...?' her voice trailed and her eyes filled with tears. 'It was just to get me out, wasn't it?'

Bear nodded.

'How could he do that?' Sarah said brokenly. 'How could he do that to his children?'

Bear put his hand over hers. 'I don't know.' His voice was gentle and their eyes locked.

'We also discovered that Mrs Annie Royal's home in Horsham was owned by Henry Royale,' Garfield interjected.

Sarah found it hard to grasp what they were saying. 'I don't understand...'

'It seems that Henry fleeced vulnerable women of their savings,' said Garfield. 'And used the money to buy property after property.'

'The point is,' said Bear, 'if we want to prove there's a pattern here, we need to find out where Kaye lived when she was married to him.'

'We've checked the other two properties, Pier Road and the house in Horsham, but Henry isn't there,' said Bear. 'We need to find that other address.'

'We're wondering if he has taken Edward there,' said Garfield.

Sarah inhaled sharply.

'It was Chichester,' Lottie suddenly said.

Everyone turned to look at her. 'When she got me out of that terrible place,' she went on, 'Kaye said she was sorry she hadn't known I was so close by. She lived in Chichester for many years before moving here.'

'Come to think of it, Lottie's right,' said Sarah. 'She once told Annie and me that she'd lived in Chichester.'

'Do you know the address?' said Bear eagerly.

Sarah shrugged helplessly. 'I'm not sure she ever said the actual address.'

Lottie's face coloured as she shook her head. 'I don't know.'

The two policemen went into Kaye's office and shut the door.

Sometime later, Bear and Garfield emerged from the office. They looked tired. 'Anything?' asked Sarah eagerly, even though she could tell by their dejected expressions that they'd found nothing.

'Let's ask Annie,' said Sarah going to the phone.

It was late, and at first Judith was reluctant to wake Annie, but once Sarah had explained everything, she brought Annie to the telephone.

'Any news?' Annie asked.

'Nothing concrete,' said Sarah, 'but Bear may be onto something.'

'I don't know,' Annie wailed when Sarah explained everything once again. 'He never talked about his past.'

Sarah heard her choking back her tears. 'Oh please don't cry, darling.'

'Oh Sarah,' Annie wept. 'What am I going to do? I feel so alone.'

'But you're not alone are you, darling,' said Sarah. 'We're all desperate to find Edward, and we don't want to leave any stone unturned. Think for a minute will you, darling. Was there anything he might have let slip?'

'Not that I can think of,' Annie sighed. 'Oh, hang on, wait a minute... I found some photographs in his secret drawer when he got arrested.' Her voice was brightening up. 'There was something written on the back of one. They're in my room.'

'Can I go and get them?' Sarah asked eagerly. 'Where are they exactly?'

'There's an old Turkish delight box on my dresser,' said Annie. 'I put them in there. You will ring me back and tell me if you find anything?'

Sarah hung up and ran upstairs two at a time, calling, 'She's got some old photographs,' over her shoulder.

She hadn't been in Annie's room since the night she took the shawl away from Edward. It was neat and tidy but his things were scattered all around. The blue elephant he liked on his bed, the rattle which always made him laugh and that yellow cardigan Lottie had spent so long knitting him. But tonight, with the others piling into the room behind her, Sarah had no time for sentimentality. 'She mentioned they're in a Turkish delight box,' she said, looking around wildly. It wasn't on the dresser.

'Is this it?' Lottie was holding it up.

'Where was it?' asked Bear.

'In the wardrobe,' said Lottie.

A minute later they were all poring over them. One was of Henry in swimming trunks. He looked much younger and even more good-looking. He stood next to a youthful Kaye who had a long cigarette holder in her hand and her hair was tied up in a white turban. The other photographs were of a man sitting on a wall and a third picture of Henry in a garden which overlooked a field.

Sarah turned over the photograph of the man sitting on the wall. On the back Kaye had written *Bunny Warren RIP*.

'So that was Bunny Warren,' said Sarah. He was tall, muscular and good-looking.

'Who is Bunny Warren?' Bear asked.

'She was going to marry him,' said Sarah softy, 'but he was killed. I think he may have been the father of her baby.'

But Bear's attention had been caught by something else. 'Look at that chap in the background,' he said, scrutinising the picture of Henry in the garden carefully. 'That's not a field. He's in cricket whites. This was taken at a cricket match.'

He flipped it over. There was something written in pencil on the back of one of the photographs. It was very faint, but using a magnifying glass, Lottie brought up from the office, they could just make out 'Priory Road August 1927.'

'I'll lay any money that that's the county cricket ground,' said Bear excitedly.

Thirty-Six

It had been frustrating having to wait until the next day, but if they were going to work out from the photograph where the house was, they needed daylight. The area where the search was to begin was stunning. They had walked all along the cricket ground in Chichester and it didn't take long for Bear to satisfy himself that this was the place which was in the background of the photograph they had studied last night. Having spent a little time trying to work out where the photographer must have stood all those years ago, he could see that little had changed.

As soon as they spotted the cottage, their suspicions were confirmed. There was a black Bentley in the driveway, registration LLD 732, but no sign of anyone inside the property. Thinking that the suspects had already flown, Bear was about to give it up as a wasted journey when Garfield lifted the lid of an enamel bucket outside the back door and found it contained soiled baby's nappies. The men retreated to the police car which they'd parked in a nearby lane and played a waiting game. In fact, they didn't have to wait there very long. Coming along the road they saw a well-dressed middle-aged woman pushing a battered old pram. The two things didn't go together at all. As she approached the cottage, Bear stepped out of the car.

'Mrs Browning?'

The woman stopped dead in her tracks. She stared at the two policemen for a second then she let go of the pram handle and began to run. Her age and her size made her slow. It didn't take much to apprehend her and a moment or two later Bear caught her arm, shouting, 'Oh no you don't!'

He and Garfield stood either side of her. 'Please don't take me to prison,' she cried.

'I have reason to believe that you have taken that child away from its mother unlawfully,' said Bear. 'You have, in fact, kidnapped him.'

'No, no I promise you,' Ada cried. 'I brought him here for his father.'

As Bear had grabbed her arm, she had let go of the pram. It was on an incline. Nobody noticed that when Ada let go of the handle, it teetered on the edge and then slowly began to move.

'But you snatched him from his pram and brought him here without his mother's permission,' Bear insisted.

'Henry was supposed to be here,' Ada wailed.

'So where is he?' said Garfield, more than a little disappointed that Henry wasn't around.

'I don't know!' Ada wept.

Unnoticed by them all, as they spoke, the pram was moving away from them and gathering speed.

'Where were you going with the baby?' Bear asked.

'I don't know,' Ada cried again.

'But you must have had some sort of a plan,' said Garfield.

Suddenly, Edward woke up and began to cry. The three of them turned around and, to their horror, saw that the pram was heading straight for a pond by the bend in the road. Letting go of Ada, Bear and Garfield raced after it with a shout.

The pram sped down the embankment, its wheels already in the water and heading towards the reed beds. As it hit a muddy ridge, it began to tip forwards. Garfield hurled himself at the handle, but Bear was already there. Just as the whole thing was about to upend itself, he steadied it and pulled it back as he skidded along the embankment. Garfield was not so lucky. He toppled and sat down in the muddy reed bank. By the time the men had got the pram back on the towpath, they both looked a mess, but they didn't care. Edward was safe and that was all that mattered.

To keep things as normal as possible while Edward was missing, Sarah took Jenny to school. When they walked into the playground, Mrs Audus told her the Headmistress wanted to see her again. Sarah went straight to her office. When she opened the door, another woman was sitting in front of the desk. She was wearing a threadbare brown coat and a floral headscarf. Sarah didn't recognise the woman but she did recognise the boy standing beside her. He was stockily built and his knees badly scabbed from frequent falls. His hair was badly cut and tousled. William Steel.

'Oh, Mrs Royal,' said the Head as she walked in. 'This is Mrs Steel and her son, William. William has something to say to you.' The child sniffed an emerging globule of mucus back into his nose and turned a tear-stained face towards her.

'Come along William,' said the Head. 'This is Jenny's mother. What do you say?'

Mrs Steel gave her son a hefty nudge. 'Mrs Audus caught him calling your girl names.'
'I'm sorry,' William mumbled.
'I can't hear you, William,' said the Head.
'I'm sorry,' said William a little louder.
'I had no idea he was upsetting your daughter,' said Mrs Steel. 'I don't know what his father is going to say about all this.'
William glanced at his mother with a worried look on his face.
'That's not all you've done, is it William?' Everybody's attention went back to the Headmistress as she laid a Stanley knife on her desk.
'Good God! That's your granddad's knife,' cried Mrs Steel. 'He's been looking everywhere for that. Did you take it out of his shed?'
'I caught William carving his initials on this desk,' said the Head sternly.
'And Jenny's initials,' William protested. 'I never meant no harm. I like her.'
'Jenny told me you've been horrid to her,' said Sarah. 'You've called her names.'
'Not now,' said William. 'I like her now.'
'School equipment is very expensive,' said the Head sternly. 'You do not carve initials onto any of it.'
'No, miss,' said William, hanging his head again.
'How long have you had Granddad's knife?' said Mrs Steel.
William looked at Sarah sheepishly. 'And I'm sorry for cutting the washing,' he said.
'It was you?' cried Sarah.
'Washing? What washing?' his mother demanded.

'Someone shredded an apron I hung on the line,' said Sarah, never taking her eyes from William.

With a face like thunder, Mrs Steel rose to her feet and thumped her son on the arm. 'You little tyke! You wait until your father hears about this.'

'Please Mum, please don't tell him,' said William, bursting into tears. 'I didn't mean to. It was an accident.'

'An accident?' his mother shrieked. 'How can cutting something with a Stanley knife be an accident?'

'I think we'd better all calm down,' said the Headmistress. 'William you realise that you've been a very naughty boy, don't you?'

Dutifully, William hung his head again. 'Yes Miss.'

'Was it you who cut Jenny's plait?' Sarah said quietly.

'It was an accident,' he cried. 'The bus jerked and it just came off in my hand.' William's head shot up. 'I never meant to do it and I gave it back,' he added defensively. 'I took it to her house, didn't I? I pushed it through her letter box.'

When Malcolm got the telephone call at his home to say Bear was on his way with the baby, he became very emotional. There was no doubt that Edward had stolen his heart too.

'It should take us about an hour to get back,' Bear explained. 'If you come straight to Worthing Hospital, you can see Edward as soon as the docs have finished with him.'

'You're taking him to hospital?' said Malcolm anxiously.

'Nothing to worry about,' said Bear, shouting over the sound of Edward's lusty yell. 'We just want him to be checked over, that's all. If I thought there was anything really wrong with him, we would have taken him to the hospital in Chichester, but I know his mother is anxious to be reunited with him as soon as she can.'

'Where did you find him?' Malcolm asked.

'I'll tell you all about it when we get back,' said Bear.

Malcolm cleared his throat noisily. 'We appreciate your care and concern,' he said. 'Thank you.' He hung up and blew his nose, then turned to the two women in his life. 'They've got him.' Seconds later they were crying in each other's arms. 'Before we go to the hospital,' he said huskily, 'I think we need to talk.'

It was a house full of laughter when Annie brought Edward back through the door of Copper Beeches later that day. Everyone crowded around, touching Edward's head or holding his hand while they smiled and cooed and made baby noises. Sarah put her arm around Annie's shoulders and hugged her gently. 'It's so good to see both of you.'

Annie smiled and leaned into her. 'Thank you, it's good to have him back.' Edward gazed at her with a puzzled expression. They sat in the kitchen while Lottie made tea and then they tucked into some of her home-made cake.

When he turned up about twenty minutes later, Bear related the whole story of what had happened, going over the fine detail again and again while everyone listened with rapt attention. He had twisted his ankle as he half fell, half threw himself down the embankment, hitting his face on the handle as the pram tipped up, with the front wheels in the water. The local ducks were startled and made a tremendous din, but fortunately the hood was up, so Edward, although he had been shaken about a bit, and was very cross, hadn't actually landed in the pond. 'You needn't worry about the little fellow,' Bear assured them. 'The doc says he was well looked after. She had kept him clean and well fed.'

'I hope you're not wanting us to feel sorry for her,' said Malcolm stiffly.

'Absolutely not,' said Bear. 'I just didn't want you to be concerned that the baby suffered in any way.'

Annie kissed her son's cheek and then wiped her own eyes.

'Why is everybody crying?' Jenny wanted to know.

'Because we're all so happy,' smiled her mother. She hugged her daughter, but it was obvious from Jenny's expression that she was still puzzled.

Edward began to wriggle, so Annie excused herself to go and feed him and, at her invitation, the children went with her.

As they left the room, Sarah asked the question uppermost in everybody's mind. 'Why did she do it?'

Bear pulled the corners of his mouth down. 'Because Henry asked her to?' he shrugged.

'But you don't go kidnapping a child just because your lover tells you to,' Malcolm boomed angrily.

'I'm sure you don't need me to tell you, sir,' said Bear, 'that Henry Royale is a cunning and manipulative man who usually gets what he wants. From what I can gather, he spun her a yarn that your daughter wasn't capable of looking after his son and that he needed to rescue the boy. Because of that, Ada Browning had convinced herself that she was doing the right thing.'

'Beggars belief,' snorted Malcolm.

'But surely, once she'd taken the baby,' said Judith, 'Mrs Browning must have realised that what she'd done was wrong.'

'No doubt she did,' said Bear, 'but by then she was in so deep she didn't know what to do.'

'Never should have done it in the first place,' growled Malcolm.

'What will happen to her now?' said Sarah.

'At the moment she's at the police station and my colleague is interviewing her,' said Bear. 'She'll go to prison, of course, but I have no doubt she will get medical care once she's been sentenced. She's not the first to fall for Henry's charms. She may have used up a sizeable chunk of her fortune, but unlike another one of Henry's victims, she hasn't jumped off the end of the pier. No, she's not a bad woman, just a very foolish, deluded one.'

Sarah felt strangely sympathetic towards Ada. She couldn't excuse what she'd done, but she knew only too well that Henry had an ability to make black seem white.

'And what about Henry?' asked Judith. 'Have you caught him yet?'

'Not yet,' said Bear, standing to his feet, 'but we will.'

'Thank you for bringing Edward back to us,' said Judith as they all stood in the hallway to see him off. 'How did you know where to start?'

Annie and the children were coming down the stairs.

'It always bugged me that Henry dressed so well and looked after his wives while he was with them, despite only ever having a very small wage,' said Bear. 'Once we found that piece of paper with instructions for selling a property in Littlehampton, we thought we would check up on the owners. Both the Horsham property and the Littlehampton property belong to Henry, so I began to wonder where he had lived with Kaye.'

Annie blinked in surprise. 'You mean my house wasn't rented?'

'That's right,' said Bear. 'Henry owned that house.'

'But we paid rent,' cried Annie. 'I remember Henry taking the rent book with him when he went to work every Friday.'

'And that landlord was Henry himself,' said Bear. 'It seems Henry was in the process of evicting the existing tenants so that he can sell it.'

Annie's mouth dropped open. 'So putting the rent up so high was simply a way to get rid of us,' said Annie.

Bear looked sympathetic. 'I'm afraid so.'

'The blaggard!' cried Malcolm. 'When I get my hands on him...'

'Do you have any real idea where Henry is?' Judith interrupted.

'No,' said Bear.

'What about Mrs Browning?'

'Apparently she doesn't know either.'
'Or she isn't telling,' said Malcolm.
'Actually, sir,' said Bear, 'I genuinely think she hasn't a clue.'
He bade them good day and turned towards the door. Sarah followed him over the threshold. They strolled together arm in arm to the gate. 'Now that this is all over, I shall speak to my superior again.' He touched her cheek affectionately and their eyes met.
'Why do they call you that? Bear?'
He smiled. 'My first name is Max,' he said, 'and someone said I reminded them of Max Baer, you know the boxer.'
'Heavyweight champion of the world,' said Sarah. 'The tender-hearted tiger.'
Bear grinned. 'You know your boxers.'
'My father used to follow all his fights,' she said. 'He admired the man for his generosity and kindness to others.'
She smiled, and for a split second, he leaned towards her. Sarah looked at his mouth and responded by closing her eyes, but when she opened them again, he was gone.

Thirty-Seven

Sarah stepped from the black car, straightened her black dress and joined Lottie outside the chapel. She had never seen so many people. She had always known that Kaye was popular, but until this moment, she'd never realised just how much she was loved. The people who lined the short path leading to the chapel in Durrington cemetery had come from all walks of life. Apart from the curious onlookers, she recognised various shopkeepers from Ham Road, the gardener and his wife from the house, and a troupe of Boy Scouts from East Worthing who stood to attention by the flint-covered arch. Kaye had been their patron and benefactor, and without her help, they would still be without a decent scout hut.

Even Vera was there. She was wearing a black hat with a small net over her face. As Sarah drew closer, she saw Vera dab her nose with the largest white handkerchief Sarah had ever seen. They hugged each other and as she stepped back, Sarah saw Bear in the crowd watching her. Managing a brave smile, Sarah turned back, keeping her eyes on the coffin in front of them.

There was also a bewildering array of other people who had known and loved Kaye inside the chapel. Some were from the BBC, high-flying men and women who worked mainly behind the scenes. Then there were the rich and famous. Francis Durbridge, the playwright, Megs Jenkins, the actress from the film *Millions Like Us*, and even Arthur English, the comedian from *Variety Bandbox*. If it hadn't been such a sad occasion, she might have expected him to begin one of the shaggy dog stories for which he was so famous. As she looked around the crowded chapel, Sarah couldn't believe how many lives Kaye had touched. She had always thought of her as a bit of a recluse, bashing away on her typewriter, her only pleasure the cigarette which dangled permanently from her lips, but so many people had a story to tell of her kindness and generosity.

Lottie seemed bewildered and very upset. It was as if she had reverted back to her old unsure and frightened self. She leaned heavily on Sarah's arm on one side and Bear's on the other and wept the whole way through the service. They sang *Abide with Me* and *In Heavenly Love Abiding*. Sarah tried to join in, but her throat was too tight and her heart too heavy. In his address, the vicar talked about true values and friendships that last, which seemed totally appropriate when it came to talking about Kaye, and as Sarah glanced around, people were nodding their approval.

The mourners walked up the hill to the graveside and Annie, red-eyed from crying, fell into step with them. 'I can't believe she's gone,' she said brokenly. 'I never really told her how much I appreciated what she did for me.'

'I think we all feel the same,' said Sarah, slipping her arm through Annie's. 'And look at all these people.'

Kaye was to be laid in a shady corner, close to an arbutus tree. Sarah was pleased about that because the garden of Copper Beeches had quite a few of them. Kaye loved the red flaking bark and the strawberry-like berries. They stood by the graveside while the final committal was read. '*Earth to earth, ashes to ashes, dust to dust; in sure and certain hope of the Resurrection into eternal life...*' And it was over. Kaye Hambledon, also known as Kaye Royale, was gone.

As they walked back to the cars and people began to disperse, Sarah caught up with Annie. 'Have you heard from Henry yet?'

Annie shook her head. 'You were right all along,' she said bitterly. 'He never intended to come back for me. He just wanted Edward.'

'It's odd that he's never turned up,' said Lottie.

'He must know the police want to speak to him,' said Sarah. She glanced at Lottie's anxious face. 'You're not afraid of him are you Lottie?'

'Not for my sake,' said Lottie, 'but for yours.'

Sarah gave her arm a little squeeze. 'We'll be fine.'

'What will you do now?' Annie asked.

'I suppose the girls and I have to look for somewhere to live,' said Sarah.

'Have you really got to move?' said Annie, suddenly sympathetic.

'Well, Kaye and Henry never divorced,' said Sarah, 'so I guess he inherits everything lock, stock and barrel.'

'That's not fair,' said Annie.

Sarah raised an eyebrow. 'Who said life was fair?' she mused philosophically.

The three women parted with hugs and Annie promising to come around the following week.

They held the wake back at the house, and thankfully Kaye's solicitor had insisted on using professional caterers. The food laid on was adequate but nowhere near as substantial as Lottie would have provided had they done the cooking, but neither woman resented the fact. They were both too exhausted by recent events to even think about catering for so many people. Bear had to go back to the station to catch up with police business, but Copper Beeches was soon packed with people; everyone, it seemed, with a story to tell.

'Sarah, dear,' said Vera coming up to Sarah and giving her a hug. Sarah stiffened. She couldn't help herself. She had just overheard Vera telling someone how much she had done in the house when Kaye died. It was clear that the woman Vera was talking to was full of admiration.

'Thank you for your help,' said Sarah.

'You're my sister,' said Vera, looking rather pleased with herself. 'I only did what anyone else would.'

'Yes, you did,' said Sarah, adding with emphasis, '...*this* time.' She saw her sister's eyebrows shoot up. 'Oh don't look so shocked, Vera. Believe me, I am grateful for your help, but it would have been nice if you'd given me a hand before. What you put the girls and me through beggars belief. Kaye, Annie and Lottie were more of a family to me than you and Bill have ever been.'

With that, Sarah turned away angrily, her cheeks flaming.

'I'm sorry,' said Vera, her voice muted.

Sarah stopped dead in her tracks and turned back. 'Excuse me?'

'You're right,' said Vera, 'and I'm sorry.'

'What made you...?' Sarah began uncertainly.

Lu-Lu crashed into them and said in a loud voice, 'Mummy, Mummy, my botty just burped.'

Sarah and her sister caught each other's eye and laughed. Sarah bent to kiss her child's head and ruffle her curls. As Lu-Lu moved on, the two sisters were still staring at each other. Neither of them could find the words, but somehow Sarah knew that from this moment on, things were going to be different. Vera could be a cow at times, but she was her sister and blood is always thicker than water.

'I'd better go,' Vera said eventually.

Sarah smiled awkwardly. 'Bye, love. See you soon.'

Vera hesitated and almost kissed her cheek. 'See you soon.'

As the party thinned out, Mr Dobbin came up. 'When would you like to hear the reading of the Will?'

Sarah hadn't given it a moment's thought. 'Do you want to do it today, sir?'

'That is the usual custom,' he smiled.

'But Henry isn't here,' said Sarah.

'I only need you and Miss Lottie,' he said.

Sarah frowned. 'Kaye and Henry never divorced,' she said. 'He may not be here, but he's still her husband.'

Mr Dobbin shook his head. 'I don't need Mr Royale.'

Ensconced in Kaye's office, Mr Dobbin got some papers out of his briefcase. 'Apart from a few charities which will each receive a legacy, the bulk of the estate will go to you, Miss Lottie. That is the house and some stocks and shares, the residue of her bank balance and her jewellery.'

Lottie was stunned. Sarah squeezed her friend's hand and sighed contentedly.

'As for you Mrs Royal, Kaye has left a substantial sum to be held in trust for your children. It will be enough to send them to a private school or to a university when the time comes.'

Sarah's mouth dropped open. She may have the problem of homelessness to face again, but Jenny and Lu-Lu's future was secure at least.

'And Henry?' Sarah asked.

'According to her will, you and Miss Lottie are her only beneficiaries,' said Mr Dobbin in a businesslike manner. 'I am also instructed to hand you this letter.'

Sarah recognised Kaye's bold handwriting on the envelope and her throat constricted again.

'I am so sorry for your loss,' said Mr Dobbin, rising to his feet. 'It may be of some comfort to you to know that you both made my client very happy.'

He left the room quietly and Sarah and Lottie looked at each other. 'Does this mean I can carry on living here?' said Lottie.

'Yes, dear,' Sarah nodded. 'It's your house, Lottie.'

'I don't think I want to be here on my own,' said Lottie, staring down at her hands in her lap. 'Would you and the girls consider staying on with me?'

'Oh, Lottie,' said Sarah, the relief flooding her whole being. 'Thank you, thank you so much...'

Later that night, alone in her room, she read the letter from Kaye.

My dear Sarah, The fact that you are reading this must mean that I have died before you. I have no idea if you are a very old lady with grandchildren, but I do hope so! I wrote this letter and put it into Dobbin's care in the early spring of 1949. I wanted to tell you how much I appreciate all that you've done for me and for Lottie. Without you, she wouldn't have blossomed and flowered the way she has. I really feel that you have given her her life back. She will never regain the first flower of youth, but I have watched her growing in confidence and ability in a way in which I could scarcely believe was possible. I have made arrangements for your girls. If they are grown women, Dobbin's firm (I guess he will be long gone by now) have been instructed to invest the money wisely until they need it for schooling or university. If they are well past that age by the time you get this, use the money to bless their lives in whatever way you think best. I hope you have enjoyed your life too, Sarah. May God bless you.

Your ever grateful friend,
Kaye.

Sarah sat dry-eyed for a long time afterwards staring out of the open window at the stars.

Thirty-Eight

When the doorbell went the next morning, Sarah was the first on her feet. 'I'll go.' Already her heart was thumping with anticipation and when she saw his outline behind the glass in the front door she felt as silly as a schoolgirl on her first date. She opened the door and he pulled a bunch of red roses from behind his back.

'Oh, thank you. They're beautiful!'

'Don't tell anyone,' he grinned. 'Policemen aren't supposed to bring people flowers.' He stepped into the hallway and the door closed behind him. They stared at each other, each with a big grin.

'Your secret is safe with me,' she whispered.

'I've been to see my Inspector,' he began.

'And?'

'And I have permission to court you.'

She lowered her eyes and smiled into the flowers, breathing in their heady scent. 'Now that you've done it, can I ask you something?'

'Anything,' he smiled.

'Can I call you by your first name?' she asked shyly. 'Max is such a nice name.'

'Oh Sarah,' he said huskily. 'My love…'

They stood for a minute just looking at each other. Sarah had never been happier. Max was wonderful – every girl's dream.

'You've gone through so much.' He kissed her hand. 'My darling, I think you've been amazing through all this. I admire you deeply for what you've done. Your girls have no idea of the hardships they've experienced and that's all down to you. You're a fantastic mother.'

As he'd put his big arms around her shoulders, he was so gentle. She felt safe ... and loved. 'I know we don't want to rush into anything...' he was saying.

'No.'

'And you want me to get to know the girls a lot better...'

'Yes,' she whispered.

'It's just that...' He stepped closer and she could

feel his hands gently caressing her arms. 'Oh Sarah, I love you so much. Will you marry me?'

'Yes...' she laughed, 'a million times yes...'

He caught his breath as she looked up at him.

'Come on, you two,' said a voice from behind the sitting room door, 'we're all waiting to get started.'

She had thought herself in love with Henry; but the feelings she had for Max were far, far deeper. He wasn't constantly trying to change her. He didn't criticise or put her down. He didn't demand anything like Henry. She, in turn, loved to please him, but she did it because she loved him, not because she was afraid he would be angry if she didn't. The girls were relaxed and happy with him and looked forward to his visits even more so than they had done with Peter Millward. She smiled to herself. Peter's wife was expecting their first child and she wondered (wickedly) if the tuft of hair in his nose would be passed on to the baby.

'What lovely roses,' cried Lottie as Sarah and Max walked into the sitting room. She jumped up to go and get a vase but Sarah said, 'Later. We'll put them in water in a minute.'

There was a bottle of sherry on the table alongside four glasses. Sarah poured everyone a glass, although Max declined because he was still on duty.

'It's been over three months since anyone last heard from Henry,' he began. 'I think we are left with only three options. One, he's moved to a totally different area, two, he's gone abroad or three,' he paused for effect, 'Henry is dead.'

'But surely if he was dead,' said Annie, 'someone would have notified you about the body.'

Max nodded. 'So that leaves us with the other two suggestions. I should really like to catch him. He's paid for what he did to you two and Kaye, but my greatest concern is that he was the instigator of the kidnap of a baby and that he's still out there breaking other people's hearts and ruining their lives.'

'What about Ada?' Sarah asked.

'She's still on remand,' said Max. 'The trial will most likely be in a few months' time and I'm afraid that means that you and your mother, Annie, will have to give evidence.'

'If Henry is Lord-knows-where,' said Annie, 'where does that leave us?'

'What happens to the houses?' asked Lottie. 'can Sarah and Annie sell them?'

'I don't think we can,' said Sarah. 'I was never legally married to him.'

'Me neither,' said Annie. They caught each other's hand and held it tight.

'They'll be part of Kaye's estate if Henry is dead, but only if he died before Kaye,' said Max. 'But we're all jumping the gun a bit. There's no body and no proof.'

He looked around at the assembled faces.

'We survived without him before,' said Sarah, 'we can do it again.'

'Speaking personally,' said Annie, raising her glass, 'I'll drink to your health, Henry, despite what you did to me, I hope you're not dead, but I hope that you never darken my door again.'

'There is one other thing,' said Max, looking back at Sarah with a mischievous grin on his face. 'Sarah may not be here for much longer herself.

She has done me the great honour of saying she will be my wife.'

And the roar of excitement and approval downstairs made the children leave their beds and creep out onto the landing to see what was going on.

About a week after Kaye's funeral, Sarah went to see Mrs Angel. Her old friend had at last heard from Mrs Rivers, Sarah's old next-door neighbour. She handed Sarah a letter which Mrs Rivers had asked her to give to Sarah. While she served a customer, Sarah tore open the envelope. '*I am so sorry for all the trouble my son has caused you. I don't want him to find me, but I did want you to know how badly I feel.*' There was no address but she sounded happy and at peace at last. She went on to tell Sarah that she had married since she'd left Worthing '*...to a good man who truly loves me...*' Apparently he owned a betting shop and took her away on holidays. Sarah was delighted. The poor woman deserved a little happiness in life. Mrs Rivers had enclosed a five pound postal order in the envelope. '*I hope this makes up for what my son stole from you that time. As soon as I could, I popped ten bob in your door, but I'm not sure you got it. Please accept this postal order with my sincere apologies. I don't want to offend you, so if you would rather not have it, use it to buy a little something for the kiddies.*'

Sarah's eyes smarted. So it was Mrs Rivers who had fed them that night. She had thought it was Mrs Angel.

The plans for her wedding were streaking ahead. Sarah had never been so happy. She made her own dress, working long hours and far into the nights when Max was on duty. The police force kept a strict eye on all its men and as soon as they were married, she and Max were expected to make their home somewhere else. The greatest fear was that a police officer would be compromised if he had to deal with people who were once numbered among his friends. Max was offered a post twenty miles away in Chichester. It was a larger town than Worthing and would be a new and exciting challenge.

On the day itself, Max looked around with a warm glow of pleasure. It was late summer, almost three months after Kaye died, and everything looked fantastic. The place where they were going to hold the reception was perfect and a little bit different from the norm. Most people used the village hall or a church hall, but he'd found a barn for the reception and persuaded the farmer who owned it to get it cleaned up. It was accessed by a brick path shaded with honeysuckle. His friends from the am-dram club had excelled themselves with the decoration. Large wooden tubs filled to overflowing with marigolds and trailing ivy stood on either side of a great oak door which gave a heavy creak as it opened. Inside, the beautifully decorated top table was covered in the last of the summer roses from the garden at Copper Beeches, which were a perfect match for the bride's bouquet.

His thoughts had been jumbled as he drove through the town on his way to his wedding. Marriage was a big step, but he was absolutely sure that he wanted to be with Sarah for the rest of his life. The girls had accepted him and enjoyed his company. Bear often kept them entertained with little tricks. Lu-Lu loved it whenever he produced a penny from behind her ear. Jenny tried to work out what he did when he folded back his thumb and moved his hand in a certain way, making it look as if he'd severed it. She would watch him put the severed digit into a match box, and then she would gasp as his finger reappeared, perfectly normal again. 'How did you do that?' she would laugh out loud.

Perhaps one day in the not too distant future he would talk to Sarah about legally adopting them. That way they would all have the same name. He didn't want Henry Royale to have any part of their lives and because of that he felt a little stab of guilt. Whatever he thought of Henry, he was still their father, but Max was determined that he would be a far better dad to the girls than Henry had ever been.

Max arrived at the church just as the first guests were going in. He looked around anxiously. Every flower, every piece of ribbon had been carefully chosen. They cascaded from the huge church pillars and the perfume of the flowers filled the air. It all starts here, he thought to himself, and a small shiver of excitement coursed through his veins. How come he got so lucky? He never thought he'd meet a girl as wonderful as Sarah.

The cameraman took his photograph next to his best man, Oscar Garfield. The minutes ticked by. His heart beat anxiously. The girls arrived, pretty in new blue dresses with brand new sandals and carrying small posies of wildflowers. They had been so excited at the thought of the wedding. He grinned at them and Jenny giggled, covering her mouth to hide the gap in her teeth. But where was Sarah? Supposing she'd changed her mind... Then all at once, there she was, walking down the aisle on Cllr Mitchell's arm. She had had no one to give her away and Annie had been thrilled when Sarah asked her father to do her the honour. He was equally pleased, having missed out when Annie had 'married' Henry.

Sarah's dress was a rich cream taffeta and her hair was elegantly caught up on the top of her head behind a small tiara. She looked so radiant, he could hardly believe his eyes. She couldn't speak of course, but he saw her give him a little wink.

After the service, as the photographer clicked away, Max was impatient. He wished it was done and dusted so that she could see the barn. The photographs seemed to take an age. He was made to stand with this person and that, to pose with the Best Man and then the bridesmaids.

Then at last, the pair of them were heading to the reception. In these austere times, their wedding breakfast was only sandwiches and cake, with wedding cake to follow, but he knew it would be perfect. Sarah was the first to step through the creaking door. She stopped and gasped. 'Oh darling!' she cried, her eyes lighting up. 'It's amazing.'

'I wanted you to have a day to remember,' he smiled. 'And many happy years to come.'

'Oh, I shall,' she whispered. She lifted her head, and when her lips brushed his, his heart melted.

'Shall I make the tea and bring it out into the

garden?' asked Sarah.

'Good idea, darling,' said Max.

It was nine months later and a beautiful June afternoon. Annie and Edward had left the sweet shop in the Steyne where she was training to be the manager (allowing Mr Richardson to retire), to join Sarah, Max and the girls for Sunday lunch at their new home on the outskirts of Chichester. Lottie, who had sold Copper Beeches in the winter of the previous year and moved into a small cottage nearby, was also with them.

'I'll get the garden chairs out,' said Max.

'Let me give you a hand,' Stan Greenaway, Lottie's gentleman friend followed him out into the garden. He was an older man, a widower around fifty-five years old with steel-grey hair and a merry twinkle in his eye.

'He's really nice,' said Annie giving Lottie a side hug as she did the last of the drying up. 'Where did you meet him?'

'He's an auctioneer,' said Sarah. 'We met him about five months ago at a sale. He and Lottie have been inseparable ever since.'

'Oooh,' squealed Annie. 'Do I hear wedding bells?'

Lottie was just about to tip the water from the washing-up bowl down the sink. Instead, she splashed Annie's arm playfully. 'Shh,' she said. 'He'll hear you.'

Sarah and Annie looked at each other and grinned.

'We're just good friends,' Lottie protested but she was blushing happily.

'How is the business?' Annie asked. 'You said

you were renting a bigger shop in your last letter.'

'Actually we got the place next door and knocked it into one,' Sarah explained. 'We've got furniture in one part and a small tea room in the other. It's doing very well, isn't it Lottie?'

'Very well,' said Lottie.

'What will you do when the baby comes?'

Sarah glanced at her friend. 'We haven't worked that one out yet,' she said.

The washing up done, Sarah put the teapot onto the tray.

'Here, let me take that,' said Max, coming back indoors. 'You shouldn't be lifting heavy things in your condition.'

'Don't be silly, darling,' Sarah laughed. 'I'm only four months pregnant.'

Outside in the sunshine, they relaxed in garden chairs with their tea. At nineteen months old, Edward toddled around after the girls, who were playing mummies and daddies in a hollowed-out area of rhododendron in the shrubbery.

'I hate to bring a small cloud into this lovely day,' said Max, 'but I have something to tell you all. Have any of you been reading the papers?'

'Who wants to read newspapers,' said Annie. 'Ever since we sent our troops to Korea, they're all full of doom and gloom.'

Lottie shivered. 'I really hoped we had put an end to war.'

'Unless we try to stop them, my dear,' said Stan, 'I'm afraid that our way of life will be gone forever and communism will rule the world.'

'The story I'm referring to hasn't been in the nationals,' said Max, 'and it's a little closer to home.' Pausing until he had everyone's attention, he reached into his back pocket and drew out his wallet. 'Developers near Horsham have found a body,' he said, handing round a small newspaper cutting under the heading *Man found dead*.

'So?' said Annie.

'It's Henry,' said Max.

Annie took in her breath, Sarah clutched at her throat and Lottie reached for Stan's hand to squeeze it tight.

'Henry?' Stan whispered. 'Is that...' and Lottie nodded.

'Darling, are you sure?' said Sarah.

Edward fell and began to wail. Annie started to get up, but Lottie said, 'We'll go and sort him out. You and Sarah need to talk. He's fine. Just a little tumble,' and jerking her head at Stan, the two of them went to the child.

'He'll have to be formally identified,' Max went on, 'but I'm as sure as I can be. I knew it as soon as they showed me his briefcase. It was found at the scene.'

'Why? What was in it?' Annie asked nervously.

'It was water-damaged having been in the ditch for so long,' Max went on, 'but it contained an expensive brooch in a box belonging to a London jeweller and papers appertaining to a house sale.'

'The Chichester house?' asked Sarah.

'The Chichester house,' said Max.

The women were silent, and for a moment, the only sound in the garden was the happy laughter of the children as Lottie and Stan chased them around the shrubbery.

'If it's any consolation to the pair of you,' Max

went on, 'you weren't the only people Henry hoodwinked. I long suspected him of having something to do with Mrs Grenville Hartley's death and I found some of her papers in that same briefcase. She killed herself because he had milked her of her fortune.'

'He was an absolute rat,' said Annie, 'and I just couldn't see it.'

'I can't believe it,' said Sarah eventually, 'that he's really gone for ever.'

'So what next?' asked Annie.

'You will be informed officially once they've checked his dental records,' said Max, 'and then there'll be an inquest.'

'Do they know how he died?'

'My guess is that he died in the ditch not long after the accident,' said Max. 'Nobody realised he was there.'

Sarah leaned forward and felt the teapot. 'The tea is cold,' she said. 'I'll go and make some more.' She stood up and went into the house. Max didn't follow. He knew she wanted a minute or two on her own.

'Before the others come back,' Max said to Annie, 'I wanted to tell you that there were some photographs in the briefcase.'

Annie took in her breath and her eyes grew wide. Max put his hand up. 'Don't worry,' he said quickly. 'They were badly damaged, and besides, there's no reason on earth why they should be made public.'

'Were they awful?' asked Annie faintly.

Max nodded. 'But we don't know who the woman is, so don't worry. The chapter is closed.'

He looked towards the house. 'I'd better go... Sarah may need me.'

'Yes, yes of course,' said Annie.

Max was getting to his feet. 'Are you all right?'

'I'm fine,' she smiled. 'And Max ... thank you.'

'There's one good thing,' he added. 'Henry's name was on the children's birth certificates. Any assets belonging to him will now come to them.'

'Surely everything will go to Kaye's estate?' said Annie.

'She survived him as far as we're concerned,' said Max. 'But even if she didn't, the three houses belong to his next of kin.'

Annie's face lit up. 'The children?'

'The children.'

Back in the kitchen, he found Sarah red-eyed and pouring boiling water into the teapot. When she'd put the lid on the teapot, he took her into his arms.

'So,' she said softly, 'it's finally over. Henry has gone forever. This is how it all ends.'

Max cupped her face in his hands and looked deep into her eyes. And just before he kissed her tenderly, he said, 'Oh no my darling girl, this is where it all begins.'

This Large Print Book for the partially sighted, who cannot read normal print, is published under the auspices of

THE ULVERSCROFT FOUNDATION

THE ULVERSCROFT FOUNDATION

... we hope that you have enjoyed this Large Print Book. Please think for a moment about those people who have worse eyesight problems than you ... and are unable to even read or enjoy Large Print, without great difficulty.

You can help them by sending a donation, large or small to:

The Ulverscroft Foundation,
1, The Green, Bradgate Road,
Anstey, Leicestershire, LE7 7FU,
England.
or request a copy of our brochure for more details.

The Foundation will use all your help to assist those people who are handicapped by various sight problems and need special attention.

Thank you very much for your help.